THE ATTORNEY

Lucas Holmes Sheridan is the senior partner of the prestigious Wall Street law firm of Porterfield, Baker & Sheridan, and is a man of great dignity and pride. He is suddenly plunged into the whirlpool of an extremely sordid murder case. Alex Moore, one of Lucas's partners, has an obsessive infatuation for Dolly Wayne, the Broadway musical star, which entangles him in a legal impropriety that threatens his own career and the reputation of the firm. When Dolly Wayne—an earthy and robustly sensual woman—becomes the victim of a vicious sexual assault and murder, Lucas's nephew, Ken Sheridan, is accused of the crime. Running counterpart to the violence is a tender love story: the deepening relationship between Lucas's daughter, Dru, and Paul Slater, the attorney for the defence. The drama reaches its shattering climax in a tense courtroom scene in which Paul Slater must make a decision that may cost him everything in the world that matters to him.

Also by
HAROLD Q. MASUR

★

THE ATTORNEY

*

HAROLD Q. MASUR

**THE
COMPANION BOOK CLUB**
ONDON AND SYDNEY

This edition, published in 1975 by
The Hamlyn Publishing Group Ltd,
is issued by arrangement with
Elek Books Limited

THE COMPANION BOOK CLUB

The Club is not a library; all books are the property of members. There is no entrance fee or any payment beyond the low Club price of each book. Details of membership will gladly be sent on request.

Write to:
The Companion Book Club,
Odhams Books, Rushden, Northants.

Or, in Australia, write to:
The Companion Book Club,
C/- Hamlyn House Books, P.O. Box 252,
Dee Why, N.S.W. 2099

*Made and printed in Great Britain
for the Companion Book Club
by Odhams (Watford) Ltd*
600871940
10.75/294

Part One

CHAPTER ONE

THE LAW OFFICES of Porterfield, Baker & Sheridan—six partners and twenty-one associates, including tax specialists and assorted drones of various categories—occupied two full floors of a tower suite high above Manhattan's financial district. Standard mid-century architecture, glass and anodized aluminium vaulting into the clouds over Broad Street, not more than fifty paces from the Classic Revival façade of the New York Stock Exchange.

An appropriate location, reflected Paul Slater, as he turned out of the teeming canyon into the relative quiet of a sterile lobby. Most appropriate, since the firm's principal clients consisted of a round dozen corporate Goliaths which it had shepherded through multiple mergers, acquisitions, and takeovers, skilfully skirting them past Argus-eyed anti-trust watchdogs and SEC examiners. Not one of the truly huge legal shops, but highly eminent and notably prestigious.

Leaving the elevator on the thirty-third floor, he experienced an abrupt dislocation, a total shift in environment. In a single moment he found himself transported into a milieu of hushed and sedate elegance. Dark panelling, oriental rug, high leather chairs, a Brancusi figure, a winding wrought-iron stairway to the floor above, and a reception desk monitored by a severely plain female of indeterminate years.

He crossed over and said, 'The name is Slater—Paul Slater. I believe Mr Sheridan is expecting me.'

She pressed a button on the intercom, spoke into the mouthpiece, then glanced up and smiled, concealing her surprise. 'Mr. Sheridan's secretary will be here in a moment.'

Not the customary procedure at all. He suspected that most visitors to the reigning partner were required to cool their heels for varying intervals, depending on prominence. And even then, only those on the policy-making level would eventually be admitted to the presence. So he felt duly flattered. And wryly amused at himself for being impressed by the churchlike atmosphere of a set-up which frequently dealt in artifice, either promoting it or frustrating its attempt by others.

Come now, he chided himself, easy on the cynicism. Not all lawyers who represent big business are unencumbered by scruples. There had to be those with some measure of social conscience. But these speculations were not what intrigued him. He was far more curious about the indirect summons from Lucas Holmes Sheridan that had brought him here. Was Porterfield, Baker & Sheridan really interested in a man with antecedents rooted in the Bronx, educated in public schools, and bearing a diploma not awarded by Yale or Harvard Law?

His mind skipped back to the meeting with Dean Julian Farquhar two days ago. In the Dean's office, overlooking Washington Square, Farquhar had been amiable but cryptic, approaching the subject from an oblique angle. He had looked at Paul through rimless glasses, the flour-white hair floating like a halo.

'We're arranging schedules for next semester, Paul. I was wondering if you'd consider an increase in your teaching load. Another class, say, in corporation law.' The clerical face, seamed and benevolent, smiled. 'Hardly an oppressive burden for a man of your energies.'

'Sorry, Julian. I'd have to beg off.' The first-name basis, unthinkable when he'd been a student of Farquhar's, now seemed natural.

'I thought you enjoyed teaching.'

'I do. Very much. Part time, though. I also have an active practice and my clients are entitled to first call. I can handle my present schedule without short-changing the students. Beyond that I'd only be fragmenting my energies.'

Farquhar sighed. 'Were your ears burning last night?'

'Now there's a *non sequitur* if I ever heard one. Who was talking about me?'

'Lucas Holmes Sheridan. You know his daughter, I believe.'

6

Paul nodded, suddenly deadpan.

'You handled her divorce.'

'Yes, I did.' Now where, Paul wondered, was this leading?

'But you never met Sheridan himself.'

'Not personally. I heard him address the Bar Association last month.'

'And your reaction?'

Suddenly Paul grinned. 'One has to read between the lines. I think Lucas Holmes Sheridan devoutly believes in motherhood, free enterprise, weak unions, and a strong Republican administration.'

'Come now, Paul. The man has credentials.'

'Ah, yes. Senior partner of Porterfield, Baker & Sheridan, a very rarified perch indeed. Former ambassador-at-large to two Presidents. Occasional adviser to the White House on Latin-American affairs. You say he mentioned my name. I hardly thought the gentleman was aware of my existence.'

'Oh, he is, my boy. Acutely aware—ever since you brought that minority stockholders action against Global Airlines. His firm took a licking on that one. It brought you to his attention. And then when that business with his daughter came up and he needed outside counsel, he discussed it one evening with me. I'm an old friend of the family, you know. He didn't want his own firm to handle it.'

'Too indelicate for them?'

'They've never been involved in divorce litigation. Anyway, he happened to mention Jim Sloane and I reminded him of your association with Sloane & Barish. He looked thoughtful and then asked me if you knew how to be discreet.'

'That divorce needed more than discretion. It needed intimidation. A contested action would have sullied the Sheridan name.'

'He suspected that, although Drusilla never told him the details. And he was impressed with the way you managed it. He told me he'd like to meet you. He asked me to arrange it.'

'I'm not inaccessible. But if he wants the inside story, he'll have to ask his daughter. I never discuss my clients' affairs with strangers.'

7

Farquhar smiled. 'He's curious, naturally. However, that's not what he's after.'

'Do *you* know, Julian?'

'He'll tell you himself. How about Wednesday, two-thirty?'

Paul elevated an eyebrow. 'All arranged? Just like that?'

'I anticipated no special reluctance. Not that you'd genuflect in his presence, but Lucas Sheridan is a man worth cultivating.'

'No argument on that.'

'Then I may confirm the appointment?'

'Why not? What have I got to lose?'

Now, in this reception room that reminded him of a chapel, he was aware of all the humming activity behind closed doors. Typewriters clacking in the stenographic pool, clerks busy at the information-retrieval files, tyros hunched over reference books in the library, staff members each diligently pursuing his own specialty. He heard a voice speak his name. 'Mr. Slater?'

'Yes, ma'am.'

'This way, please.'

He admired the clench of muscles in rounded buttocks as they preceded him up the winding stairway, speculating on his reaction to the old man. He recapped what he knew of the man's history. Lucas Holmes Sheridan, *Law Review* at Harvard, clerkship under the aegis of a Supreme Court Justice, thence to Porterfield & Baker with a personal introduction to Millard Porterfield himself, that iron-willed old predator who had joined forces with scholarly Asa Baker upon the latter's retirement from the Appellate Division.

An effective combination, those two. Porterfield, the polished courtroom orator; Baker behind the scenes constructing briefs, whole segments of which often appeared in the Court's decision. Specialty of the house—corporate law. Mergers, reorganizations, dissolutions, and endlessly defending against the encroachment of governmental authority. A natural habitat for young Lucas Sheridan. He had settled comfortably and nimbly into this background.

Now Millard Porterfield was dead, dying in harness, felled by a massive coronary while arguing an appeal in Washington.

Asa Baker, for all practical purposes, had retired, but several times each year his chauffeur would drive him down from Scarsdale, a misty shrunken legend, and wheel him up to the library where he would argue in a thin reedy voice with juniors researching precedent. One hour of this, and then back to his limousine.

So it was inevitable that Lucas Holmes Sheridan, through an amalgam of ambition, drive, presence, and intellect, would ultimately establish his suzerainty. And not until this position was unchallengeably established had he taken a leave of absence to serve various administrations on diplomatic missions.

The girl pronounced Paul's name.

From behind a bare desk in a corner of the vast room, its windows hermetically sealed, Lucas Sheridan elevated himself, hand outstretched, cold grey eyes alert, measuring and evaluating.

'Good of you to come, Slater. I've been wanting to meet you for some time. Dean Farquhar speaks most highly of you.' He indicated a chair drawn close to his desk. 'Please sit.'

Paul settled himself and crossed his knees.

'First,' Sheridan said, 'I want to thank you for the way you handled my daughter's divorce. I don't know how you managed it, but it was precisely the solution I'd hoped for.'

'Your daughter's marriage to Gordon Frazer was doomed from the start.'

'Did you meet Frazer personally?'

'In his lawyer's office, yes.'

'How did he strike you?'

'I prefer to stand mute. As an attorney, I know the penalty for slander.'

Sheridan shook his head ruefully. 'You know, in a way I was partly responsible. Frazer was one of our clients and I introduced him to Dru.' He paused, looking uncomfortable. 'I've heard rumours. Are they true?'

Paul made him say it. 'Would you be more specific, sir?'

'Does the man have homosexual tendencies?'

'On information and belief, yes.'

9

Sheridan's face tightened. 'Then why in the name of God did he marry her?'

'The usual reasons, I suppose. She provided a cloak of normality, of respectability. In a pinch, Frazer can probably handle women, though he'd prefer not to. He is also, I've been told, a collector. He covets beautiful possessions. Your daughter became one of them, another item in his collection.'

Sheridan sat back, his mouth sour, a tall spare man with an air of austere durability. 'May I assume that his allegations were false?'

'They were a gross distortion.'

'I'm curious, Slater. How did you persuade him to discontinue and agree to an out-of-state decree?'

'By convincing him and his attorney that a contested action in New York would be inadvisable.'

'As simple as that.'

It had not been simple at all. Paul added, 'Ordinarily, I don't touch matrimonial actions. I took this one as a favour to Jim Sloane.'

Sheridan sat back, folding his hands on top of the desk. 'Incidentally, what is your professional relationship to Sloane & Barish? Are you a member of the firm?'

'No, sir. We have a very loose and fluid association. Sloane is a politician; he generates the business. Barish handles all the paperwork. They retain me as counsel in charge of litigation.'

'Would you consider leaving them?'

There was a brief silence. Then Paul said, 'Not without a good reason.'

'Let me phrase it this way, Slater. Do you find their practice a challenge worthy of your talents?'

'Sometimes.'

Sheridan smiled ruefully. 'Such as the Global Airlines case?'

Paul smiled back. 'That's a pretty good example.'

'We had one of our best men on that matter.'

'I remember him. Alex Moore.'

'He tells me you gave him a very bad time indeed.'

'There was nothing he could sink his teeth into. Global's officers were guilty of a breach of trust. We caught them with their pants down. They had no authority to——' A placatory gesture stopped him.

'You made us quite aware of the facts,' Sheridan said. 'Moore thought he saw a loophole.'

'That loophole had been plugged two years ago.'

'We know that now. Somehow our research team missed it. Moore chopped a few heads on that one.'

'It was an obscure decision.'

'Perhaps. Dean Farquhar tells me that your graduate seminar on corporate law is one of the most heavily attended in the school's history.'

'That may be less of a compliment to me than an indictment of the profession.'

'How do you mean?'

'Corporations can afford big fees. It draws too many of the top men away from the practice of criminal law.'

'But you yourself rarely appear in the criminal courts these days.'

'Nothing interesting has come my way.'

'Do you object to the corporate set-up?'

'On the contrary. Corporations serve an essential function. My beef is with the people who run them.'

'In what way?'

'Price fixing. Specifically, those charges of criminal conspiracy to gouge the utilities. And they never denied it. All we got was a *nolo contendere*.'

'Yes. I agree. That sort of thing can and must be avoided.' His gaze was searching. 'Industry can use a man like you to pull the reins.'

'Me? The government has dozens of powerful regulatory agencies. Why me?'

'Because a man of your calibre, familiar with all those agencies, could anticipate, advise, and prevent.'

'Would they listen?'

'If you had the right affiliations, yes.'

'You mean Porterfield, Baker & Sheridan?'

'That is precisely what I mean. Corporate officers would not only listen, they would heed your advice.'

Paul quirked an eyebrow. 'Are you offering me a job?'

'Would you be amenable?'

'Probably not. My days as a hired hand are over.'

'Would you consider an invitation to join the firm? My partners have authorized me to discuss it with you.'

He needed authorization, Paul thought, like the man in the Kremlin needed permission to light a cigarette. A partner in Porterfield, Baker & Sheridan! Good God!

Paul could not help wondering whether Dru had anything to do with all this. He immediately rejected the thought. Lucas Sheridan was unaware of his daughter's social activities. His face revealing nothing, he considered the offer. Porterfield, Baker & Sheridan, solidly entrenched, rich in prestige, with yearly retainers running into seven figures.

'Have you discussed this with Jim Sloane?' he asked.

'Sloane is a reasonable man. I don't think he'd stand in your way.' Sheridan gathered his brows. 'You seem hesitant.'

What the hell, were they expecting him to fall all over himself? 'Except in emergencies,' he said, 'I never make snap decisions.'

'Naturally. Well, you know our position. Any organization can benefit from an infusion of fresh blood. We can offer you challenging problems, questions on constitutional law, appearances before the Supreme Court. And I think we can make it worth your while financially.'

Paul smiled. 'It's an interesting prospect. Porterfield, Baker, Sheridan & Slater.'

There was a frosty loss of expression. Sheridan gave him a startled look. 'Well, now, that seems a little premature. The firm already has six partners and there's a sensitive matter here of seniority.'

Short on humour, Paul thought. He said, 'It's a tempting offer, Mr Sheridan. I need time to think about it.'

'Of course. We're prepared to keep the offer open for——' The telephone buzzed and he reached for it. 'Yes?' A flash of irritation crossed his face. 'Absolutely not. You'd better discuss that with Moore. And tell Moore I want to see him in my office. You come along too. There's someone here I want you to meet.' He broke the connection and looked up. 'Donald Baker,' he explained. 'Asa Baker's son.' His tone was flat and expressionless.

It was general knowledge that Donald Baker's connection with the firm was due to neither competence nor sagacity, but simple nepotism. A cross borne with irascible fortitude by Lucas Sheridan. Baker's legal chores had steadily dwindled until he'd been relegated to a position as office manager and general factotum on all matters unrelated to litigation.

A moment later he appeared. Donald Baker was a soft, paunchy man in his middle forties, with a balding head and anxious mannerisms. His handshake was moist and, like his smile, uncertain. 'Moore will be along in a moment,' he said. 'May I offer Mr Slater my congratulations?'

'Not yet,' Sheridan told him. 'No decision has been reached.'

Baker said, 'You know, Mr Slater, we screened over a hundred possibilities for this offer. You were second on the list.'

'Who was first?' Paul asked dryly. 'The Chief Justice?'

Baker blinked as a knock sounded and the door opened. A smiling man shambled directly to Paul, hand outstretched. 'Hello, Slater. Pleasure to see you again. We're still reeling from that shellacking you handed us in the Global matter. I don't mind telling you, it was a chastening experience. I left that courtroom with my tail between my legs.'

Paul warmed to the man instantly. Alex Moore was overstating it. He had been a formidable opponent, resourceful, informed, articulate. Garbed in loose brown tweeds and carrying a meerschaum pipe, his attire in this office seemed incongruous. There was a vigorous masculinity and assurance in his manner, no hint of insecurity that some newcomer might jeopardize his own seniority.

'The law was on our side,' Paul said.

'So you instructed us. And we paid the tuition fee.' He turned to Sheridan. 'Have you spoken to him, Lucas?'

'Yes. He's taking it under advisement.'

'Well, we'd like to have you aboard, Slater.' No hard sell, no cataloguing of advantages, no condescension.

'How many are in the firm?' Paul asked.

Don Baker supplied the answer. 'All told, forty-two. Not including secretaries and filing clerks.'

'Oh, there are larger firms,' Moore admitted. 'But they need the manpower because they produce more boiler plate.'

Boiler plate—that exhaustive and deadly dull paperwork involved in registration statements, trust indentures, re-organizations, precisely the sort of work Paul felt would stifle him.

Lucas Sheridan must have read his mind. 'We have our share of routine operations, Slater, but we wouldn't expect you to bother with them.' He started to rise. 'I know you're a busy man. There's no point in meeting other members of the firm unless you reach an affirmative decision.' He offered his hand. 'Incidentally, would you be free this weekend? Some people you might find interesting are coming out to Sands Point. My summer place. If you can make it, we'd like to have you.'

Paul almost laughed. He had asked Dru for a date over the weekend. She had begged off, saying she had promised to spend it with the family. 'I'm free,' he said with alacrity, 'and I accept.'

Sheridan smiled. 'Let us know what train you're taking and I'll have someone pick you up at the station.'

'I'll probably drive.'

'Then my secretary will send you instructions.'

The amenities were formal and polite. Donald Baker accompanied him to the elevator. Outside, he flagged a cab. And sitting back on the way uptown, he examined the offer from various angles. Certainly it would mean a precipitate boost in income. But money had never been a major factor in shaping his goals. There were, however, other aspects. Senior partners of Porterfield, Baker & Sheridan were part of the power structure. Random names clicked through his mind, prominent members of the Bar who had passed into other areas of public life. Wendell Willkie, Henry Stimson, Tom Dewey, Wild Bill Donovan. . . .

Paul knew that he was not immune to such inducements; they could provide a man's place in the sun. Easy now, he told himself. Down, boy. Play it cool. Sleep on it. Plenty of time for a decision. Maybe ring his father tonight, discuss it with him. The old man would appreciate that. Eventually, he would say, 'Paul, you've chosen your own options since you were six.'

Philip Slater, high school mathematics teacher, retired, a widower now living in St Petersburg, Florida. A thoughtful, logical man who still retained a level-headed perspective in matters concerning his son. Memories swept in. As a boy, Paul had been underweight, blade-thin, bookishly haunting the public library. It was, in the end, his father who had steered him resolutely to the local Y, determined to broaden his son's activities. And with customary fervour, Paul had attacked his new hobby. Two hours every afternoon, groaning under the weights, sweating on the parallel bars. Observing with adolescent pride as the muscles toughened in arms and shoulders, ridging across his chest.

He remembered that birthday when he got his first tennis racquet and how he had haunted the city courts, learning by trial and error. He strove fiercely, his style unconventional, somewhat awkward, redeemed by tenacious retrieving. And three times he had reached the finals in the boys' division by driving his opponents into error.

Even now, the ritual was immutable. Twice a week, weights, squash, sauna, rubdown.

The cab let him off at Rockefeller Plaza. There was a backlog of work waiting at the office and a lecture on evidence to prepare for his evening class.

CHAPTER TWO

'IF WE CAN GET this evidence before a jury,' Abe Barish said, 'then we've got a chance.'

Paul nodded. 'One way or another, I'll manage it.'

It was late in the afternoon and Barish had brought him some notes for a trial brief. Barish was a slight, puckish man in his late fifties, with a high-domed forehead and bright humorous eyes behind heavy glasses. He could draw a contract so meticulously airtight that it could neither be broken nor even dented by a Caterpillar tractor. The two men enjoyed a warm, working relationship. Paul knew how much he would miss Abe if he ever left Sloane & Barish.

Earlier, a messenger had arrived with detailed motoring instructions to the Sheridan place at Sands Point. Paul had tried without luck to reach Dru and guessed that she had already left the city.

A voice boomed at them and they turned to find Jim Sloane's bulk filling the doorway. He was still wearing his hat and coat. 'Get set for a big one, gentlemen. We've got a new client. Small electronics outfit being raided by a gang of conglomerate cutthroats. The bastards are setting up a proxy fight. Tell you more on Monday.'

And he was off, launching himself down the corridor, a huge florid man, flamboyant and profane, with the lexicon of a mule skinner. A hearty backslapping member of many organizations from the Knights of Columbus to the Benevolent and Protective Order of Elks. A prodigious drinker, socializer. womanizer, storyteller, and procurer nonpareil of new clients, A wily advocate, but too active courting business to ply his trade.

Because of this, and because Abe Barish lacked the temperament for trial work, they had wooed Paul Slater with a set-up attractive to all parties. After his graduation, Paul had served five years as an assistant U.S. attorney for the Southern District of New York. His courtroom experience was extensive. Teaching had broadened his base of knowledge. Sloane & Barish supplied all office facilities and he handled their trial work on a percentage arrangement. He was entitled to develop his own practice. After the first year, they had offered him a full partnership, but Paul preferred to maintain his current status. Both older men were amiably resigned.

It was Jim Sloane who had first discussed Dru's divorce with Lucas Sheridan. And Sloane who had ushered her into Paul's office that unforgettable morning six months ago.

Gordon Frazer had served his wife with a summons and complaint, alleging adultery. This alone was most unusual. The divorce laws of the State had been liberalized to allow grounds far less drastic than adultery, which would involve accusations, denials, unsavoury publicity. So Paul's antennae instantly quivered.

'Mrs Frazer,' Jim Sloane said, 'this is Paul Slater. He's in charge of your case.'

Paul was quite unprepared for the physical impact. He'd seen pictures of her in the papers. They had captured only the visual image, missing the vibrant immediacy of her presence. A kaleidoscope of images flickered across his memory. Miss Drusilla Sheridan at the Cotillion, astride a horse in Connecticut, clinging to the mast of a sloop off Barbados, at the America Cup races, at the opening of a new musical. To society editors she was photogenic and newsworthy. Her marriage to Gordon Frazer had commanded half a page.

She was not, he saw, a spectacular beauty. Her figure was slender and athletic, her complexion a honeyed tan. Her eyes, almost violet, were large, eloquent, and challenging.

He stared at her like a schoolboy.

'Mr Slater,' she said, one eyebrow quirked with amusement.

He bounced up and pulled a chair close. He did not know at first that Sloane had left them alone. She found a cigarette and he quickly snapped the desk lighter. He noticed then a slight tremor in her fingers.

They studied each other for a moment and then broke the ice with self-conscious smiles. Her sculptured mouth was only lightly touched with colour. She had one small automatic mannerism, a way of lowering her lashes and then quickly lifting them to reveal fleetingly an unexpected vulnerability.

She asked, 'Am I in the presence of one of New York's outstanding divorce lawyers?'

'I'm afraid not, Mrs Frazer. What gives you that idea?'

'The fact that my father selected you. His recommendations are generally a guarantee of top quality. At least, almost always.'

'Why almost?'

'He also introduced me to Gordon Frazer. And he really believed Gordon was a great catch.'

Paul cocked his head quizzically.

'I know what you're thinking,' she said. 'I'm a big girl, all grown up, capable of making my own decisions. Quite true. I was taken in. I was flattered to be singled out by the great Gordon. He is handsome, dashing, and disgustingly talented. And utterly impossible. Do you know anything about him?'

'Only that Frazer is one of Broadway's most notable lyricists. That he collaborated with Brian Wirth on several successful musicals.'

'Not just successful, Mr Slater. The jackpot. A smash hit every time. *The Melody Man. Hats Off. Go For Broke.* Each worth the weight of its leading lady in platinum. Have you seen any of them?'

'Yes, he's good.'

'As a wordsmith, he's peerless. As a husband, perhaps even as a man, he's a false alarm. Nothing. A zero with the rim removed. Instinct should have warned me off. But I was dazzled by all the glamour. Even Dad thought he was a prime quality candidate. Old family, the right schools, fat royalties rolling in. Such a shiny surface, such a vacuum inside. And to add insult to injury, he lacked one truly important qualification.'

'What's that?'

'I don't want to shock you, Mr Slater.'

'I don't shock easily.'

'All right then.' She spoke without bitterness, a touch of self-mockery in her voice. 'After our honeymoon, Gordon seldom performed his connubial duties. And on those banner occasions when he did condescend, it was highly unsatisfactory. To put it bluntly, Counsellor, my husband prefers men to women.'

Paul kept his face imperturbably expressionless. 'Are you telling me he's a homosexual?'

'I am indeed.'

Paul studied the affidavit supporting Frazer's complaint. It named a co-respondent. Billy Clark. The name was vaguely familiar. It alleged that a private detective had entered Clark's apartment and found Drusilla Frazer in the bedroom. Both parties were in a state of undress. He picked up the affidavit and read the paragraph to her.

Anger coloured her face. 'You think I'm depraved?'

'Human, perhaps. I'm not here to judge.'

'Well, now, that's mighty big of you, Counsellor. An admirable display of tolerance. But quite unnecessary. So let us straighten this out right now. If that complaint says I committed adultery, it's a damned lie. Yes, I was in Billy Clark's apartment and nothing happened. First, that little oaf never laid a finger on me. I wouldn't let him. Second, he's just as queer as Gordon. Third, I don't sleep around; that's not my style. Fourth—oh, what's the difference, you probably don't believe me.'

Paul was delighted. He liked her reaction. Even more, he liked what she said. And his change in mood must have been infectious because her anger suddenly dissolved and she was smiling back at him.

He said, 'As a matter of fact, I do believe you.'

'Why? You hardly know me.'

'Intuition. It hasn't failed me yet. Is this the same Billy Clark, the song-and-dance man who's kicked his way through most of Frazer's shows?'

'It is.'

Paul remembered him as a very fruity specimen. He tapped the complaint. 'Was there no attempt to work out an amicable settlement?'

She shook her head. 'None. I had moved out of Gordon's apartment and taken my own place. And that truly bugged the great Gordon. Nobody had ever walked out on him before.'

'Would you settle for an uncontested out-of-state divorce?'

'Good Lord, yes. I suggested it myself, but he wouldn't even discuss it. He wanted me around. It added to his illusion of masculinity. Then, after I walked out, he planned that raid on Billy Clark's apartment, setting me up. He's vindictive because I know the truth about him. He can't tolerate my contempt. He wants to even the score by humiliating me.'

'Tell me about the raid.'

She made a face. 'Do I have to?'

'If you want me to help. I need all the facts and you'll have to provide them. That's our only chance of avoiding a public spectacle. Besides, everything you say in this room is privileged.'

'So I'm to have no privacy.'

'It's already been invaded. As you say, you're fair game for the papers. Nothing boosts circulation more than the erotic antics of prominent citizens.'

'I am not prominent.'

'Your father is. So don't expect reticence or good taste from the journalists.'

She sighed. 'What happened makes me seem rather foolish.'

'Mrs Frazer, I——'

'Please. I hate that name. When can I resume my own?'

'After the divorce.'

'That's too long to wait. You'll have to call me something else.'

'How about Drusilla?'

'That's reserved for my father. Make it Dru.'

'All right, Dru. Start at the top.'

He listened to her with marked intensity. In the beginning, if there had been any hint of sexual aberration, she was completely oblivious, blinded by the whirlwind courtship of a worldly, urbane, and spectacularly successful suitor.

'I was really quite naïve at the time. And he gave me the full treatment. A young and impressionable girl thrust into an exciting new world, dazzled by all those famous show people. It would have turned the head of an experienced courtesan. Even Ken was impressed.'

'Ken?'

'My cousin. He's taking his first year at Harvard Law. He was only six years old when he came to live with us after his parents died. My own mother was an invalid at the time. That threw us together more than we might have been. He was a strange child, which made me even more fiercely protective, although there wasn't that much difference in our ages. Anyway, Gordon had us all fooled. I suppose I was infatuated, which may not be love but is close enough to be mistaken for love. So he proposed, and I accepted.'

'When was that?'

'Three years ago.'

'All of it bad?'

'Except for the first few weeks. Gordon had chartered a boat for a cruise through the Caribbean. Then, without warning, he suddenly lost interest. We abandoned ship at St. Kitts and flew home. Business, he said. And that was it. For all practical purposes the end of our sex life. It took a bit of time for me to recognize the problem. It came as a terrible shock, a ghastly discovery for a young bride. I felt unused, like surplus stock mouldering on a shelf.'

It had all been bottled up and she was talking now without restraint. In the past, Paul's tendency had been to cut clients short on personal revelations, but he found himself with an insatiable hunger for information about Dru.

'Why didn't you cut out and leave him sooner?'

'Pride, I suppose. It's a family characteristic. We hate to admit defeat. But then it just got too utterly unbearable. I couldn't discuss it with Dad, though Ken knew about it. He encouraged me to break it off. When I asked Gordon for a divorce, he was adamantly opposed. I was trying at all costs to avoid a courtroom confrontation. For Dad's sake, really.'

'When did he find out your marriage was on the rocks?'

'After I moved out and took my own apartment. Dad really isn't able to cope with this sort of thing. He finds domestic quarrels terribly distasteful.'

'I take it you knew Billy Clark through Frazer?'

'Yes. Billy's been in most of Gordon's shows. He's a harmless little clown and I had no idea there was anything between them. He was amusing and full of deliciously bitchy gossip about theatre people. Occasionally he'd get house seats to some Broadway opening and for a while it was fun.'

'What happened at his apartment that night?'

'It was the first time I ever went there. Actually, we'd stopped off to see a friend who lives in the same building. It's a converted town house. I'm sure you know her name. Dolly Wayne.'

'Who doesn't?'

'Well, when we left Dolly's, Billy suggested a nightcap at his place. He fixed a drink, one drink only, and it got to me. Looking back now, I'm dead certain he put something into it. Because I have no recollection of the raid or what happened. Not until I saw a snapshot Gordon sent me.'

'Do you still have it?'

'Not likely. I tore it into a thousand pieces. Of course, I know they still have the negative.'

Paul's eyes had grown cold, his voice thin; the sudden change startled her. 'Conniving jackals. No doubt about it. Frazer set it up. And Clark co-operated. Look at it. If a man attempts to seduce his friend's wife, he makes pretty goddamn sure they won't be caught. He double-locks the door and he sure as hell wouldn't answer the bell. That private eye was supplied with a key or else Billy Clark left the latch open for him. It reeks of collusion.'

'And the most disturbing part was that I had thought Billy Clark was my friend.'

'You were duped. You could not contend with Clark's sexual preferences or his reluctance to offend Frazer, who controls future employment.'

She shuddered. 'Ugh! Do I have to go to court and testify that both my husband and my alleged lover are homosexuals?'

22

'I intend to keep you out of court.'

'You don't know Gordon.'

'Gordon doesn't know me.' Paul's smile was tight and humourless. 'I believe we have a handle that will change his mind.'

She studied him curiously. 'You know something, I believe you. I'm beginning to feel more confident. How many lawyers are there in New York?'

'I never counted. Perhaps ten or eleven thousand. You might get an accurate figure from the Yellow Pages. Why do you ask?'

'The odds were against me. I guess I'm lucky.' She stood up.

He reached for his pencil. 'Where are you staying?'

She gave him the address. 'Will I hear from you soon?'

'This evening. Are you free for dinner?'

Her eyes sparkled with amusement. 'More legal consultation?'

'Our lawyer-client relationship ends at the door to this suite. When I pick you up at seven-thirty the name will be Paul. Try it on for size.'

'Paul.'

'You're an excellent study.'

CHAPTER THREE

SANDS POINT, on the north shore of Long Island, had once been a highly fashionable retreat. More recently, a mild parvenu invasion was hastening the area's fading elegance. Nonetheless, a few of the older families, jealous of the Point's natural beauty, still clung to their enclaves of stately mansions.

Paul's directions had given him a precise fix. It was a cloudless day with that uniquely invigorating flavour of Indian summer. He drove with a keen sense of anticipation, looking forward to a full weekend in Dru's company. He let his mind wander, recalling that meeting in the small Italian restaurant when he told her to get ready for a trip.

'You are going to fly to the Dominican Republic, where a gentleman named Señor Felipe Morales will greet you and escort you to the posh El Embajador Hotel in Santo Domingo. The next morning he will pick you up and convoy you to the Palace of Justice for a brief hearing. Frazer will have signed a notice of appearance but will not appear to contest. By noon you will be unhitched and on your way home.'

'*Paul!*' She was ecstatic. 'I can't believe it. How did you manage?'

'First, I went to see Billy Clark. I told him we'd put him on the stand. We'd show his deviant relationship with Frazer. To say the least, that would cast considerable doubt on his credibility as a co-respondent. He might also be charged with perjury and conspiracy. Clark was frightened. He's a man who melts under heat. So he opened up. And of course we were right. That drink he fed you carried a dollop of chloral hydrate commonly known as a Mickey Finn. It knocked you out, after which he removed some of your clothes, then his own, and waited for the private eye with his little Brownie. This whole scenario was written, produced, and directed by your husband. It was easy to draft Billy Clark because he knew that future jobs depended on Frazer's good will.

'Next, I arranged a meeting with Frazer and his lawyer. I showed them a deposition Billy Clark had signed. The lawyer was shocked. He was shocked even more by evidence that Clark and Frazer were seen dining together soon after the alleged raid. This is not the kind of conviviality usually harboured between a cuckolded husband and the man who betrayed him. Frazer wouldn't have a prayer. He'd be open to a charge of conspiracy and perjury.'

Delighted, Dru leaned over and kissed him.

Paul had decided not to mention the rest of it. The sudden eruption, the livid rage, Frazer roaring in blindly with his fists flailing. It would have been heartless to prolong it. So Paul had measured his man carefully, stepped inside, and decked him with a single blow. Frazer sat on the carpet, his mouth loose, his eyes glassy.

Paul towered over him. 'Don't be a fool, Frazer. It's time to cash in your chips.'

The lawyer went over and offered a helping hand. Sullenly Frazer pulled his arm away and manœuvred on spaghetti legs into a chair. The lawyer stood in front of him and began to speak in a low intense voice. He had advised against the charge of adultery from the start. Now, if Frazer persisted, he wanted out. He wanted no part of it. He would not go into court and make a fool of himself.

Then Paul added the clincher. 'Financially you'll be getting off scot-free. Your wife is demanding no alimony, no settlement. She wants a clean break. Give us a notice of appearance and she'll fly to the Dominican Republic and you'll be off the hook.'

Frazer glared in frustration, but with all the legal talent lined up against him, he eventually conceded defeat.

He heard Dru clapping her hands. 'Oh, Paul, Paul, the best news I've had in months. We have to celebrate.'

'Fine. Let's finish dinner and go some place to dance.'

'Not a chance, Counsellor. Tonight I'm not sharing you with anyone. We're going to my place.'

He had left Grand Central Parkway some miles back and could now smell the bracing air of Long Island Sound. He pulled over for a quick look at his instructions. Another half-mile and he found the entrance between low stone walls. It led him along a gravelled driveway towards a rambling structure, an antique hybrid of weathered shingles, with a mansard roof, dormer windows, and the gingerbread ornamentation of a by-gone era. It was saved from actual ugliness by the magnificent setting. Beyond, on the glittering water, silhouetted against the sky and the distant Connecticut shore, he could see the sails of weekend mariners.

Off to one side there was an all-weather tennis court with a game in progress, its participants a chunky tan girl and a tall muscular youth. Several guests were watching on redwood chairs under peppermint-striped umbrellas. Then the driveway curved away towards the other side of the house. Paul felt an exultant lift at the sight of Dru's bottle-green Porsche.

Almost immediately a door under the portico opened and a black man in an immaculately white jacket with an even whiter smile approached. 'Mr Slater?'

Paul acknowledged his identity.

'We've been expecting you, sir. Mr Sheridan is out on the water. He told me to put you in the east wing and to make sure you were comfortable. If you need anything, please ask. The name is Quintus.'

It was a large room, sparsely furnished, with a single large window and an ancient brass bedstead. He dropped his bag on the luggage rack and looked out the window. It opened on the Sound. By craning his neck he could see the tennis court and the game in progress. The thought occurred to him that neither confiscatory taxes nor the high salaries for domestic help had completely foreclosed a way of life familiar to him only through early films portraying an elite society. There was a knock on the door.

'It's open,' he said.

Dru came in, her face alight. 'Paul! What a wonderful surprise! I found out only this morning from our housekeeper. Why didn't you phone me?'

'I tried. You'd already left.'

She cast a quick conspiratorial glance over her shoulder, came close, kissed him fleetingly, and stood back. 'I decided to come out ahead of everyone else. But what's all this with Dad? I didn't even know you'd met him.'

'Strictly business.'

'Law business?'

'In a way.'

'Don't just stand there. Tell me.'

'He's asked me to join Porterfield, Baker & Sheridan.'

She gaped, momentarily speechless.

'You look surprised,' he said.

'I'm thunderstruck. These bulletins keep flashing at me without warning. And I know Dad's firm specializes only in corporation law.'

'Happens I conduct a graduate seminar on the subject.'

'Paul! You never told me.'

'I was brought up to be modest.'

She regarded him expectantly. 'Well?'

'Well, what?'

'Have you accepted the offer? Is that why you're here?'

'The answer is no to both questions. I've reserved decision on the first and I'm here because I wanted to see you.'

'But you will take him up on it eventually, won't you?'

'Probably not.'

She was frowning.

'I don't understand.'

'Look, Dru. Your father's clients are single-mindedly consecrated to the pursuit of money. I'm not sure I want to devote the rest of my professional life helping them to achieve that ambition, worthy as it may be.'

She braced for argument. 'But Porterfield, Baker & Sheridan is——'

'Yeah.' He was abrupt to the point of discourtesy. 'What's our programme for this afternoon?'

She looked momentarily startled. 'Don't you even want to discuss it?'

'No.'

She stared at him, then smiled opaquely. 'You mentioned something about tennis. Did you bring any equipment?'

'Never travel without a spare outfit.'

'Then change your clothes. I hope you're good enough to provide some action for Ken. He's ex-varsity and down from law school for the weekend.'

'That large young quarterback type I saw on the court as I drove by?'

'Yes, indeed. He's warming up now with Peggy Wayne. I've arranged a doubles match for us.'

'This Peggy a guest here too?'

'She's Dolly Wayne's daughter. They're neighbours. You can see Dolly's place from the pool.'

Paul knew that Dolly Wayne had been the leading lady of all the Frazer-Wirth musicals. She was also the widow of Brian Wirth, her second husband. The composer had died earlier this year.

Dru paused at the door. 'I'll wait for you on the veranda.'

'I'm not bashful,' he said. 'You can stay while I change.'

'Please. Quintus is a very proper gentleman. And he's been watching over me since I was a child.'

'Quintus. An interesting handle. Where did he get it?'

'He says his father worked for a Latin professor. He was the fifth son of eleven children. We adore each other.' She stepped out and closed the door behind her.

He changed swiftly into white tennis shorts and shirt, pulling a sweater over his head. When he joined her five minutes later, she looked at the new steel racquet and said, 'Is that thing any good?'

'I'm not a power hitter. It gives me a little more whip.'

They started across the lawn. 'Seriously, Paul, can you really play?'

'I reached the boys' finals in Central Park.'

She laughed delightedly. 'The things I don't know about you.'

'All you have to do is ask. It's the best way to get information. For example, suppose you fill me in on those people
sitting around the court.'

'There's Dolly Wayne and Alex Moore. Have you met
Alex?'

'Yes.'

'Well, they seem to have a thing going between them. Alex is
staying at Dolly's place. Peggy is sweet on Ken. Has been ever
since she was a knobby-kneed kid. And the other couple is
Ernest and Janet Stoufer. They're staying with us.'

'Stoufer, Wingate & Company, the brokerage firm?'

'Uh-huh. They're clients of Dad's.'

As they drew closer, he said under his breath, 'Hey, now,
look at that Dolly Wayne. The footlights hardly do her justice.'

'Down, boy! She's too old for you. Besides, Moore would
challenge you to a duel.' Her hand fastened on his arm.
'Watch Ken serve.' There was pride in her voice.

The youth was tall and rangy, with a look of resilient fitness.
Cool, self-confident. He tossed the ball high, arched his back,
and a thundering serve exploded across the net with projectile
velocity.

The chunky girl lunged. To Paul's surprise, she managed
a return. But Ken had moved up and now he angled it
sharply out of reach.

'Hey!' Paul said. 'Doesn't he ever let up, even against girls?
He's giving that child no quarter.'

'Peg doesn't need any and she'd be insulted if he did. She's
the club champ, female division. Eliminated me in the quarter-
finals last year.'

'Cute, too.' Paul was admiring the healthy pneumatic look,
pulsing with youthful vitality. Solar exposure had turned the
pert round face a lovely tan. She had durable legs and dark
hair cut short in a choppy hoyden style.

'And hopelessly mad for Ken,' Dru said. 'Watch this one. He
can't beat her from the baseline.'

They were engaged in a long-distance exchange now, holding everyone's attention. There was a musical sound to the ping
of a tennis ball against tightly strung gut. The point ended as

29

Peggy whipped a backhand down the line, and play was suspended for introductions.

Alex Moore's cordial greeting was lightly scented with bonded whisky. Glasses and set-ups lay on the shaded table. He presented Dolly Wayne with a proprietary air. In the merciless glare of bright sunlight, behind her dazzling smile, Paul saw the barely visible network around her eyes. Still, in some indefinable way, she had managed to retain a youthful quality. There was more than a hint of sensuality in the warm configuration of her mouth. And the flair, the presence, the sheer animal magnetism would make her stand out in any group.

'So you've challenged our youngsters to a set of doubles. I warn you, Mr Slater, they're a pair of tigers. They have no respect for their elders.' But her words carried a note of pride and affection.

Ernest Stoufer came to his feet, hand outstretched, a quizzical solemnity in his appraisal of Paul. He was a solid, bulky man with the face and bearing of a Roman senator. 'Well, Slater, you look a pleasant enough chap. I had you tagged as some sort of ogre after that Global Airlines fiasco.'

Paul lifted an eyebrow.

'Were you involved in that?'

'Peripherally, my dear chap. Stoufer, Wingate & Company were the underwriters of a bond issue for Global just two weeks before you lowered the boom.' He turned slightly. 'I'd like you to meet my wife.'

Janet Stoufer was a large, amiable, anxious woman in a summery outfit with a loud floral design enhanced by a considerable amount of bizarre costume jewellery. Some glandular imbalance, or over-indulgence, had padded her grossly. Her body seemed a loose assemblage of sagging components insecurely attached. But her grip, when she shook Paul's hand, had a steamfitter's crushing power.

Stoufer said, 'I'm a betting man, Mr Slater. Would you like a little wager on this match?'

Paul shook his head, smiling. 'Afraid I'll have to pass. Betting tightens my game.'

'How about you, Alex? I'd like a little action.'

'Not a chance, Ernie,' Moore said. 'I've never seen Slater play before.'

'You've seen him in court.' A suggestion of irony in the comment.

'In a law court, not on a tennis court. Don't you get enough action five days a week on Wall Street?'

Stoufer gave a barking laugh.

Dru said quietly, 'I'll take your bet, Ernie.'

'How much?'

'You name it.'

'Fifty dollars.'

'You're covered.'

'Hey, now!' Ken said. He was standing by, waiting to be introduced. 'You're putting me on a spot, Dru honey. I don't want to cost you money.'

'Don't worry about it. If it makes our guest happy, I'm satisfied. Ken, Peg, this is Paul Slater.'

Ken Sheridan smiled crookedly, the lines of his face accentuated by sharp bone structure. Peg was grinning widely, her arm linked in his. 'I'm ready whenever you two are,' she said. 'Suppose Ken and I rest a few minutes while Dru warms you up.'

Paul thought it was a fine idea. Ernie Stoufer removed a single fifty-dollar bill from his wallet and anchored it under a bottle of Jack Daniels. 'Your credit is good enough for me. Dru,' he said, clamping a cigar happily between his teeth.

Dolly Wayne treated them to one of her hallmarks, a silvery glissando of laughter.

They volleyed for five minutes. Paul realized instantly that Dru was the product of long-time professional coaching, her style fluid and classic. By contrast, he felt a little awkward in his self-taught game. The steel racquet suited him fine. Quite unlike that first Harry C. Lee, which had all the resilience of an old snowshoe.

Then Dru joined him as Ken and Peggy Wayne crossed to the other side of the net. 'How about a little side bet?' Peg asked. 'Losers pay for the movies tonight. There's a great double bill at the drive-in. Horse opera and a new skin flick from Sweden.'

'Not on your life,' Dru said. 'The last thing I need is four solid hours of gunplay and eroticism in a cramped car with two libidinous adolescents.'

'Are you talking about my little girl?' Dolly Wayne demanded.

'Your little girl is all growed up, Mother,' Peggy told her.

'I'll believe it when your hair is white and you need a walking stick. You're still a child.'

Paul smiled inwardly. This nubile eighteen-year-old, so flamboyantly packed into a velvety hide, exuded the impact of a *Playboy* centrefold. He spun his racquet. Ken called it accurately and elected to serve. Dru took the forehand court to receive first.

Ken toed the baseline. He smiled pleasantly and leaned into the ball. It rocketed into the corner of the service box, well out of Dru's reach.

'Ah, well,' she said fatalistically. 'He can't do that every time. He'll probably miss as many as he makes.'

Paul got set. Ken's first serve was a fault. He followed his second to the net. Paul tossed a lob neatly over his head and Ken reversed, galloping back to make a futile stab at the ball. He shook his fist in mock anger and stood there laughing.

'Not elegant, but effective,' he said.

From there on, it was touch and go, with no service break until the fifteenth game, when Dru knocked a backhand down the line to catch Peggy flatfooted. Tasting victory, she served the final game with a sudden burst of energy. On the crucial set point, Ken drove hard and Paul lunged to retrieve. He thought his return was out.

'Sorry,' he told Dru.

'Sorry nothing,' Ken said. 'It nicked the line. Your set. How about a return match?'

'Not today,' Dru said. 'You and Peg can knock yourselves out if you want to. We've had it. Tomorrow morning maybe.'

'Same bet?' Ernie Stoufer asked her.

'Sure. Paul and I are an unbeatable combination.' She

fielded the fifty dollars and made an elaborate ceremony of folding and tucking it into her bosom. 'What would you say to a long cold drink?' she asked Paul.

'I would say the sooner, the better.'

'Tom Collins?'

'Perfect.'

While she mixed the ingredients, he stole another look at Dolly Wayne. The phenomenon of fame had always intrigued him. His memory leapfrogged with pleasure to the last Frazer-Wirth musical in which she had starred. The last because after that her husband had suffered his final illness. And after Brian Wirth's death, Paul had read somewhere that Gordon Frazer was searching for a new collaborator. He was aware of the oddly interwoven relationships that existed among all these people. A sense of fitness, sensitivity perhaps, would probably keep Dolly Wayne from inviting Gordon Frazer to her own place here at the Point.

'Anyone for the pool?' Dru asked. 'The water's heated this time of year.'

Alex Moore stretched to his feet. 'We brought our swimsuits with us. How about it, Dolly?'

Dru walked Paul back to the house. 'I really don't know how we did it. I haven't won a set from that pair all summer.'

'Tactics,' he said, tapping his forehead. 'We out-generalled them.'

She quirked an eyebrow at him. 'Aren't there some things you can't do at all?'

'My God, yes. Algebra, cartwheels, sky-diving, the minuet, among many others. About the game, though, your young cousin goes for broke on every shot. I try to keep the ball in play until there's an opening. That way the plodders often top the grandstanders.'

'Well, the system works and it was a very sweet victory. And a joy to take Ernie's money.'

'Do you always bet with Stoufer?'

'This was the first time. Dad says Ernie never makes a wager except on a sure thing. I resented his automatic assumption that we'd lose.'

'He took it in good spirit.'

'Sure, because he expects to win it back tomorrow.' She grinned mischievously. 'Let's disappear in the morning and deprive him of the chance.'

Paul laughed. They reached the house and she told him to meet her at the pool.

When he emerged in trunks, she was already gliding through the water with the sleek grace of a porpoise, wearing no cap, the light hair plastered to her skull. Alex Moore and Dolly Wayne were stretched out on a pair of plastic lounges. Compared to the others, Paul's skin seemed incongruously pale. There had not been much time for exposure during the past summer. But he was grateful for the health club that had kept his body lean and hard.

He dived in alongside Dru. They swam the full length of the pool three times, pacing themselves idly. He did not see Janet and Ernie Stoufer and guessed that they had retired for a nap before dinner. When Peggy and Ken appeared they began churning the water with unbridled energy, driving Paul and Dru to refuge on the apron.

Dru said, 'There's enough sun left to give that white hide of yours a nasty burn. You want some lotion.'

He shook his head. 'I hate the stuff.'

She regarded him with approval. 'At least you look fit. We've had members of Dad's firm out here with enough blubber on them to fry a moose.'

'Occupational hazard,' he said. 'Law is a sedentary profession.'

'That's no excuse. How come you manage?'

'Habit. And necessity. I seem to function better when I'm in condition.'

She said accusingly, 'You're staring at Dolly Wayne again.'

'She's a prime example of what I mean.'

Dolly, in a bikini, unabashedly exposed, lay on her stomach. Her body was remarkably well preserved, its rounded contours firm and smooth, invitingly mature. Moore, propped on one elbow, leaned over, rubbing suntan lotion into her shoulders and back. They seemed oblivious of their surroundings, as if no

34

one else in the world existed. He would squeeze fresh oil into his palm. His strokes were slow, caressing, lingering along her spine. As Paul watched, he noticed a change in the man's face. It grew heavy and took on a humid faraway look.

Paul, vaguely embarrassed, was about to turn away when Dolly rolled languorously over and sat up. Her mouth was slightly swollen and her eyes had a glazed, unfocused quality. There was a tacit, unspoken communication between them. Moore stood up and reached for her hand. He pulled her off the lounge and they started across the lawn towards Dolly's house and disappeared over the slope.

'All right,' Dru said. 'Eyes front and centre. Don't let those two give you any wild ideas.'

'So you noticed too.'

'I've seen that routine before.'

He glanced towards the pool. Peggy and Ken were splashing, ducking each other, absorbed in themselves, the centre of their own special universe, totally unaware of the scene just played out.

After a while Dru started to rise. 'I think you've had enough sun, Paul. Besides, it's getting to be about that time of the day. I'm going up for a shower. Cocktails at six. Dinner around seven.'

CHAPTER FOUR

QUINTUS was handing Lucas Holmes Sheridan a drink when Paul entered the large living room, its screened doors opening on a terrace. Sheridan was dressed informally in grey flannels, an open sports shirt, and a navy blazer. His afternoon fishing on the Sound had put a mahogany polish on the high broad forehead. He welcomed Paul in his peculiarly reserved manner, inquired about his accommodation, and hoped he would be comfortable.

'We seem to be the first ones down,' he said. 'I would like to make a suggestion. Quintus mixes the finest martinis this side of paradise. It has my unequivocal recommendation.'

Paul smiled at Quintus. 'If you please.'

'I suppose you're wondering about the name. Shall we tell him, Quintus?'

'He's the fifth son,' Paul said.

'Ah, so Dru told you.'

'Yes, sir.'

Quintus brought him the cocktail. 'Very dry, sir. I would suggest no more than two of these if you plan on going out this evening.'

'Depends on your tolerance quotient,' Sheridan said. 'I should think one would be plenty.' He chuckled softly. 'A year ago Alex Moore miscalculated his capacity and had three of them on an empty stomach. It paralysed him. He sat through dinner with an idiot grin on his face and ate not one single morsel throughout the entire meal.'

Paul laughed. He tasted the martini. It was pure nectar. He nodded his approval to the houseman, deciding nevertheless to make it last, that one would be quite enough.

Sheridan studied him quizzically. 'I was under the impression you were a scholar, not an athlete. I hear you gave my nephew a tennis lesson this afternoon.'

'I had Dru's help. The boy beat himself. Youth flexing its muscles. If he'd concentrate more on tactics than on raw power, we shouldn't have stood a chance.'

'He needs seasoning. Ken is studying law, you know.'

'Yes, Dru told me.'

'I'm rather proud of the boy. He's lived with us ever since my brother died. He's more of a son than a nephew.'

'Will you take him into the firm when he graduates?'

'If he decides to join us, yes. I'm generally not in favour of nepotism, but we set a precedent with Asa Baker's son, Donald. As a matter of fact, Ken has been working at the office during his last two summer vacations. I think he has the makings of a lawyer. Sharp mind, retentive memory, good analytical ability. Ah, here he is now.'

Ken Sheridan stood grinning in the doorway. 'Couldn't help overhearing that last remark.' He crossed over to join them. 'Whatever they're drinking, Quintus, I'll have the same.' He turned to Paul. 'Dru tells me you teach law besides practising it.'

'On a part-time basis.'

'Uncle Lucas thinks I have a tendency to coast along at school. He says I don't study hard enough. But I've never flunked an exam yet. Does a chap really have to be a grind?'

'Not if he's a genius. Do you fit that category?'

The grin widened. 'I never gave it much thought. What's your specialty, Paul?'

'General practice. Trial work mostly. What area of the law appeals to you, Ken?'

'I'm not sure. But I've read biographies of Clarence Darrow, Earl Rogers, Bill Fallon. Great stuff. Those boys had a field day in court.'

'Your uncle says you might join his firm. I don't think you'd find that kind of excitement in corporation law.'

'That may be. But I'm willing to bet those lawyers weren't deskbound bookworms.'

'You'd lose, Ken. The top men in any profession spend long

grinding hours at their work. Especially trial men. He might have to be thoroughly familiar with medicine, pathology, serology, anatomy, ballistics, finance, art—you name it. And one can't absorb that kind of knowledge by osmosis. You simply stick your nose in the appropriate source and sweat. And that's only the beginning. During the trial you may be up most of the night, studying and analysing the previous day's testimony, preparing your cross-examination. Is it a grind? Drudgery? My God, yes. A man has to believe in what he's doing.'

Lucas Sheridan was watching the boy's reaction from under lowered brows.

Ken shook his head. 'I see what you mean. I never thought of it like that.'

'Does it shake you up? Well, never mind. It has its compensations.'

Then, as the Stoufers joined them, the conversation became general. With her ear-rings and bracelets, Janet Stoufer jangled with jewellery. Her husband's face was puffy with sleep. He headed straight for the bar and sluiced down a martini in a single draught. It perked him up at once. Almost immediately, Dolly Wayne arrived with her daughter and Alex Moore, and the cocktail hour picked up momentum. Dru was the last to arrive. She wore a pale yellow outfit of knitted silk. Paul manœuvred her into a corner of the large room.

'Do you always dress like that for dinner?' he asked.

'We're going out later, visiting friends in the area. Is that a Quintus cocktail in your hand?'

'It is.'

'How many have you had?'

'This is the first. Your father warned me.'

'What were you two gabbing about?'

'This and that. Then Ken joined us. He seems very proud of the boy.'

'So am I. I think we did rather a good job of raising him. It was my responsibility mostly, Dad's been away so much. But Ken is the son he never had and the brother I always wanted. We missed him dreadfully after he went off to school.' Something caught her attention and she peered over his shoulder. 'Mrs Shanahan is signalling me. Dinner must be ready.'

He turned and saw a short bustling woman with rimless glasses.

Dru semaphored with her eyebrows and Mrs Shanahan nodded.

'Time to collect our guests,' Dru said.

She had been trained as her father's hostess under varied conditions in many places, and Paul noticed how efficiently she herded everyone towards the dining room.

Dinner was simple: a leg of lamb carved and served by Quintus with Lucullan generosity, baked potatoes, broccoli and mint jelly, all prepared with an old-fashioned savoury skill. Appetites were zestful after the day's vigorous activities, and conversation was temporarily suspended. Lucas Sheridan had broken out a treasured burgundy and it added to the pleasant glow.

When coffee came, conversation picked up. Dolly Wayne told several amusing anecdotes about her experiences while shooting a film in Hollywood. Alex Moore must have heard the stories many times before, but he listened attentively and laughed heartily along with the others. Ernie Stoufer recalled his boyhood days as a runner on Wall Street. He claimed he was only a block away when the historic bomb exploded in front of J. P. Morgan & Company, though it seemed to Paul, judging from the man's age, that he had to be stretching his dates. Janet Stoufer made no contribution at all. Her small, busily chomping mouth was totally occupied in dispatching a second portion of Mrs Shanahan's apple pie, ear-rings bouncing in concert with her jaws.

Sensing everyone's reluctance to leave the table, Lucas Sheridan said, 'Brandy now, Quintus. The Polignac.'

Peggy Wayne turned towards Paul and said with rare seriousness, 'Ken has been talking about a career in criminal law, Mr Slater. He doesn't know what kind of people he'd be dealing with. I think he'd listen if you told him.'

'What kind of people are you talking about, Peggy?'

'You know, gangsters, pimps, whores, narcotics peddlers, people like that.'

Her mother looked shocked. 'Now, where in the world did you learn about——'

'Please, Mother, stop being so old-fashioned.'

Paul smiled. 'A lawyer doesn't have to consort socially with his clients, Peggy. He doesn't pal around with them. He merely represents them in court. The man's vocation is irrelevant. It's the lawyer's job to see that he gets a fair trial. That happens to be the fundamental right of everyone living in this country.' He shook his head ruefully. 'I wish I could say this without sounding pedantic.'

'Say it any way you like,' Dru told him.

'Well, crime is not a monopoly of gangsters, Peg. Have you read a newspaper lately? Every single issue carries a piece about some criminal violation being charged against bankers or brokers, politicians, students, labour leaders, almost anyone you can think of. Not all of them are guilty. Some of them may be innocent. So if all the good lawyers were to shun the criminal courts, who'd go to bat for them? You may not know this, but some of our most notable figures have appeared as defence attorneys. Alexander Hamilton and John Adams, to name only two. Seems to me that travelling in such company would be an honour.'

Alex Moore grinned sardonically. 'What's more, bankers and brokers can afford very substantial fees, can't they, Ernie?'

Stoufer laughed. 'Well, if I ever got my finger caught in the till, a good lawyer would be worth anything he charges.'

Paul said, 'Fat fees may be a minor consideration.'

'That so?' Stoufer had raised an eyebrow. 'Then what would interest him?'

'Justice. Fighting for the dignity of man. And I mean any man, rich or poor. But especially the poor. Because an attack against human rights generally starts at that end. And nobody seems to care. Nobody gives a hoot in hell for the poor hapless indigent caught in the jaws of our criminal process. After all, he's nobody. A cipher, without a job perhaps, without a family or friends. Who needs him? Society can get along very nicely without him. So you have apathy and indifference. And right there is the fracture point. Right there the Bill of Rights begins to collapse. And once it starts, some clown like Hitler comes along and grabs power. Then people become the tool of the State, instead of the other way round. So you see, Peg, we need able lawyers to defend those rights. We simply cannot afford to leave it to bunglers. The risk is too great.'

His speech had a sobering effect. Alex Moore said, 'You're putting an awful burden on the legal profession.'

'Well, who else is trained to do the job?'

Dolly Wayne lifted her glass. 'A toast. I want to thank you, Paul.'

He looked at her curiously. 'What for?'

'For talking to my daughter like an adult, which I seldom do. For exposing her to the realities of life, when I have a tendency to protect her from them.'

He was embarrassed, but Dru brought it mercifully to a quick conclusion. She glanced at her watch and started to rise. 'That's it, people. Please excuse us. We have to run.'

'Where to?' Lucas asked her.

'Small bash at the Websters'.'

CHAPTER FIVE

AT NINE O'CLOCK on Saturday morning Ernie Stoufer stepped aboard the scrubbed teak deck of Lucas Sheridan's ketch, *Flagship II*. He knew that sailing had long been the awyer's chief hobby. He himself was indifferent to the sport; he was susceptible to motion sickness, and had swallowed two Dramamines before leaving the room. At the door, he'd paused for a look at Janet's puffy face. She was snoring like a drunken pipefitter, her hair tangled across the pillow. He had not been gentle closing the door. Nothing less than a ten-gun salute could wake her.

He spied Alex Moore hunkered down and rummaging in a pail of live bait. Ernie Stoufer felt a mild stab of guilt. A sudden vivid memory flashed across his mind, bringing with it, unbidden, that nagging visceral twist. Jesus H. Christ, he thought, that Dolly Wayne! Like a goddamn bucking bronco. He'd hung on to the bedposts just to stay aboard. And if he hadn't been half out of his skull, he would probably have needed a couple of seasick pills right then and there. He still couldn't believe his luck.

He greeted Moore, and called out to Sheridan, who was checking the mizzen and mainsails, 'How does it look, Lucas?'

'Just enough wind so we don't have to use the auxiliary.'

'Where's Slater?'

'He should be along any minute.'

'Never thought you'd be able to cut him loose from Dru. They seemed to hit it off.'

Moore said, 'He's never been fishing. She insisted he try it.'

'This will be a short run,' Sheridan said. 'Couple of hours at the most.'

Stoufer didn't care for fishing himself. Those wall-eyed scaly little bastards held no attraction for him except boned, skinned, seasoned, and broiled. Not enough action. The long intervals waiting for those lipless jaws to take a hook made him edgy and impatient. He took a deep breath and smiled inwardly, immensely pleased with himself. He felt an expansive euphoria and knew that its source was easily identifiable. Yes, sir. Dolly Wayne for one. And that new underwriting for another. Especially with Stoufer, Wingate & Company as the syndicate manager. By God, the world was turning into one very sweet piece of real estate. He produced a silver flask.

'Shot of bourbon, Alex?'

'At this time of morning?'

'Does your stomach look at a clock? This is a celebration.'

'For what?'

Stoufer could reveal only half the truth. 'For your sterling efforts, my friend, in steering that Calox issue past the SEC. We're pricing the bonds at a healthy premium and the syndicate is being cleaned out in advance.' He took a short pull of bourbon and put the flask away. 'Which is my rod?'

'Help yourself.'

'You gonna bait a hook for old Ernie, Alex. I wouldn't touch one of those things with a window pole.'

'They don't bite, Ernie.'

'Neither does crap. But that doesn't mean I have to handle the stuff.'

Moore smiled at Stoufer's coarseness; Lucas Sheridan showed no reaction.

Stoufer waved. 'Here comes our young lawyer friend. Hop aboard, Slater. We're ready to shove off.'

'Sorry to keep you waiting,' Paul said.

'You're just in time,' Sheridan told him. 'All right, Alex. Pull in the lines.'

Moore cast off and began hoisting sail. From his post at the wheel, Sheridan half turned to indicate the equipment. 'There's your tackle, Paul. Any instructions you need, Moore's in charge.'

Paul reached for a fibreglass rod. 'What's available in these waters?'

'Bluefish, sea bass, fluke, flounder—all of them are good eating.'

'This is my third time out,' Stoufer said, 'and I never had a nibble. If you should need a little libation, Counsellor, I have the makings.' He patted his hip pocket.

'Not at the moment. Thanks anyway.'

Stoufer was sizing him up. Fit-looking chap. Trim, hard, somewhere in his middle thirties, with a face of blunt flat planes and sceptical eyes. His movements positive and precise. Sharp mind, judging from last night, and a tough core of integrity, physical confidence, all radiating an air of restlessness. This morning, however, he looked a trifle drawn. Stoufer wondered if he was bedding down Lucas's daughter. Now, there was a prime piece of merchandise. A shade slender perhaps, but he wouldn't mind taking a hack at that himself. Provided Dolly hadn't drained him. Jesus, he thought, if they could only read my mind. They'd say I was a dirty old man. But what the hell, I was a dirty young man too.

If they only knew. Especially Alex. . . .

Flagship II was on an easterly course now, Sands Point and Glen Cove astern, canvas slack under the desultory breeze. They had their lines over the side. Stoufer knew that Sheridan would employ the auxiliary only as a last resort; he had the sailor's contempt for internal combustion.

Ernie Stoufer was feeling more expansive by the moment. 'Anybody here like to pick up a little easy money?' he asked.

'How?' Moore was suddenly attentive.

'Old Wally Bassett is retiring from an active role in Global. Chairman of the board, you remember. He's loaded with common, been exercising options for thirty years. Now he wants to diversify. Block that size shouldn't be traded on the floor. We're offering it on a secondary, below market, no commissions. It's over-sold now and one of these days it'll go through the roof. We're holding a fair-sized piece for our own portfolio.'

'Earmark five hundred for me,' Moore said.

'You, Lucas?'

'Same. Five hundred.'

Stoufer gave Paul a quizzical look. 'After what you did to us

44

on the Global lawsuit, Slater, you're not entitled. But I'm not a hard man. And I am in a forgiving and generous mood. So speak up.'

'What's the current market?'

'Thirty-two and a quarter at Friday's close.'

'Price-earnings ratio?'

'Twelve times.'

'Put me down for a hundred.'

Stoufer grinned happily. 'You're a member of the club now. Insider stuff. How do you like it?'

'Fine. So long as nobody gets hurt.'

Alex Moore came erect. 'Oh-oh, I've got one.' His line had gone taut. He leaned over the rail and watched the silvery flash of scales in the frothing water. Moore was crooning half to himself, 'Ah, come along now, come to daddy, you fat lovely monster.' He played the line out with skill, and when the fish tired at last, he pulled in a large sea bass.

At that precise moment there was a heavy tug on Slater's line. He felt a surge of excitement and braced himself. His drag was set too tight and the reel whined as something went streaking through the water in a breathless rush.

'Jesus!' Stoufer breathed. 'You got a barracuda there, boy.'

Sheridan chuckled. 'Not in these waters. Play him easy, Paul. Don't let him get away.'

Slater fought it gallantly, enjoying the contest. But he was inept, inexperienced, and suddenly the line snapped, leader, hook, bait, everything gone. He turned to Alex Moore, looking mortified.

'Don't worry about it. Better luck next time.'

'So I'm the only virgin here,' Stoufer observed complacently. 'Maybe the goddamn fish don't like me. Well, I don't like them either.' He leaned back and closed his eye to the sun, tipping his hat forward.

They could have the fish. He had the Calox deal. He'd nailed it just right, outbidding First Boston, Goldman Sachs, half a dozen others. A coup. Compared to those Goliaths, Stoufer, Wingate was a pygmy. Ah, what a day that had been! First the winning bid, and that same afternoon the business with

45

Dolly. It might kill him, but what a way to go. Under the brassy sun, he let the scene drift back across his mind. . . .

The Policy Committee was in session. Miles Wingate, a short paunchy man with a computerized brain, had the floor. He also had, Stoufer knew, a tendency to caution.

'Then we're all agreed,' Wingate said. 'We've been invited to participate in the Texarkana offering. And we've accepted. That much is settled. The question is, how much? The Dillon group suggests five million. Can we afford a slice that size? I think it's too much for the firm at this time.'

'Query,' he said. 'How's our inventory moving?'

'Slowly. We still have close to a million left on those municipals.'

'Suppose we dump them at a discount. We'll more than make it up on Texarkana. The terms are attractive. It's non-callable for five years. They've applied for listing. It's priced right for our institutional investors. And if our sales people get on the blower, those bonds will walk out of here in forty-eight hours.' He levelled a look at Karl Hydek, head of research. 'Any comment, Karl?'

Hydek, the economist, a spidery man with owlish eyes, lured from a teaching post in the Midwest, had proved his worth on a dozen deals. He cleared his throat. 'Interest rates are headed down. 'Nuff said. The Texarkanas should respond favourably. I suggest we retain a sizable batch in the house account.'

Stoufer's eyes encompassed the assembled faces. He slapped the desk sharply. 'No further debate. We're for the lot.'

Wingate didn't like being stampeded. He started to object. 'Now, just one moment——'

Stoufer cut him off. 'Miles, have we ever lost money on Hydek's judgement?'

'But this is a tight money market.'

'Mr Wingate,' Hydek said, 'I have a report on my desk. Texarkana's profit margin is close to the highest in the industry. Working capital more than adequate. Debt financing sound. If you——'

'All right.' Wingate threw his hands up in surrender.

46

The door opened and Stoufer's secretary came towards him He scowled. What the hell! She knew better than this. Meetings of the Policy Committee were sacrosanct. Not to be interrupted except for emergencies.

She bent over and whispered in his ear.

Ernest Stoufer pushed himself away from the table and stood up. He saw the curiosity in their eyes. 'Carry on, gentlemen. I'll be available in my office.'

Dolly Wayne, he thought. What the hell gives?

Stoufer walked briskly along the aisle past account executives talking to customers on the telephone in low, sincere voices. Up front, ever-changing quotations crawled across the screen. Stoufer had never done business with Dolly Wayne, but he knew that she was a market plunger. He had invited her down several times, offered her lunch at the Bankers' Club, a personally conducted tour of the Exchange, but she had always put him off.

She was seated in his office, the bright smile not touching her eyes. 'Hello, Ernie. I hope you don't mind my barging in like this.'

'You're welcome any time.'

Her looks never failed to amaze him. About the same age as Janet, barely marked by the years, her complexion smooth as a baby's rump, the hourglass figure firm and solid. How in hell did she manage it? Even ten years ago Janet had begun to spread, breasts sagging, thighs waffled, tiny broken veins visible in her legs, hair losing its colour. Damned unappetizing. Their sex life had never been anything to cheer about; now it was non-existent. How long since he'd touched her? Over a year at least. And he was building up one hell of a backlog.

Dolly said, 'I was hoping you wouldn't be too busy to see me.'

'Never.' He sat behind his desk and searched her worried face. 'Problems?'

'To put it mildly. I want you to look at something for me.' She took a sheet of paper out of her purse and handed it to him.

He saw a long list of securities with dates of acquisition and cost. His impression was one of gross incompetence. Large

47

positions had been taken in highly speculative and unseasoned issues bought at the peak of a bull market. Since then prices had plummeted disastrously.

'Your current holdings, Dolly?'

She nodded without comment.

'Who suggested this junk?'

'My investment counsellor.'

Stoufer exploded. 'He's no investment counsellor. He's an idiot—maybe worse. How in Christ's name could anybody recommend such crap?'

'He said it was a hedge against inflation.'

'My aching back! Those prices discount the hereafter. Any imbecile should have been able to calculate the downside risk. The man should be drummed out of the profession, if I may be permitted to dignify stock forecasting with the title.'

'I told him I could afford some risk. He knew I wanted capital gains.'

'And presumably he had a crystal ball. He knew the formula, did he?'

'Is there one?'

'Dolly, I've toiled these vineyards all my life and I never found it. Anybody knows the secret, he'd own all the money there is.' Stoufer tapped the sheet of paper. 'There's a lot of money involved, and you've been taken to the cleaner's. You're being too soft on this joker. Matter of fact, I'd like to see all your brokerage statements. He may have been illegally churning the account for commissions.'

'Forget it, Ernie. I am not going to proceed against the man in any possible way.'

He shrugged. 'Up to you. Good thing, though, Brian is well heeled and able to take care of you.' He was thinking of Brian Wirth's illness, thinking that Dolly might soon inherit a mint.

She shook her head. 'It's not that simple. Brian and I haven't been getting along. The sicker he gets, the more impossible he becomes. At the moment we're not even talking. He sleeps in the guest room. I can't and I won't ask Brian for money. As you know, his last show closed over a year ago. So I haven't worked since. With nothing on the horizon.' She made a help-

less, appealing gesture. 'I need your help, Ernie. Is there anything you can do to salvage my account?'

'You're asking me to take over?'

'I'm begging you.'

He studied the list again. He sighed. 'All right, Dolly. I'll
try. First off we have to liquidate the lot. Nothing here is worth
holding. Then we find solid situations that hold genuine
promise. I'll need the certificates. Who has them?'

'My broker.'

'You'll sign a transfer request and we'll start as soon as they
arrive. I still think you ought to sue.'

'I'd lose. My lawyer is a fossilized antique I inherited from
my first husband. He came with the estate.'

Stoufer cocked a brow.

'Doesn't Moore represent you?'

'Alex is a friend, not my lawyer. He's Brian's lawyer.'

Stoufer sat back, eyes half closed, his mind winging. Dolly
not sleeping with her husband. This vital, robust woman,
smouldering, hot-blooded, looking like she needed it almost as
badly as he did. It was worth exploring. The possibilities
intrigued him. He wasn't over the hill yet, by God, not by a
long shot. Given half a chance, he could still cut the mustard.
His imagination conjured erotic visions, a shimmering Koda-
chrome of Dolly, the flesh tints, the velvet textures, pinned
down by a strenuously active Stoufer, moaning and crying his
name while he pumped her into a demented frenzy.

He felt weak, dizzy. Was it possible? Perhaps. If he could
rejuvenate her finances, make her healthy again. He'd done it
before. His track record was good. He had a knack for timing.

Dolly said plaintively, 'Ernie, isn't there one single company
worth holding?'

'Maybe one.'

'Then shouldn't we buy more at these prices?'

'Dolly, averaging down killed more suckers than Hitler.
What you need is a lesson in high finance. And I think we ought
to start tonight. Will you have dinner with me?'

She looked startled. It shaded slowly into speculation. 'What
about Janet?'

He flipped a hand in dismissal. 'Janet's no problem. I often work late.'

He felt no twinge of disloyalty. He had married one woman and the years had turned her into something else. Indolent, bovine, lack-lustre in bed. In a way, the change had liberated him. Freed him from emotional obligations and allowed him to concentrate fully on Stoufer, Wingate & Company. Now it was time for a little extracurricular activity, time to feed other hungers. And here was Dolly. He suspected he could reach her through avarice. He had observed the role it played in her make-up. Jesus, just looking at her started the glandular juices, the burgeoning tumescence.

Shouts brought Ernie Stoufer out of his reverie with a start. Alex Moore had landed a bluefish. It took a moment to orient himself. Lucas Sheridan was tacking the *Flagship II* against the wind, heading back towards Sands Point.

CHAPTER SIX

ALEX MOORE climbed the graded lawn towards Dolly Wayne's. It was a ranch house of slate, glass, and California redwood. Elvira, Dolly's black maid, intercepted him. Dolly, she said, was taking a nap and did not wish to be disturbed. He felt a distinct letdown. In his room, he sat in a rocker with his attaché case in his lap, riffling through some papers but unable to concentrate. He was deeply troubled. Some subtle and incomprehensible changes were taking place between himself and Dolly.

From one day to the next he never knew where he stood. Without warning, her mood would shift from warm response to cold indifference. Yesterday had broken the ice after two weeks. Today she was avoiding him. Moore was keenly aware of Dolly's physical needs. Just to contemplate infidelity stabbed him with intolerable anxiety. He thrust the notion aside and let his mind dwell on yesterday's session. It was vividly engraved on his memory. They had left Sheridan's swimming pool and strolled back to the house. She had carefully locked the door behind them. Peggy was thoughtless and might barge in uninvited. He remembered how careful they had tried to be when Brian was alive. But not, apparently, careful enough.

Dolly did not speak. She did not look at him. She kicked off her bikini and tumbled back at once upon the bed, her eyes half closed, a vein pulsing in her throat. As her thighs parted in abandoned invitation, he fell upon her without preliminaries, like an animal racked with fevers.

No delicacy, no tenderness, no murmured words of affection, none of the practised devices to please or delay. She was ready and blindly demanding, her haunches limber, flexing, heaving to meet him. Instantly he was lost in an obliterating fog of

51

carnality. No other woman had ever affected him like this. She had become an obsession, an overwhelming compulsion. She churned and whinnied in thready gasps, greedy and urgent. And then, within minutes, her head thrown back, muscles straining, features eroded with passion, her mouth broke open to cry, 'God! Oh God, oh God . . .' For a single measureless instant his own senses soared in a cataclysmic spasm that drained him utterly.

For several heartbeats they remained locked in quivering union. Dolly's pulse slowed to normal. As her blood cooled, the scissored thighs loosened and she turned flaccid beneath him. She put her palms against his chest and pushed him away. She rolled out of bed and said in a flat, indifferent voice, 'I'm going to take a shower. You'd better go back to your own room, Alex.' She disappeared into the bathroom and closed the door.

Just like that. As though he were some random stud casually picked up in a bar.

He forced his mind back to the papers in his lap. But the print held no meaning. He could not work. Dolly pre-empted all other thoughts. If she was trying to get rid of him . . . The idea made him physically ill. He wouldn't hold still for it. She owed him. She owed him plenty. After what he'd done for her. . . .

After her shower, Dolly had stretched out luxuriously on the bed. She was pleased with herself, pleased with the world. The future looked brighter. Money problems a thing of the past. And Gordon Frazer had called recently about a new show. If he came up with a winner, her cup would be full. She might even take a piece of it. She could afford a flier now.

She had even discussed it with Ernie, who was handling her financial affairs. He was ready to loosen the purse strings if he liked the script. Dear, dear Ernie! There was so much about him that she admired. He was forceful, independent, and so damned delightfully vulgar. And to top it off, he had developed into a lover of genuine dimension. An accomplished voluptuary, insatiable, with the ardent enthusiasm and physical stamina of a young man.

She ran a hand along the velvet smoothness of her body. It had endured even better than her face. She reached for a hand mirror and inspected herself critically. The marks of time were barely perceptible. Constant care and some adroit plastic surgery had erased the telltale lines around her eyes. Only one trouble spot. Her neck and throat. And there was damn little she could do about that. Soon, perhaps, she'd have to buy some colourful scarfs.

She heard the growl of a car engine as it came highballing up the driveway, spraying gravel against the side of the house. Brakes squealed under the south portico. Unmistakably identifiable. Ken Sheridan's Volkswagen. He drove that silly little projectile as if he were competing at Le Mans against Mario Andretti. It worried her every time he called for Peggy and they went speeding off to God knew where.

Dolly was pleased with her daughter. Peg had blossomed from shy adolescence into a bounding extrovert. Dolly hoisted herself on one elbow and peered out the window. The kids, returning from the pool, were heading towards the back door and the refrigerator. Naturally. Peg was wearing a short terry robe. Chunky, but appealing. And so exuberantly healthy. Too bad the dominant genes had belonged to her first husband. Keeping Peg's weight down called for constant vigilance. Dolly never stopped warning her about calories. Not that it did much good. This whole new breed of youngsters never listened. They were optimistically convinced that youth was eternal, that life was immortal. That nothing could harm them. So they blithely consumed vast quantities of pizzas, Cokes, hamburgers, sundaes.

Dolly knew that underneath all the exuberance, Peg was really quite sensitive. She hoped Ken was serious. Because Peg had, with childlike candour, indicated her total commitment. She hoped Ken would not take advantage of the child. She knew that Peg was far more vulnerable than herself. Peg had been sheltered, had never been forced to survive the early vicissitudes of a stage career.

She saw Ken stop suddenly and pull Peg around to face him. His hands went around and dropped, cupping her young

53

buttocks. Peg raised up on her toes, seeking his mouth. Dolly knew the kiss was deep. She saw the pelvic thrust, saw her daughter respond. She turned quickly away, and lay back in bed, disquieted. Probably it was her fault. She herself had never practised restraint. She had never set Peg much of an example. Peg probably knew about her and Alex.

The notion shifted her thoughts. That lapse yesterday had been a mistake. She had been drugged by sun and cocktails and the rhythmic stroking of oil on her back. Like an aphrodisiac. Alex knew exactly what he was doing.

She frowned and shrugged away her misgivings. At least Ernie had not been around to see them. So nothing much lost. Call it a reward to Alex for past favours. Actually, she should never have invited him. But he had been so persistent. She wished she had the courage to tell him outright. She wanted his friendship, but nothing more than that. There was no really tactful way of telling him. Oh well, there were other ways of communicating. Indifference, faultfinding, breaking appointments. Not subtle perhaps, but effective. Alex would just have to learn that nothing lasts for ever.

CHAPTER SEVEN

'DAMN!' Dru said with feeling. 'Damn, damn, damn!'

She sat huddled in a far corner of the front seat. Paul was driving slowly along the dark, unfamiliar road. The sky overhead was cloudless, reeling with stars.

'Still upset?' he asked.

'Those stupid people! Inviting Gordon and me at the same time. And Gordon flaunting that despicable Billy Clark. It was inexcusable. I'm so angry I could spit.'

'Go ahead. Only roll down the window first.'

'Seriously, Paul, weren't you embarrassed?'

'At one point I thought I might have to hang one on Frazer, but it wouldn't have been worth the effort. Incidentally, did I tell you how much I enjoyed the tennis this afternoon? Even more than yesterday.'

'All right. Change of subject. It was fun. Even Dad came down to watch. I'm glad we split sets. I don't think Peggy could have survived another loss. What do you think of that young lady?'

'Cute and nubile.'

'Nubile. You know, I always planned on checking that word in the dictionary. What exactly does it mean?'

'Marriageable. Ripe. Ready for action.'

She said with mock indignation, 'Do I detect a note of lechery in your voice?'

'Hardly. The child is not my type.'

'I'm most interested. Just what is your type?'

'You mean like blonde or brunette, tall or short, flat or round? Sorry. Colour and measurements are secondary considerations. The qualities that get to me I can't define.'

'You mean looks aren't important?'

'They help. But I couldn't stomach the most breathtaking beauty if she had an obnoxious personality.'

'I know men who are married to very disagreeable types.'

'Happens all the time. Shows how a man's judgement can be adulterated by glandular compulsions.'

'And are you immune to those compulsions?'

'More immune now than ten years ago. I was impetuous then and less discriminating.'

'Keep talking, sir.'

'About what?'

'Yourself. I have an inexhaustible curiosity about you, Paul. You haven't been living in a monastery. Whom did you court before me?'

'Well, nobody until I was seven. And then I was smitten by a female with pigtails. In high school it was a cheerleader. In college, a philosophy major with unplucked eyebrows. At law school I was moonstruck by a sculptress in Greenwich Village with a fragile talent and an extraordinary bust.'

'Did you have affairs with any of them?'

'Not with the seven-year-old. And you'll never get a straight answer about the others. Sex talk is for kids.'

'And you never considered marriage?'

'I came close with the sculptress. But I saw the light just in time. Only her talent was fragile. She herself was tough, ambitious, and hopelessly frustrated.'

'What happened to her?'

'She became an interior decorator. Very expensive little shop and an exclusive clientele. Happens I'm her lawyer. All very businesslike.'

'Please keep it that way. And watch out now, the entrance is just ahead.'

Paul swung through the gate and followed the driveway to the parking area. In the moonglow, moisture glistened like teardrops on the lawn and insect sounds filled the night air.

'Are you tired?' Dru asked.

'Not very.'

'Then let's sit on the deck of Dad's boat for a while.'

She took his hand and they strolled down to the dock. Paul

helped her aboard. Dru found a large padded mat and rolled it out on the afterdeck. They stretched out, side by side, faces turned upward, fingers intertwined. It was a time for silence. The boat rocked gently against its mooring, timbers creaking. Far above, the moon hung like an open porthole in the sky.

After a while Dru said, 'Have you made a final decision about Dad's offer?'

'I'm turning it down. I don't think I'd be content as a small cog in a large machine.'

She accepted it without argument. 'Tell me something. Did the sculptress sour you against women?'

'It made me a little wary, that's all. But a man never stops looking.'

'For what?'

'An emotional investment he can live with.'

'My God, Paul, it's not like buying a share of stock.'

'Indeed not. You make a bad investment in the market, all you lose is money. A bad investment in love, the scars are much deeper.'

'How does one judge?'

'I'm hardly an expert. Chemistry is part of it. Otherwise marriage can be a very sterile exercise.'

'You know something, Paul?'

'What?'

'Lawyers talk too much.'

He laughed and rolled over on his side. Her face was blurred in the moonlight. He kissed her, savouring the sweet warmth. He already knew the flavour and texture of her mouth, and it was a heady experience. Her arms tightened convulsively, pulling him close. He covered her with his body and she arched strongly against him. The kiss turned savage, almost brutal. It grew within him, a bursting need, almost primitive in its intensity. His hand had a life of its own, exploring the smoothness of thigh, and she responded with a shudder. Her body changed, became softer, more supple, tremulous with movement. His fingers began working at fasteners, exposing, liberating.

'No, Paul,' she whispered. 'Not here.'

57

But it was too late. She had unleashed forces beyond restraint. Her words were slurred, lacking conviction, and even as she spoke she was shifting, parting to accommodate, the breath caught in her throat. It was no gentle merging. In some vague hidden alcove of the mind he knew that gentleness would come later. The urgency now was despotic. Dru cradled and rocked him, moaning words of love. And in this timeless ritual he instinctively sensed her tempos and rhythms.

Just before the end, it came as a blinding revelation. He had found something immeasurably priceless. This woman, this ribbed cage, this laughing spirit and tangle of hair, she was fire in his blood, a touch of magic, the end of searching. He felt the vibrations. She cried his name and he quickened to her need. It was a moment of communion with eternity, an instant of living death, of unbearable sweetness. And in that explosive moment of completion, the whole world tilted, casting them adrift in a drugged and melting languor.

Later, Paul sighed. 'I guess there's no help for it.'

'Help for what?'

'I'll have to make an honest woman out of you.'

'How quaint, darling. Am I pregnant?'

'More than likely.'

'Is this a proposal?'

'It is. Now, wait a minute, Dru. Don't say anything yet. This is not a spur-of-the-moment decision. It has nothing to do with moonlight or sex. I've lived alone for a long time. And while it has compensations, being a bachelor is not unalloyed bliss. Something vital has been missing.'

'A companion?'

'I've had companions. I want more.'

'What took you so long to decide?'

'Caution, probably. As a lawyer I've been involved in some corrosive divorce actions. Always there was animosity and greed. Maybe it affected my judgement. But it never stopped me from liking women.'

'And you like me?'

'All right, Dru. You want me to say those three words, that hackneyed and threadbare phrase. Let me put it this way. The thought of living my life without you would be a barren prospect indeed, meaningless, empty, and quite unendurable. Yes, damn it all, I love you.'

Her eyes were swimming. He kissed her and tasted her tears.

'Just hold me,' she said in a muffled tone. 'Don't say any more. Just hold me.'

A long moment passed. Water lapped at the hull of the boat. The night breeze was a soft caress.

Then Dru sat up and thumbed the corners of her eyes. 'Damned mascara!' She dipped her chin. You're sure now? It wasn't just agitated hormones?'

'They are not agitated at the moment, believe me. They are more tranquil than at any time since puberty. Though I don't expect it to last very long. Anyway, I know the difference between lechery and devotion.'

'It's leap year, darling. If you hadn't spoken, I guess I would have brought it up myself.'

'All right then. Name a date.'

'Are you in a hurry?'

'Yes.'

'Let's see. This is Sunday. How about next week?'

'Fine with me. How will your father take it?'

'I'll present him with a *fait accompli*. I won't have a replay of that last disaster. He launched me like a national asset, big posh glittering affair, hundreds of people I didn't even know, Dad's clients, Gordon's theatre friends—and look at the result. Acrimony and divorce. No, thanks. Not again. This time, a simple quickie at City Hall, if that's all right with you.'

'Let's skip the City Hall bit. I'll ask some judge to perform in chambers. Anybody you want as a witness?'

'I'd like Ken, but I don't want him to stay away from school.'

'Then I'll ask my associates, Jim Sloane and Abe Barish. One thing more . . .'

'Yes?'

He changed his mind. 'Forget it.'

'Never pique a woman's curiosity.'

'You may have to readjust your style of living. Both your father and Frazer have——'

'Oh, shut up, darling. Let's go back to the house. I wish we could sleep in the same room tonight. I miss you already.'

'Patience. Two more days.'

Lucas Holmes Sheridan broke the news to Alex Moore as they were driving back to New York on Monday morning. 'Slater's not joining us.'

'When did he tell you?'

'Last night.'

Moore shrugged. 'It's a free country, Lucas.'

'It's not rational, damn it. Doesn't the man have aspirations? How can he prefer an outfit like Sloane & Barish?'

'He probably figures he'd be lost in the shuffle at a shop like ours. Why didn't you offer him a partnership?'

'He'd have to earn it like everyone else.'

Moore chuckled. 'Count your blessings, Lucas.'

'What are you talking about?'

'We happen to like Porterfield, Baker & Sheridan just as it is. Slater's a maverick. He might have shaken us up. There could have been repercussions. Not everyone would have taken kindly to him.'

'Dru seems to like him well enough.'

Moore touched the horn and changed lanes. He made no comment. The night before, plagued by insomnia and Dolly's indifference, he had been wandering the grounds and had seen Slater and Dru as they crossed the lawn, obviously returning from Lucas's boat. They had paused under the moonlight and Dru had amply demonstrated her feelings.

At precisely nine-thirty a.m., shortly before leaving chambers to ascend the bench, His Honour, Arthur J. Holomon, justice of the New York Supreme Court, donned both his robes and a look of solemnity, and performed the ritual that changed Drusilla Sheridan's name to Drusilla Slater. Jim Sloane and Abe Barish smiled throughout the ceremony. Lacking time that morning for the selection of an appropriate ring, Paul had picked up a temporary substitute at Woolworth's. Dru adored it.

Paul watched as Judge Holomon kissed the bride with an enthusiasm hardly befitting his judicial garb. The judge stood back admiringly. 'Daughter of Lucas Sheridan. Didn't think the old fox had it in him. Where are you off to, Counsellor?'

'I'll take the Fifth, Your Honour.'

Holoman laughed. 'I hereby enjoin you from appearing in any domestic relations court as a litigant.' He nodded to his clerk, who kept pointing urgently at the clock. 'I'm leaving, I'm leaving. Good luck to both of you.'

Dru received properly avuncular pecks from both Jim Sloane and Abe Barish. Sloane said, 'It's not much, but four days is all you have. Make the most of them.'

Paul's secretary had cancelled and shifted appointments to clear the meagre four days for a honeymoon. They flew to the Bahamas and settled in a small beach-front hotel. Once installed, Dru called her father and broke the news. Paul sat beside her on the bed and listened.

'No, Dad, not an impulse. We've been seeing each other for weeks. I've just been waiting for Paul to ask. . . . Well, that's exactly what we were trying to avoid—another Hollywood spectacular. That's why we did it this way. . . . Yes, he's right here.' She handed Paul the phone.

'Paul?'

'Yes, sir.'

'Congratulations.'

'Thank you, sir.'

'Where are you staying?'

'The Bahamas.'

'Shall I send Quintus with the car to meet you when you come back?'

'No, sir. We'll call you over the weekend.'

Silence for a moment. 'All right. Give Dru my love,' he said, and broke the connection.

It was an idyllic interlude. A time of search and discovery. They roamed the beaches, swam in the surf, dined leisurely, talked endlessly, and spent a vast amount of time in bed. Dru was a constant source of wonder, an amalgam of innocence and bawdiness, of naïveté and sophistication. They argued often, but without heat. She had a bizarre sense of humour and laughed easily. He found her flexible and open to persuasion. There were other people at the hotel, but they invited no intrusion.

On their last day Dru said woefully, 'I don't want it to end.'

'It's not ending, honey. It's beginning. We're leaving here together.'

'Yes, but here we spend twenty-four hours a day in each other's company. In the city, you'll have to march off to work every morning.'

'Only five days a week. Like men all over the world. Even savages abandon their huts every morning to hunt and provide food.'

'We're not savages. We live in New York. The supermarkets have plenty of food.'

'They want money for it.'

'Mother left me a trust. We have enough money to eat ourselves into a coma.'

'Save it. We may come to that later.'

She sat up in bed. 'I have a wonderful idea. If I learn typing and shorthand, will you give me a job? I'll work at the office. And you can exploit me. It would be very economical.'

'You'll be too busy having babies.'

Her eyes widened. 'How many?'

'Enough to frighten the authorities about a population explosion.'

'Not me,' she said emphatically. 'Maybe three at most.' She frowned. 'Dad always used to bring home a briefcase full of work and he'd spend all evening studying papers. Will you have to do that too?'

'Probably. Especially if I'm on trial. Litigation requires a lot of work.'

'And what is a lonely wife supposed to do?'

'She is supposed to minister quietly and unobtrusively to her husband's needs. To nourish and comfort and safeguard his privacy.'

'Are you nuts or something? Women's Lib would drum me out of the corps.'

62

'So you go to work and I'll stay home and take care of the kids.'

She shook her head. 'Oh no. I like your way better. Will I be on salary?'

'You'll have an allowance.'

'What else?'

'Selfless devotion.'

'What else?'

'All the sex you can handle.'

'I love you, Mr Slater.'

'Likewise.'

'Then please demonstrate,' she said, walking her fingers across his bare stomach.

He reached for her, amazed at his own recuperative powers. A word, a glance, a touch, and he was instantly revitalized. It was a slow, sweet blending, with Dru's transfigured face staring at him, the sheer physical pleasure multiplied a thousandfold by their deep emotional involvement, knowing in their use of each other, giving and taking, a rising joy, the sudden plaintive call and the roaring response, and then tumbling together into gentle lassitude, hearts slowing, flesh cooling, Dru offering small quick kisses and murmuring in a drunken little voice, 'I love you, I love you, I love you.'

Part Two

CHAPTER ONE

DOLLY WAYNE had inherited the East 65th Street town
house along with the rest of Brian Wirth's estate. She occupied
the first two floors and rented the third to Billy Clark. The
initial suggestion had come from Gordon Frazer. And since
the Wirths did not need the extra space, and were fond of the
dancer, it seemed a good idea.

With Peggy away at school, there was no need for a live-in
maid, and Dolly had arranged for Elvira Wilcox to come in
every other weekday morning. Elvira was huge, competent,
and proudly black.

On Thursday morning in the third week of October, Elvira
arrived at her usual hour, nine-thirty. She had her own key and
went silently about her chores while Dolly slept late on the
floor above. Elvira worked with unhurried diligence for two
hours.

A warm, casual, and somewhat irreverent relationship
existed between the two women. Elvira had seen most of the
Frazer-Wirth musicals from a seat provided by Dolly in the
orchestra, fifth row centre. At home she had a record player
and a complete set of Dolly's show tunes, constantly on the
turntable.

At eleven-thirty Elvira headed for the kitchen. Dolly's
unvaried regimen called for juice, one poached egg, a slice of
dry toast, and a pot of strong black coffee. Elvira arranged
these ingredients on a tray and carried them upstairs. She
knocked once and entered, simultaneously uttering a cheery
good morning.

Nothing in Elvira Wilcox's forty-one years, much of which
had been spent observing savagery and violence on television,
had prepared her for the sight laid out on Dolly's bed. Her

eyes bulged and the breakfast tray fell from her fingers. Then her mouth opened in an agonized scream that kept repeating itself over and over again.

On the floor above, Billy Clark was fussily preparing eggs Benedict when the first piercing howl arched his spine and lifted the hairs at the back of his neck. He stood for a moment, trembling and indecisive. As the cries rose in crescendo, he whirled excitedly towards the hall phone.

The squeal was relayed by radio to a patrol car in the area. Its driver touched the siren and stamped the gas pedal to the floor. Less than ten minutes after Billy Clark's call, the car braked sharply and two policemen tumbled out, unbuckling their holsters.

Elvira stood at the front door in a state of shock, her face the colour of wet sand. She made inarticulate noises and gestured towards the stairs.

The officers took them two at a time, saw the open bedroom door, and froze on the threshold. The first man turned chalky and gagged. The second went racing back to the street to report on the patrol-car radio.

By the time Detectives First Grade Barney Krehm and Lou Schatz arrived, the victim's identity was known and the laboratory men were already at work. Krehm, a craggy-featured veteran, stared at the body and emptied his lungs. 'Je-sus!' he exclaimed.

Schatz, heavy-set and moon-faced, shook his head and blinked. 'My God! Dolly Wayne! It's gonna hit the fan on this one. Looks like we got us a vampire on the loose.'

'Vampires go for the throat, not down there,' Krehm said. He turned to one of the technicians. 'You know what we want, Carl. Comb it clean. Every latent, every grain of dust, every strand of hair, threads, skin under fingernails, the works.' He sighed. 'On the lieutenant's day off, too. See if you can reach him at home, Lou. Then take a shot at that maid. Maybe she's in condition now to cough up some information. I'll talk to the guy from upstairs.' He sent a patrolman for Billy Clark.

Although the dancer's mannerisms were not especially re-vealing, Barney Krehm knew instinctively and at once that he was dealing with a queer. Krehm couldn't have cared less. Whatever the goddamn fruit wanted to do in private was okay with him so long as he stayed away from young boys. Billy Clark was jumpy, sweaty, agitated. It took a bit of time to settle him down and fill in the background.

'You say you heard sounds of a scuffle yesterday afternoon?' Krehm asked.

'Yes, sir. More than a scuffle. A fight of some kind.'

'You remember the time?'

'About twelve forty-five.'

'Can you describe the sounds?'

'There was some angry yelling back and forth, and some thumping, and then I heard something like a crash.'

'Could you recognize the voices?'

'Well, I knew one of them was Dolly Wayne. The other I can't place.'

'Male or female?'

'Male.'

'Did you do anything about it?'

'Well, I tiptoed down one flight and listened at the door and I heard someone moving around. But by then everything was quiet, so I went back up. I tried to call her later, but I got a busy signal. I figured she was all right.'

Schatz came into the room and shook his head. 'I got her name and not much else. Elvira Wilcox. She came to work this morning and found the body about two hours later.'

'How about Lieutenant Varney?'

'He's on his way.'

It was inevitable that all news media would give the murder a big play. Dolly Wayne was, after all, a celebrity. Dru heard it on the radio and phoned Paul at once. She sounded so dis-tressed that he left his office immediately and went straight to her. Janet Stoufer's message caught her husband at a stormy policy meeting and he instantly secluded himself in his office. He knew that his face revealed too much. He could not help

66

wondering if he had caught a note of malicious pleasure in Janet's tone.

Lucas Sheridan heard about it before Alex Moore and broke the news as gently as he could. Peggy Wayne's paternal grandparents drove to Poughkeepsie and picked her up at school.

Lieutenant Charles Varney, in charge of the investigation, had clamped a tight lid on all information. One enterprising reporter, however, managed to unearth a few of the more lurid details. These were highlighted, amplified, and ultimately distorted. Since Varney had no jurisdiction over the medical examiner or the morgue attendant, rumours leaked from one source and another. In order to keep the record straight, he reluctantly decided to grant a press interview.

Varney was a spare, dry man with cold eyes in a grey slab of face. His manner was brusque and impersonal. He seemed as insulated from civilian life as certain high-ranking military officers. He had fashioned his life for one job exclusively, enforcing the law. And while he offered the men under his command little cause for affection, he had nevertheless earned their respect and loyalty.

Television cameras focused, flash bulbs exploded, and voices came at him from a dozen directions. He shook his head and pointed at various reporters, allocating one question to each man.

'Lieutenant, is there any truth to the rumours that Dolly Wayne was sexually molested?'

'Yes.'

'Have you found the murder weapon?'

'Plural. They are attached to her assailant. She was strangled.'

'Did she suffer other injuries?'

'Yes. Bruises, contusions, lacerations. Probably caused during an attempt to defend herself. Also certain mutilations caused by teeth. We will not go into that at this time.'

'Do you have any leads?'

'Several. We expect an arrest within forty-eight hours.'

'Would it be a stranger or someone she knew?'

67

'You will be able to judge for yourself when the suspect is in custody.'

'Was there a forcible entry into her apartment?'

'There was not.'

'May we assume, Lieutenant, that she admitted the killer voluntarily?'

'Any assumptions at this time would be premature.'

'Is it true that her apartment was burglarized?'

'Certain articles of jewellery appear to be missing. This will have to be checked against her insurance records.'

'Can you tell us——'

'That's all, gentlemen.' Varney nodded abruptly and ended the interview.

CHAPTER TWO

PAUL LOOKED DOWN at the young faces, predominantly male, which made up his class in criminal law. At this stage of the fall semester he was able to associate most features with names. Several would always remain an amorphous blur; a few would stand out.

The young man in the third row—gangling, with serious, owlish eyes peering out from behind thick lenses—already showed considerable promise.

The slender girl, seated just behind him, would also bear watching. Bright and challenging, a Slavic tilt to her mercurial eyes, she tended, when Slater permitted, to keep discussions in a ferment. Two standouts, he thought, in a class of twenty-three. Not bad.

They had somehow slipped into a discussion of moral responsibility. It was the girl who posed the question. 'How can a lawyer really extend himself if he decides that his client is guilty?'

'The lawyer who makes that decision is usurping the function of a jury. Under our system, no defendant is guilty until a jury says he's guilty.'

The young man flagged his attention. 'That's a crock, Professor. Pure sophistry.'

'Boil it down for me, Booker.'

'Well, if the jury returns a verdict of guilty, then the defendant had to be guilty before they said so. How else could they reach that verdict?'

Paul smiled. 'We're quibbling about semantics. Perhaps I should have said *presumed* innocent until the verdict is in. Under our system of jurisprudence, we leave the decision of innocence or guilt to the combined intelligence and common sense of twelve ordinary men. The lawyer has one job. To provide his client with the best defence and protection available under the system. Doesn't that seem reasonable?'

'No, sir,' the girl said. 'I don't think it's reasonable.'

Paul lifted an eyebrow. 'Why not?'

'Well, any decision *that* important shouldn't be left to twelve ordinary men. Twelve *ex*traordinary men would be better.'

The boy applauded. Paul laughed and the class joined him.

'I see your point,' Paul said. 'On the other hand, how would you go about selecting these so-called *ex*traordinary men? By committee? Educational standards? Property? Ability? And how would you judge their lack of bias? Freedom from prejudice? Their sense of fair play? Yes, I grant you, the system has its faults, but if you're looking for absolute perfection, I'm afraid you're not going to find it this side of paradise, if paradise exists.'

'All right,' she conceded grudgingly. 'But isn't it only human for the lawyer to reach a private conclusion? After all, he has to talk to his client and evaluate the man's story. He can't turn his mind blank.'

Paul said, 'Whatever the lawyer's private opinion, the accused is still entitled to representation. No man should be deprived of life or liberty without due process. It's up to the state to prove him guilty beyond a reasonable doubt. The Constitution guarantees every accused the right to counsel. It makes no exceptions. It does not exclude murderers or rapists or draft-card burners. No matter how odious the crime, every word of testimony against the accused should be tested on cross-examination. By any standards, humane or juridical, I would say that is something worth cheering about.'

The class was silent. But the girl did not surrender easily.

'Suppose the client in confidence admits his guilt?'

Before Paul could answer, the door opened.

Dean Julian Farquhar came down the aisle and leaned towards Paul to whisper, 'Telephone. Your father-in-law. It seems urgent. Take it in my office and I'll finish the class for you.'

Paul's throat went dry. He felt a cold spasm of apprehension.

70

Something about Dru? Farquhar made a gesture of ignorance. Paul left the room and quickened his pace along the corridor. Farquhar's secretary pointed to the inner office. 'On the Dean's line, Professor.'

He snatched the instrument. 'Lucas?'

Sheridan's voice was strained and hoarse. 'This is an emergency, Paul. I'm leaving the office at once. Please wait at the school, main entrance.'

Paul said sharply, 'Damn it, Lucas. Don't hang up. Tell me now. Is something wrong with Dru?'

'Dru is all right.' The voice broke. 'It—it's Ken. He's been arrested.'

'For what?'

Sheridan's tone was leaden. 'Homicide. They're charging him with the murder of Dolly Wayne.'

Paul stood frozen, incredulous. Ken? Dru's adored cousin? Lucas Holmes Sheridan's nephew? It sounded insane. 'Where is Ken now?'

'At the 19th Precinct.'

'Can he hold his tongue?'

'The boy is not an imbecile. He demanded and they allowed him one call.'

'All right, Lucas. I'll be waiting.'

He went down to the street and stood facing Washington Square Park, oblivious to the milling activity, the garish anachronistic costumes. His brain churned. Considering Lucas Sheridan's prominence at the bar, his eminence in the political and social structure, his aversion to publicity, the implications were overwhelming.

The plea for help was understandable. No one at Porterfield, Baker & Sheridan would be able to cope. None of the staff had any notion of criminal procedures. They would be helpless in dealing with the police or the district attorney's office. He wondered how deeply he himself would be involved. Hopefully, it was all a ghastly mistake.

A cab pulled up and the rear door swung open. He climbed in. Sheridan sat back, stiff with restraint. The driver took off instantly.

71

'Preposterous!' Sheridan snapped. 'An outrage! Paul, I want that boy out of custody at once.'

'If possible, Lucas.'

The older man flared. 'What the hell are you talking about?'

'Slow down, Lucas. We have a pretty good police department. They don't usually climb out on a limb. If they put the arm on Ken, they have a reason, or think they do. And if they charge him, he'll have to appear before a magistrate, who could hold him for the grand jury.'

Sheridan spoke between his teeth. 'On what grounds?'

'You put me into the picture less than twenty minutes ago. That's something we have to find out.'

Sheridan was silent for a moment. 'So help me, if they lay a hand on that boy——'

'Oh, for Christ's sake! Let's not go off the deep end. You're not dealing with some hillbilly sheriff manhandling a vagrant.' Paul modified his tone. 'And what the hell are we snapping at each other for? We're supposed to be on the same side. Let's get organized here, Lucas. They know who Ken is. And even if they didn't, they'd be careful. Ever since the Miranda decision the police have been instructed on how to treat a suspect in custody.'

Lieutenant Varney swivelled back in his chair. He looked up at Ken Sheridan without expression. For once, things had been simple. The boy had driven down from Boston to attend Dolly Wayne's funeral and they had collared him at his uncle's apartment. No need for extradition. And a very cool customer, he thought. Relaxed. Smiling. No sign of nerves.

Varney nodded at Detective Krehm and said, 'All right, Barney.'

Krehm took out a dog-eared slip of paper. He knew the contents by heart, but read them anyway. 'You are hereby advised that you have a right to remain silent and you do not have to say anything until you choose to do so. Do you understand that?'

Ken nodded. He seemed more like a curious observer than a suspect.

'Anything you say may be used against you in a court of law. It is your right to have an attorney present with you during any questioning now or in the future. If you cannot afford an attorney, the court will appoint one to represent you. You have a right to remain silent until you consult with him. Have you got an attorney?'

'I expect one shortly.'

I'll bet, thought Lou Schatz, leaning against the wall. And maybe more than one. Maybe a whole battery of them. Well, they'd followed the routine to the letter. Nobody was going to reverse this one on the basis of some stupid technicality.

'You know why you're here?' Varney asked.

'Yes. These two gentlemen told me.'

'Is there anything you'd like to say?'

'About what?'

'Dolly Wayne. For openers, son, why did you kill her?'

Ken threw his hands up. 'Come off it, Lieutenant. You don't seriously believe that, do you? Dolly Wayne was a very good friend. I'm practically engaged to her daughter. We got along fine. I was devoted to her.'

'Devoted enough to knock her unconscious, rip off her clothes, and climb up on top?'

Ken gave him a pitying look. 'You got to be kidding. Dolly was twice my age.'

'You mean you don't go for older women?'

'Not like that. A peck on the cheek maybe, if the occasion calls for it.'

Varney put a cigarette between his lips and offered the pack. 'Smoke?'

'No, thanks.'

'You don't care to socialize with the lower classes?'

The old ploy, Krehm thought. Pricking the skin. Trying to open him up a little. But the boy refused the bait. He shook his head affably. 'Not at all. But the label says that cigarette smoking may be hazardous to your health. And I don't like to take unnecessary chances.'

Varney smiled. He took a deep drag. 'I understand you're a law student.'

73

'Yes, sir.'

'Going to school up at Cambridge?'

'That's right.'

'And you say you drove in for Dolly's funeral. When did you get here?'

'Thursday evening. The day they found her. My uncle called and told me to come right home.'

'How about the day before? Wednesday? Were you here then too?'

'That's the day Dolly was killed, isn't it?' Ken shook his head in mild admonition. 'What I see, Lieutenant, over there on top of that filing cabinet, is a tape recorder with what looks like a highly sensitive mike, and unless I'm mistaken, it happens to be plugged in right now. So an affirmative answer might conceivably be incriminating, and you'd have it on record. I don't mind, really, because I've got nothing to hide. But my uncle gave me strict instructions to stand mute until he got here. So don't you think it would be better if I waited before answering any more questions of that nature?'

'Better for whom?'

'Everybody concerned, including yourself.'

'You got something to hide, sonny?' Schatz asked.

'No, sir. But the fact is that you gentlemen are old hands at this sort of thing. Very wise and maybe even a little devious. I'm pretty green, you know, wet behind the ears, inexperienced. So it would be silly of me to waltz around with you. You've got a crime to solve, and you need a scapegoat. You've cooked up some wildly implausible hypothesis and it seems I'm elected. I'm not half clever enough to figure out why or how you're trying to tie me into this thing. So the advice of someone who can cope with you gentlemen is clearly indicated. You just read me some words on a piece of paper. I should take them literally. After all, they practically emanate from the United States Supreme Court.'

Varney, Krehm, and Schatz stared impassively. At that moment the desk phone buzzed. Varney put it to his ear and listened. 'All right,' he said woodenly. 'Send them in.'

*   *   *

Lucas Sheridan's stony gaze made a circular sweep and encompassed the room, focusing finally on his nephew. 'Are you all right, Ken?'

'I'm fine, Uncle Lucas.' His smile was bland and guileless. 'These civil-service gentlemen are quite civilized. No threats, no violence, no third degree?'

'Did they advise you of your rights?'

'They've been absolutely meticulous. As a matter of fact, it's all down on tape, on that little recording device over there.'

Sheridan glared. He aimed a finger. 'I want that thing shut off . . . *now.*'

Varney nodded at Schatz, who went over and flipped the switch.

Sheridan turned to Varney. 'Are you in charge here?'

Varney nodded. 'Detective-Lieutenant Charles Varney. Detective Krehm. Detective Schatz.' He was brusquely courteous. Brusque by nature; courteous because it was politic. He knew that Lucas Holmes Sheridan's prestige and influence reached far beyond the area of his own circumscribed jurisdiction.

'You know who I am. This is Paul Slater. He represents my nephew. Now, what is this all about? Why is my nephew here?'

'Because he is under suspicion of homicide. We have reason to believe that he was involved in the death of Dolly Wayne.'

'Preposterous!' The word was explosive. 'You're floundering, sir. According to the newspapers, the motive appears to have been burglary. You don't seriously contend that my nephew is——'

'We are not responsible for journalistic speculations. At this moment we are not sure of the motive. And with all due respect, neither are you.'

'The medical examiner's report says she was killed on Wednesday. At that time my nephew was attending school in Cambridge, Massachusetts, two hundred and thirty miles away.'

Varney shook his head.

'He was right here in New York, sir, and we can establish that as an incontrovertible fact.'

Lucas stiffened. He stared at Varney in stunned incredulity. He turned slowly towards his nephew. 'Is that true, Ken? Were you here on——'

'Hold it, Lucas!' Paul snapped, abruptly taking command. 'There will be no further talk until we've had a chance to confer with the boy privately.' He looked at Varney. 'Are you prepared to make a formal charge, Lieutenant?'

'We are.'

'Is there a room here where I can talk to him?'

Varney stood up, his gesture directing Krehm and Schatz to follow him. They disappeared into the corridor, closing the door behind them. Paul walked over to the filing cabinet and turned on the recorder. He reversed the tape and played it back, listening without expression. He reversed it again, and then, with a wolfish grin, ran it through once more, erasing the material.

He swivelled to his father-in-law. 'Lucas, I haven't been involved in a criminal case in over three years. Are you sure you want me to handle this thing?'

'Yes.'

'Ken?'

The boy smiled. 'Sure. So long as I can't have Clarence Darrow. But I really don't need a lawyer. Somebody around here is——'

'We'll dispense with the editorial comments,' Paul said shortly. 'I'm going to ask you some questions, Ken. You're being charged with murder one. Apparently they believe they have enough evidence to bind you over. I don't know what it is and there's a damn good chance I won't find out until it's sprung in court. If the case ever goes to court—which I hope to Christ it doesn't. So I want to meet them head-on. Nip it at the start. Try to prove they're wrong. To do that, I need the facts. Everything. I want you to open the bag. No double-talk. No holding back. No lying. If you lie to me, Ken, I'll take a walk. Is that clear? Do you read me?'

Lucas Sheridan looked bewildered, as if seeing his son-in-law for the first time. 'Why are you talking to the boy like that? What's happened to you, Paul?'

'I'm establishing authority. So there will be no mistake about it, now or later. Any comment, Lucas?'

The older man blinked. He pointed to the recorder and said plaintively, 'Yes. What did you do to that machine?'

'I erased the tape.'

'*What?* You . . . isn't that tampering with evidence in an alleged homicide?'

'They'll never know, will they, Lucas? They may suspect but they'll never know. They may even think the equipment was at fault. And there wasn't any evidence there worth a damn anyway. Only that Ken here was treating them like a bunch of idiots, which is a very easy way to commit suicide.'

'But that man Varney just gave us the courtesy of his office.'

'So you think he's a gentleman. He observes all the Marquis of Queensberry rules. Bullshit, Lucas! He knew you were on your way here. He shouldn't have tried to pump the boy. Okay? Can I get on with it now?' He swung towards Ken, who was grinning at him. 'Wipe it off. And think twice before you answer. On Wednesday, October eighteenth, the day Dolly Wayne was murdered, did you come to New York?'

Ken turned uncharacteristically sober. 'Yes, I did.'

Lucas Sheridan said heavily, 'You mean you drove into town and then left without calling either your cousin or myself?'

'I didn't have time, Uncle Lucas. I had to get back to school. If I——'

'Let's stick to the issues,' Paul broke in. 'Did you see her?'

'Yes.'

Sheridan went stark under sudden pallor. He started to say something, then changed his mind.

'What did she want?' Paul asked.

Ken averted his face, looking stubborn. 'It—it was something personal.'

Lucas Sheridan made an explosive sound. 'No, sir. We will not accept that, Ken. When I took on the responsibility of raising you I asked neither credit nor gratitude. And I will not demean our relationship now by demanding a reciprocal obligation. But you're in trouble, boy, and it may have tragic

77

consequences. To your future, your freedom, the reputation of the family. You need help and I intend to render it to the fullest extent of my resources. For your part, you've got to co-operate. Answer Paul's question.'

Ken was clearly troubled.

Paul said, 'A personal matter indeed. Are you so naïve you think the police are in the dark about it too? Well, let me disabuse you, friend. They know a hell of a lot more than you think they do. And any assumption to the contrary is sheer stupidity. The fact that you're here, under detention, is proof enough. You feel sensitive about something? Tough titty! They've got an army working on it. I don't. It's going to come out anyway. You can't afford the luxury of reticence.'

Ken put a thumb knuckle between his teeth, frowning. He took a breath.

'She wanted to see me about Peggy.'

'What about Peggy?'

'She's pregnant.'

Lucas Sheridan flung his hands up.

'Are you responsible?' Paul asked.

'I guess so.'

'Aren't you sure?'

'I'm sure she never fooled around with anyone else.'

'We discussed that,' Sheridan said heavily. 'I asked you not to get involved until you finished school. Moral aspects aside, I at least gave you credit for some small amount of sophistication. Couldn't you take precautions?'

'Only once, Uncle Lucas, just once, I lost control.'

'You sure lost something. Thank God she's over eighteen.'

Paul considered the news from various angles. He did not condemn the boy. Considering Peggy's exuberance and devotion, unlimited opportunity, the new permissiveness, not many youngsters would have been able to resist. So Dolly found out and wanted to talk to Ken. Not unreasonable. He said, 'How did Dolly know about it? Did Peggy tell her?'

'No, sir. Peggy wasn't feeling well, so Dolly sent her to a doctor. He examined her and finked.'

'And she called you?'

78

'Yes, sir. On Tuesday. I had no classes Wednesday, so I drove in.'

'Do you remember the exact time?'

'I left Cambridge at eight a.m. and got to Dolly's place about noon. She was waiting for me.'

'How long did you stay?'

'Not more than half an hour.'

'Was she upset? Angry?'

'Maybe a little upset. But not angry. She hadn't discussed it with Peggy yet, and she wanted to know how I felt about it. If I had any choice, would it be marriage or an abortion?'

'And your answer?'

'Well, I was surprised. She sprang it on me without warning. I knew how Uncle Lucas felt about finishing school first. At the same time I felt my obligation to Peggy took precedence. I wasn't going to make a decision without consulting her. If she wanted the baby, okay, we'd get married. I could still finish school. And under the circumstances I was pretty sure Uncle Lucas would understand.'

'What was Dolly's reaction?'

'She said that was exactly what she wanted to hear. She asked me if I loved Peggy and I said yes.'

'Did she berate you for what happened?'

'No, sir. She was very philosophical about it. She said she guessed people couldn't deny their erotic natures. She would have been happier if we had restrained ourselves, but there was no use crying over spilled milk.'

'And you left her on that note?'

'Yes.'

'At what time?'

'The latest, twelve-thirty. Probably earlier.'

'She was alive and well?'

'She was smiling. She even kissed me on the cheek.'

'Do you know anything about what happened to her later that afternoon?'

Ken met his eyes directly. 'No, sir. When they told me, I was shocked. I even cried.'

'Did Dolly take you to the door or did you let yourself out?'

'I'd been there before. I let myself out.'

'Does the door have a snap lock?'

'Yes.'

'Did you hear it catch when you left?'

'I think so.'

'Did anyone see you leave?'

He hunched his shoulders. 'There were people in the street, but I don't know if they'll remember seeing me.'

'When did you get back to Boston?'

'Not later than four-thirty. Earlier, I think.'

'So it took you about four hours.'

'I made very good time.'

'All right. In a couple of minutes Lieutenant Varney is coming back to this office. He'll be itching to talk to you, but he probably thinks because I'm here, you've been muzzled. So let's surprise him. If this thing is a mistake, let's kill it now. I'll tell him you're ready to answer questions. Whatever he asks, look at me first. If I touch any part of my face, you have nothing to say. Otherwise tell him the truth. You have an academic degree, cum laude. Presumably you have a brain. Use it. Don't try to outsmart these men. They're professionals. And volunteer nothing. Just stick to the particular question.'

Lucas Sheridan shook his head. 'I don't think he should give them the right time.'

Paul stared at him fixedly. 'Are you prepared to take this case into court and try it yourself, Lucas?'

Sheridan pulled himself erect. 'I'm not sure I like your tone, Paul.'

'I haven't got time to practise diplomacy. I thought I made my position clear. If I'm handling Ken's defence, I don't want you or anyone else second-guessing me.' Paul relented a bit. 'But if it makes you feel any better, I'll tell you why I'm doing it. I want to hear Varney's questions. Just possibly they may clue me in on his thinking.'

Paul turned away and opened the door. He saw a fourth man conferring with the detectives. He recognized the man at once and felt a reflexive tightening of nerve ends. He was not really surprised at the presence of an assistant district attorney.

Since the ultimate responsibility for prosecution fell on the D.A.'s office, its participation now was routine. But Paul had collided on a previous occasion with John Nicoletti and had sampled the man's disciplines, the bulldog tenacity, the steel-edged acuity.

He nodded briefly and said, 'We're ready, gentlemen.'

CHAPTER THREE

THE CRIMINAL COURT BUILDING at 100 Centre Street was a tall structure, cold, antiseptic, undistinguished. As architecture, purely functional. Around the corner on Leonard Street, a second entrance opened on a small lobby with elevators which ran up to the offices of the district attorney of New York County. The Homicide Bureau was located on the sixth floor. Here, none of the windows could be raised more than three inches, on the theory that a guilty suspect might elect a quick fatal dive to the pavement below rather than risk conviction and long confinement.

Assistant D.A. John Nicoletti sat at his desk, hunched over a sheaf of documents, his brow crimped in concentration. Behind the deceptive façade of low-pressure amiability was a toughly incisive mind. He was a dark man, with flat cheeks, a lantern jaw, and close-cropped wiry black hair.

His father, Carlo Nicoletti, had arrived as an immigrant while still a young boy. Carlo had struggled through a primary-school education, had bulled his way through night school, and had managed to pass the civil-service exams for postman. Carlo's social contacts were largely limited to the local Democratic Club, where he performed an assortment of chores. His own parents, long since gone, had exhorted him to educate their grandson, young Giovanni.

It needed little coaxing. Giovanni was a quick, eager, diligent student. In high school he Anglicized his name to John. At City College he graduated third in a class devoted to scholarship. Then, with characteristically single-minded resolution, he had worked his way through Brooklyn Law.

John, too, joined the Democratic Club. And again he was an indefatigable worker. At first he ran errands. Later, during election times, he tacked up posters, rang doorbells, and harangued listeners on street corners. He became adroit at handling audiences, fielding questions, manipulating his voice. Inevitably, the district leader took notice and began to rely on him for more sensitive assignments. And ultimately, law degree in hand, John Nicoletti was rewarded. He landed his first appointment to the Manhattan district attorney's staff.

Nicoletti had served his apprenticeship through various bureaux—Complaint, Indictment, Rackets, Appeals; and then, due to tenacity and skill, he had risen to a position as one of the stellar performers on the trial staff, specializing in felonies and homicide.

On weekends old Carlo would often break up a game of boccie by whipping out a packet of clippings from which he would quote excerpts about his son's unremitting war against the underworld. Occasionally Carlo would call in sick and later appear at the Criminal Court Building and squeeze out a place for himself on a forward bench, where he could observe his son in action, his heart bursting with pride.

Remembering his parents' devotion, their deprivations caused by moving to a 'better neighbourhood' for the sake of the boy, the vicissitudes endured with stoicism, the implacable drive to claw their way up from a peasant heritage, John Nicoletti managed despite a back-breaking schedule to spend one evening a week with the old man, especially now since his mother's death.

Nicoletti was able to pinpoint precisely that moment in adolescence when he decided to become a lawyer. It happened at the movies, a courtroom melodrama viewed at a Saturday matinee. He could not, of course, remember the plot, but the climax, counsel's eloquently impassioned plea for justice, had so inspired and enthralled the boy that he was unable to leave the theatre. He sat mesmerized through two additional double features, finally racing home to a family frantic with apprehension.

Carlo, arms folded, demanded, 'You know what time it is?'

'It's late, Pa.'

'So where were you?'

'At the movies.'

Carlo Nicoletti's meaty palm caught his son a thundering clout over the left ear that left the boy glassy-eyed. 'Why?' he shouted. 'Nine, ten hours like a dummy in a stinking movie house. Tell me why?'

And, tearfully, Giovanni had spilled out his glowing account and a fervent plea for his newly discovered ambition.

A lawyer! Carlo smiled broadly, a miraculous transition from rage to benevolence. He grabbed his son and gave him a noisy kiss. He superintended the consumption of heroic quantities of pasta. He ate himself a second time just to keep the boy company.

So the goal was set. Young Giovanni haunted the library for books about lawyers. When he grew older he attended night court, observing, absorbing, sensing intuitively the fundamental rules of evidence. Often, with the dramatic instincts of youth, he would stand before a mirror, his imagination conjuring a rapt courtroom, and he would declaim and plead, developing a stock of custom expressions from which he would select the one most appropriate for intimidating witnesses or beguiling jurors.

Now on the D.A.'s staff, he had mastered his craft well enough to survive several changes of administration. In court, when guilty of skirting restrictions, his blinking innocence at a chiding judge would invariably soften the rebuke. Expert witnesses who had been subjected to his exhaustive examination of their specialties remembered the ordeal with awe and embarrassment. He was a relentless prosecutor but he had never tried to improve his batting average at the cost of his conscience.

He was squinting at a deposition through the upward swirl of smoke from a cigarette pasted between his lips when the phone rang. It was the district attorney's secretary. 'Mr Nicoletti, the chief would like to see you, if you're free.'

He correctly interpreted the diplomatic phrasing to mean *on the double*.

The Rt. Hon. Philip Lohman, district attorney for New York County, had been attending a convention of state prosecutors in Albany and had returned the previous evening. Lohman was a tall, grey, angular man with rimless glasses on a high-bridged nose. He was dressed in his customary dark suit, the collar of his shirt starched and white. Nicoletti knew that his courtly and somewhat clerical appearance concealed an instinct for the jugular. He was a capable administrator, permitting his deputies considerable latitude until adversity surfaced, and then he would land on the offender with withering censure. A veteran of the political wars, the beneficiary of various patronage plums, he took special relish in his present eminence.

He rose to press Nicoletti's palm.

'Good to have you back, sir,' Nicoletti said.

'Thank you, John. About that Dolly Wayne case, how is it shaping?'

'We have enough now for the grand jury to vote a true bill.'

'Do we have enough for a conviction?'

'I believe we can lock it up tight when our investigation is completed.'

Lohman pursed his lips thoughtfully. He tugged at an earlobe. 'Rather a ticklish situation. I happen to know old Lucas Sheridan personally.'

Nicoletti made no comment. His face was expressionless.

Lohman smiled. 'Has he applied any pressure?'

'Nothing we haven't been able to handle.'

'Don't misunderstand me, John. I'm not suggesting silk gloves. On the contrary. Even if I were so inclined, this is far too hot. I want you to proceed with all available facilities. Who's in charge at the police end?'

'Lieutenant Charles Varney.'

'A good man. I don't suppose Sheridan is appearing personally for the boy.'

'No, sir. His son-in-law. Paul Slater.'

Lohman raised an eyebrow. 'I wonder why. He can easily afford Bailey or Williams or someone in that league.'

Nicoletti shrugged. 'Maybe he wants to keep it in the family.'

'You've locked horns with Slater before, haven't you?'

'Once.'

'What's your impression?'

85

'I wouldn't mind having him in my corner if I were in trouble.'

'Any feelers out for a plea?'

'No, sir. They're convinced the boy is innocent.'

'Naturally. You read about this sort of thing. It never roosts on your own doorstep. Are you working on anything else at the moment?'

'The Freeman case.'

'Turn it over to Donenfeld. The Wayne homicide is your baby, John. I want you to concentrate on it. Take whoever you need from the Investigations Bureau. I'll pass the word.' His closed fist thumped the desk. 'I'll back you all the way. Just stick to established policy regarding the press.'

Established policy meant that all statements for publication emanated from the chief himself. Well, Lohman was head of the office, the elected official, responsible for its record. He was entitled to the plaudits. But first he wanted to know the current status.

'We're set for the preliminary hearing tomorrow morning. And I have an appointment in one hour with Slater.'

'What's he after?'

'Probably wants to establish the ground rules.'

'He knows we're going for murder one?'

'I made it very clear.'

Lohman looked him squarely in the eye. 'One thing more, John. Muncie is retiring at the end of the year. His job as chief assistant is up for grabs. Keep it in mind.'

When Paul Slater was ushered into Nicoletti's office, the two men regarded each other warily. Nicoletti's desk had been cleared of all reports, statements, and depositions. Lieutenant Varney had suggested that he be careful. Something about a tape recorder. Nicoletti indicated a chair.

'If you're thinking of a deal, Counsellor, save your breath. I repeat, we're going for broke.'

'On purely circumstantial evidence?'

'That's right. In how many homicides can we produce an eyewitness with twenty-twenty vision and an accurate memory?

Zero, Counsellor. Never in my experience. Even so, we have a pretty good record for convictions.'

'And you think a jury will buy it?'

Nicoletti showed his large square teeth. 'You fishing, Counsellor?'

'Only for enough of your case to know whether or not I ought to waive the preliminary hearing. Could save us both a lot of time and trouble. Besides, you know my attitude on discovery.'

'Yeah. It's coming out of my ears. You're working to liberalize procedures. You oppose secret testimony before a grand jury. You'd like the names of all State witnesses and an opportunity to examine them before trial. We say no dice. I have my job and you have yours. Mine is to nail the bastards. Yours is to help 'em beat the rap.'

'Not quite, John. Just to make you prove they're guilty.'

'Sure. By opening our hand in advance. Not a chance. You defence lawyers say you're interested in justice. Only, your clients are hanging in there every time trying to subvert it with lies, trickery, intimidation, and violence.'

'Only the professionals. You're not suggesting that every suspect is a pro? Including Ken Sheridan.'

'Tell you the truth, Counsellor, I don't know what the hell he is. I haven't got his combination by a long shot. That breed is light-years away from my background. I know what I think he is. And I'm willing to find out if a jury agrees with me.'

'Will you give them all the facts?'

'All the facts I've got.' His smile now showed a double row of teeth. 'And you'll get them at the same time. You sure don't need my help. That Warren Court made it easy for you.'

'Johnny boy, you're beginning to sound like a born cop.'

'Bullshit! You ought to know better. You were a federal prosecutor once. So you ought to know the problems. And in a city like this, triple 'em in spades. We got a jungle here, mister. Carnivores on the loose. It's a perpetual war. I read those bleeding hearts telling us we're doing it all wrong. Prisons only make 'em worse. So lead them to Jesus or the couch. They're maladjusted, disadvantaged, misunderstood; they come from

87

broken homes, they never had a chance. Crap! Offer any one of those hyenas an honest job and he'd spit in your eye. Work is for suckers like you and me.' Nicoletti pulled his thumb, cracking the knuckle. 'And what the hell made me sound off like this?'

'Maybe you're not sure of your reasoning,' Paul suggested.

'Ah, spare me the amateur psychology. Just give me one good argument why I should open up.'

'How's this? I'm essentially a single practitioner. Look at the personnel and financial resources you've got behind you.'

'Come on, Counsellor. Don't tell me Lucas Holmes Sheridan is sewing up his pockets. You'll get all the financial backing you need.'

'Money won't help.'

'What will?'

'When are you going to the grand jury?'

'Soon.'

'How about a look at the minutes?'

'Don't even bother to make a motion. If I stuck my neck out that far, Lohman would chop it off.'

'You're forcing me to test your evidence at the preliminary hearing.'

Nicoletti shrugged. 'You won't get much.' He frowned thoughtfully and pinched his bottom lip. 'I'll tell you this. We're gonna prove that young Sheridan came in from Boston and was in Dolly Wayne's apartment at the time she caught it. He says she was alive when he left. But he also says she was in a good mood. Well now, we have a witness who can testify that she was in a raging fury because he knocked up her daughter. Wild enough to cut off his marbles.'

'Who?'

Nicoletti smiled and yawned.

'I'll know anyway when you put him on the stand.'

'You will at that. Okay. Gordon Frazer.'

Nicoletti saw the slow loss of expression on Slater's face. He knew that Frazer had been Paul's predecessor at the altar and he had sensed the undercurrents of animosity in Frazer's manner.

'So we know how Dolly Wayne felt when young Sheridan got to her apartment,' he added. 'And we also know there was a bang-up donnybrook at the same time.'

'Another witness?'

'Yes. Dolly Wayne's tenant.'

'Billy Clark? You know the kind of impression he'll make.'

'So he's queer. That makes him a liar?' Nicoletti flexed his shoulders and stretched. 'And we have more, Counsellor, much more.'

'How about bail?'

'You got to be kidding.'

'The boy won't powder, John. Set it up in any amount you like.'

'Not a prayer. The uncle could post the whole bundle himself. And how would that look, with a tank full of poor slobs who can't even afford a lawyer?'

'That's it then,' Paul said. 'See you in court.'

CHAPTER FOUR

ON THE SURFACE, nothing seemed changed at Porterfield, Baker & Sheridan. Routine matters were handled as usual. Open discussion of Dolly Wayne's murder was avoided. Outside, however, staff members pursued the topic with debate, speculation, and rumour. It kept the stenographic pool, where most of the girls knew Ken from his summers at the office, in a state of avid excitement.

For three days after the funeral Alex Moore failed to appear. On the fourth day Lucas Sheridan sent for him. He was shocked at the change. Moore looked gaunt, brooding, apathetic, his mouth inverted and bitter, as though he had recently emerged from a long siege of illness.

Sheridan said, 'Alex, you've got to get a grip on yourself. I know how you felt about Dolly. And I sympathize. But she's gone and there's nothing you can do about it.'

'Nobody knows how I felt about Dolly.' Moore looked up, kneading his fingers. 'You know, I asked her to marry me.'

Sheridan nodded.

'You understand that Ken had nothing to do with it. The boy is innocent.'

'It's difficult to believe otherwise.'

'Not difficult. Impossible.'

'I've been in seclusion, Lucas. No papers, no radio. What are they basing it on?'

'They know that Peggy was pregnant and that Ken drove here to talk to Dolly about it. Paul is meeting with the D.A. now. He'll stop by to see me after his talk. We'll know more then.'

He leaned forward. 'Alex, I am neither blind nor gullible. Ken has his faults. But rape, plunder, murder—no, sir,

I'll never buy it. This was the work of an intruder, a psychopath. She probably surprised somebody in a burglary attempt. Anything else is inconceivable. I need your help, Alex.'

'Lucas, I haven't cracked the penal code since law school. I'd be useless.'

'That's beside the point. I need a reliable sounding board. I respect your common sense and judgment. The actual defence will be in Slater's hands.'

'Have you considered alternatives?'

'A few. Williams and Bailey are unavailable. Messinger is too flamboyant, too theatrical, a publicity hound. All this of course is confidential. I wouldn't want either Dru or Paul to know about it. So we're riding with Slater. The decision is final.'

'You know he's independent, a maverick.'

'Yes, but not unreasonable. And he's a first-rate trial man. You've been up against him. You recommended him to this firm.'

'I'm not questioning his competence. But Slater fragments his energies. He has obligations, classes to teach——'

'No problem. He's on leave of absence from the school. I've spoken to Dean Farquhar. And Jim Sloane assures me he and Barish will clear the decks for Paul at their end.' Sheridan glanced at his watch. 'I want you to sit in with me when Slater gets here. Council of war.'

'If you wish.'

'I appreciate it, Alex. I know it may be painful at times.' Sheridan sat back. 'Do you know how many men are available to the district attorney for investigation?'

'No.'

'I inquired. About fifty on the grand jury squad alone, all trained police officers, specially selected, headed by a captain. Plus a staff of civilian experts attached to the Investigation Bureau. Heavy odds, wouldn't you say? If my memory serves, didn't we once use a private detective in an industrial espionage matter?'

'Roy Burroughs.'

'He's a good man?'

'Fifteen years with the FBI. Heading up his own agency now. His work for us was impressive.'

'Call him on the phone now. See if he's free. We'll get him for Paul's use.' The buzzer sounded. He picked up the phone. 'Send him right in.' He looked up. 'Slater's here.'

They listened in sober silence while Paul gave them an account of his meeting with John Nicoletti. The corners of Sheridan's mouth turned down and he said tightly, 'So Gordon Frazer is back in our lives. I thought we'd seen the last of him. The son-ofabitch! He'll never hold up in court. I want you to tear him apart, Paul.'

'Let's hear his testimony first.'

'Any talk of a deal?' Moore asked.

'What kind of a deal?' Sheridan snapped. 'The boy is inno-cent. They want to negotiate, let them drop charges.'

'They're going all out,' Paul said. 'First degree.'

'Can they pinpoint Ken's presence in Dolly's apartment?'

Paul shrugged. 'They may have a witness who saw him leave. It's essential to their case and they've got the manpower to check it.'

'Which brings up a matter I want to mention,' Sheridan said. 'Does the name Roy Burroughs ring a bell?'

Paul reflected. 'Head of a private detective agency, I believe.'

'Yes, and a damn good one too. Would you accept his help if it were available?'

'I need all the help I can get. How big is the outfit?'

'He has at least a dozen men,' Moore said.

'I'd want that many to try and locate Dolly's jewellery. If we could find who has it, the State's case would collapse.

'Burroughs will hire all the men you need. I'll give him full authority.'

'All right, Lucas. Have him get in touch with me as soon as possible.' Paul was encouraged. He knew from past experience how a lack of resources could cripple an effective defence. It was virtually impossible for any accused to compete with the State on that basis. Still, a few dedicated investigators could often tip the balance.

'What's your next step?' Sheridan asked.

'First, another talk with Ken. I want an accounting of every second and every move he made from the time he left Cambridge until he returned.' He turned to Moore. 'I'm sorry about this, Alex, but I have no choice. I want Burroughs to dig into Dolly's background over the past year or so, probe her appointments, winnow her friends, turn over every stone he can find. Obviously, that puts you in the picture. But we know about you. It's the people we don't know about that might give us a clue. In the meantime, I'll file every motion in the book for discovery. It will keep the prosecution busy and may do us some good.'

'And you'll keep us appraised?' Sheridan asked.

'No, Lucas, I will not.'

Sheridan arched back, his eyes wide. 'I beg your pardon. What did you say?'

'I'm saying that I will not be obligated to render periodic reports. Let's have a clear understanding now. I am rejecting, unequivocally, the imposition of any outside pressures. I expect to be totally immersed. And I will not be available for additional conferences. I must have and I demand complete autonomy. That is not a negotiable condition. And it's the only way I'll accept responsibility for the boy's defence.'

Sheridan's voice was icy. 'Ken is my nephew, almost a son; he's lived with me most of his life. He needs my help. Are you closing the door on me?'

'What I'm trying to get across, Lucas, is that I will not operate on a committee basis.'

'You seem to forget, this office is not without prestige, resources, brainpower. Good God, man, make use of it.'

Paul said, tightly controlled, 'Every man jack at Porterfield, Baker & Sheridan, consigned his knowledge of criminal law to mothballs the day he entered the firm. That kind of brainpower I don't need. You've already made your personal resources available through Roy Burroughs. As for prestige, you try peddling influence here and it may blow the game. Nicoletti would sure as hell make an issue of it. We don't need a bad press.'

'May I voice an opinion?' Moore said.

'Go ahead.'

'I've met Philip Lohman. So have you, Lucas. He's an ambitious man who's going to exploit every angle of this prosecution. You couldn't pull strings anyway.'

Sheridan shook his head. 'You don't leave me any choice, Paul. I hope to Christ you know what you're doing.'

The bed was positioned so that Dru could manipulate the curtains for a view of the East River. She was staring out at the water traffic, tugs, barges, an occasional tanker. As dusk fell, night-time lights flickered over Queens and smokestacks etched a calligraphy against the darkening sky. She saw the distant glow of a DC-9 as it circled for its landing pattern into La Guardia.

She had managed a kind of numbed acceptance. For the first few weeks after Ken's arrest, life had taken on a nightmare quality. It had pre-empted her thoughts and invaded her dreams. When it began to affect her health, she'd caught hell from the obstetrician. He had warned her to maintain some semblance of normality. She owed it to the baby. And for Paul's sake too; because he had to contend with the case all day, she had trained herself to assume a brave front.

She heard Paul in the shower. He had come home fairly early, his face drawn with fatigue. She closed her eyes and pictured him, foaming with suds, and toyed with the notion of joining him, scrubbing his back. But he generally ran the water so hot it made her dizzy. So she resisted the impulse and stretched her legs and waited for him.

When he came through the bathroom door, wearing a short shave-coat, he paused for a moment and stood admiring her. She crooked a finger and said, 'It's awful lonely in this big bed.' He sat alongside her and placed his hand flat against her stomach. She covered it with her own. 'Feel anything in there?'

'Not yet. When is he supposed to start kicking?'

'About the end of the fourth month. And what makes you think it's a he?'

'Just a figure of speech.'

94

'Would you be disappointed if it was a girl?'

'Girls are my favourite.'

'Then you're not particular?'

'I'd be happy with either one or a combination of both.'

'I hope you mean twins.'

He laughed. 'What does the doctor say?'

'It's too early to tell.' She moved his hand up to her breast. The nipple responded instantly. She pulled him down and fitted herself against him. He captured one of her flanks between his thighs. She turned her mouth to his and dug closer. Suddenly he tasted the salt moisture of a tear, and she shuddered deeply.

'I'm sorry, darling,' she said in a muffled voice. 'I try so hard to forget.'

'Everything is going to be all right, Dru.'

She moved back and searched his face. 'Are we putting too much pressure on you, too much responsibility?'

'In my line of work, pressure is an occupational hazard.'

'It isn't just another case, is it, darling?'

'You know better than that.'

'I keep worrying about Ken, how they're treating him.'

'The boy amazes me. Most suspects become apathetic and despondent. Ken acts as if this whole thing were a fascinating school assignment.'

'That's because he's innocent. He knows they can't hurt him.'

'We don't have to prove his innocence. They have to prove his guilt. But we're bucking a system that stacks the cards against us. The mere fact of an indictment sometimes influences a jury.'

'You're frightening me, Paul.'

'I don't mean to. But I won't soft-soap you either. I think you ought to know what we're up against. A lot of political capital can be made out of this case. For one thing, I need information and they're trying to keep it from me. This afternoon I wanted to look at Dolly Wayne's apartment and I found it guarded by cops. Which means I may have to get a court order just to inspect the scene of the crime. And of course I'll have to interview all our witnesses, wherever they are. In the next few days I'm driving up to Cambridge to see Ken's class-mates. You can help too. I need background information. It may help me to understand the boy. How old was Ken when his parents died?'

'He was six.'

'How did it happen?'

'An automobile accident. Ken was home with a sitter. Uncle Hugh and his wife had gone to a New Year's party in Stam-ford. It had begun to snow when they left about three a.m. He'd been drinking, I suppose, and certainly he was driving too fast when the car skidded on the Turnpike. It hit an abut-ment and they both died instantly.'

'Before that, what did he do?'

'Uncle Hugh was one of the early rebels, the absolute anti-thesis of Dad. He quit school and shipped off on a freighter as an able-bodied seaman, travelling around the world. In Singa-pore he met an English girl and married her. Ken's mother, my Aunt Elizabeth. About that time he'd begun to sell some articles to left-wing magazines, and they came back to the States. He despised the system and he never saw eye to eye with Dad on one single thing. So naturally they seldom came to see us. And because Dad was out of the country so much, Ken was the only relative I had for long periods of time. We took vacations together and I gave him his first tennis lesson. This brought us closer together.

'Ken was such a sad sack when Dad brought him home, remote, withdrawn, a little suspicious. But within a year he seemed to blossom. He was quick and bright, though a little unsettled at times and odd, but that may have been my fault. Perhaps I spoiled him.'

'Did his father leave any insurance?'

'Hardly. That wasn't Uncle Hugh's style.'

'How about Frazer before your divorce? Did he like Ken too?'

'There was no room in Gordon's affections for anyone but Gordon. He took pleasure in baiting Ken with snide remarks. At first Ken was no match for him. But then at a dinner party one night Ken responded, and my God, did it light a fuse!'

'Tell me.'

'We had guests, about twelve people. Gordon was being more obnoxious than usual. He made some gratuitous remark about Ken's physique, implying that Ken was muscle-bound all over, including his head. Ken looked up at him very innocently and sweetly and said, 'I have to keep exercising, old top, in order to protect my chastity. I never know when you might take a fancy to me.'

'Good God!' Paul breathed. 'What happened?'

'Gordon turned dead-white. Ken just kept smiling at him. Physically, of course, they were no match. Then someone laughed and that tore it. Gordon jumped up and stalked out of the apartment in a cold fury. The party limped along after that until everyone went home. And it was the last time Ken came to see us until after I left Gordon.'

Paul mulled it over. 'Would Frazer be capable of lying in court just to get revenge?'

'I wouldn't put it past him. You know something?' she said, abruptly changing the subject.

'What?'

'I think I'd like a pastrami sandwich.'

He laughed. 'I was wondering when this sort of thing would begin. You mean you want me to get dressed and go down to a delicatessen?'

'Nope. There's some in the fridge. I ordered it this afternoon. But first I want a kiss.'

'If you start that, you may not get around to the pastrami for another hour.'

'Boaster,' she said and wrapped her arms around him.

He took her gently.

It seemed to get better all the time. 'Hey!' he said suddenly, 'how many more months have we got before I get orders to cease and desist?'

'About four.'

'And after delivery, how long do we have to wait?'

'That depends, darling, on whether you get me a private room or a semi-private room.'

CHAPTER FIVE

ABE BARISH had a rumpled face and the melancholy look of a scholar. When he was a boy on the Lower East Side, his chie companions were books. Eclectic in taste, he read everythin, from Horatio Alger to Immanuel Kant. Like most immigran parents, his were maniacally possessed with the notion of a professional career and had aimed him like a crossbow with law school as the target. The ratiocinative process, finely honed throughout his youth, resulted in a notable academic performance. Upon graduation, knowing that his reserve and self-effacing diffidence would probably prevent his attracting potential clients, and armed with an enthusiastic recommenda tion from one of his professors, he had sought a connection and been employed by a medium-sized firm. There, consigned to a small cubicle, he had drawn the most airtight contracts and the most closely reasoned briefs the firm had ever submitted

He remained with them for six years, his competence recog nized but unrewarded. Until Jim Sloane, another member of the staff, had approached him with a proposition. Why not cut loose and open their own shop?

Barish required exactly one-third of a second to reach a decision. They shook hands over it.

In personality, the two men were diametric opposites. Sloane was a bluff, beef-faced, professional Irishman, hearty, aggres sive, gregarious. Within a year he had generated enough business to keep Abe Barish behind his desk twelve hours a day. At first he was constantly organizing tenants' committees to fight rent increases. Lately he had been ferreting out news of executive shenanigans and originating minority stockholders' actions.

Sloane & Barish became a profitable union of talents. When

Paul Slater joined them as trial counsel, a singular rapport soon sprang into existence among the three men.

Now, working at his desk, correcting syntax and checking annotations, oblivious of passing time, Abe was suddenly surprised to hear his name. Paul Slater stood in the doorway, greeting him.

'I'd like a word with you,' Abe said.

'I'm listening, Abe.'

'You're off the hook on the Maddox trial. We got a two-week adjournment and then Sloane will take over. The malpractice suit at York General was settled this morning. Which clears you completely for the Sheridan defence.'

'Thank you, Abe.'

'You're welcome. And there's something else on my mind. Granted criminal law is not my forte, I want in. I think I can be of some use. I want to help. I'd consider it a favour.'

'A favour, Abe?'

'Life is like food. It needs a little spice. All my work is on dull cases—breach of contract, probate, a real-estate conveyance, an almost total concentration on property and money. I want to do something for people. Yes, Paul, it would be a *mitzvah*, a favour.'

'There won't be any fee in this case, Abe.'

'Who needs it? How many steaks can I eat anyway?'

'Can you afford the time?'

'So we don't sign up any new business for a while. I already spoke to Sloane. It's jake with him.'

Paul was touched. 'You're hired, Abe. Maybe that devious brain of yours will conjure up some vital nugget of wisdom.'

'When are you putting me to work?'

'Right now. I suppose you've been reading the papers.'

'Avidly.'

'Anything there that bothers you?'

'Hints, insinuations. Am I to understand that the deceased was—er—injudiciously handled?'

'You know almost as much as I do, Abe. The State has been disgorging information with all the prodigality of a slot machine.'

99

'So we'll demand a bill of particulars.'

'In the criminal courts, you'll never get full disclosure.'

'How about the medical examiner's report?'

'Confidential to the police department.'

'You attended the funeral. How did she look?'

'Sealed casket, Abe.'

'May I offer a suggestion?'

'Please.'

'Maybe the undertaker has a loose tongue. He had to see the remains in order to embalm them, no?'

Paul grinned. 'You may have something there, you old ghoul. What gave you that idea?'

'My reading habits. Along with Blackstone and the Talmud, I also enjoy detective stories.'

'Keep reading, Abe. Unconventional thinking in our orthodox profession is a welcome novelty.'

'More to the point, what should I read in the line of criminal law?'

'We'll come to that later. You know that a man is presumed innocent until he's proven guilty, don't you?'

'A fine ringing doctrine.'

'It sometimes rings against deaf ears, Abe. When a man is accused, only his friends believe he's innocent. Most people think he's guilty, why else would he be in the dock? And that worries me.'

The library phone buzzed and Barish reached for it. He listened and offered the handset to Paul. 'For you. A Miss Peggy Wayne.'

Paul had seen Peg at the funeral, but had not spoken to her. He knew that she had called Dru after Ken's arrest, semi-hysterical, sobbing her belief in his innocence. He could tell from her voice that she had only a tenuous grip on herself. He said quietly, 'Hello, Peg.'

'I—I was wondering if I could see you, Paul.'

'Of course. When?'

'This afternoon?'

'Any time after four o'clock. I'll be tied up until then.'

'I'm going to need a lawyer.'

'You, Peg? What for?'

'Well, there's Mother's estate and everything.'

'Wouldn't Alex Moore be a more logical choice?'

She hesitated. 'My grandparents say I can choose my own.'

'Suppose we talk about that when you get here.' He hung up and said, 'Abe, there's something I'd like to discuss with you.'

'Probate Dolly Wayne's estate?' Abe Barish looked doubtful. 'Is it proper? Can you defend young Sheridan on a homicide charge and at the same time represent the victim's estate?'

'The victim's daughter, actually,' Paul said. 'And we're not soliciting the girl. She comes to us voluntarily. It's splitting hairs, of course. But there are fringe benefits. Prospective jurors would hear about it.'

'How?'

'We'd leak the news. Retaining us is a sign of confidence in the defendant. Naturally, I personally wouldn't handle it. Sloane & Barish would be attorneys of record.'

Barish sighed. 'I wish there were clear lines of conduct.'

'You'd have to feed these particular facts into a computer and hope for a printout that applies. Considering the infinite variations, how could you programme the machine? You make the decision, Abe. When it comes to ethics, your standards are good enough for me.'

'Is it a big estate?'

'Dolly inherited from Brian Wirth.'

Barish was impressed. 'Very tempting. The fees would be substantial.'

'Substantial fees!' boomed a voice from the doorway where Jim Sloane's massive bulk had suddenly materialized. 'An interesting phrase. For us, Abraham?'

'It's a possibility. Paul wants us to be attorneys of record in the probate of Dolly Wayne's estate.'

'So what's the problem?'

'A matter of propriety,' Paul said. He explained the situation.

'I have an old pal on the Ethics Committee. I will ask for an adjudication.'

'Like right away,' Paul said. 'Use the telephone. The girl will be here later this afternoon. And thanks for the use of your partner.'

'You may need him. Who else can juggle a precedent with so much guile and sagacity?'

Barish chuckled. 'You see, Paul. With such honeyed words the Irisher wooed me into this partnership.'

'It worked on you, Abe. But I couldn't sell our young professor here. Nevertheless, I am not affronted. He also turned down his father-in-law.'

Barish widened his eyes. 'You had an offer from Porterfield, Baker & Sheridan? And you refused?'

'Not so much reverence, Abe. It's a law firm, not the Holy Trinity. Where did you hear about it, Jim?'

'I have unimpeachable sources, my boy. I am flattered, but mystified.'

'Where would I fit into a set-up like that? They'd bury me under fifty tons of boiler plate a day.'

'Don't knock it; it's profitable work.'

'Subject closed, if you please.'

Sloane beamed an amiable look at his partner. 'Your first criminal case, Abe. Enjoy yourself. Just remember, when it's over, you'll have to work twenty-four hours a day correcting my mistakes.'

Paul's desk phone buzzed.

'A Mr Roy Burroughs,' the receptionist told him. 'He says he has an appointment.'

'Show him in,' Paul said, and broke the connection. 'I want you to sit in on this, Abe.'

Jim Sloane waved expansively and disappeared.

Roy Burroughs was a flinty man in his middle forties, with precise eyes and a flat uninflected voice. He looked more like a minor executive of some utility company than a private investigator. He wore brush-cut hair and a neat, unobtrusive business suit. In anticipation of Paul's request he had already begun to accumulate a biographical file on Dolly Wayne.

He hitched up a trouser leg and crossed his knees. He

listened without expression while Paul put him in the picture, speaking carefully and succinctly.

'The nature of the crime,' Paul concluded, 'the condition of the body, the stolen jewellery, all make the boy's guilt inconceivable. So far as I know, the case against him is purely circumstantial. This is your line of country, Mr Burroughs. Do you have any suggestions?'

Burroughs sat back. 'We proceed on an assumption of the boy's innocence. Ergo, someone else is guilty. Here we have two alternatives. Some character with a real or a fancied grievance. To find out, we have to ransack her private life, acquaintances, associates, intimates, everybody.'

'How many men can you put on it?'

'Depends on the budget.'

'Were you told to submit your bills to Sheridan senior?'

'I was.'

'Then don't stint. Whatever the freight, he can afford it.'

Burroughs nodded. 'The other alternative is a stranger. Perhaps a hophead looking for a quick score. Miss Wayne surprised him and he did what he had to do to cover his tracks. I understand there was some mutilation of the corpse. Do you have any specific details on that?'

'Not yet.'

'Can you get them?'

'We're trying.'

'An addict could explain that kind of violation. The large jewellery haul was an unexpected dividend. I'll need a complete list and description from her insurance company.'

'You'll have it by tomorrow morning.'

'We could run into a snag. With all the publicity a real pro would lay low, break the stuff up for sale in South America. On the other hand, a junkie needing a quick fix would probably start unloading at once. Soon as I have the list, we'll start checking known fences and pawnshops.'

Paul nodded. 'I may have other suggestions from time to time. One additional item, Mr Burroughs. About your reports——'

'They are confidential to the people who employ me.'

'That needs clarification. Mr Lucas Sheridan is paying the bills. Period. But you're working for me. Exclusively. All reports will be made to me personally or to my deputy here, Mr Abe Barish. There are no exceptions. Should Mr Sheridan or anyone else make inquiries, refer him to this office. Any questions?'

'Not at the moment.'

'I take it you're prepared to give this matter precedence.'

'I am.'

'Anything else you want to contribute, Abe?'

Barish shook his head. 'I think you've covered it.'

Paul stood up. 'Keep in touch, Mr Burroughs. Time is of the essence.' He had looked at his watch and seen that it was almost four o'clock.

'Please, Paul,' Peggy Wayne pleaded. 'Couldn't you fix it for me to see Ken?'

She had only a precarious control, her lips trembling, her hands shaking. Paul felt a sharp twinge of compassion. It seemed as though a large pitiless fist had squeezed all the exuberance and vivacity out of the girl. She looked wan and bleak, her eyes tortured.

'Later maybe,' he said. 'They're very strict about visitors.'

'I—I guess I'm a mess.'

'That's understandable, Peg. You've been through an ordeal.'

'And there's so much more to come, isn't there? If they only knew Ken like I do. How is he?'

'Confident.'

'Does he ask for me?'

'All the time. And he wants you to know that everything is going to be all right.' Paul found himself covertly looking for telltale signs of a bulge, but found none. Apparently it was too early. He wondered what, if any, plans she had made.

'Nobody tells me much,' she said. 'My grandparents try to shield me. I want to know, Paul, did Ken really come to New York that day?'

'Yes, Peg.'

'But why?'

'Your mother asked him to.'

'I—I don't understand. He drove in from Cambridge?'

Paul leaned forward. 'Peg, I'm going to give it to you straight. You're a big girl now and I think you ought to know some facts. You weren't feeling well and your mother sent you to a doctor. After you left the doctor's office, he called her and told her that you were pregnant.'

She laced fingers over her mouth. 'Oh, no . . .'

'Your mother was deeply concerned. She knew you weren't an easy mark, sleeping around. And she knew how you felt about Ken. So it had to be him. Naturally she wanted to discuss it with him.'

'Who else knows?'

'Ken's uncle, the prosecutor; it's not public knowledge.'

'Did Mother carry on? Did she——'

'They had a very friendly talk, Peg. Ken told her he would abide by any decision you made. If you wanted to get married, fine. If you decided not to have the baby, he wouldn't be happy about it, but he'd go along with that too.'

She turned away, blinking back tears. 'Mother hated to talk to me about things like that. No matter what she did with her own private life, she had me on some kind of crazy pedestal.'

'Do your grandparents know about the baby?'

'Not yet.'

'I think you ought to tell them. And you'll have to make a decision. Soon. Don't wait too long.'

She said vehemently, 'That's why I have to see Ken. I won't decide anything without talking to him first. It's his baby too.'

She was an odd amalgam of naïveté and sophistication, suspended between adolescence and maturity, agonized by events beyond her control. 'I'll try to arrange it,' Paul said. 'Will you be going back to school?'

'Not this term. I want to be near Ken during the trial.' She leaned towards him, pleading. 'Paul, isn't there something I can do to help?'

He nodded slowly. 'There may be. You see, Peg, one way to exonerate Ken would be to find the man actually responsible.

It could have been a stranger. Or someone she knew. If the latter, maybe you can help us identify him. You often spent weekends at home. You knew the people she saw. You may have overheard conversations on the telephone. I know this is a delicate subject, Peg. If you find it too painful, just shake your head and I'll understand.'

Her chin came up. 'Mother is dead. I'm resigned to that. I have to think about Ken now. I'll tell you anything I can.'

She had more iron than he'd suspected. 'Do you recollect any incidents that seemed odd, any change in the pattern of her normal behaviour?'

Peg frowned. 'I guess it's no secret that Mother was having a sort of thing with Alex Moore.'

'When did that start?'

'Soon after Brian—you know, Brian Wirth, my stepfather—died. Alex was very helpful. He was Brian's lawyer and he had always been attentive to Mother, especially after Brian went to the hospital.'

Had it progressed beyond the point of friendship even at that time? Wirth had been ill for almost a year. And Dolly had not been one to deprive herself. He remembered Dru's laughing revelation about Dolly's libido. 'She was tipsy at the time,' Dru had said. 'She told me she had never been without a lover since her sixteenth birthday. She was terribly frank. "Some sort of glandular imbalance, dearie. Hormones or whatever overactive, I suppose, in a constant ferment. Going without makes me nervous. Even gives me insomnia. To say nothing about raising hell with my complexion. Besides, Dru dear, I happen to like sex. It's such a lovely diversion. And it keeps a woman looking young and feeling young too".'

He saw that Peg was frowning at some elusive memory, and then looking uncertain as it crystallized. She thought about it and decided to tell him. 'I was home one weekend. It was just before Brian went to the hospital that last time. I couldn't sleep and I got up to get a glass of milk. I remember passing Mother's room and they were arguing. Brian was furious. He accused Mother of having a lover. He said he was going to make a new will and cut her off without a cent.'

'Did she deny the accusation?'

'Oh, yes. She said he'd always been insanely jealous. Then Brian came stumbling out and headed for the guest room. I didn't even have time to hide.'

'Did he see you?'

'He must have. But Brian never paid much attention to me anyway. He just sort of tolerated me, something that came with Mother, like her career and her wardrobe. They'd been feuding quite a bit and it embarrassed me, so I went back to school early the next day.'

'Are you comfortable with your grandparents?'

'They're kind of old and always fussing. They say I ought to sell Mother's house because taxes are so high. They wanted to take me to their lawyer, but I insisted on coming to you. Could you take care of things for me, Paul?'

'Did Dolly leave a will?'

'I don't know. She was always talking about it, but you know Mother, everything *mañana*.'

'I'm not turning you down, Peggy, but it would be better if my associates here at the office were attorneys of record. My name would not appear on the papers.'

'Whatever you say, Paul.'

'And I'll want you to attend the trial, as a mark of confidence in Ken. It won't be easy for you. You may have trouble with reporters.'

Her lips tightened. 'They're on my neck now, ringing at all hours, annoying my grandparents, photographers waiting in the street.'

'It's the price one pays for celebrity. Your mother was in the public eye. I may or may not arrange a brief press conference. In the meantime, say nothing to anyone. Can you do that, Peg?'

She said with quiet determination, 'I can do anything I have to do.'

'Good girl. Now let's go meet Mr Abraham Barish.'

CHAPTER SIX

THE LAMBERT FUNERAL CHAPEL was a sedate two-storey structure on upper Madison Avenue. Its sepulchral atmosphere evoked subdued whispers. It held various reposing rooms and a chapel in which, with adroit manœuvring, a steady stream of defunct clients could receive their last rites. Below ground was the workroom of a macabre cosmetician skilled in the use of rouge and embalming fluids.

Fabian L. Lambert was no stereotype. Paul had expected an unctuous and melancholy specimen. The portly man behind the desk had tax-collector eyes and a preacher's flexible voice. He could assume a mask of sympathy while simultaneously gauging the financial resources of bereaved relatives. Paul wondered what prompted a man to enter this dreary traffic in death. He abhorred the pagan ritual, the homage to clay, the harrowing cortège, the finality of new-dug earth. Fabian L. Lambert inquired politely how he could be of service.

'I would like some information about Dolly Wayne.'

A slight arching of one eyebrow. Lambert was not sure he had caught the visitor's name. Paul produced a card and was inspected with fresh interest.

'Aren't you the attorney for young Sheridan, the boy responsible for her death?'

'The boy is a long way from conviction, Mr Lambert.'

The undertaker smiled primly. 'What information are you seeking?'

'Information about her injuries. Since your establishment prepared the remains for interment, I thought you might describe them for me.'

'Were you at the funeral, Mr Slater?'

'I was.'

'Then you must know that the body was not on display. The casket was sealed under instructions from the family. I am not sure that it would be proper for me to disregard their wishes now.'

Paul's face and manner took on that special quality he could invoke when it became necessary to extract information. It was largely reflexive. It came into operation without any conscious volition, a penetrating intensity, eyes suddenly bleak. Without other leverage, his voice changed, became icily uninflected.

'Have you been paid for your services, Mr Lambert?'

'I expect to be.'

'By the estate?'

'Naturally.'

'Miss Peggy Wayne is the sole legatee of that estate. I am her attorney. I suggest that you pick up that phone and ask her permission to discuss details with me.'

Fabian Lambert suddenly felt uncomfortable. 'I—I don't have much time for conversation, sir.'

Paul said evenly, 'You only think you have no time, Mr Lambert. A young man is locked up in a cell downtown. When he goes on trial I can subpoena you and have you sequestered in a waiting room, cooling your heels for days until I decide to put you on the stand. It might be wise to take time right now and satisfy my curiosity.'

The undertaker wavered. He opened his hands in surrender. 'What can I tell you, Mr Slater? We did not even embalm the remains. You must understand that a post-mortem had been performed. When the medical examiner released the body to us, it was . . .' He gestured vaguely. 'Surely you must know how difficult it is to describe injuries after an autopsy.'

'Try,' Paul said.

Although the man's commerce was corpses, he seemed genuinely distressed. 'There were many bruises and—er—teeth marks.'

'Where, specifically?'

'On the breasts, the thighs, around the—er—pudenda.' Lambert's voice rose. 'Like some damned vulture had been at the woman. . . .'

Or a psychopath, Paul thought. Inflamed by dark forces that lurk in sick minds. He was both repelled and heartened. Repelled by the act; heartened because it conformed to no pattern observable in Ken.

'Would you by any chance have a photograph?' he asked.

Fabian L. Lambert was deeply aggrieved. He lifted his chin with heavy dignity. 'Sir, this establishment was founded by my grandfather over forty years ago. And never, not once in all that time, has anyone ever impugned our methods or our integrity. No, we did not take photographs, although handsome offers were made by certain publications. We are responsible businessmen, not ghouls. If you want photographs, I am sure the police can accommodate you. Photographs taken from every conceivable angle.' He paused, and added as if to reassure himself, 'This is an old and a very highly regarded establishment.'

'That may be,' Paul said. He stood up. 'I may even recommend your services.' He turned and left without ceremony.

Even the street, with exhaust-polluted air, seemed oddly pleasant in contrast to the sickly sweet aroma so pervasive in these institutions. He flagged a cab and headed south towards Foley Square. He remembered vaguely a court decision that might implement Lambert's disclosure. He would have to alert Abe Barish. It was unlikely that Nicoletti would volunteer any information. The prosecutor would prefer to spring it in court, too late for an adequate response.

The attendant at Manhattan's House of Detention asked for no identification. He greeted Paul with a single word, 'Counsellor,' and turned the book for his signature.

An elevator lifted Paul to the seventh floor. He sat in the lawyers' waiting room until they brought Ken to the large chamber on its right. Small cubicles lined both walls, each containing a table and two chairs. Out of earshot on a bench at the rear sat a guard, eyes constantly moving and alert. Two other lawyers were conferring with their clients in hushed tones.

Despite the shock of his sudden transformation to a strange and hostile environment, Ken's assurance and equanimity remained unruffled. All the more surprising in view of his associates in this cheerless place, denizens of an unfamiliar world to whom he could not in any sense relate. He knew of course that he had the support and devotion of influential relatives. Two weeks of confinement had faded the sun-browned face to a light tan.

He was eager for news, and Paul brought him up to date, a cheerless procedure. Then, because nothing of a positive nature for the defence had yet emerged, Paul once again took him carefully and painstakingly through his movements on the fatal day, checking and rechecking every step, all the people he had spoken to.

He explained that what he needed was something beyond a mere denial of guilt. Prosecution witnesses had to be refuted, neutralized, demolished.

He said, 'Think back, Ken. You saw Dolly that day. You spoke to her. Did she give any indication, by words or manner, that she was expecting other company after you left?'

'Not that I recall.'

'Did she seem impatient to finish her talk with you?'

Ken's frown quirked into a slow smile. 'Would it help my case if I said yes?'

Paul stared at him. He said sharply, 'Hold it right there, damn it! I am not putting words in your mouth. I'm making no suggestions. You will testify to nothing but the absolute truth. One lie, one little distortion, one evasion, and our friend Nicoletti would tie you into knots.'

'"Oh, what a tangled web we weave, when first we practise to deceive?"'

He had turned the Walter Scott quotation into a query. 'And you better believe it,' Paul told him. 'Anyway, it's academic. You probably won't even take the stand.'

'Why not? I can handle myself.'

'Against whom? Your classmates at school in a mock trial?' Paul referred to notes taken on a previous visit. 'We have you leaving Dolly's apartment about twelve-thirty and getting back to Cambridge about four-thirty. Is that right?'

'On the nose.'

'Four hours exactly?'

'Just about.'

'And you went straight to your lodgings?'

'Yes.'

'You said your room-mate was there studying. His name is Cliff Eldon?'

Ken nodded. 'I felt stiff from all that driving. Eight hours in one day. Boston to New York and back again. I wanted to loosen up. So I suggested a game of touch football, and Cliff got the two guys next door. There's an empty lot across the street and we went down there and roped in a few passers-by and started to horse around.'

'The boys would remember that?'

'Damn right. Because the Duke dumped me. You know the rules. He wasn't supposed to tackle me but he did. He brought me down hard and my nose began to bleed. It was squirting like a crushed tomato.'

'The Duke?'

'Howard Pirie. We call him Duke because he spent a year at Oxford and suddenly he has a British accent. We went back to the house and Hadley got some ice from the landlady.'

'Which one is Hadley?'

'The Duke's room-mate. Frank Hadley.'

'All studying law?'

'Except Duke Pirie. He's on a scholarship doing post-graduate work in economics.'

Paul added the new names to his notebook. 'I'll want to talk to the boys.'

'They may not be able to get away from school.'

'Then I'll call on them.'

'Pre-trial preparation?'

'That's right. Were you very friendly with them?'

'With Cliff Eldon mostly. We roomed together as under-graduates.'

'He knows about Peggy?'

'That she is my girl friend?'

'No, that's she's pregnant.'

Ken shook his head. 'I wasn't sure myself. I knew she was a

little late, but it wasn't the first time, and I figured she'd come around all right.'

'I spoke to her yesterday. She says she'll have the baby if you want her to.'

'I don't think she should, Paul. We're too young to assume that responsibility. And we'll have plenty of time later on.'

'You don't mind subjecting her to the operation?'

'Ah, Paul, it's legal now. No big deal. No more than a little plumbing. She's in the hospital twenty-four hours and out the next day maybe batting a tennis ball around.'

'You're sure of that?'

Ken grinned, confidentially, man-to-man. 'Look, I once got into a jam with another girl. Cost me three hundred bucks. The boys took up a collection and I'm still paying it off out of my allowance. But the girl was out dancing the next night.'

Paul made no comment. He remembered his own youthful escapades, from bumbling shyness to reckless abandon. The clerics, the civil authorities, the Mosaic laws through the Napoleonic Code to Anglo-Saxon proscriptions had all tried to curb man's innate eroticism, with a total lack of success. So who was he to condemn?

'Peg would like to see you, Ken, and talk it over.'

He looked up eagerly. 'Can you fix it?'

'I promised her I'd try. But if the thing is going to be done, the sooner the better.'

He nodded. 'Okay. Then you tell her how I feel about it.'

Paul stood up. 'Is there anything you need?'

'Yeah,' Ken said wryly. 'Cigarettes, clean sheets, air conditioning, a copy of *Playboy*, and food. Christ, the slop they feed you here.'

Paul smiled sympathetically. 'Just hang in there, boy. We'll try to get this thing rolling as soon as possible.'

He drove steadily in the centre lane. Monster trucks howling alongside kept him alert. He would have preferred the Parkway, but Ken had travelled the Thruway and now Paul was timing the trip. He made it to Cambridge in slightly over four hours.

Ken's address was a two-storey building of red brick with strands of ivy clinging to its façade. It contained a dozen utility apartments occupied largely by graduate students. Paul had phoned Cliff Eldon in advance. When he pushed the button a metallic voice on the annunciator demanded identification. He spoke into the mouthpiece and a buzzer released the catch.

Eldon, a sandy-haired, blue-eyed young man, was waiting at an open door on the second floor. The living room held a meagre assortment of wicker furniture. On one of two tables a high-intensity lamp burned brightly over an open casebook. It reminded Paul of his own student days, the endless hours of study, eyes gritty with strain.

Eldon waved at the book. 'Exam in negotiable instruments tomorrow morning.'

'Then I won't take up too much of your time.'

'Oh, I didn't mean anything like that, Mr Slater. Ken's welfare comes first. And I've just about got it licked anyway. So there's no hurry at all. Try this chair. The cushion is still pretty good.' He shook his head. 'God, it jolted us. I still can't believe it. The whole law school was buzzing for days. Everybody who knows Ken is sure it's a mistake. I room with the guy, Mr Slater. I've roomed with him for over three years, and it just doesn't make sense. Those cops must have blown their marbles.'

'We appreciate your faith in him, Cliff. But we need more than faith. We need something that will carry weight with a jury.'

'You're not the only one. Those New York detectives are still looking too.'

'They were up here?'

'A pair of real sharpies named Krehm and Schatz.'

Paul's expression did not change. It was inevitable. If nothing else, they were thorough. Nosing around up here, rubbernecking, checking the times of arrival and departure, prising any information out of Ken's classmates, would be basic to their investigation. 'You spoke to them, Cliff?'

'I had no choice. They were waiting for me when I got back from class. Smiling and friendly, and oh, brother, so persistent.'

'Tell me about it.'

'Well, they asked me when Ken got back to Cambridge that day. I said about four-thirty. I told them how we got the guys next door for a game of touch football. One of them kept talking to me while the other sort of wandered around.'

'Did they have a search warrant?'

Eldon looked sheepish. 'I didn't ask. They were, you know, overwhelming.'

'Did they take anything from the apartment?'

'I wouldn't know. It could have been in his pocket. They wanted to know what Ken was wearing.'

'I'd like to know too.'

'Blue jeans, a maroon turtleneck, and a golf jacket.'

'Are they still here?'

'The detectives didn't find them. I'm not sure, but I think Ken wore them back to New York after Dolly Wayne was killed and his uncle called him.'

'Did you tell that to Krehm and Schatz?'

'Hell, no, Mr Slater. I didn't volunteer any information at all. I told them I didn't know where Ken kept his clothes, I wasn't his valet.'

'Were you trying to help Ken?'

'I guess I was. Those two were not a very lovable pair of characters. And we're not on the same side. Right or wrong, they want a conviction. So I just decided not to co-operate.' He looked at Paul somewhat anxiously. 'Did I do something wrong?'

'You did exactly right. How did Ken look when he drove back here that day?'

'The same as usual, except for the mud.'

'What mud?'

'Well, it had been raining earlier that afternoon and Ken said he'd slipped taking a short cut across the lot.'

'Then it was still pretty sloppy when you fellows went out there to play touch football.'

Cliff Eldon grinned. 'We didn't plan on wallowing in it. And it wouldn't have been too bad if Duke Pirie hadn't brought Ken down. Tackled him like a Green Bay linebacker, the s.o.b.

Ken landed smack on his nose. Christ, did it bleed! He must have lost a pint.'

'All told, there were six of you in the game?'

'Uh-huh. Ken and I. Frank Hadley and the Duke. And the two guys we picked up on the street. Wise guys. When the Duke tackled Ken, they piled up on top.'

'Can you identify them?'

Eldon shook his head.

'Will you get their names for me if you see them around?'

'Sure.'

'Did Ken seem very tired after his long trip?'

'Ken? He's all iron, man. Like we took off one Christmas vacation for St Pete, with Hadley, three of us, travelling in Ken's Volkswagen. He wouldn't let anyone else touch the wheel. Drove right through, all day and all night, only stopped for burgers a couple of times. What I mean is, that bug really flew. Hadley and I slept half the time. So from here to New York and back again was a breeze for him.'

'Were you here when Dolly phoned, asking to see him?'

'Yes. We were studying. I heard him say, "Okay, I'll be there." Then he hung up and said, "Shit! I have to go to New York tomorrow." I asked him what cooked, and he said, "Small problem. No sweat."'

'Did he seem worried?'

'Not specially. Nothing fazed Ken. He took everything in stride. Even exams. Most of us would be studying half the night; Ken cracks a book once and has it all filed away. I have to read everything three times and write it down twice. There must be a better way. Like attaching a pair of electrodes to the brain from a tape recorder and having it pumped in while you sleep.'

Paul laughed. 'Easier maybe. Not better. A little sweat makes it stick.'

'Ken talked a lot about you, Mr Slater. He once said if he could learn ten per cent of the law you knew, he'd be satisfied.'

'Ten per cent wouldn't even get him past the Bar exam.' Paul rose. 'May I use your bathroom?'

'Through the bedroom, door on the left.'

Paul ran the water, opened the cabinet over the washbasin, and inspected the contents. Razors, shaving cream, toothbrushes, aspirin, hair lotion, and a small plastic bottle with no pharmacy label. He shook out two tablets, touched one of them to his tongue, could not identify its composition, and on impulse folded them into a piece of tissue and tucked it away in his pocket. He flushed the bowl and while the water was still gurgling he rejoined young Eldon.

'Incidentally,' Paul said, 'when the case somes to trial I may need you in court.'

'You mean as a witness?'

'Yes. One day at the most. You'd come down the night before and we'll put you up at a hotel. All expenses paid, of course.'

'That would help. My old man's pretty tight-fisted.'

'If they should cross-examine you about expenses, tell them the truth. But we can discuss that later. Where is your home, Cliff?'

'Buffalo. My dad is in real estate. He'd like me to go back up there to practise. I'm afraid he's in for a disappointment. Have you ever been to Buffalo, Mr Slater?'

'I've never had that pleasure.'

'A pleasure it's not, believe me. Especially with my old man around. Mom calls him the Emperor. Compared to him, Ivan the Terrible was a cream puff. If my grades don't hold up, the next day he's on the phone bellowing at the Dean.'

'Well, if you lose any schoolwork because of this case, Cliff, I'll bring you to New York at my expense for a week of personal tutoring.'

'How about that! You got yourself a deal, Professor.'

As he walked down the hall, Paul thought that Cliff Eldon would make a good witness. He had the frank, ingenuous quality that appeals to jurors. The names Howard Pirie and Frank Hadley were on the last door of the corridor.

Frank Hadley was an Ivy League throwback—crew-cut hair, collar-advertisement features, button-down shirt—a living anachronism amongst his shaggy and bewhiskered schoolmates. The small apartment was an exact duplicate of the one Paul had just left.

'When you opened the door, I thought you were Duke Pirie.'

'There's no resemblance at all,' Hadley said. 'What gave you that idea?'

'I hear he's majoring in economics. You look like a junior executive on the way up.'

Hadley smiled. 'Then you're due for a surprise. The Duke is one of the sloppiest guys at Cambridge. But he's got it up here, where it counts.' Hadley tapped his forehead. 'That grey stuff must have been installed by I.B.M. The Duke says brains are a marketable commodity regardless of packaging.'

'Where is he now?'

'At the library, I guess. He's working on his thesis.'

'When do you expect him?'

'I don't. He's in and out all the time. Tell me about Ken, Mr Slater. How is he?'

'As well as can be expected.'

'He's innocent, you know. He never did anything like that.'

'We're going to do our damnedest to prove it to a jury.'

'Some of us at the law school are talking about cutting a few classes and coming down to watch the trial. We'd like to see you in action.'

'You'll have plenty of time for that after you graduate. And there's a chance you'd be barred as a spectator.'

Hadley looked startled. 'Me? I don't understand. Why?'

'I may need you as a witness. If we invoke the rule, prospective witnesses are kept away from the proceedings until after they testify.' Seeing Hadley's look of disappointment, he added, 'After all, our main job is exonerating Ken, don't you think?'

'Oh, sure.' Hadley hesitated. 'May I ask you a personal question?'

'Let's hear it.'

'Ken told me that his uncle had invited you to join Porterfield, Baker & Sheridan, but you turned it down.' Hadley shook his head. 'Half the guys in our class would give their right arm for a chance to join a firm like that.'

'It all depends on what a man wants out of life, Frank. I enjoy teaching. I like to defend an occasional underdog. Neither of those activities fits into any pattern that Porterfield, Baker & Sheridan has in mind for its members. They specialize in bales of paperwork before the alphabet commissions. The financial rewards are commensurate, but money alone has never been my bag. Okay? Does that answer your question?'

Hadley nodded, unconvinced. 'Sure.'

'You know by now that Ken drove into New York to see Dolly Wayne.'

'Yes.'

'Tell me about that afternoon when he returned.'

Hadley's recital followed the script. He and Duke Pirie had been idling in the apartment when Cliff Eldon rang the bell and conned them into a game of touch football. They drafted two strangers and had been slogging around for about twenty minutes when Duke Pirie changed the rules.

'Ken's a bleeder, you know. Whenever we start a little rough-house, his nose is off and running. God, he was sore at the Duke. We had to hold him back.'

'Were you in any of Ken's classes?'

'All of them. Same year, same courses.'

'You and Cliff Eldon are his best friends?'

'Here at school, yes.'

'How about outside of school?'

Hadley backed off. He scratched the back of his head and regarded Paul obliquely. 'Is it important?'

'It could be.'

Hadley thought about it. After a moment he mustered an admiring smile. 'That Ken! Best damned operator I ever saw. I'll tell you something in confidence, Mr Slater. We were cruising around in his bug one night—last semester it was—and we got as far as Newton. We'd built up a thirst and we started looking for a tavern. You know, a few laughs and a couple of beers. The joint we found was kind of sleazy, but it had a juke box belting rock, and a chick smack in the middle of the floor dancing by herself, go-go, waving it around at the customers. Seventeen, eighteen, hair bleached almost white, local gash, but built for it. Jesus, was she built! Flaunting her goodies so you could see all the ways to Timbuktu. No bra. Swinging those pineapples.' Hadley rolled his eyes. 'Wild! Even the truckers were glassy-eyed. Ken and I were breathing through our mouths. This was a dish, Mr Slater. Ken watched for a little while and then he stood up and zeroed in. He put an arm around her and they started dancing. But close, I mean locked in there tight. You could smell the smoke. When the music stopped he brought her back to the table. He said, "Frankie boy, this is my dream girl. Say hello to the man, Amy. Amy Kowalski." The minute she opened her mouth I knew this was no finishing-school product.

'I could see it coming,' Hadley went on. 'The old heave-ho. In two seconds flat he was dumping me. He said, "You don't want to keep those people waiting, Frankie. You're gonna be late for your appointment. I'll drive you to the bus".' He shrugged charitably. 'What could I do? If Ken had a chance to rack up a score on merchandise like that, he was entitled. So I bowed out.'

'And did he rack up a score?'

Hadley looked down his nose. 'I never asked. And Ken doesn't rap much about stuff like that. The Duke now, you get it all, in clinical detail. Between the two of them, though, I'd say Ken was the top virtuoso around this plant. All I know is he couldn't get up for classes the next morning. He slept till late in the afternoon.'

'Was it hit-and-run? Or did he see the girl again?'

'I heard him on the phone a couple of times, making dates. And some weekends he had to invent excuses for Peggy.'

'How long did it last?'

'Couple of months maybe. He lost about eight pounds. When it finally broke up I asked for her number. Boy, did he hit the ceiling! He told me to lay off, to keep away from her.'

'Did you ever go out on double dates?'

'Not with Ken. He likes to be alone with girls. He'd spend his allowance and mine too. Always borrowing.'

'Does he still owe you money?'

'Sure. He told me not to worry about it because when we

graduated he'd get me a job with his uncle's firm. Cliff Eldon too. Maybe in fifteen years we'd change the name of the firm to Porterfield, Baker, Sheridan, Hadley & Eldon. Wouldn't that be something?'

'It would indeed. Porterfield, Baker & Sheridan is a fine, distinguished outfit.'

'You know something, Mr Slater? A lot of the bleeding hearts around here kid us about it. They say we're selling out. They say they're gonna join up with some public defender.'

'Each to his own.'

Hadley was suddenly defensive. 'All those New Left clowns keep blasting the establishment for every goddamn problem in the country. Ken laughs at them. He says who do they think supports the school if not those establishment corporations. He tells them to look at the university's investment portfolio and see where the dividends come from, dividends that pay for scholarships and salaries.'

Paul was hardly in the mood for undergraduate rationalizations and philosophy. There was still no sign of Duke Pirie. He was certain, however, that Pirie's story would support Hadley's version of the football game. He thanked Hadley for his time, shook hands, and promised to contact him at a later date.

Outside, he patronized a telephone booth. He dialled information and learned that only one number was listed in the Newton directory under the name of Kowalski. Samuel. He tried the number, listened while it rang for a long time, then hung up. He reversed the charges and called his office. There was a message from Roy Burroughs. The detective wanted to see him regardless of the hour.

Twilight was shadowing the landscape as he entered the southbound lane of the New England Thruway. He timed the trip back to New York. Four hours and twenty minutes.

Roy Burroughs, draped in a loose terry-cloth robe, hair rumpled, said, 'Glad you came, Mr Slater. I wanted to see you personally. I didn't think this particular piece of news should be in writing. Bourbon?'

'Please. Jack Daniels if you have it.' Drink in hand, Paul settled back attentively.

'It's about Dolly Wayne. You know, of course, that she was being courted by Alex Moore, that he wanted to marry her.'

'Yes.'

'That relationship was on the verge of being terminated.'

'By whom?'

'The woman. Evidence from various sources indicate that she had developed a new attachment.'

'You know the man's name?'

'Mr Ernest Stoufer.'

Paul's eyebrows shot up. 'Are you serious?'

Burroughs nodded. 'Interesting, no?'

'Interesting, yes.' Paul was surprised. Ernie Stoufer and Dolly Wayne. He had observed them together and detected no sign. Outwardly circumspect, never furtive. It raised a number of high-priority questions. Had Alex Moore suspected? Had he identified his rival? Was Janet Stoufer in the dark? How long had it been going on? 'Tell me about it,' he said.

'You stressed research on Dolly Wayne's activities. So I put several investigators on it. When the first indications came in, I took over myself. The most likely source was the victim's maid, Elvira Wilcox. At first we ran into misguided loyalty. She was guarding her employer's reputation. But she's an intelligent woman, open to reason. If she had any information that might solve the crime, then revealing it was an obligation she owed Dolly.' Burroughs smiled. 'Excuse the garrulity, Counsellor, but it took a lot more words than this to open her up. At any rate, over the past few months, Stoufer's visits averaged out at approximately two a week. Mrs Wilcox didn't even know his name until Dolly inadvertently mentioned it.'

'No possibility of mistaken identity?'

'The description tallies.'

'Business conferences, perhaps?'

'In the bedroom, Counsellor?'

'She never mentioned this to the police?'

'Mrs Wilcox does not admire our law-enforcement officials.'

'What time of day did they meet?'

'During the evening occasionally; mostly in the afternoon.'

Early-bird games, Paul thought. Matinees for the broker. A vigorous man no longer stimulated by the familiar and suety flesh of an unattractive wife. Nicely primed for some extra-curricular activity.

'Not that you need rule out business conferences,' Burroughs added. 'She needed those too, and that's probably where it started. Her financial condition was exceedingly rocky at one time. We learned that she called on Stoufer for investment advice.'

'I was under the impression that Brian Wirth left her very well heeled.'

'He did. This happened before Wirth died. She had a dis-cretionary account with a very hungry joker who damned near churned her into bankruptcy. Short-term stuff, highly specula-tive, parlaying losses, averaging down, every stupid ploy in the book. Like that, Counsellor, anybody can get killed. So she took her troubles to Stoufer. He pulled the account, sold off the crap, and got her fairly healthy again.'

'Did Alex Moore know he had a rival?'

'A moot question. My vote would be yes, though it's possible for a clever woman to keep two men dangling.'

'How about Mrs Stoufer?'

Burroughs shrugged. 'Your guess is as good as mine.'

'Look into it.' Paul studied the investigator for a moment. He was impressed. 'I'd like to hear your opinion on all this.'

Burroughs sat back, pinched his bottom lip. 'Dolly Wayne was a vital, attractive woman. Moore was solidly hooked. A man in his position wants and demands an exclusive. On the other hand, she had a liberal attitude. It certainly raises an important query. Suppose he found out. How far would a bruised ego lead him?'

Paul nodded speculatively. 'It sure as hell opens a new door.'

'You want another candidate, Counsellor? Here's one with motive and possible opportunity. He could have gained access without breaking down the door.'

'Yes. And it brings up a matter which may be related. I have information that Brian Wirth threatened to change his will in order to disinherit his wife. Moore handled his legal affairs at Porterfield, Baker & Sheridan. I want a much closer look at that angle. With extreme delicacy, need I say?'

Burroughs, frowning, tugged at an earlobe. 'That's one I can't delegate. I'll have to handle it myself.'

'And don't forget Mrs Stoufer. She might have learned about her husband's philandering.'

'We'll check her movements.'

'And one more item, Mr Burroughs. Are you in touch with a good chemist?'

'One of the best.'

'Have these analysed.' Paul produced the two tablets he had taken from the medicine cabinet shared by Ken and Cliff Eldon. 'They came from a bottle with no label, and I'm curious. No rush.'

Burroughs dropped them into an envelope and made a mark of identification in his own peculiar hieroglyphics. He looked up and cleared his throat. 'I had a call this afternoon from Lucas Holmes Sheridan.'

Paul's face went blank. 'About what?'

'He wanted to know if I had turned up any useful evidence.'

'And your response?'

'I suggested that he discuss it with you.'

'His reaction?'

'He hung up on me—with a bang.'

'It's something I anticipated. Don't let it worry you.' Paul stood up and offered his hand. 'You can go back to sleep now.'

Dru lay in bed, trying to read. It was an exercise in futility. She had absorbed nothing of the last few pages. Ever since her father's call she had been unable to pick up the thread. His voice had been brusque with contained anger, demanding that Paul call him back whenever he returned. Breaking the connection without explanation. It had left her uneasy and brooding.

Her hand rested lightly on her abdomen, testing for some sign of life. She glanced at the bedside clock, noticing the hour with growing concern. She remembered thinking how deeply

she would cherish her independence after the divorce from
Gordon. A defensive mechanism against new commitment
which quickly dissolved under Paul's courtship. The sudden
memory of Gordon brought echoes of queasiness. She thought
she had banished him for ever, but the mind is perverse and
obstinate, not easily controlled. Besides, how could she forget
him now? He was going to be a witness against Ken. She knew
she could not be a spectator on the day he testified. It might
trigger unpredictable reactions.

She was suddenly alert, imagining she had detected a faint
stirring of life inside her body. She spread her fingers gently.
The doctor kept admonishing her to get a decent night's sleep.
Such a glib and easy suggestion, so difficult under the circumstances. She heard the door open and called Paul's name.

He came directly to the bedroom, still wearing his coat. He
bent over and kissed her. 'What are you doing up at this hour?'

'Waiting for you—with a message.'

'From whom?'

'Dad. He phoned and wants you to call him back.'

'All right. Tomorrow morning.'

She shook her head. 'Tonight. He said whenever you
returned. He sounded emphatic and I think a little ferocious.'
Her eyes searched his face. 'Is there something wrong between
you two that I ought to know about?'

'A small difference of opinion.' He shucked off his coat and
threw it over a chair. He reached for the phone on the night
table and dialled his father-in-law's number.

Lucas Sheridan answered in a curt bark on the first ring.
'Paul? Where in Christ's name have you been all day? I called
your office four times. Is that secretary of yours tongue-tied?'

'I've been out of town.'

'At a time like this? Where?'

'Cambridge. Collecting prospective witnesses. I talked to
several of Ken's classmates.'

'What in hell are we paying Burroughs for? Can't you leave
all that to him?'

'He's working on something else.'

'Yes.' There was a tight pause. 'And that's why I called. I

spoke to Burroughs earlier today and asked him for a progress report.' Lucas Sheridan emptied his lungs with harsh irascibility. 'He had the unmitigated effrontery to ignore my request.'

'He was following my instructions, Lucas.'

'Am I or am I not footing the bills? What's all this cloak-and-dagger nonsense? Why all the secrecy?'

'That's the way I want it.'

'Well, damn it, don't I have the right to know what's going on?'

'Lucas, you retained me as chief strategist. I assume you have confidence in my judgement. Or am I mistaken?'

'No, you are not mistaken.'

'Then let me handle it my own way. I won't have Burroughs duplicating reports or being coached from the sidelines.'

Sheridan's indignation faded into plaintiveness. 'Is there any harm in keeping me appraised?'

'Perhaps not. Only I insist on evaluating his information before discussing it with anyone else. We're dealing with a criminal investigation, Lucas, which is my line of country, not yours. I'm asking you to keep your hands off.'

'You're acting like a prima donna.'

'It's a complaint I've heard before. Would you prefer someone more tractable?'

Silence for a moment. Then Lucas Sheridan said, 'You must be tired, Paul. You're saying things you don't mean. Let's sleep on it and we'll talk tomorrow.'

Paul felt no sense of triumph in having faced the old man down. He saw Dru frowning at him.

'What's wrong, darling?' she asked.

'Your father and I seldom see eye to eye.'

'Be patient with him, Paul. He's terribly worried about Ken and he's not used to opposition.'

'Yeah.' He changed the subject. 'I need a hot tub.'

He went to the bathroom and opened the tap. He felt saturated with weariness, muscles and joints creaking from the constricted position of the long drive. He kicked off his clothes and sank into the steaming water, relaxing slowly under the healing therapy of heat. He soaked himself for ten minutes, then towelled himself and donned fresh pyjamas. Back in the bedroom, he stretched out alongside Dru.

She made a transparent effort to divert him. 'Like father, like son. I felt him kicking a little while ago.'

'Him?'

'I think so. Is it too early to decide on a name?'

'He'll have my last name. You go ahead and pick the first.'

'Could we name him after Dad?'

'Sheridan Slater? Too pompous.'

'No, silly. Lucas Slater.'

'Too old-fashioned. How about my father?'

'We could use both names.'

'Lucas Marcus Slater? Or Marcus Lucas Slater? You really want to tie a handle like that on to some poor defenceless kid? Give the boy a fighting chance, Dru.' Paul grinned at her. 'It could be a girl, you know. So why not brainstorm the problem later on.'

She tilted her face for a kiss.

'Pay attention now,' he said. 'Here's one that drove the Maharani of Jalopore half out of her mind.'

'Mm-m,' she murmured. 'The Maharani must have been frigid. It's driving me right out of my nightgown.'

'Easy now,' he said without conviction. 'Are you sure it's all right?'

'If one is inventive, of course. And I'll let you know when it's time for abstinence.'

She rolled over on her knees, straddling him, and abandoning the accustomed familiarities or readying gestures, poised teasingly for a moment before engulfing him in the heady textures of union while his hands traced the soft lines of her back. She bent forward with a shuddering sigh, eyes unfocused, and covered his face with quick kisses, hearing his smothered whisper against her searching mouth, 'Ah, Dru, Dru, Dru . . .' in cadence to the tantalizing rhythm of an ancient and ever-new ritual, a temporary anodyne that blocked out for them all the pressures and problems and fears, and left them whirling alone in space. He had not realized how urgent his need was.

And Dru, reading the clues, the importunate tumult, brought him quickly to a blinding release, holding gently, while his breath dwindled and his thundering heart slowed and he sank back in lassitude.

'My God!' he muttered. 'You're getting better all the time.'

'Practice,' she said.

'Let's get married.'

'We are married.'

'That's nice,' he said, and fell asleep.

CHAPTER SEVEN

ABE BARISH sat hunched over a yellow legal pad of scrawled notes, elbows propped on the desk, chin cradled in the V formed by both hands. For weeks he had been checking citations and abstracting points of law. It was familiar work, with each decision carrying additional references until the mind boggled at the sheer volume of annotations.

Paul had explained his position. For the time being he was not interested in those philosophical aspects which might be appropriate for a brief on the appellate level. He needed cases in point, citations he could quote in support of a motion. It was frustrating work. Barish knew how rarely a researcher found precedents whose facts were precisely tailored to the problem at hand. Now he thought he'd found a promising case, 243 New York Supplement 457. People against Jimmy Courtney. It fit. It fit perfectly. Justice Geller had ruled that a medical examiner's report is a record made by a public official, which gave the defendant every right to inspect it.

Barish settled back with a serene smile. Since the Sheridan case was already on the calendar, scheduled for trial, he would have to act at once. He called for a stenographer and began to dictate the necessary motion papers.

Paul related the incident to Lucas Sheridan at dinner that night. Dru listened attentively. The three of them seemed lost in the long baronial dining room. Lucas Sheridan occupied an eight-room apartment fourteen floors above Fifth Avenue, in a building that was a pre-war pile of turreted limestone standing in solid contrast to the sterile warrens proliferating on all sides. After the death of his wife and Dru's marriage, the apartment was admittedly too large for his current needs.

Sheridan, however, was not a creature of change. He was bitterly opposed to the demolition of old landmarks, erasing all flavour of the past. Having foreseen the trend years ago, he had organized like-minded tenants and arranged a conversion of the property to co-operative status.

He had personally selected a burgundy to go with Mrs Shanahan's duck, and Quintus kept it flowing. At first they had made an effort to discuss other matters, but the impending trial was a dominating obsession, and they had finally succumbed. Sheridan was intensely curious about Nicoletti's background and abilities. Paul gave it to him straight.

'However,' he said, 'I'm hoping we'll be ahead on points by the time this thing goes to a jury.'

'Points?' Dru said. 'You make it sound as if it were a game.'

'In some strange and terrifying way, it is. That's the adversary system. Two surrogate gladiators in combat. And more often than not the outcome depends on personal skill, counsel's thoroughness in preparation, his ability to cross-examine, the impression he makes on a jury.'

'Then Ken should take the stand,' Sheridan said.

'Why?'

'Because of the impression he'll make. If the jury sees him and hears him, they'd have no choice but to judge him innocent.'

'That decision is a little premature,' Paul said. 'I haven't even considered it yet.'

'Why not?' Dru demanded. 'Don't your clients always take the stand?'

'Not in criminal cases. The law protects a defendant against self-incrimination, and the jurors are not supposed to draw unfavourable inferences from his failure to testify.'

'I would,' she said. 'No matter what the judge instructed me. I couldn't help but draw an unfavourable inference against a man who failed to speak up in his own behalf.'

'Then you'd never sit on a jury of mine.'

'But an innocent man has nothing to hide.'

'He might. A lot would depend on his ability to hold up under cross-examination.'

'Exactly,' Sheridan said with emphasis. 'And that's when Ken would shine. He's sensible and bright. And any attempt by the prosecutor to bully him would only prejudice the jury.'

'Dad is right, Paul. I know he is.'

Paul shook his head. 'It's still premature. I'll make no decision until I have a chance to evaluate the State's case.'

Lucas Sheridan set his jaw stubbornly and was about to comment, but held back with an effort. Quintus served coffee and was offering to lace it with brandy. 'We'll take it in the library,' Sheridan said.

Dru fell into a chair and hooked a leg over the arm. She laced fingers over the nape of her neck, elbows out. When Quintus approached with the brandy she shook her head. She listened with faint amusement to her father's waspish peroration against what he termed the too liberal interpretation of constitutional rights by a couple of bleeding hearts on the Supreme Court.

'Not a couple,' Paul said. 'The Warren Court had a majority.'

'Doesn't society have the right to protect itself?'

'Certainly. But not at the expense of the individual. You of all people ought to be aware of that, now that a member of your own family is in trouble.'

'I'm talking about organized crime.'

'Which is composed of individuals, Lucas. And the individual always needs protection.'

'The individual has his remedy.'

'What remedy?'

'Obey the law, damn it! The option is his. Stay out of trouble.'

'Ah, how simple, Lucas. So quixotic. And so far out of sight no human being may ever see it.'

'I say put the blame where it belongs. On the felon. Let's stop blaming society.'

'The trouble could be right there, you know.'

'So if we change the system, will everybody then turn into saints?'

'Probably not. Maybe it's man's legacy from his prehistoric predators. Maybe evolution needs more time.'

'This prehistoric legacy hasn't affected me, or Ken, or you.'

'That's because we have a sense of moral values and we've learned to exercise control.'

'My point exactly. The criminal has neither. And our courts compound the problem by providing him with too many escape hatches.'

'Safeguards would be a better term, Lucas. And since those safeguards apply to Ken, they have to apply to everyone else too.'

Sheridan shook his head in frustration. 'Where in hell did you learn how to debate? That's the kind of dialectics that misleads milky old men on the bench.'

Paul laughed. 'Maybe we can put it to good use on Ken's behalf.'

Dru said, 'Have you seen or spoken to Peggy?'

'Yes. She wants to attend the trial. It's a good idea. A show of faith in Ken's innocence could be an asset.'

'What about her pregnancy? Is she going to have the child?'

'She says she'll make that decision after speaking to Ken. Incidentally, she asked me to probate Dolly Wayne's estate.'

Sheridan's brows leaped.

'I'm not sure that would be proper.'

'I suggested Sloane & Barish for the job. After all, I'm not a partner in the firm.'

Lucas nodded slowly. 'At least the girl is financially secure. We represented Brian Wirth, you know. He left Dolly a sizable estate.'

'Then Porterfield, Baker & Sheridan probated his will?'

'No will. As I recall it, he died intestate. Alex Moore was in charge.' Sheridan reached for the brandy, poured, and knocked it down in a single gulp. His gaze settled fixedly on Paul. 'Let's get down to brass tacks now. What's all this secrecy with Burroughs?'

Paul had been waiting for him to bring it into the open and his expression instantly chilled. 'Burroughs is investigating certain sensitive matters that are highly confidential.'

Without moving his eyes, Sheridan said, 'Would you leave the room, Dru? I want to talk to Paul alone.'

'No.'

'I beg your pardon.'

'I said no. I don't know what's going on, but a referee may be needed and I'm staying.'

'Very well. I don't know what you're driving at, Paul. Confidential matters. Are you impugning my judgement or my discretion?'

'I thought we settled this, Lucas.'

'To your satisfaction, not mine. I'm opening it up again.'

'Then I'll put it as plainly as I can. It is essential for me to have full control. Absolute dictatorial control, if you will. The exclusive prerogative to field every decision before trial and in the courtroom. The pressure is growing. I cannot and I will not have anyone else quarterbacking the plays. If I'm expected to report all developments, then clashes of judgement and temperament would be inevitable. Especially in your case. Because you're in the same profession and you're emotionally involved.'

'So you're sticking to your guns.'

'Yes.'

Sheridan turned his back and walked to the window. He stood rigidly for a moment and then faced them again. His face was devoid of expression. He had not capitulated, but it was clear he was not going to pursue it at this time. 'Do you know the name of the judge?'

'Albert Chaffee.'

Sheridan made an explosive sound. 'That hack!'

'He knows his limitations. So he'll try to be fair. And if he makes an error, it will give us something for the record.'

'God help you, Dru. You have married a wilful, headstrong man.'

'What's more, I did it with my eyes open. But he has other traits too. Shall I enumerate?'

'I'm interested.'

'He's tender and protective and sentimental and——'

'What is this?' Paul said. 'A commercial?'

'Just an attempt to enlighten my myopic parent.'

Paul tapped his head. 'Pregnancy impairs the brain, Lucas.'

'I believe it.'

'And it also requires rest,' Dru said. 'I think it's time you took me home.'

Sheridan accompanied them to the door. 'Paul?'

'Yes.'

'We're counting on you.'

Part Three

CHAPTER ONE

ON TUESDAY MORNING, when Justice Albert Chaffee arrived at chambers in the Criminal Court Building, his clerk said, 'They're starting early down there, Judge. Hell of a mob outside your courtroom.'

Chaffee raised an eyebrow.

'For the jury selection?'

'Looks like it. Mr Nicoletti is waiting inside.'

'Slater?'

'Not here yet.'

Chaffee glanced at his watch and saw that defence counsel still had another five minutes. He lifted his nose and sniffed. 'Coffee's on?'

'Yes, sir.'

'Three cups, then.'

While conferences in chambers were always informal, Albert Chaffee would have preferred wearing his judicial robes. The vestments of office imparted a special feeling of dignity and importance, cloaking his customary modish suits. It was an ingredient of Chaffee's vanity to appear more youthful than his years, even to the point of restoring dark tints to his thick wiry hair.

Emerging from law school with an indifferent record during a depression, Albert Chaffee had entered politics as a bridge to survival. He had served his apprenticeship with unflagging industry, working coincidentally under the same district captain as old Carlo Nicoletti, the assistant D.A.'s father. He had been rewarded with various political sinecures and had been feeding at the public trough for most of his professional life. One term on the City Council, two in the Assembly. And then came the break he had been yearning for. Shortly before the opposition party returned to power, a lame-duck administration had appointed him to fill out the term of a defunct Civil Court judge.

Aware of his limitations, Chaffee had laboured mightily, familiarizing himself with, if not mastering, the complex rules of evidence. Persevering indefatigably, he had managed to turn in a modestly creditable performance. Two years later his elevation to the State Supreme Court was assured when he won the bipartisan approval of both political parties. And since he had been assigned to the criminal courts where important money judgements were not involved, the offstage power structure endured his unexceptional talents with benign tolerance.

His ultimate goal as a lawyer had been achieved. He knew that not infrequently in the history of the bench, the impartiality of judges had been subverted by a toxic gall bladder, a rancorous ulcer, or domestic upheavals. So Albert Chaffee had reason for complacency. He had for three decades been married to a devoted woman who kept him well fed, physically comfortable, and sexually pacified.

As Chaffee turned to join Nicoletti, Paul Slater appeared at the door of the anteroom. Chaffee waved him in and they entered chambers together. Amenities were brief and cool. Coffee arrived but only the judge seemed interested.

He sipped and looked up over the rim of a paper cup. 'Well, gentlemen, how much time do you anticipate we'll need for this trial?'

Nicoletti said, 'The State can probably complete its case in less than a week. Provided the defence co-operates.'

'Co-operates?' queried Paul. 'How do you mean?'

'Minimizing obstructive tactics. Eliminating emotional appeals. Suppressing frivolous objections.'

'Anything else?' Paul's tone was sarcastic.

'That should do it.' Nicoletti showed his large square teeth in a smile.

'This is a two-way street, Your Honour. If Mr Nicoletti limits his witnesses to admissible testimony, then I won't have any reason to object, will I? On the other hand, I owe a duty to my client. The defence will require only that amount of time necessary to prove his innocence.'

'May we figure on about two weeks, Counsellor?'

'So long as you don't hold me to it. I'd prefer to remain flexible.'

'Naturally.' The judge transferred his gaze from Paul to Nicoletti and back again. 'Shall we invoke the Rule?'

'Absolutely. I insist on it,' Paul said.

'Just a moment,' Nicoletti snapped. 'The defence has no right to insist on anything. The exclusion of witnesses is a matter of discretion for the judge.'

'Not in a capital case.'

Capital punishment is no longer an issue in this State.'

'Please, gentlemen,' Chaffee intervened. 'We're starting on a hostile note. I'd like you to keep the bickering down. And I will exercise my discretion in favour of separating the witnesses. So that's settled. Now, how about a reasonable time limit on the voir dire?'

'Suits me,' Nicoletti said. 'I'm not eager to spend a couple of weeks picking a jury.'

'Mr Slater?'

'A reasonable time, yes. But I'd still prefer to remain flexible. I cannot waive any of my client's rights.'

Chaffee's response was tinged with annoyance. 'The Court is not asking you to waive any of your client's rights. I simply want to get this trial under way and keep it moving. You know the situation in this county. The detention cells are over-crowded. Our docket is so far behind that——'

'I understand, sir. But my client is hardly responsible for a jammed calendar. The system's inadequacies cannot be permitted to hamper his defence.' Paul's smile was frosty. 'I will promise, however, not to dawdle.'

Chaffee sighed. 'Good enough. Then I take it we're ready.'

'The State has been ready since nine o'clock.'

'And you, Mr Slater?'

'No, sir. I'm sorry. The defence is not ready.'

Nicoletti and the judge sat erect. They stared at him sharply. Chaffee sounded querulous. 'What now, Counsellor?'

'Just this, Your Honour. The prosecution has not yet complied with an order of this court granting my motion for an inspection of the medical examiner's report. That report may be vital to our case. I cannot in all good conscience proceed until it is made available.'

Chaffee cocked an inquiring brow at Nicoletti.

'It's news to me,' the prosecutor said. 'I gave instructions to my people.'

'Well, damn it,' Paul said, 'somebody goofed.'

'Then I apologize, Counsellor. And I give you my personal guarantee you'll have it this afternoon.'

Chaffee spread his fingers in a conciliatory gesture. 'That should give you plenty of time, Mr Slater. We still have a jury to select. And if experience serves, it will probably take a few days. I am anxious to avoid further delay. So, gentlemen, shall we proceed?'

Paul had no further objections.

As Justice Chaffee entered from the robing room, Francis X. Kearney, the court crier, intoned his ritual: 'All rise, the Honourable Judge of the Criminal Court in and for the County of New York.'

Most of the available space was occupied by prospective jurors, who were staring at the back of Ken Sheridan's head. He sat at the defence table, flanked by Paul Slater and Abe Barish. Now the jurors looked up at the judge, unconsciously aware of the medieval flavour imparted by the black robes.

Chaffee mounted the dais and spoke to them in measured tones. He explained that they were about to select a jury in a homicide case which might take several weeks. If for any substantial legal reason any of them could not be available to serve that long, he should state the fact when his name was called. Once a juror was selected, the Court would entertain no excuses. Chaffee nodded at the prosecution table. 'You may proceed.'

John Nicoletti rose and walked slowly to the rail. He stood for a moment in grave deliberation, studying the attentive faces. All conversation died.

'My name,' he said, 'is John Nicoletti. I am the assistant district attorney whose duty it is to prosecute this case. The defendant, Kenneth Sheridan, sits at the counsel table over there with his attorneys. He is represented by Mr Paul Slater and Mr Abraham Barish. The indictment in this case charges the defendant with murder in the first degree. It does not involve the death penalty. With several exceptions that need not concern us here, the death penalty has been abolished in the State of New York. The present indictment does not involve one of those exceptions. I emphasize this point to reassure those of you who may not wish to serve in a capital case.

'Now, ladies and gentlemen, I have here a list of names. I would like you to pay close attention as I read them because it includes prospective witnesses who will appear for the State. Many of them are law-enforcement officials. If you are acquainted with any of these people, you will so state when and if you are called to the jury box.'

It was not a dry recital. As a practised hand, Nicoletti knew how easy it was to lose their attention, so he lifted his voice to a commanding ring. He finished the list and returned to the prosecution table.

Chaffee then addressed the entire panel with a few questions designed to weed out those members who would be clearly ineligible. Had any of them read about the case? If so, had they formed an opinion? Had any of them, or members of their family, been victims of a crime of violence? No one spoke in the affirmative. Chaffee then nodded to the clerk.

The spinning drum yielded up twelve names, and their owners were ushered into the jury box.

Paul had, on occasion, doubted the value of the jury system. On the whole, however, twelve men, whatever their intellectual or economic status, would of necessity bring to their judgements a variety of backgrounds and experience no judge could hope to match. Nevertheless, like any system, it had its drawbacks. Prejudice and incomprehension. So the selection of an impartial or sympathetic juror was sometimes a matter of instinct, sometimes a matter of subtle evaluation. And if his own personal assessment faltered, he had to risk the loss of a valued peremptory challenge; after all, he had only twenty chances to exclude a juror without explanation. At times, in a calculated attempt to preserve these challenges, he had accepted some dubious prospect with a show of satisfaction, hoping thereby to gull the opposition into immediate rejection. He doubted that Nicoletti would fall prey to any such ruse.

The voir dire itself was an attorney's first opportunity to establish a rapport with the jury. What Paul wanted were people of decent intelligence and flexible attitudes, certainly no one so case-hardened by years that he automatically resented youth. To that end he had prepared a searching list of questions designed to elicit the slightest taint of bias.

He studied the panel board containing the names, addresses, and occupations of the first twelve prospects. Four of them appeared to be substantial citizens. Did he really want the blue-ribbon conservatives favoured by most prosecutors? Or the blue-collar worker who might harbour some resentment against Ken because of his privileged background? And how about the women? Would they tend to feel charitable and motherly towards an appealing young man in dire adversity? Or would the brutality of the crime and the sex of the victim create such anathema that it would blunt their judgement against any accused? How could he possibly get at the truth? How could he open their skulls or read their hearts?

He heard Nicoletti say, 'Permission to approach the bench.'

'Granted.'

Paul followed him.

'I would like to state, Your Honour, that the victim suffered considerable physical violence. As a consequence, some of the evidence and photographic exhibits may be highly distressful to women jurors. Perhaps the Court should point this out and permit the more sensitive prospects to withdraw at the outset.'

Paul was surprised. Inflammatory evidence of this kind generally favoured the prosecution. And Nicoletti was a man who seldom gave anything away. What, if any, clever gimmick did he have concealed up that neatly pressed sleeve?

'Counsellor?'

'I agree with the district attorney, Your Honour.'

Chaffee made the appropriate comments. One of the women, a stringy, prim-mouthed spinster type, took advantage of the offer with obvious relief. She was excused from the box. Barish said in a dry whisper from behind his hand. 'Saves you a challenge.'

He was right, of course. Paul would have had to reject her out of hand. The clerk spun the drum and pulled out another card which he inserted in the panel board. Thomas Carey, Negro, taxi driver.

'And that saves me another,' Paul whispered to Barish.

'How come?'

'Taxi drivers have a natural aversion to policemen. Nicoletti will excuse him.'

The twelve prospects rose at the clerk's request and Chaffee administered the oath. 'Each of you do solemnly swear that you will make true answers to all questions asked of you by the Court or counsel for either side regarding your service and qualifications, so help you God?'

They murmured assent. It could be assumed that they had some knowledge of their function as jurors. Like army draftees exposed through training films to the hazards of random cohabitation, these veniremen had attended a film entitled *The True and the Just*, designed to inform them of their responsibilities. Although Paul approved this innovation, he suspected that it rendered them no more expert on the subject of jury service than the GI had become on the subject of gonorrhea.

The first prospect took the stand and Nicoletti moved towards him. 'Your name is Martin Grady?'

'Yes, sir.'

'And you are employed as an office manager?'

'By the Fidelity Life Insurance Company, yes.'

'How long have you been employed there?'

'Eleven years.'

'Have you ever been engaged in any litigation involving Mr Slater or the firm of Barish & Sloane?'

'No, sir.'

'No association whatever with any of the participants in this trial?'

'No, sir.'

'What newspapers do you read?'

'The *Post* and the *Daily News*.'

'Then you must be familiar with certain aspects of this case.'

'Only what I read in the paper, sir. Nothing specific.'

As the methodical probing droned on, Grady emerged as a stable enough citizen, candid and honest. He exhibited no apparent eagerness to serve on the jury. And yet he must have been hopeful, Paul thought. He would continue to draw his salary, plus the juror's per diem. It would make him a stellar attraction at the office. The willowy little typists would listen to him with round-eyed avidity. His name might even appear in the papers. Even so, he had not denied all familiarity with the case. He was intelligent enough to know that only a blind, illiterate deaf-mute would be uninformed.

Barish whispered, 'He made a slip. This is the first time anybody ever put my name before Jim Sloane's.'

'He won't make many of them,' Paul said. He was pleased with Ken's appearance. Mrs Shanahan had sent over a dark suit and a freshly laundered white shirt set off by a maroon knitted tie. He had entered the courtroom with a show of diffidence. He sat now, the quintessence of sober young manhood, clean-cut, dependable, upright.

Nicoletti said, 'No objection by the People,' and turned away.

Paul moved close. Grady was tall and cranelike, the skin around his mouth marked with traces of boyhood acne. But the mouth itself was a good one, with none of the fanatic's tightness. He said, 'You understand, Mr Grady, that the indictment in this case is not evidence. It is merely a piece of paper drawn up for the purpose of bringing the defendant into court. It proves absolutely nothing against him.'

'Yes, sir. I know that.'

'Have you ever served as a juror in a criminal case before?'

'No, sir.'

'Do you understand that a man is presumed innocent until proven guilty beyond a reasonable doubt?'

'Yes, I do.'

'And will you extend that presumption of innocence to this defendant regardless of the nature of the charges?'

'Yes, sir.'

'With no mental reservations whatever?'

'None that I know of.'

'If the judge tells you that the State must prove every element of the crime charged beyond a reasonable doubt, and the State fails to prove one single element to your satisfaction, do you think you could stand firm against any pressures the other jurors might bring against you?'

'I believe I could.'

'And the mere fact of being in a minority would not influence your vote?'

'Nobody can tell me how to think.'

'Good, Mr Grady. You understand that the Court will instruct you as to the law, but you will be the sole and exclusive judge of the facts?'

'Yes, sir.'

'Am I correct in believing that you have been an office manager for eleven years?'

'Not quite. I have been employed by Fidelity Life for eleven years, only the last three of them as office manager.'

'And before that?'

'I started as filing clerk, then was put in charge of records.'

'As an employee of an insurance company, you must know that when a person's death is caused by some outside agency, all premiums stop and payment on the policy becomes immediately due.'

'Yes, sir, that seems a fair enough statement.'

'Do you think you could render an impartial verdict where such a death occurred?'

Grady smiled fleetingly. 'Yes, sir. It doesn't come out of my pocket. That's what insurance is all about.'

Paul returned his smile. 'Are you married?'

'No, sir. Single.'

'Do you have a college degree?'

'The best I could manage was a high school equivalency diploma.'

'Was there any special reason why you cut your education short?'

'The best reason there is, I guess. Money. My father died when I was fifteen and I quit school to go to work and help the family.'

'Would you be envious of someone whose relatives were able and willing to finance his education?'

'Not at all.'

'Will you give this defendant an impartial hearing and wait until you have heard all the evidence on both sides before forming an opinion?'

'Yes, sir, I will.'

When it emerged that Ken had lost his own parents, it might create through a sense of identification some measure of sympathy in this juror. 'Mr Grady,' he said, 'is acceptable to the defence.'

It seemed a miracle. No challenge by either side on the very first prospect examined. Any optimism, however, on an early completion of the panel was premature. In succession, eight veniremen were excused for cause, and a number of others through the exercise of peremptories. And so they moved into the afternoon session.

Late in the day a slight, spidery man with tightly stitched mouth tucked under a large nose, weighing no more than a jockey, took the stand and kept bobbing his head at Nicoletti's questions. He was openly eager to serve and Nicoletti had no objections. But Paul's antennae quivered warningly. He could picture the prospect as a frail unattractive boy, lacking co-ordination, contemptuously dismissed by his contemporaries, standing on the sidelines in frustration and bitterness. Would these traces of resentment linger into maturity? Would he be unconsciously prejudiced against a handsome and strapping athlete?

Paul excused him out of hand, relinquishing another challenge from his dwindling stock of peremptories.

Just before adjournment, the second juror was finally seated. Leo Bernhard, electronics engineer, a stolid, thoughtful man in his middle years. Paul felt that Bernhard's training and background would enable him to weigh the evidence, reason logically, and when the time came, present sound arguments to his fellow talesmen.

Then, admonishing the two jurors not to discuss the case, Chaffee adjourned court until the following morning.

The spinning drum continued to supply candidates from the city's huge reservoir and Chaffee kept reciting his memorized ritual as the procession moved on. By mid-afternoon Paul had accepted a third juror. Richard Kee, Chinese-American, a certified public accountant.

He was relying on a cherished theory that many members of a minority group tended to identify with an individual they felt was being persecuted. The district attorney, representing authority and power, was instinctively distrusted. For this reason, apparently, Nicoletti had rejected two blacks. He had, however, no objection to Kee.

With a third black, Nicoletti began to explore new territory. Arthur Atwood, chief of a maintenance crew in a Madison Avenue skyscraper, was a burly man with an underplayed air of competence.

'You understand, Mr Atwood, that a man committing murder seldom does so in front of eyewitnesses.'

'I understand, of course.'

'So that we often have to rely on circumstantial evidence. Would you be willing to draw the logical inferences from facts proven to you beyond a reasonable doubt?'

'Yes, sir.'

'Have you known any homosexuals, Mr Atwood?'

The courtroom stirred and grew silent. Chaffee leaned forward. Ken glanced curiously at Paul, who knew that Nicoletti was preparing the ground for Gordon Frazer and Billy Clark.

'Known them how?'

'I don't mean intimately, Mr Atwood. I mean socially.'

'I've met a few. They're all over the lot these days.'

'Would you be able to recognize one?'

'I might. Not always, though.' He smiled broadly. 'Couple of years ago I met one who looked like a professional wrestler.'

'Does the notion of homosexuality sicken or revolt you?'

Atwood gave it some thought. 'Each to his own,' he said finally. 'It's just not my scene. I'm a married man.'

'Would you be able to give full credit to the testimony of a witness even though he suffered from some sexual aberration?'

'Well, I don't think it would necessarily make him a liar.'

Nicoletti nodded. 'Mr Atwood is acceptable to the People.'

Paul stood. His eyes met Atwood's unflinching stare. He waved companionably. 'The defence will accept this man's promise that he will do his best to render an impartial verdict.'

Judge Albert Chaffee had always found jury selection a tedious proceeding. He allowed his eyes to rest on the defendant. Chaffee was not immune to normal curiosity. Young Sheridan seemed like a decent young citizen. He wondered what evidence they had against the boy. It must have been a terrible shock to old Lucas. A man like that! The shame and ignominy.

Cary and I, he thought, are lucky. No kids. He hadn't always considered sterility a piece of good fortune. In the third year of their marriage they had endured all sorts of tests before the doctors had determined something was wrong with Cary. For a brief time they had contemplated adopting a child. But he had always been so damned busy, running, running, hacking out a career. And now, in these last few years, they could laugh about it. What if they had spawned one of those wild-haired, bearded, anarchist types? The last thing a State Supreme Court judge needs.

He turned his attention back to the prosecutor, now examining a woman prospect. He remembered that he himself had never been especially adept at jury selection. Too many imponderables. Nicoletti, he saw, had that combination of instinct and acuity, and the tenacity to ferret out oddball tendencies.

The woman was a handsome brunette with a generous mouth and thrusting cheekbones, a fashion co-ordinator for one of the uptown department stores. Despite a precision of speech, she had a warm earthy quality. No, she asserted, she was not in the least squeamish. She could look at blood without fainting. Yes, she had read the newspapers, but she had no opinion as to the guilt or innocence of the defendant.

Chaffee tried to project a telepathic message of approval to the prosecutor. She would be a diverting piece of scenery during those inevitably dull passages when the technicians testified. He was mildly startled at his occult powers when Nicoletti failed to challenge.

Paul glanced at the panel board. The woman's name was Edith Hume, but there was nothing to indicate her marital status. He inquired about it.

'I'm single,' she said, her tone implying that any applicant staking a claim of exclusivity would have to prove himself first.

Paul decided to take her, but tied up a few loose ends first. 'In weighing the testimony of a witness, would you carefully consider any prejudice or bias that witness may have towards the defendant?'

'Of course.'

'You realize that the burden of proving the defendant guilty rests on the prosecution, and the defendant need not introduce any evidence whatsoever?'

'If that is the law.'

'The judge, I am sure, will so instruct you. If he does, would you require the accused to satisfy you of his innocence?'

'No, I would not.'

'You will not hold it against him if he fails to take the stand in his own defence?'

'That is correct.'

'Have you ever been the victim of a crime?'

'Yes, I have.'

Paul's hand stopped in mid-gesture. 'Will you tell us about it, please?'

'My car was stolen.'

'When did this happen?'

'About three years ago.'

'Was it recovered?'

'Two days later. In Yonkers.'

'Anything missing?'

'A tankful of gas.' Her smile was dazzling.

147

Paul relaxed. 'One last question, Miss Hume. Do you believe there is any distinction between the district attorney and myself simply because he holds an official position?'

'Nothing that would cause me to respect his word more than yours.'

Paul nodded his acceptance and Edith Hume took her place. By late afternoon two additional veniremen had been seated. Frank Hilsop, a real-estate broker, and Barney Young, a portrait photographer. Seven, all told. An equal number was now required to complete the panel and provide two alternates.

Chaffee adjourned for the day.

Conally's was a sunless oasis on the other side of Foley Square. It was patronized mostly by lawyers, judges, politicians, bureaucrats, and bail bondsmen. A large array of bottles on the polished bar contained exactly what their labels proclaimed. The chef specialized in beef, an unchanging standby, varied daily by only one additional selection. Booths were separated by high solid partitions that kept private conversations inviolate.

Paul left the telephone booth and found Abe Barish at a rear table.

Barish was staring awestruck at the heroic side of beef on his plate. 'My God!' he said faintly. 'Do these people regularly consume such portions?'

'They do indeed.'

'How is that possible?'

'The stomach is elastic. It expands.'

'And stays expanded. Half of Mr Conally's customers look pregnant. Which reminds me of Dru. How is she?'

'Worried as usual about Ken. I just spoke to her on the phone, told her we'd be working late at the office. She'd like you to come for dinner next week.'

'I accept. Wednesday would be fine. And we must not lunch at Conally's that day. Excuse me, please.' He conveyed a forkful of beef to his mouth, eyebrows rising in appreciation. 'Well, to hell with my diet.'

They dined in silence, drinking from steins of Heineken.

Finally, Barish settled back and caressed his swollen stomach. 'Enough is enough. I must leave room for coffee.'

It came, hot and black. They talked about the work they would do that night on the trial brief. Barish remarked on Ken's absorption in the process of jury selection. 'The boy soaks it up like he's in a classroom. And I need some instruction myself. Why, for example, did you accept the Chinese?'

'Kee is a member of a minority group who I hope will feel sympathetic to an underdog.'

'Ah, but Ken is a WASP, his family saturated with entrenched privilege.'

'That is not how Mr Kee will see it. He will see a young man with the whole massive power of the State lined up against him. Besides, he's an accountant. He has, I hope, a precise and accurate mind. He should be able to hear evidence and judge it dispassionately. I like the man.'

'So does Nicoletti. And I notice he generally boots them off when you like them.'

'That works both ways, Abe.'

'I'm curious. Why did you take the woman?'

'Why not? Maybe I think women are naturally stubborn. If things go against us, she could be the lone holdout for a deadlocked jury.'

'Against all those men?'

'I'll try to get another woman on the panel for moral support. There are no hard-and-fast guidelines, Abe. I remember accepting a smiling, outwardly agreeable prospect once who turned out to be a stone-hearted sonofabitch in the jury room whose mind was made up before he heard a single word of testimony.'

Barish sighed. 'I prefer my books. What I see in print reassures me.'

'Not me, Abe. I've read decisions that not even Solomon could interpret.' He saw Barish peering beyond him and turned to find Nicoletti approaching their booth on his way out.

'Working late tonight, Counsellor?'

'I have to, John. The State doesn't provide me with a staff of bright young assistants.'

'I'll trade a dozen of them for Barish here.'

'No deal.'

Nicoletti grinned. 'Did you get a copy of the medical examiner's report yesterday?'

'As promised. You're a man of your word.'

'A beaut, isn't it?'

Paul shrugged. The report had shocked and horrified him. He said, 'Think we can complete our jury tomorrow?'

'We can if you stop being so choosy.' He waved lightly, saying as he turned, 'See you in court tomorrow.'

CHAPTER TWO

IN THE FIRST HOUR of the morning session three additional jurors were seated. A bank teller, the manager of a luggage shop, and the co-owner of an art gallery. The next five were disqualified for cause, Paul expended two peremptories, and then got his second woman. Mrs Irene Bishop, housewife, a stout, motherly type, formerly a registered nurse.

The selection of Mrs Bishop accelerated the pace and started a parade into the box. Astonishingly, the panel was completed before court broke for lunch. Nicoletti informed the judge that he would be ready with his opening address when they reconvened at one o'clock.

The jurors were sworn, received the usual admonition, and filed out in custody of an attendant. Several spectators chose to forgo nourishment and retain the franchise on their seats.

Somewhere in the Criminal Court Building there seems to be a ghostly transmitting station which broadcasts eventful developments. News that a jury had been selected in the Sheridan case brought a rush of visitors to Chaffee's courtroom. Lucas Holmes Sheridan received a call at his office from Dru, who heard it on the radio. He knew that she was resolved to attend at least part of the trial and he had arranged for two seats just behind the rail, adjacent to Peggy Wayne.

Courtroom pundits who had observed John Nicoletti in action expected his opening to be clear, trenchant, concise. He arose at the judge's signal, but instead of addressing the jury, he faced the bench and said, 'It was my understanding, Your Honour, that counsel for the defence had invoked the Rule.'

Chaffee nodded. 'You understand correctly.'

151

'I believe the Rule excludes *all* the witnesses. I see one of them sitting in the courtroom at this time.'

Paul came upright, bristling. 'Which witness is the district attorney referring to?'

'Miss Peggy Wayne. Daughter of the deceased. Seated in the front row. A highly cynical attempt to influence the jury into believing that——'

'The district attorney is mistaken. The defence has no intention of calling Miss Wayne. She is a friend of the accused. She has a special interest in this case. She has every right to attend the trial.'

Nicoletti's square teeth showed in an innocent smile. 'The defence may not intend to call her. But the prosecution does. I now request Your Honour to exclude her from these proceedings.'

Paul's face went stiff with restraint. *Bastard!* he thought. So that's how you want to play. Every trick in the book. No holds barred.

'Counsel will approach the bench.'

He stalked forward, Nicoletti alongside him. He said, 'I would like to point out, Your Honour, that Miss Wayne's name was not endorsed on the information. Up to this moment no mention of her appearance as a witness has ever been made by the People.'

The judge lifted an inquiring eyebrow. 'Mr Nicoletti?'

'The prosecution has never stopped investigating this case, Your Honour. It reserves the right to be at least minimally flexible. Whenever an additional witness seems expedient, we expect the Court, in the interests of justice, to admit such testimony.'

'Since when is the district attorney interested in justice?' Paul's voice was ominously calm. 'What can the People possibly hope to prove with this witness?'

'That remains to be seen,' Nicoletti said. 'If the defence insists, the People will now move to amend its information so as to include Miss Wayne's name. The prosecution needs no instructions from Mr Slater on how to present its case.'

Chaffee gestured waspishly. 'That's enough, gentlemen.

Motion to amend is granted. If the prosecution intends to call the girl, I will exclude her.' He raised his voice. 'Miss Wayne will please rise.' Peggy rose nervously. 'The attendant will escort you to the witness room, and I caution you not to discuss this case with any of the other witnesses.'

Paul turned. Peggy gave him a tearfully beseeching look. He shrugged impotently, seeing Dru at the same time, and mustering a grim smile.

Nicoletti was smiling too, a smile of half-suppressed irony. He turned it off as he faced the box, his expression sober, his voice clear and measured.

'May it please the Court, ladies and gentlemen of the jury. The State will prove beyond a reasonable doubt that the defendant, Kenneth Sheridan, is guilty of homicide in the first degree, in that he did wilfully, feloniously, and with malice aforethought, physically attack the deceased, Dolly Wayne, beating her, violating her, and finally causing her death by strangulation. . . .'

As he continued in a carefully worded statement of what the People intended to prove, all the damning evidence that would emerge, several jurors, wearing troubled frowns, glanced uncertainly at the defendant. Paul knew that Nicoletti's words were barbed arrows piercing Dru's armour. He hoped he could persuade her to stay away from the trial. Perhaps if he enlisted the help of her obstetrician. . . .

'Mr Slater?'

He looked up at the judge. Chaffee nodded, a signal for the defence to open. Paul had briefly considered reserving his opening statement. Now, after listening to Nicoletti, he realized the risk involved. He could not allow the district attorney's words to stand unchallenged. They had made too deep an impression.

He stood for a moment in the silent courtroom and cleared his throat. 'Your Honour. Mr Foreman. Ladies and gentlemen of the jury. You have just heard a statement by the district attorney outlining what he hopes to prove in this case. It was a most eloquent and persuasive statement. But that is all it was. A statement, words, nothing more. It was not evidence. There is only one kind of evidence in this case.' He pointed. 'The testimony you will hear from that witness stand. And not just the words of the witnesses, but words you can believe, words that hold up under cross-examination.'

He raised his hand like a traffic officer. 'I show you my palm. It is not my whole hand. You can see that only when I turn it around. The analogy is clear. There are two sides to every story. So far you have heard only accusations, once in the reading of the indictment, and again just now in the prosecutor's opening statement. But please bear this in mind, Mr Nicoletti is not a witness. He has not been sworn. His words are not evidence; they have no probative value. He knows less about this case than you will know after its conclusion. *After* you have heard all the testimony. We ask only that you keep an open mind, that you reach no decision until you have heard both sides of the case, because the version of the defence is quite different from that of the State. We contend that Ken Sheridan did not commit this crime. Before God and before this jury he unequivocally denies the charge against him. He asserts his innocence. And we expect to satisfy you by the accumulated weight of *all* the evidence that he speaks the truth. We will prove that Dolly Wayne was murdered by someone other than the defendant.' He paused to take a deep breath.

'In the course of this trial you will hear evidence that carries a special nastiness. We do not deny that nastiness. It happened. You will be outraged. You will feel revulsion. These are perfectly normal reactions. I feel them myself. Any decent human being would be repelled by the events of that dark afternoon. I ask that you do not allow these emotions to lead you to strike back blindly at the first individual nominated by the State for punishment. The State is not infallible. Like anyone else, it makes mistakes. The history of mankind is saturated with injustices perpetrated by the State.

'We have talked about the presumption of innocence. That is not an idle phrase. It is a mandate clearly imposed by law. It protects every accused in the courts of this country. We must cherish and defend it as one of our most precious rights. It cloaks the defendant with the right to stand mute. He does not have to prove anything. But the People do. They have to prove his guilt beyond a reasonable doubt. They have to overcome this presumption of innocence. We say they cannot do this and they will not do this. We say a man cannot be convicted simply because of a prosecutor's speech. We ask that you keep an open mind, that you listen to all the evidence, that you weigh it carefully. If you do that, I am confident that you can reach only one conclusion, that the State has failed to meet its task of proving Ken Sheridan guilty beyond a reasonable doubt. And that you will then return a verdict of not guilty.'

There was a moment of hushed silence as he returned to the counsel table.

Judge Chaffee cleared his throat. 'The People may call their first witness.'

Deliberately and methodically John Nicoletti began to construct the foundations of his case. In the formal phase of proving and marking into evidence diagrams of the scene and photographs of the victim, he adhered meticulously to the rules of evidence. Distances had been measured, chalk marks drawn, fingerprints dusted.

During this initial phase, Paul sat looking either supremely unconcerned or mildly sceptical. Very little of the early evidence was in dispute. He examined these preliminary witnesses briefly and politely, content merely to establish an image of the courteous and fair-minded advocate.

Nicoletti spoke to the attendant, who went to the waiting room and called one of the State's witnesses. A stumpy, middle-aged man with tufted brows over tired eyes in a crabbed, impatient face came forward to be sworn.

'You do solemnly swear to tell the truth, the whole truth, so help you God?'

'I do.'

Nicoletti advanced. 'What is your name, please?'

'Dr Simon Bukantz.'

'You are a duly licensed physician?'

'I am.'

'Will you tell the court where you received your medical training?'

'I am a graduate of the Cornell University Medical College. I interned at Bellevue Hospital in the city of New York. In 1958 I became a resident in pathology and later served as chief of the department for five years. At the end of that period I received an appointment to the office of the chief medical examiner of this city. I have been there ever since and I am now the deputy chief.'

'Do you hold any teaching positions?'

'I am an assistant professor of pathology at the Post Graduate Medical School of New York University, and a lecturer in criminological medicine at the New York Police Academy.'

'Have you written any books on the subject?'

'I am co-author of a standard textbook called *Forensic Medicine*.'

'What precisely does the term "forensic medicine" mean, Doctor?'

'Forensic medicine is that branch of pathology that relates to law and the administration of justice.'

Impeccable background, Paul thought, an old hand at testifying, with no flavour of boasting.

He waved his hand.

'The defence will concede Dr Bukantz's qualifications.'

But Nicoletti wanted none of it. Additional background could only add weight to his expert's testimony. 'We are pleased to find the defence so co-operative. Nevertheless, the People will continue to qualify their witness.' He turned back to the doctor. 'Are you a member of any professional societies?'

'I have been certified as a diplomate by the American Board of Pathology and I am a member of the New York Pathological Society.'

'What is the function of your office, Doctor?'

'We examine the remains of all persons who die suddenly and unexpectedly, wherever criminal cause or negligence is suspected.'

'And that includes the performance of autopsies?'

'Yes.'

156

'How many of those does the medical examiner's office perform each year?'

'Between seven and eight thousand.'

'And how many autopsies have you personally performed?'

Bukantz smiled sourly. 'I have never kept score, sir. At a conservative estimate, I would say at least several thousand.'

'Have any of those involved death as a result of traumatic injury?'

'I take it you don't mean automobile accidents.'

'I mean death as a result of violence committed against the victim by another human being.'

'Then my answer is yes. A very high percentage.'

'Now then, Doctor, were you on Thursday, October nineteenth of this year, summoned to the home of Dolly Wayne?'

'I was.'

'Would you tell the court what you found?'

'I found a dead female identified as Dolly Wayne. She was sprawled across the bed, her head hanging over the far side. Her hostess gown had been ripped open so violently its buttons had popped off, leaving her body naked and exposed. She had suffered extensive injuries, multiple lacerations of the face and body, contusions, with marked signs of strangulation on the throat. Her mouth was open, tongue protruding. Rigor mortis was complete. Her face had cyanosed——'

'Would you explain that term for us, Doctor?'

'Blood sagging into the dependent parts of the body turns blue, especially where asphyxia was the cause of death.'

'Were you subsequently able to confirm that conclusion?'

'Yes. Later in the day after I had completed the autopsy.'

'What did you find?'

'There were four crescentic marks on each side of her neck, fingernail marks, just under the angle of the jaw. I found a fracture of the larynx and extensive injury to the trachea. Depriving the body of oxygenated blood causes irreparable damage to the brain and death generally results from within five to eight minutes, leaving numerous tiny haemorrhages scattered throughout that organ. These were clearly visible.'

'Can you tell us what time death occurred?'

'Not with pinpoint accuracy. We can, however, approximate the time fairly well.'

'How is that done?'

'By measuring the temperature, observing the state of rigor mortis and post-mortem lividity, and the degree of decomposition, we place the time of death somewhere between noon and certainly not later than two o'clock of the previous afternoon.'

'Had the deceased been sexually molested?'

'She had been raped. There were signs of forcible entry and traces of semen.'

Nicoletti turned and stood for a moment, looking at the jurors. It seemed as if all breathing in the courtroom had been temporarily suspended. In a carefully measured voice, Nicoletti said, 'Now, in that connection, Doctor, did you particularly note any unusual evidence of injury?'

'Yes, I did.'

'Would you please elaborate on that?'

'There were lacerations on the victim's thighs, the upper part of her thighs, in the pelvic region, where she had been—well, injudiciously handled. These lacerations were unmistakably caused by human teeth.'

'Are you saying she had been bitten?'

'Yes.'

There was a concerted exhalation, nervous shuffling of feet. At last the spectators were being rewarded for their patience. Chaffee tapped his gavel warningly.

Nicoletti pivoted to one of his trial assistants and received a document. 'I ask you to examine this paper, Doctor. Is it your complete autopsy report?'

'It is.'

'The People offer it in evidence.'

'The defence has no objection.'

'It will be received and marked,' Chaffee said.

Nicoletti inquired about specific details and then, abruptly, his direct examination was completed. 'No further questions,' he said and sat down at the prosecution table.

Paul walked casually towards the witness. He kept his voice

low-keyed and conversational. 'You have stated, Doctor, that you are the deputy chief medical examiner.'

'That is correct.'

'Would you say that your duties are primarily administrative?'

'I would.'

'It is my understanding that work in the medical examiner's office is divided between two groups, tour men who are called to the scene to inspect the corpse and those assistants who perform actual autopsies at the morgue.'

'That is right.'

'And as a general rule, the tour men do not get involved in actual laboratory work, do they?'

'Well, sir, over thirty thousand deaths a year are referred to our office for investigation. The tour men have enough work to keep them busy.'

'Would you explain why, as the deputy chief, you personally went out on this particular assignment?'

'Everything considered, sir, the prominence of the victim, the degree of violence, we anticipated that this case could build into a very complicated piece of business, involving special expert testimony. The chief himself suggested that I take the call, perform the laboratory work, and keep myself available as a witness.'

A blind alley. Paul moved back a step. 'Would you describe the condition of the bedroom itself?'

'In complete disarray. Chairs knocked over, clothes pulled off hangers, chest drawers open and their contents strewn over the floor.'

'Indicating, wouldn't you say, that the room had been searched?'

'Objection,' Nicoletti said. 'Counsel is calling for a conclusion on a subject concerning which this witness is not an expert.'

'Withdraw the question.'

The seed had been planted anyway. And Paul had no argument with Dr Bukantz. Dolly's death was an incontrovertible fact. She had been assaulted, violated, and strangled. *Res ipsa loquitur.* The thing speaks for itself. Bukantz knew nothing about motive or culprit. Nothing in his testimony had implicated Ken.

'You *are* an expert on bodily injuries, are you not, Doctor?'

'In all modesty, I would agree with that statement.'

'Then what conclusions would you draw about the perpetrator of this crime?'

Bukantz hesitated. 'I would say that quite possibly he was under the influence of some irresistible sexual impulse.'

'Abnormal, would you say?'

'Without question.'

Paul was satisfied. All the jurors had to do was look at Ken. A portrait of normality. 'No further questions,' he said.

'You may step down,' Chaffee told the witness.

The media had profiled Gordon Frazer so fully that everyone in the courtroom was now familiar with his relationship to the principals. They found most intriguing the knowledge that he had once been married to the defence counsel's wife. It promised some degree of fireworks when he came under cross-examination.

Frazer was Nicoletti's first witness in the damning process of linking the defendant to the crime. Taking the stand, he felt a sense of satisfaction. The humiliating experience inflicted at the time of Dru's divorce still rankled. Like some men of erratic sexual inclinations, his disposition was spiteful, and in Frazer's case, extended now to all members of her family. Besides, in testifying against Ken, he was tasting a sweet sense of reprisal against the boy himself.

Nicoletti elicited information about his career and long professional association with the deceased. He knew the defendant well and had at one time been a member of the Sheridan family through marriage.

'You are now divorced?' Nicoletti asked.

'I am.'

'Was it an amicable arrangement?'

'Not entirely. There is always some discord when two people separate.'

'Do you feel any hostility towards your former wife?'

'None at all.'

'Now, Mr Frazer, in addition to your professional association with the deceased, were you also a close friend?'

'Exceedingly. Her husband had been my collaborator for years and she had starred in many of our productions.'

'When did you last see Miss Wayne?'

'The day before she was murdered.'

'That would be Tuesday, October the seventeenth, would it not?'

'Yes, sir.'

'Where did you see her?'

'In Miss Wayne's apartment.'

'And what was the occasion of this visit?'

'She invited me to lunch. We were going to discuss her participation in a new musical now in preparation.'

'What time did you arrive?'

'Shortly before noon.'

'And did you have lunch?'

'Yes, sir.'

'Can you recall anything unusual that happened during your discussion with Miss Wayne?'

'There was a telephone call. Miss Wayne had gone to the kitchen and she asked me to take it.'

'Please tell the court what happened.'

'I recognized the caller's voice as soon as he spoke. It was a Dr Allan Truscott. He happens also to be my personal physician. We exchanged greetings and then he asked me to put Dolly on the line.'

'Did you hear any part of the conversation she had with him?'

'I heard her side of it.'

'Will you tell us what she said.'

Paul stood. 'If it please the Court, I am going to object to this whole line of testimony regarding anything the deceased is alleged to have said, since the defence cannot possibly test the accuracy of her remarks.'

'Counsel will approach the bench.'

Paul and Nicoletti moved to the sidebar. Judge Chaffee peered down inquiringly at the prosecutor.

'What is your position on this, Mr Nicoletti?'

'Your Honour, I believe that Miss Wayne's side of the conversation on the telephone falls within certain exceptions to the rule. The exception of necessity. Because she is dead and obviously cannot testify, certain facts would be lost to the People by excluding her statements. My authority is Jendresal v. Metropolitan Life, 70 N.E. 863.'

'Mr Slater?'

'Your Honour, the mere fact that a person is dead does not in itself render her statements as competent. They must be supported by certain independent facts, not yet provided by the district attorney. Even if statements by the deceased are the *only* available evidence.'

'Would the Court request a citation on that?' Nicoletti said.

'The defence volunteers it without a request.' Anticipating an argument on the point, Barish had armed Paul with the appropriate authority. 'Brown v. General Insurance, 70 N.M. 46.'

Nicoletti snorted. 'New Mexico. I am sure His Honour is aware of a trend in *this* State towards a more liberal interpretation.'

'No, Mr Nicoletti, the Court is not inclined to be quite so liberal.'

'Then the People offer it as part of the res gestae.'

Chaffee pinched his lower lip, looking thoughtful. 'Mr Slater?'

'The actual crime took place on the day following this conversation. We object to any statements she may have made twenty-four hours earlier as being too remote.'

'You have a valid point,' Chaffee said. 'Mr Prosecutor?'

Nicoletti had one last card up his sleeve. It proved to be an ace. 'The People ask the Court to admit Miss Wayne's statements, not to prove accuracy of content, but merely as evidence that statements were made and subject to linking them later with additional supporting evidence.'

'What supporting evidence?' Paul demanded.

'Dr. Truscott will testify to his end of the conversation. And Mr Slater is free to examine him until he's hoarse.'

Chaffee sat back. After a moment he said, 'The Court will admit the statement for that purpose.'

'Exception,' Paul said.

'You have it. Now let us proceed.'

Paul resumed his seat and Nicoletti turned back to the witness.

'All right, Mr Frazer. You handed the phone to Miss Wayne and heard her speak to Dr Truscott. What did she say?'

'She said, "Did you see Peggy, Doctor? How is she?" She listened and turned pale and said, "Oh, my God! Are you sure? No, no, Doctor, I'm sorry. Of course you don't make mistakes like that. Thank you for calling." And she hung up.'

'What happened next?'

'She started cursing. She was positively ranting. She said, "I'll kill that Ken Sheridan. The miserable, whoring little sonofabitch! Debauching my child. I'll cut his goddamn root off." Then she ran to her desk and found an address book and made a long-distance telephone call.'

'How do you know it was long distance?'

'By the number of digits she dialled, an area code first. She got someone and said, "Put Ken Sheridan on the line." And after a moment I heard her speak to him in a very harsh voice. "Ken? I want to see you. I want you to get that stupid carcass of yours into New York on the double. We have some business to transact. Now look, young man, don't take that tone with me. I just spoke to Peggy's doctor. She's pregnant." Dolly listened and said, "All right. Tomorrow, around noon. I'll expect you." And she slammed the phone down.'

Ken leaned towards Paul and whispered, 'He's lying. She wasn't angry at all.'

Nicoletti said, 'Did she make any comment to you, Mr Frazer, any explanation?'

'Yes. She said, "I'm sorry you had to hear this, Gordon. I'm so angry I could spit." I tried to calm her. I told her the world hadn't come to an end, that she wasn't the first mother to face this problem, and certainly not the last.' Frazer smiled

163

ruefully. 'She said, "Please. Spare me the platitudes. I don't care what happened to anyone else. I am not happy about an abortion and I'm not sure I'd like Peggy to marry the Sheridan boy." She said she had a splitting headache and would I mind calling in a few days. I told her I understood and I left.'

'Did you see Dolly Wayne again after that?'

'Yes. Three days later.'

'Where?'

'At the Lambert Funeral Home. She was dead.'

'Thank you, Mr Frazer. Your witness.'

Paul rose to cross-examine. He stood for a moment, hands clasped behind his back. Frazer waited, eyes veiled and wary. The first question came in a quiet, courteous tone.

'How long have you known the accused, Mr Frazer?'

'About three years.'

'Under what circumstances did you first meet him?'

'I was courting his cousin Drusilla Sheridan.'

'Whom you subsequently married?'

'Yes.'

'And you saw him frequently in her company?'

'Yes.'

'You know they were deeply devoted to each other?'

'I suppose so.'

'Well, now, you knew that for a fact, did you not?'

'I was not privy to all her emotional alliances.'

He's caught the drift, Paul thought, and he's skirting a direct answer. 'That may be,' he said, 'but you must have heard her speak of the defendant from time to time.'

'She mentioned him.'

'In any but the most affectionate terms?'

'Her judgement of people has always been flawed.'

'Was it equally flawed when she accepted your proposal of marriage?'

Frazer's eyes turned stony. Before he could frame a reply, Nicoletti flagged the bench.

'Objection. Counsel is baiting the witness. And a further objection on the ground that all this is new material not developed on direct.'

'It goes directly to the question of bias, Your Honour.' Paul's tone was now sharp. 'I'm entitled to show prejudice.'

Chaffee had always appreciated a neatly executed entrapment. He was curious as to how Frazer would disentangle himself. 'I'm going to let the question stand. The witness will answer.'

The brief exchange had apparently restored Frazer's presence of mind. He said, 'On rare occasions my ex-wife showed flashes of good sense.'

'Is she an attractive woman?'

'Yes.'

'And you consider that her choice of you, above all the men available to her, was an exercise in good judgement?'

Frazer held his tongue. Instinct warned him of the danger in an affirmative answer. What sagacity lay in marrying a man whose sexual quirks had doomed the union from its inception? He backed away quickly. 'It—er—may have seemed so at the time.'

'But she was mistaken, wouldn't you say?'

'I'm not sure I understand——'

'Well, sir, the marriage ended in a divorce, did it not?'

'Yes, we were divorced.' An edge of surliness in his voice.

'Who initiated the action?'

'My wife.'

'You testified on direct that it was an amicable arrangement. Would you now like to reconsider that answer?'

'It depends on how one looks at it.'

'Well, tell us how *you* look at it, Mr Frazer. Were there any heated discussions, recriminations, resentment, bitterness?'

'Some.'

'As a matter of fact, the proceedings involved considerable acrimony and rancour, did they not?'

'You ought to know. You were her lawyer.'

'Oh, *I* know, Mr Frazer. I just want to make sure the jury knows.' Paul turned to Chaffee. 'Would the Court direct this witness to be more responsive.'

'Counsel's questions demand a specific reply, Mr Frazer. Your answers must be affirmative or negative, as called for.'

Frazer glared. He spoke through clenched teeth. 'Yes. There were hard feelings.'

'Thank you.' Paul had made his point. Implicating Ken might be Frazer's way of retaliating against the defendant and his relatives. He said, 'So disregarding the question of your former wife's judgement, sir, right or wrong, wouldn't you say that her attitude towards Ken Sheridan was always one of deep affection and high regard?'

Frazer nodded in grudging admission. 'Yes.'

'Are you here in court subject to a subpoena?'

'No.'

'I take it you volunteered of your own free will?'

'In the performance of my duty as a citizen.'

Paul's eyebrows shot up. 'Bravo! Most exemplary, sir. So you consider yourself a conscientious citizen keenly aware of your civic obligations, is that your position?'

'It certainly is.'

'Then let me direct your attention to September of last year. Were you at that time called in for a tax audit by the Internal Revenue Service?'

Frazer sat motionless. A flush darkened his face. Nicoletti came to the rescue, heaving himself upright.

'Objection. How much leeway are we going to allow the defence, Your Honour? Where is the materiality or relevancy in this line of questioning?'

'If it please the Court,' Paul said blandly, 'I am merely pursuing a matter opened by the witness himself. He asserts virtue as a conscientious citizen. He claims to be a citadel of integrity. I submit we're entitled to test that assertion.'

Chaffee nodded. 'Objection overruled.'

Nicoletti remained half out of his chair, fists propped against the table.

Paul said, 'We're waiting for your answer, Mr Frazer.'

Their eyes met in silent conflict. 'Yes, I was called down for an audit.'

'And is it not a fact that you were charged with making fraudulent returns over a three-year period?'

'There was no prosecution.'

166

'Indeed. Will you tell us, then, why the government was so
lenient?'

The warning flags were up again. Frazer compressed his lips.

'No reply, sir? Was it because you made a substantial settlement of the government's claim?'

Silence. Only the white patches on Frazer's cheekbones
betrayed his emotions.

'You must answer,' Chaffee admonished.

Frazer dipped his chin fractionally and said in a barely
audible voice, 'There was a settlement.'

'I believe the figure was very close to a hundred thousand
dollars, was it not?'

'Yes.'

'Did you demand an official hearing in tax court?'

'My attorney advised against it.'

'So for all practical purposes you conceded liability.'

'Well, I signed a waiver.'

'And paid the assessment?'

'Yes.'

Paul's voice was suddenly freighted with heavy irony. 'Do
you consider an attempt to swindle the government out of a
hundred thousand dollars the act of a conscientious citizen?'

Nicoletti's growl came at once. 'The People object to
counsel's characterization and use of words. There is no evidence on the record that——'

'Withdraw the question,' Paul said indifferently. 'And would
the Court direct the prosecutor to sit down. Standing there,
glowering like that distracts the jury's attention from the witness. We appreciate his zeal in trying to preserve Mr Frazer's
alleged credibility, but——'

'That will be quite enough, Mr Slater.' Chaffee was firm.
'Have you any further questions for this witness?'

'Yes, I do, Your Honour.' He waited for Nicoletti to resume
his seat. He folded his arms and looked scornfully at Frazer.
'So as a conscientious citizen, the instant you heard of Dolly
Wayne's death you went sprinting to the district attorney's
office of your own volition to volunteer information against
this boy.'

'I did not sprint.'

'But you lost no time. You got the information to the district attorney without delay. This so-called information?'

'I told him what I heard.'

'With no malice in your heart?'

'None.'

'Nor any embroidery on your tongue?'

'That's right.' It came out in a splenetic hiss.

Paul flicked his hand in a gesture of contempt. 'No further questions.'

As Gordon Frazer moved to step down, Nicoletti waved him back. 'Just a moment, Mr Frazer. When you came to the district attorney's office you were referred to me, were you not?'

'Yes.'

'Did I make any suggestions about your testimony?'

'No, sir.'

'Do you remember my exact words?'

'You instructed me to tell my story exactly as it happened.'

'Thank you, Mr Frazer. That will be all.'

When he vacated the witness stand, Frazer did not remain in court. He stalked down the aisle, eyes straight ahead, moving faster than usual, and left the courtroom. Chaffee glanced at the clock and started assembling his notes.

'Court will adjourn until tomorrow morning. You members of the jury are not to discuss this case among yourselves or with anyone else. You are not to form or express any opinion of the guilt or innocence of the defendant until the case has been finally submitted to you for your decision.' His robes billowed out as he hurried briskly from the courtroom.

Ken was all smiles and laudatory adulation. 'Beautiful, Paul. Absolutely beautiful. God, did you have him squirming!'

The attendant touched his shoulder and beckoned. Ken turned to smile at his uncle and to wink at Dru. She signalled to Paul that she would be waiting.

'He's right,' Barish conceded. 'It was beautiful. But what exactly did it accomplish?'

'Several things,' Paul said, stuffing notes into his briefcase.

'First, reasonable doubt. They counted on Frazer to place Ken at the scene of the crime. I wasn't going to help them do that. So we create uncertainties wherever we can. Second, Nicoletti got my back up. After that little subterfuge of his in getting Peggy out of the courtroom, I decided to try everybody in the city except the defendant, especially the prosecution witnesses. He wants a bare-knuckle fight, we'll accommodate him.'

Reporters clamoured around Paul as he stepped into the corridor. Questions hammered at him from all angles. 'Mr Slater ... Mr Slater ... Is the defence going to——'

He elbowed his way roughly towards Dru and her father. 'It's only the first round, gentlemen. I have no comment to make while this trial is in progress. Let us pass, please.'

They ran the gauntlet. Lucas Sheridan's car was at the kerb, with Quintus at the wheel. 'How is Mr Kenneth, sir?'

'In better spirits than anyone has a right to expect, Quintus.'

The car lurched through stop-and-go traffic. Dru sat between them. She looked pale and tired. Sheridan touched the automatic control and rolled up the windows, effectively insulating them from street noises. He said, 'I lost control of my daughter when she reached her fifteenth birthday. Perhaps she'll listen to you, Paul. Tell her she'll be better off not attending this trial.'

'I've already told her. You had control for fifteen years. I never had control at all. Incidentally, I think the day went rather well.'

'It could have gone better.' Sheridan's eyes were flat ahead.

'Oh? How do you mean?'

'Well, damn it, you know what Frazer is.'

'I thought he was a highly successful lyricist.' Paul felt Dru's fingers tighten on his in a silent plea to avoid conflict.

'That's not what I mean. The man is a practising homosexual.'

'So?'

'The jury should know about it.'

'Why?'

'To help them evaluate his character.'

169

Paul rubbed his jaw slowly. 'Well, now, Lucas, I'm not sure about that. In the first place, we'd have to argue its relevance. In the second place, it could have alienated the jury. And third, while I admit Chaffee is no heavyweight, how many side excursions is he going to allow in this trial?'

'You could have tried. Perhaps I'm labouring under a mis-apprehension, but I thought defence counsel's job is to destroy opposition witnesses.'

'Not the witnesses, Lucas. Their testimony. His job is to create a reasonable doubt. And I think we accomplished that. So why hold the man up to public ridicule? Why not leave him with just a little dignity?'

'Because he doesn't deserve it. Because Ken's future is at stake. Because I think we should spell out exactly the kind of witnesses the People are relying on.'

Paul held himself in check. 'My sense of decency is only a part of it, Lucas. There is also a matter of tactics. Gratuitous debasement of a witness sometimes militates against the lawyer. I've seen it happen. We have an intelligent jury here. Instead of revulsion, it might arouse sympathy. I'm prepared to dis-credit testimony but not the man himself if it serves no special purpose.'

Sheridan flushed angrily. 'Scruples, Paul? At a time like this?'

Dru intervened hastily. 'Oh, stop it. I have an announce-ment to make. I saw the doctor this morning. He thinks I may be having twins.'

It broke the rising tension. Paul smiled secretly to himself, surmising that it was pure invention. Lucas appraised her with sudden concern.

'Twins? My God, can you handle it?'

'You brought a daughter into this world, Father. Not a piece of fragile china. A woman can handle whatever she has to handle.'

Paul played the game.

'Could he determine their sex?'

'He thinks they're boys, one hippie and one square.'

Lucas Sheridan managed a dry chuckle, then lapsed into a

distant silence that lasted until he dropped them off at their apartment.

On their way up, Paul reminded Dru that Abe Barish would be joining them for dinner.

Their guest arrived promptly at seven. Dru planted a vigorous kiss on his cheek. Barish touched the spot with his finger. 'The last time a female did that, it must have been maybe five years ago.'

'Was she pretty, Abe?'

'She was fifty-six and she weighed two hundred and thirty pounds. I had just won an appeal that doubled her bank account.' He accepted a martini and lifted an approving eyebrow. 'Who prepared this concoction?'

'Dru did,' Paul told him.

'You were aware of this gift when you married her?'

'Of course.'

'May I have the recipe, Mrs Slater?'

'Tanqueray gin and dry vermouth applied with one squeeze of a perfume atomizer. Stir with cracked ice and serve with a lemon peel.'

'I will remember it. Earlier in life it might even have led to a successful romance.'

There was an unspoken pact to avoid any talk of the trial at dinner. It was a long, leisurely affair. Later, in the afterglow of wine, Abe Barish became more expansive than Paul had ever seen him. His conversation was spiced with dry wit and gentle iconoclasm. He recalled with nostalgia his memories as an immigrant child on New York's Lower East Side, revelations fascinatingly alien to Dru's experience. She was endlessly curious as he talked of struggles, ambitions, prejudices, excursions into hostile territory.

'Was it an unhappy time?' she asked.

'Not at all. We are a people who make a joke of our problems. We laugh to keep ourselves from crying. We are fatalistic, and perhaps even a little arrogant.'

'Arrogant, Abe?'

'Yes. You see, we call ourselves God's chosen people.' He

171

cocked his head quizzically. 'But chosen for what? To be persecuted for two thousand years? To be the world's scapegoat? To wander the earth looking for a home? And now that we have one, how long will it last?' He shrugged expressively, his eyes smiling. 'Ah, but we survived, and we made our contributions to mankind. We gave our tormentors Jesus, Marx, Freud, Spinoza, and Jonas Salk—and how many more must I name? Enough to make God's green footstool a little better place for His benighted children.'

Dru looked at him with earnest intensity. 'Do you really mean to include Karl Marx? Do you think he made this world a better place?'

'In practice, no. But his theories are not without merit for certain places. Do not blame Marx for the inhuman slaughter of Stalin.' He pressed a palm against his chest. 'For me, for this country, never. At least you must admit that the history of my people produced no Stalins, no Attilas, no Genghis Khans, no Hitlers, to name a few.'

'I'm beginning to understand your pride.'

'Yes, we are a proud people. We believe in man exercising his brain, not his sword. That is why I find law so rewarding.'

'And you have no prejudices, Abe?'

'Ah, but I do. I am a man of many prejudices. I am prejudiced against bigotry, against tyranny, against injustice, against anything that stifles man's freedom and spirit.'

She made a lugubrious face. 'Is there any hope for us, Abe?'

He looked at her reflectively. 'I do not know. I have no crystal ball. Man's potential is unlimited and so, apparently, is his capacity for evil. Perhaps this new generation has some answers. I can only hope.' He leaned back ruefully. 'I do not mean to burden you with my personal philosophy.'

'But I asked for it, Abe. And I think I've learned something. You are a very wise man.'

'Which is one of the reasons I asked him here,' Paul said. 'We have much work to do and I need his help. Will you forgive us, darling? And please don't wait up.'

'I can take a hint.' She kissed Abe's cheek again. 'Will you come back? Soon?'

'I am a bachelor,' he said. 'My evenings are free. Invite me.'

'You're invited. Sunday.'

When they were alone, Barish heaved a deep, heartfelt sigh. 'The mistakes I made, Paul. I should have got married years ago.'

'It's not too late, Abe.'

'Who would have an old man?'

'An old lady.'

Barish laughed. 'No, sir. Not me. I long for a Lolita.'

'Then emulate our Supreme Court Justice, the one who keeps getting them even younger than Dru.'

'He is more distinguished than I am, and more learned. Handsomer. And certainly more vigorous. He even climbs mountains. I get winded on a short flight of stairs. No, Paul, I'm afraid I am doomed to looking and admiring. Enough, already. Let us get to work.'

CHAPTER THREE

DR ALLAN TRUSCOTT was sworn and took the stand as the first witness of the day. He was a tall, spare man, irascibility stamped into the lines of an angular face. Nicoletti qualified him as an internist who had been actively engaged in the practice of medicine for twenty-two years. When he started to enumerate his long list of affiliations Paul conceded his accomplishments, and this time the prosecutor accepted.

'Now, Dr Truscott,' Nicoletti inquired, 'did you on October sixteenth receive a telephone communication from Dolly Wayne?'

'I did.'

'What was the substance of that conversation?'

'She told me that her daughter Peggy had not been feeling well. The girl seemed to be suffering from cramps and nausea. Miss Wayne wanted me to see Peggy the following day and I managed to fit her in.'

'Did Peggy Wayne appear at your office?'

'Yes, sir.'

'Did you examine her?'

'I did.'

'And what was your diagnosis?'

Paul's instant challenge blocked Truscott's response. He was on his feet, hand out in warning to the doctor. 'Objection, Your Honour.'

'On what grounds, Mr Slater?'

'A physician's findings are privileged unless waived in open court by the patient. The patient has not waived, and as her representative I now claim that privilege.'

Chaffee was frowning.

'Her representative?'

'Yes, Your Honour, she has consulted with me and retained me as her attorney.'

'I will sustain the objection.'

Nicoletti was not in the least troubled. He had expected the objection and was prepared to circumvent it. He turned back to the witness.

'All right, Doctor, without disclosing your diagnosis, or any treatment you may have prescribed, what did you do after you examined the girl?'

'As soon as she left I phoned Dolly Wayne and told her that Peggy's condition was out of my line. I told her the girl needed an obstetrician, not an internist.'

Paul's reaction was involuntary; he slapped the defence table savagely and shot a blistering glare at Nicoletti. He'd been out-manœuvred. Barred from eliciting a direct response, the prosecutor had sneaked it in through a side door. These jurors were not illiterate. They knew the functions of an obstetrician. Paul's anger faded with the quick realization that he had not lost much. Gordon Frazer had already let the cat out of the bag. Incongruously, he felt a touch of resentment at Chaffee's half-concealed smile of amusement. Not because he'd been outflanked, but because there was too much at stake for even tacit approval of adversary subterfuge. Well, he'd always known that Nicoletti was a dangerous opponent.

'Did you advise the girl of her condition?' Nicoletti asked.

'I did.'

'Did you ask her who was responsible?'

Paul started to rise, and then thought: The hell with it. He would object when it served a purpose.

'Yes,' Dr Truscott said. 'She told me in effect that it was no one's business.'

'What was her general reaction to the news?'

'She was upset. She didn't want anyone to know about it. She asked me for some pills. I told her it was too late for that.'

'Why did you feel it necessary to call her mother?'

'Because I was concerned. I've known the family for many years. I felt it was my duty to notify her mother and I did so as soon as Peggy left my office.'

'Who answered the telephone?'

'Mr Gordon Frazer.'

'You recognized his voice?'

'Of course. I've been his physician for many years.'

'What was the substance of your conversation with him?'

'We merely exchanged amenities and then I asked for Dolly Wayne.'

'And he summoned her?'

'Yes. I heard him call her name. She came to the phone and I reported my findings on her daughter.'

'How did she react?'

'Well, sir, I could not see her face. But she sounded shocked. She gasped and said, "My God, are you sure?" I told her of course I was sure. She was breathing harshly. She thanked me and hung up.'

'Thank you, Doctor. No further questions.'

Paul was inclined to pass the witness, but he was still smarting over what he believed was Truscott's complicity in skirting the rules. He stood slowly and regarded the witness with impassive solemnity.

'Now, Doctor,' he said, 'you testified that Peggy Wayne came to your office and you examined her. Was it a thorough examination?'

Truscott snorted. 'All my examinations are thorough.'

'Webster's dictionary defines the word 'thorough' as complete, painstaking, exact about details. Would you agree with that definition?'

'Absolutely.'

'Well, then, let us see how thoroughly you examined Miss Peggy Wayne. Did you take blood samples for analysis?'

'I saw no need.'

'How about urine samples for an Aschheim-Zondek test?'

'Well, not exactly. You see——'

Paul's eyes opened wide with incredulity. 'Not even for the egg test on female toads?'

Truscott looked shaken. 'That is not my speciality.'

'Did you try administering hormones to hasten possible menstruation?'

176

'It—it did not occur to me.'

'Did you check basal metabolism?'

'No, because——'

'So, as a matter of fact, Doctor, you performed none of the standard tests for determining pregnancy, did you?'

Nicoletti rose to the rescue. 'Counsel is not allowing the witness to complete his answers.'

'I am not asking the witness for his subjective reasoning,' Paul snapped. 'My queries are directed to his specific actions, what he did or did not do.'

'Are you objecting, Mr Nicoletti?' Chaffee asked politely.

'Most forcefully.'

'Overruled.'

Paul restrained a smile. Too bad Dru wasn't here. She would have appreciated this. It was, after all, her own pregnancy and his insatiable curiosity about every aspect that had supplied all this information.

He pressed ahead.

'Did you examine the patient's heart?'

High colour stained the doctor's cheekbones. 'Of course I examined her heart.'

'By palpation?'

'Yes.'

'Electrocardiogram?'

'I did not think it necessary.'

'Then, by any definition, Doctor, your examination was considerably less than thorough, wouldn't you say?'

'It was thorough enough by my standards.'

'Your standards apparently leave something to be desired. How effective is the Aschheim-Zondek test?'

'About ninety-five per cent effective.'

'And the failure to bring about menstruation after administering female hormones?'

'The same.'

Paul threw his arms wide in a gesture of astonishment. 'Yet you failed to perform either of those tests? Are you at least a specialist in gynaecology, sir?'

'I am not.'

'How about obstetrics?'

'I am an internist.'

'I did not ask you what you were, Doctor. These jurors will decide that for themselves. Your answer then is no.'

'I am not an obstetrician.'

'Obviously. The point is, why didn't you refer your patient to a specialist in that category?'

'It did not seem indicated.'

Paul turned away.

'No more questions.' He went back to his seat, shaking his head in disbelief.

Nicoletti rose, quick to rehabilitate. 'How *did* you arrive at your diagnosis, Doctor?'

'There was plenty of evidence.'

'Would you please elaborate for the jury.'

'I found the breasts enlarged, with the appearance of tiny blood vessels in that area. The uterus was swollen and the cervix was softer than usual. The patient complained of fatigue, shortness of breath, drowsiness, nausea, increased bladder pressure.'

'And all those symptoms were present?'

'Yes, sir. Every last one of them.'

'In a case of this kind, have you ever been misled into a faulty diagnosis?'

'No, sir. Never.'

'And at the time you considered them sufficient for an accurate medical conclusion?'

'I did, and I would stake my reputation that I was right.'

'Thank you, Doctor. You may step down.'

'Just a moment, Dr Truscott,' Paul said, half rising. 'The laboratory tests I suggested are generally considered far more conclusive than all these symptoms you just mentioned, are they not?'

'You may put it that way if you wish.'

'I certainly do wish, Doctor. Once again, you did not perform these laboratory tests, did you?'

'No.'

'Pass the witness.'

Truscott's rapid stride took him out of the courtroom with a speed suggesting that he would again appear as a witness only through irresistible compulsion.

Paul knew that Nicoletti was not in the least disturbed. These minor ripostes of defence counsel were Pyrrhic victories at best. Nicoletti had made his point. The pregnancy was established and Gordon Frazer's testimony confirmed. All of which he would elaborate and emphasize on summation.

'Call your next witness,' Chaffee said.

Nothing in his past experience as a seasoned stage performer had prepared Billy Clark for the merciless glare of a public trial. He sat stiffly in the witness chair, ill-at-ease, gripping his knees hard to conceal a tremor in his hands. He would gladly have relinquished this opportunity for free publicity.

Nicoletti established his background, his connection with the deceased, and the fact of his tenancy in the converted town house owned by Dolly Wayne.

'On what floor is your apartment, Mr Clark?'

'The third floor.'

'Miss Wayne occupied the first two, did she not?'

'Yes, sir, she did.'

'How long have you been a resident at that address?'

'About four years. I signed the original lease with Brian Wirth, Miss Wayne's husband, shortly after he bought the property and renovated it.'

'Are you presently employed?'

'Not at the moment. Gordon Frazer is scheduling a new production and has asked me to stay available.'

'Then you're free to spend a considerable amount of time at home?'

'Yes, sir.'

'I call your attention to the early afternoon of Wednesday, October eighteenth. Do you recall that date?'

'I remember it well.'

'You were at home?'

'Most of the day. I did not leave until the evening, about seven o'clock.'

'Did anything occur on that particular day to make it stand out in your memory?'

'Yes, sir. I was doing some limbering-up exercises when I suddenly heard yelling from the floor below. There were two people and Dolly Wayne's voice sounded furious.'

'This other voice, was it male or female?'

'It was a man's voice.'

'What time was this?'

'Between twelve forty-five and one.'

'Could you recognize the man's voice?'

'Well, I can't identify it, if that's what you mean.'

'Did you hear anything else besides those voices?'

'Thumping and scuffling sounds, like a fight, you know. I heard Dolly scream several times and then a noise, a heavy noise, like someone falling. After that it was quiet.'

'Did it occur to you that Miss Wayne might need help?'

'Yes, it did. I went to the telephone and dialled her number. I got a busy signal. I figured she was talking to someone and that everything was all right.'

'You made no further attempt to contact her?'

'No, sir. I didn't want Dolly to think I was prying into her affairs.'

'Pass the witness,' Nicoletti said.

Paul took his time rising. He was puzzled at the brevity of Nicoletti's direct. Puzzled, too, that the prosecutor had concluded on an implication that Dolly was alive and well and using the telephone after the violence had apparently ended. He recalled Ken's statement that he had left the apartment at twelve-thirty. Paul was eager to underscore the time clearly.

'You testified, Mr Clark, that you heard this noise between twelve forty-five and one o'clock, is that correct?'

Billy Clark looked at him nervously. There was a light sheen of perspiration along his upper lip.

'Yes, sir.'

'Are you telling us that the struggle lasted a full quarter of an hour?'

'Oh, no, a couple of minutes at most.'

'How can you be sure of the time?'

'I was listening to the radio. WLCA. They play fifteen minutes of show tunes every Wednesday starting at twelve forty-five. I remember this one, a recording of *When In Rome*, because it was an early Frazer-Wirth musical. The first they ever wrote, I think.'

'Was this programme still playing when you dialled Miss Wayne's number?'

'It was just ending.'

'Then it would be safe to assume that it was close to one o'clock when you called her.'

'Yes, sir.'

'There is no doubt in your mind about that?'

'No, sir.'

'And her line was busy?'

'Yes.'

'Did you by any chance look out the window to see who, if anyone, left the building?'

'No, sir.'

Paul nodded. 'No further questions.'

Chaffee recessed for lunch.

When court reconvened, Nicoletti's first two witnesses were Detectives Barney Krehm and Lou Schatz, mortar to bind the foundation blocks of his case. Nothing here for the defence. Paul passed them without cross.

Chaffee seemed pleased at the progress.

The People's next witness was Lieutenant Charles Varney. Sitting with the erect posture of a drill sergeant, he handled himself under direct with the assurance of a professional who is no stranger to courtroom procedures. Paul bent forward, listening with sharp attention as the prosecutor guided him through his preliminary investigation.

'Now, Lieutenant, after you spoke to Gordon Frazer, and made all these inquiries, you decided that the defendant should be brought in for questioning, is that right?'

'Yes, sir.'

'And you sent Detectives Schatz and Krehm to pick him up?'

'That is correct.'

'Where did they find him?'

'In the apartment of his uncle, Mr Lucas Sheridan.'

'Do you know what he was doing in New York at that time?'

'Only what he told me, that he came here to attend Dolly Wayne's funeral.'

'Did you or any of your men advise the defendant that he was entitled to a lawyer and that he need not make any statement until counsel was present?'

'He was so advised.'

'Did he nevertheless waive that right and elect to talk freely?'

'He did, but only at the beginning of our interrogation.'

'Was a tape recording made of that interrogation?'

'It was.'

'Do you have it here in court?'

'No, sir.'

'Will you tell the court why?'

'It seems to have been erased while his lawyer was in my office without any supervision.'

Paul was bitterly resentful. Nicoletti had to bring it in, implying that the material was so damaging, counsel had felt an urgent need to deliberately sabotage the tape. He did not challenge it. His turn would come later.

'We have been told that the victim's apartment was in disarray. Did your examination of the premises indicate that anything was missing?'

'Yes, sir. A jewel box had been ransacked. We learned that Miss Wayne kept a considerable amount of valuable jewellery in the apartment. None was found there or in her safe-deposit box. All of it appears now to have been stolen.'

Paul frowned.

Was the prosecution now usurping the defence contention of burglary as the motive?

'Did you institute a search, Lieutenant?'

'Yes, sir.'

'Under what circumstances?'

'We obtained a complete list with detailed descriptions of all the missing items from Miss Wayne's insurance carrier,

182

National Indemnity. This list was routinely circulated among various agencies and pawnbroking establishments.'

'Did it bring any results?'

'Yes, sir. One week later we were notified by the Empire Loan Company that one of the items had been pledged in their establishment.'

'Where does Empire Loan conduct its business?'

'In Boston, Massachusetts.'

'That would be right adjacent to Cambridge, would it not?'

'Cambridge is a part of Boston.'

'It is also where the defendant attends school, is it not?'

Paul sat tense, feeling a sudden dryness at the back of his throat. He heard Abe Barish's quick intake of breath. He glanced at Ken and saw the placid smile.

'What steps did you take, Lieutenant?'

'I personally flew to Boston and recovered the item. A gold pin in the shape of a praying mantis with emerald chips for eyes.'

'Did you also examine the pawnbroker's records?'

'Yes, sir. The pin had been pledged by a man who gave his name as George Blake.'

'On what date?'

'Thursday, October nineteenth.'

'That would be the day after Dolly Wayne was murdered, would it not?'

'Yes, sir.'

'Did you attempt to locate this George Blake?'

'I did. There was no one by that name at the address given.'

'Who is the proprietor of the Empire Loan Company?'

'A Mr Max Kassel.'

'Was he able to describe George Blake?'

'He was. The description conformed very closely with the appearance of the defendant.'

'Were you able to confirm that description?'

'Yes, I was.'

'How?'

'We showed Mr Kassel a photograph of the defendant and he made a positive identification. We also examined the borrower's signature in Empire Loan's receipt book. It carried the name George Blake, but our handwriting expert confirmed it as the signature of Kenneth Sheridan.'

Paul reeled with shock. He felt a sickening contraction of his stomach. Ken leaned over and whispered in his ear. 'No sweat, Paul. I can explain everything. There's nothing to it.' He hoped to Christ the boy had an explanation that would hold water.

He stood. 'Your Honour, the defence would like to know if this so-called handwriting expert will be available for cross-examination.'

'He will,' Nicoletti assured him.

'And the pawnbroker Kassel?'

'Mr Kassel is in court under subpoena and will be the People's next witness.'

Paul did not like the way the jurors were staring at Ken. Nicoletti produced the pin and offered it in evidence.

Paul challenged.

'If it please the Court, I think we ought to hold back on this offer until a positive first-hand identification is made by the pawnbroker himself.'

'Yes,' Chaffee agreed.

Nicoletti shrugged with the air of a man who could afford to indulge all these picayune objections. Paul was overruled on his next objection when the court allowed the prosecution to introduce a deposition from Jacques Sutro, a Parisian jeweller who had designed the pin and sold it three years ago to Mr Brian Wirth. The jurors were free to draw their own conclusion that Wirth had bought the pin as a gift for Dolly Wayne.

And there was more to come. The prosecution was using Lieutenant Varney as one of its main batteries. Nicoletti shuffled through several of the State's exhibits that had been introduced and marked earlier in the trial.

'Will you identify this picture, Lieutenant?'

'It is a picture taken by a police photographer of Dolly Wayne's bedroom shortly after her body was discovered.'

'I specifically direct your attention to a night table alongside the bed. What do you see?'

'The table is lying on its side. Near one of its legs is a princess-type telephone.'

'In what condition is the telephone?'

'The handset has fallen off and lies approximately fourteen inches from the instrument itself.'

'Was it in that condition when you arrived at the scene?'

'It was.'

'In cases of this kind, what rules are the police instructed to follow?'

'Absolutely nothing is to be touched or disturbed until the scene has been photographed and the room checked for fingerprints.'

'The first officers who arrived have testified that they followed that injunction to the letter. Now, Lieutenant, if anyone were to dial Miss Wayne's number from an outside phone, what response would they get?'

'A busy signal.'

'One of the State's witnesses, Mr Billy Clark, testified that he called Miss Wayne after hearing sounds of a struggle. Since he received a busy signal, he was under the impression that Miss Wayne was using her telephone. Under these circumstances, would that assumption be correct?'

'No, sir. Clark got a busy signal because the receiver was off the hook.'

Nicoletti was satisfied. He turned to Paul with a soft, catlike smile.

'You may examine.'

Paul rose, feeling the spurt of adrenalin that sharpened his brain. The prosecution had shot down one of his most cherished defences. His cross-examination of Billy Clark had been cancelled. Those courtroom pundits who had called it a draw would now be changing their tune. So it called for a heavy salvage job.

'The Homicide Squad employs many technicians, Lieutenant, does it not?'

'It does.'

'Photographers, fingerprint men, laboratory assistants,

detectives, a few patrolmen, all swarming over the scene, together with an assistant medical examiner and a representative from the district attorney's office?'

Varney immediately caught the drift and grew wary. 'I would not call it swarming, sir.'

'But they would all have been there in Dolly Wayne's bedroom.'

'Not at the same time.'

'Not all, perhaps, but many of them.'

'Several of the men could have been moving around at the same time, yes.'

'And in all that turmoil and confusion, it is possible, is it not, that one of those men could have knocked or kicked the receiver off the telephone?'

'It is possible but not probable.'

Paul had his point and did not pursue it. 'You testified that a tape recording of your preliminary conversation with the defendant had been erased.'

'That is correct.'

'Do you recollect any of that conversation?'

'All of it.'

Paul was leery of his next question. It was unexplored territory and could open a Pandora's box. But it was a calculated risk and he had little choice. If danger lurked in this line of inquiry, he suspected that Nicoletti would long since have dug it up.

'Was anything said by the defendant that might implicate him in this crime?'

'Yes, sir.'

Paul held his breath. He couldn't leave it hanging. He had to go ahead.

'Tell the court what he said.'

'He told us that he had driven to New York and was in Dolly Wayne's apartment on the day she was killed.'

'Did he also tell you what time he left her apartment?'

'Yes, sir.'

'Again, please, tell the court.'

'He said he left at twelve-thirty.'

186

'That would be twelve-thirty in the afternoon, would it not?'

'Yes.'

'And what time did Billy Clark say that he heard sounds of a struggle in Miss Wayne's apartment?'

'Between twelve forty-five and one p.m.'

Paul nodded. 'Now, if you please, Lieutenant, let us return to the tape recorder you spoke about. Did you attempt to play back any of the conversation you held with the defendant before my arrival at your office?'

'No, sir.'

'Then you do not know for a fact that it was working properly, do you?'

'I checked it before he was brought to my office.'

'Are you certain it was turned on?'

'Yes, I am.'

'How could you tell?'

'The reel was spinning.'

'But it is still possible, is it not, that you failed to depress the recording switch?'

'I have never failed to do so in the past.'

'Well, Lieutenant, there is always a first time for everything. Did you at least attempt to shut if off before you left the office?'

'No, sir.'

'It was still running at that time?'

'I believe so.'

Got you! Paul thought triumphantly. He stepped back, his eyes wide with astonishment, scandalized. 'Well, certainly, Lieutenant Varney, you know that any conversation between an attorney and his client is privileged. How dare you attempt to record it!' He pivoted towards the bench. 'I ask the Court to openly censure this witness for a gross breach of conduct. It is inconceivable——'

Nicoletti came up shouting. 'This is a grandstand play, Your Honour, long overdue from counsel——'

Chaffee was banging his gavel. 'Sit down, Mr Nicoletti. *Sit down!* I will have none of this in my courtroom. The jury will draw its own conclusion about the witness's behaviour. Get on with your examination, Mr Slater.'

For the first time Varney's calm was shaken. He sat rigid, his face tight and bloodless. Paul stood looking at him, shaking his head in silent reproach.

'I trust, Lieutenant, that your actions in other areas of this case were more circumspect. Did you permit the defendant to make a telephone call as required by law?'

Varney nodded curtly. 'Yes.'

'And he called his uncle?'

'He did.'

'You knew that Lucas Holmes Sheridan was a prominent attorney in this city?'

'I knew.'

'And you know that when an attorney notifies the police that his client is not to be questioned any further, then the interrogation must stop at this point?'

'There is no record of any such call,' Nicoletti growled from the prosecution table.

'Naturally. Because the switchboard officer had his instructions. Mr Sheridan was unable to get through. He was, in effect, foreclosed from exercising his rights and protecting the accused.'

Nicoletti sprang to his feet and shouted, 'Objection! Counsel is overstepping——'

On the bench, Chaffee was a man tried beyond human endurance. He banged the gavel repeatedly. 'Now, gentlemen, I am not going to warn either of you again. This is not a forum for debate. Any legitimate comments should be addressed to the Court. Mr Slater, do you have any further questions for this witness?'

'No, Your Honour.'

'You may produce your next witness. Mr Nicoletti.'

'One more question on redirect, if the Court please.' The prosecutor stood with his hands on his hips. 'Lieutenant Varney, I ask if you deliberately left the tape recorder running when you left Mr Slater in your office with the defendant?'

'I am not sure that it was turned on at all. I had forgotten about it. If indeed it was still connected, that would have been inadvertent on my part.'

His testimony had been damaging but contestable. Nicoletti's next witness, Max Kassel, sole proprietor of the Empire Loan Company in Boston, was a balding, pear-shaped man with disillusioned eyes.

He sat with a pawnbroker's receipt book in his lap and in short order identified the praying-mantis pin and the pledger's signature.

They were introduced into evidence and marked.

'Now, Mr Kassel,' Nicoletti said, 'the individual who pawned this pin, who signed the book as George Blake, do you see him in this courtroom?'

'Yes, I do.'

'Will you point to him?'

Kassel aimed an accusing finger at Ken Sheridan.

'That's him.'

'You're positive? No doubt in your mind?'

'None whatever.'

Nicoletti waved his arm, inviting Paul to cross-examine, and sat down.

'No questions.'

Chaffee seemed mildly startled. This was damaging testimony. How could the defence let it go unchallenged? Clearly they'd been taken by surprise. But Chaffee knew that in the course of a trial, sentiments ebb and flow, first in favour of one side, then the other. All that really mattered in the end was how the jurors felt when they retired to deliberate. He craned his neck to look at the courtroom clock.

'I believe we have time for one more witness,' he said.

A tall, reed-thin man with a high forehead was called and sworn. Karl Herter, a handwriting expert with impressive qualifications. The People had obtained a specimen of Ken's signature from his school records. This, together with the name George Blake taken from the pawnbroker's receipt book, had been reproduced and highly magnified so that it was clearly visible to the jury from an easel set up for that purpose. No attempt, apparently, had been made to disguise the calligraphy of George Blake. Herter indicated unmistakable points of similarity between the two signatures and offered his expert opinion that both had indisputably been signed by the same individual.

Paul did not cross-examine. He was certain he could not shake the man's testimony.

Chaffee adjourned court for the day and peered down over the dais.

'I would like to see counsel for both sides in my chambers without delay.' He tapped his gavel in sharp annoyance. 'You there—you reporters will stay seated until the jury retires.'

Members of the press were acting skittishly, like horses at a starting gate, anxious to sprint for telephones. The prosecution, they felt, had scored heavily in this afternoon's session.

CHAPTER FOUR

FROM CHAMBERS, Paul went directly to the Tombs. When they brought Ken into the conference cubicle, Paul said without preamble, 'Tell me about the pin.'

'Peggy gave it to me.'

'Are you suggesting that Peggy stole it from her mother?'

'Ah, Paul, come off it. Nobody stole it. They're trying to make a big deal out of nothing. Just listen to me before you start blowing your top.'

'All right. I'm listening.'

'Dolly never liked that pin. She hated it from the moment Brian Wirth gave it to her, and after he died she offered it to Peggy. Peg wasn't crazy about it either, so when I couldn't come in for a date one weekend because I was strapped for cash, she mailed it to me and told me to sell it. I didn't, because I had already borrowed some money from my room-mate.'

'That's the truth?'

'The gospel. I wouldn't lie to you about something like that.'

Paul didn't think he would. It was too easily checked. No one had anticipated its introduction at the trial and there had been no opportunity for Ken to conform his version with Peggy's. He was suddenly buoyed with hope. Nicoletti had presumably shot down a vital defence theory and now he could retaliate in kind.

'What about "George Blake"? Why use a fake name at the pawnbroker's?'

Ken looked sheepish. 'It's a habit I have. I always invent names when it doesn't mean anything. All my friends know that, and it's always good for a laugh. And I thought what the hell, Peggy doesn't want the pin back and I was never going to redeem it, so I wrote "George Blake" purely on an impulse.'

'You pawned the pin after Dolly was dead. Didn't you know that was a stupid thing to do?'

'But I didn't know she was dead at that time, Paul. I pawned it in the morning and nobody notified me until late that afternoon.'

'How much did you get for the pin?'

'Two hundred dollars.'

'Didn't you think it might be worth a lot more?'

'Sure. But who would buy the damned thing? I was glad to get the two hundred.'

It held water. Ken had a native shrewdness and intelligence. Only a cretin would pawn merchandise stolen from a murdered woman. Nevertheless, he wanted confirmation.

'All right, Ken. I may be back later.'

He found Peggy Wayne at the home of her grandparents. She'd heard the news and was chafing with excitement. 'Oh, Paul, I called your office and I called you at home. I even called Mr Barish and he said you were in a conference with the judge. They're making a terrible mistake. If they think Ken stole that pin from Mother, they're crazy. I gave it to him.'

'Tell me about it.'

'My stepfather bought it when he was in Paris. I guess he forgot how much Mother hated insects, even as ornaments. And she thought the praying mantis was especially ugly. Once, at Sands Point, a praying mantis landed on her shoulder and she got hysterical. Anyway, a couple of months ago I was in her room when she was rummaging through some things and she came and threw it on the bed where I was sitting and she said, "Here, baby, here's a present for you. Only don't wear it when I'm around." She didn't even want to see it again.'

'Go ahead. What happened?'

'Well, a couple of weeks before she died we had a date, Ken and I, but he couldn't come into town because he was broke. He doesn't get a very big allowance, you know, and he spends most of it for expenses at school. So I sent him the pin. I never liked it much myself, and I told him he could pawn it or sell it or do anything he liked with it.'

Paul probed the troubled face. It was disingenuously innocent, incapable of dissemblance.

'Have you any idea why he used the name George Blake?'

She giggled. 'He was always doing things like that. He would introduce himself and say, "My name is Spalding; you've played with my balls." Or he would autograph books and sign the author's name. He even wrote *Best Wishes* on the flyleaf of our Bible and then signed it *God*.'

'Find the Bible and bring it to my office.' He gave her a broad smile. 'All right, Peg. You're going to be a defence witness, after all.'

Paul's explanation eased Dru's distress. The Cassandras on the six o'clock newscast had doomed the defence unless it could pull a rabbit out of its hat. She fell weakly into a chair and shook her head. 'What damnable timing! I was sick with fear. You'd better call Dad. He's been trying to reach you.'

Paul relayed the explanation to his father-in-law and heard the heartfelt sigh of relief.

Later, while he was studying a transcript, Dru joined him and said, 'Something I wanted to ask you.'

'Shoot.'

'That day in court—I think I recognized one of the jurors.'

'Which one?'

'Third from the left in the front row.'

He had committed their names and positions to memory. 'Howard Williams.'

'Does he own an art gallery?'

'Yes. International Graphics.'

'I've been there a few times.'

He stiffened and looked at her sharply. 'Have you ever bought anything from him?'

'I never saw anything I really wanted.'

'Does he know who you are?'

'I doubt it. We never spoke to each other.'

He relaxed. 'All right. No harm done. But you had me worried for a minute. I don't think you ought to mention this, not to anyone.'

'I don't understand.'

'Look, Dru, a juror might be inclined to favour the client of a lawyer whose wife was a customer of his, and might become one again. Jurors are not supposed to have had any dealings with any of the participants or members of their family.'

She smiled wryly. 'Maybe I should have given him some business.'

'Yeah, and put me under an obligation to notify the court.'

'Would you, Paul, even if it helped Ken?'

'I would have to, Dru. And anyway, if the judge found out, he'd be forced to declare a mistrial.'

She was silent for a moment. 'Why did you put Williams on the jury?'

'Because that whole art business is under investigation by the Consumer Frauds Division of the attorney general's office. Too many forgeries. So you might expect the dealers to be somewhat unsympathetic towards anyone in an official position.'

'Very tricky,' she said. 'I always suspected you were a shifty operator. As long as you're in the mood to conduct classes, why did you seat that engineer?'

'Leo Bernhard? Because he's trained to demand proof, and proof is what the State must supply. He said he reads only trade journals, so he may be the only juror who really comes to this case with no preconceived notions. And we haven't had a very good press.'

'Surely you don't think the black man will identify with Ken?'

'Not on the level you're thinking about. But he'll be serving with a jury of whites and may run across an undercurrent of prejudice. I'm not averse to a few incompatible members. Too much harmony in a criminal case can pose a threat to the defendant. If the trial goes against him, some discord and wrangling may result in a hung jury.'

'Paul,' she said with a catch in her voice, 'you don't think that possibility really exists?'

'Merely playing it safe. A good lawyer is prepared for all contingencies.'

*　　*　　*

Judge Albert Chaffee was in an expansive mood. He had enjoyed a good night's sleep, and the morning paper had carried a complimentary editorial on his handling of the Sheridan case. He stepped quickly into the courtroom, nodded at the jury, and got the proceedings briskly under way.

'We're ready for your first witness, Mr Nicoletti.'

Patrolman Francis X. Molloy was less than six months out of the Police Academy. His young face was fresh, unblemished, and needed the application of a razor blade only twice a week. He had used one this morning. His state of mind was accurately indicated by the patch of plaster on his chin. The surge of confidence he generally felt at the simple act of donning his new uniform had failed to materialize.

Patrolman Molloy had never before appeared as a witness. The prospect had made him nervous ever since he had first spoken to the D.A. That Nicoletti, Jesus, the guy had wrung him dry and then, grinning broadly with those big square teeth, had clapped him enthusiastically across the back.

A sharp observer might have detected the quaver in his voice when he took the oath. Still, this was his moment of canonization. His first bleat for recognition. After today the brass would be aware of his existence. But he felt the dryness in his throat and the moisture in his armpits.

'Will you state your name and occupation?'

Molloy had to clear his throat to get it wired for sound. 'Francis X. Molloy, Patrolman, New York City Police Department. Shield number 4343621, attached to the 19th Precinct.'

Nicoletti took him back to Wednesday, October 18. 'Were you on duty that day?'

'Yes, sir, I was.'

'Did your tour of duty cover the area on 65th Street between Madison and Lexington avenues?'

'It did.'

'What were your specific duties?'

'I was issuing summonses for parking violations.'

'Parking is restricted on that street?'

'During the day, yes, sir. No parking between eight a.m. and seven p.m.'

'Are official records kept of all ticketed violations?'

'Yes, sir, by the Traffic Control Bureau.'

'Do you have those records with you at this time?'

'I do.'

'You may refer to them to refresh your recollection. Now, Officer Molloy, would you tell us if there were any cars illegally parked on 65th Street on that day?'

'Yes, there were. There always are.'

'Did you issue a summons to any foreign vehicle?'

Molloy made a pretence of glancing at the records even though he knew the facts like his own front teeth. 'I wrote out a parking ticket for a Volkswagen bearing licence plate 1C-4125.'

'Do the regulations require you to make a precise notation of the time the summons is issued?'

'Yes, sir, they do.'

'And at what time, according to the records, was this Volkswagen tagged?'

'At one-fifteen p.m.'

Paul's newborn optimism took a precipitous dive. He cursed savagely under his breath. Molloy's testimony threw the whole timetable out of kilter. Ken claimed he'd left Dolly's at twelve-thirty. He heard Ken's urgent whisper in his ear: 'That's not true, Paul. He's mistaken. I walked over to Lex for a sandwich but I was only there a few minutes.'

Nicoletti said, 'Did you subsequently check with the Motor Vehicle Bureau to determine the ownership of the Volks-wagen?'

'Not at that time. Later.'

'What prompted you to make this inquiry?'

'Well, sir, as you know, this Sheridan case is getting a lot of publicity. Everybody is talking about it, especially the men in my precinct, where it happened. I heard that the defendant was supposed to have driven to New York in a Volkswagen. And since there are always a couple of cars illegally parked on that street, I thought I ought to take a look at the records and check. So I did.'

'What information were you given?'

'The vehicle bearing licence plate number 1C-4125 was registered in the name of Kenneth Sheridan.'

Nicoletti offered the records into evidence. Paul moved in for a quick check. There seemed no legitimate way of keeping them out. And they placed Ken not only in Manhattan but in the immediate vicinity of the murder scene at the critical time. With that, Nicoletti relinquished the witness.

Paul's mind raced, pondering the problem. He could not let the testimony stand without challenge. But how? Molloy was obviously sincere. He was also nervous. Paul saw the telltale signs that betrayed his youth and lack of experience. The moistening tongue, the squaring of shoulders, the false bravado masking apprehension as the cross-examiner bore down on him. Paul had in the past encountered witnesses so uneasy they had even stumbled over their own names. He decided on a shot in the dark. But not just yet. A few harmless questions first.

'Have you ever made any mistakes in reporting parking violations, Officer Molloy?'

'None that I know of.'

'But mistakes have been made.'

'I suppose so.'

'With the new computer system, a number of complaints about mistakes have been lodged, isn't that so?'

'I've heard it mentioned.'

'People being dunned by the Traffic Control Bureau for violations they never committed?'

'I don't know about that.'

'Do you carry a pocket watch, Officer Molloy?'

'No, sir, a wrist watch.'

'The same watch you were wearing on October eighteenth?'

'That's right.'

'Will you look at it and tell us the time?'

Molloy shot his cuff and glanced down. His mouth opened and stayed agape. Sudden consternation stamped his face. It flamed with colour, totally disorganized. Paul was instantly aware that his gamble had paid off. He knew exactly what had happened and why. Molloy's eyes came up incredulously, searching for the courtroom clock.

'Your wrist watch,' Paul said, his voice like the snap of a whip. 'Not the courtroom clock. What time is it on your wrist watch?'

The witness swallowed hugely, 'I have—er—two-twenty . . .' His voice was faint.

'Two-twenty.' Paul repeated it for the benefit of the jury. 'You may now look at the courtroom clock. What time does it read?'

'Ten-fifty,' Molloy stammered.

'The courtroom clock is obviously accurate. How long have you had that wrist watch, Molloy?'

'It was a high school graduation present.'

'Have you had it checked recently? Cleaned? Oiled?'

'No, sir.'

'It isn't very accurate, is it?'

'This is the first time.'

'So you say. But we can't be sure, can we?'

'I—I guess not.'

'And it might also have been wrong on the day you tagged the Volkswagen, couldn't it?'

'I don't think so.' Molloy's voice lacked conviction.

'But you're not certain.' Paul cast a meaningful look at the jury. How could they convict on such tenuous evidence? He returned to the defence table.

Nicoletti's shadow fell across the witness before Paul was seated. He thrust his hand out. 'May I see your watch, please.'

Molloy unstrapped it. Nicoletti held it to his ear. He gave it back. 'What time is it now?'

Molloy blinked. 'Two-twenty.'

'Still two-twenty. No change at all. Look at the second hand, if you please. Is it moving?'

'No, sir.'

'Tell me if you can hear the watch ticking.'

Molloy brought it to his ear and shook his head, sudden light dawning in his eyes. 'No, sir.'

Nicoletti took it back and paraded the watch in front of the jurors, allowing each one of them to read the dial. He wheeled back and returned it to the witness.

198

'Will you wind the stem a few times?'

Molloy did so.

'Is the second hand moving now?'

'Yes, it is.'

'When do you generally wind your watch?'

'When we stand muster at the precinct. I check it with the stationhouse clock.'

'Did you report for muster this morning?'

'No, sir. I was excused because I had to be in court this morning.'

'And that was a break in your regular routine, was it not?'

'Yes, sir, it was.'

'Have you ever appeared in court as a witness before?'

'This is the first time.'

'Were you nervous about coming here to testify?'

Molloy was not unintelligent. He managed a lame smile. 'I was petrified. I hardly slept all night.' He offered the People a small bonus. 'In fact, I left my coat and had to go back for it.'

Laughter broke and Chaffee silenced it with a single slap of his gavel.

'Has anything like that ever happened before?'

'Never.'

'It is possible then, is it not, that on this one unique occasion, because of your anxiety, because of the break in your routine, that you simply forgot to wind your watch this morning?'

'I'm sure that's what happened.'

'The defendant's Volkswagen was not the only car you ticketed for a parking violation on the eighteenth of October, was it?'

'There were many others.'

'And did you note the specific time of violation on each of those summonses?'

'Yes, sir.'

'You would have noticed it, would you not, if your watch had not been working and you had to write the same identical time on each ticket?'

'No doubt about that, sir.'

'Then you remember now without question that the hands

on your watch had advanced each time you wrote a ticket?'

'Absolutely.' Molloy was gaining confidence.

'You are certain that it was operating in a satisfactory manner that day?'

'Yes, sir.'

'Thank you, Officer Molloy.'

There had been considerable rehabilitation, but Paul waived his right to re-cross. It could still leave ammunition for his closing. Why, for example, had the People failed to produce other records for that day actually showing different times on other summonses?

More than once Paul was to be jolted by an aspect of the case on which his protests were unavailing. The surprise witness. Howard Pirie was the first of an unforeseen list.

It was easy to see why he was known to his classmates on campus as the Duke; Pirie was a tall, indolent-looking youth with a cool, faintly condescending air. He identified himself as a graduate student of economics at Cambridge. He had known Ken Sheridan since their sophomore year and was now a neighbour of the defendant in the same apartment building. Yes, Wednesday, October 18, was fixed clearly in his mind.

'Does any particular incident stand out in your mind?' Nicoletti asked.

'Yes. I spent most of the afternoon in my room studying. Late that day, after five-thirty I remember, Ken Sheridan came along and wanted to start a touch-football game. They had already lined up my own room-mate, Frank Hadley. I thought they were crazy. It had been raining earlier and the lot across the street was muddy; we'd be wallowing in it like pigs. So they called me chicken and I said okay, I could take it if they could. We went down and started tossing the ball around and then we pulled a couple of strangers into the game.'

'Did you know these boys?'

'No, sir. They were not students.'

'What happened in the game?'

Paul only half listened. The time element had come back to haunt him. Ken claimed he'd returned to Cambridge at four-thirty. Now Pirie was bringing him back at least an hour later. And Pirie was the only one of the four he had not interviewed. Detectives Krehm and Schatz must have interviewed him on their own trip to the school, and had then put him on ice.

'The game got a little rough,' Pirie was saying. 'Somebody tackled Ken and the rest of us piled on top. By that time we were all pretty messy, so it didn't make much difference. Ken got sore and sailed into the two chaps we didn't know. Fists were flying, so we broke it up.'

'And after that?'

'We went back to take showers and change our clothes.'

'Did you see the defendant in the shower room?'

'No, sir. I got there first. I was on my way back to the room when I saw him in the hall.'

'What was he doing?'

'He was shoving his sweater down the incinerator chute.'

Nicoletti cupped his ear. 'Would you repeat that, please?'

'He was throwing his sweater down the incinerator.'

'Did you say anything to him about that?'

'I said it must be nice to have a rich uncle and just burn your clothes when they got dirty.'

'Can you describe the sweater?'

'It was a maroon crew-neck.'

'Did you see the defendant earlier that morning when he left for New York?'

'Yes, I did. I had an early class and I walked him to his car.'

'Was it the same sweater he was wearing at that time?'

'Yes, sir, it was.'

'When he first came into your room to start the game, did you notice anything peculiar about the sweater?'

'Yes, sir. It was covered with mud.'

'Covered with mud? Even before the game?'

'That's right.'

'Thank you, Mr Pirie.' Nicoletti sat down.

'If it please the Court,' Paul said, 'the defence would like a fifteen-minute recess.'

Judge Chaffee gave it to him.

*   *   *

'What was that all about?' Ken asked.

Paul leaned close, eyes grim. 'He's intimating you destroyed the sweater because there was blood on it.'

'Of course there was. My nose was bleeding.'

'Not your blood. Dolly's.'

Ken paled. 'Oh, Christ! But that's crazy.'

'It's more than that. It's terrifying. Why didn't you send the sweater to the cleaner? Why destroy it?'

'Jesus, Paul, it was beyond repair. One of those goons I sailed into got his claws on it and half ripped off a sleeve. The sweater was junk—muddy, bloody, and torn. Nobody could fix it. Ask Cliff Eldon. Ask Frank Hadley.'

'All right,' Paul said. 'The jury's coming back. Look unconcerned.'

The judge reminded Pirie that he was still under oath. Paul started his cross-examination in a low-keyed, friendly tone.

'They call you Duke at school, do they not?'

'It's sort of a nickname.'

'Mind if I use it too?'

'Suit yourself.'

'Are you here voluntarily to testify against your friend?'

'Well, they asked me to come and tell what I saw.'

'And how did the prosecution know what you saw?'

'A Detective Schatz came out to Cambridge and asked me a lot of questions. He wanted me to come to New York and talk to the district attorney.'

'Who paid your fare?'

'They gave me a ticket.'

'And your hotel bill?'

'The State of New York, I guess.'

'Spending money?'

'Some. I had to buy food.'

'Sort of a picnic for you, isn't it—a free trip to town, pocket money, the limelight?'

'Not really. I haven't had much chance to cruise around.'

'Pity. They should have been more generous. Do you consider yourself a friend of the defendant?'

'Hardly. I never visited him in New York or in Sands Point.'

'You mean like Cliff Eldon and Frank Hadley?'

'That's right.'

'Not very polite of Ken. You resented that, did you?'

'Why should I? Who needs it?'

'Nevertheless, you were quick enough in volunteering information to Detective Schatz that you thought might injure the defendant. Eager enough to repeat it to the district attorney. Not at all reluctant to testify under oath in court. And you still say you harbour no ill-feelings against Ken Sheridan?'

Pirie's mouth had turned petulant. 'I only told what I saw.'

'And you saw mud on the defendant's sweater before the game?'

'It's the truth.'

'He's generally quite neat, is he not?'

'Yes.'

'Didn't you ask him where the mud came from?'

'No.'

'Weren't you curious?'

'Not much.'

'Have you played touch football with the boys on other occasions?'

'Several times?'

'You know the rules?'

'Well enough.'

'You testified on direct that someone tackled the defendant, did you not?'

'Yes.'

'As a matter of fact, wasn't that "someone" you?'

'It might have been.'

'Now, Duke, surely you remember whether or not you lunged at Ken Sheridan and brought him down face-first on a muddy field?'

'All right, I guess I did.'

'Can you tell us why?'

'Just horsing around.'

'Did you tackle Cliff Eldon?'

'No.'

'Did you tackle Frank Hadley?'

'No.'

'Did you tackle either of those two strangers?'

'No.'

'Only Ken Sheridan. Didn't you deliberately pick him because you don't like him?'

'Look, he didn't get sore at me. He started throwing punches at those strangers.'

'Because they piled up on top and made it even worse, wasn't that the reason?'

'Well, yes. . . .'

'And do you remember Eldon and Hadley leading the defendant back to his room for some ice?'

'I have a vague recollection.'

'Well, now, Mr Pirie, isn't it odd that you're quite positive about certain aspects of this incident and vague about others, especially if they seem to favour the defendant? Didn't they need the ice because the defendant's nose was bleeding?'

'I remember now.'

'Good. And can you also remember that in the melee after you tackled the defendant, his sweater was badly torn?'

'It was torn, but I don't remember how badly.'

'Have you ever seen Ken Sheridan walking around with torn clothes?'

'No.'

'Now, Duke, if you had a sweater that was muddy, bloody, and ripped beyond repair, that could not be rewoven, what would you do with it?'

No response.

'Let the stenographer note that the defendant failed to answer. I have no further use for this witness.'

CHAPTER FIVE

AN INCREDIBLE BREAK, Paul thought. But one fraught with unforeseeable consequences. Could he use it? Or more to the point, could he afford not to? He looked at the phlegmatic face of the investigator and said, 'All right, Burroughs, let's have it again. From the top, please.'

Roy Burroughs crossed his legs. 'You had information that Brian Wirth might have changed his will and you wanted me to look into it. The problem was where to start. Getting information from Porterfield, Baker & Sheridan was a little chancy. So I examined my options. Wirth died in a hospital. Under those circumstances a man is dependent on the people who take care of him. I learned that Wirth had been attended by nurses around the clock, two registered and one practical. This last had the night shift when Wirth was under heavy sedation, and I eliminated her as a possibility. Of the other two, I wound up with a Miss Elizabeth Harmon, fat, forty, and talkative.

'Three days before Wirth lapsed into his final coma, he had two visitors. The first was Dolly Wayne. She had not been there for several days and he was visibly upset by her arrival. Harmon sensed animosity and bitterness. They started to argue and Harmon called a staff physician, who asked Miss Wayne to leave.

'The second visitor was Gordon Frazer, who'd been there almost every afternoon. As usual, Miss Harmon withdrew to the adjoining toilet facility to keep herself instantly available. She claims that she did not mean to eavesdrop but that it was unavoidable under the circumstances. Neither Wirth nor Frazer were making any effort to keep their voices down. Wirth had something to say and a need to get it off his chest. He told

Frazer that Dolly had cuckolded him and that he had drawn a new will disinheriting her.'

'Hold it,' Paul said. 'Did he seem rational at the time?'

'Completely.'

Odd, Paul thought. And inconsistent with the facts, because Dolly had inherited Wirth's entire estate.

'What happened next?'

'The visit taxed Wirth's remaining strength. Frazer left soon after. That was at two o'clock. The patient was due for another shot and Harmon administered it. At noon he fell into a coma and never came out of it. At five Miss Harmon was relieved by her alternate.'

'No other visitors or phone calls that day?'

'None. I checked it out. Any calls he made would have gone through the switchboard and appeared on his bill.'

'Anything else?'

'Yes.' Burroughs cracked a thumb knuckle. 'In my line of work you sometimes get lucky. I approached several girls in the secretarial pool at Porterfield, Baker & Sheridan. One of them had been regularly assigned to take dictation from Alex Moore. Her name is Fern McFee. She is no longer with the firm, having left a few weeks ago for a better job. She doesn't like Moore and is genuinely distressed about Sheridan's nephew. She had known the boy during the summers he worked at the office. At first she was a little suspicious, but when it finally got through to her that I was working to help young Sheridan, she talked freely.'

Burroughs uncrossed his legs and leaned forward. 'This should interest you. Brian Wirth visited Porterfield, Baker & Sheridan several days before his final trip to the hospital. He wanted to revoke his old will. Moore had Miss McFee bring the Wirth file to his office. After Wirth left he called her back and dictated a new will. He said it was a rush job and would she please type it during her lunch period because Wirth was coming back to sign it. According to Harmon, the will did indeed cut Dolly Wayne off without a cent.'

'Who signed as attesting witnesses?'

'Moore himself and Donald Baker, one of the partners.'

'There's something you'll have to do.'

'Yes?'

'I want you to see Miss McFee as soon as possible, when you leave here as a matter of fact; find out if there was a prenuptial agreement between Wirth and Dolly Wayne in which the parties waived their respective rights to inherit from each other. I understand that Wirth had been married once before, and that he had a son somewhere. This is urgent. Check it out.'

Burroughs nodded. 'Will do. Now listen to a very curious coincidence. Several days after Wirth died, a letter came into the office from one of those appraisal firms. They knew that Porterfield, Baker & Sheridan were the attorneys for the estate. They offered their services, appraising jewellery, paintings, objects of art, that sort of thing.'

'For tax purposes,' Paul said. 'Go ahead.'

'Moore had been out of town for a few days, so the correspondence was turned over to Miss McFee for filing. She got the Wirth folder and put the letter in with the new will.'

'She actually saw the will at that time?'

'Yes.'

'And remembers its provisions?'

'She does.'

Paul was expressionless. 'Then she can verify its existence after Wirth died. Tell me, Burroughs, have you drawn any conclusions?'

'The obvious one. Somebody must have destroyed the will. Because in probating the estate, Porterfield, Baker & Sheridan filed administration papers. I understand that means Wirth was supposed to have died without a will.'

'Intestate,' Paul said. 'You understand this has to be kept in the strictest confidence.'

'Naturally.'

'And I'll have Mr Barish draw a deposition for her to sign.'

Burroughs pulled a paper out of his breast pocket. 'I anticipated the request and wrote one out in longhand when I questioned her.'

'Signed?'

'And notarized.'

207

Paul glanced at the statement. 'I see you're also a notary public.'

'It saves time and trouble.'

The man was worth his weight in platinum. 'Will Miss McFee take the stand and testify?'

'I asked her, and she said with pleasure.'

'Go see her right now.' Paul stood and offered his hand. 'Get what information you can about an ante-nuptial agreement and call me right back.'

Alone, he dialled Abe Barish and relayed the information. Barish was silent for a long moment, and then said softly, 'I don't like it, Paul.'

'Neither do I.'

'Are you going to use it?'

'I don't know. Some damned effective defence lawyers attempt to try everyone but the client. Look at the situation. We know that Dolly Wayne had formed a new emotional attachment. If Moore destroyed that will because he loved her, so that she would inherit Wirth's estate, and then learned that she was dumping him for another man . . . well, you see where it takes us. It gives the jury something to think about. Someone else with motive. Reasonable doubt.'

'My God, Paul! A lawyer violating his trust. A partner in Porterfield, Baker & Sheridan. You know what will happen?'

'The shit will hit the fan, Abe.'

'Are you willing to take that chance?'

'Do I have a choice?'

'Lucas Holmes Sheridan is your father-in-law.'

'Goddamn it, Abe, don't you think I know that? Or what that firm means to him? But the boy is my client, not the firm. And he's on trial for murder one. Where is my primary obligation?'

'You'll have to answer that for yourself. Only think what it would do to Moore. He could be disbarred.'

'I wouldn't be surprised.'

Barish exhaled. 'A man like that . . . to risk his honour for money.'

'His reason was adulterated by sexual obsession. It's not so

208

unusual. Bankers have embezzled from their own institutions. Senators have taken bribes. Directors have manipulated the stocks of their own companies.'

'We're talking about a lawyer in a fiduciary capacity.'

'Lawyers are people, Abe. I don't enjoy holding a man's reputation in my hands. And he may be guilty of something worse than a gross breach of ethics.'

'Think it over carefully, Paul. Sleep on it.'

But he could not sleep on it. He stayed awake most of the night, mulling it, twisting it, examining it from every possible angle. Moore had drawn the will cutting Dolly off. Its disappearance entitled her to inherit. A large sum was involved, well over a million dollars, and he knew that Dolly was in a financial bind. He was in love with her. He wanted to marry her. He had reason to believe she would accept him. He had access to the will. He took Wirth's estate through probate. He drew the petition for letters of administration. He had to file an affidavit that a search was made and no will could be found. He had sold his honour.

Late that night the phone rang. He snatched it off the cradle before it could awaken Dru.

'Paul?' It was Sheridan, sounding tense, on edge.

'Yes, Lucas, what is it?'

'I just had a call from Alex Moore. The prosecution served him with a subpoena for tomorrow morning. What in Christ's name is happening?'

So Nicoletti had finally taken the decision out of his hands.

Alex Moore was not reached until mid-afternoon. Nicoletti recognized the risks. Putting him on the stand demanded a certain audacity. As soon as he was sworn, Nicoletti requested permission to approach the bench.

Paul joined him at the sidebar. Chaffee directed an inquiring look at the prosecutor.

'As Your Honour knows, this witness is a partner in the firm of Porterfield, Baker & Sheridan. We have reason, therefore, to believe that he will be a hostile witness. Nevertheless, he is vital to the People's case. Since we anticipate opposition and evasion, it may be necessary to ask leading questions and perhaps test his response. We ask the Court's indulgence so that——'

Paul cut him short. 'The defence objects to characterizing the testimony of this witness before he has demonstrated his attitude by a single answer. Why don't we just wait and see?'

Chaffee nodded. 'Put your questions, Mr Nicoletti. The Court will make its rulings at the proper time.'

'So long as the Court is aware——'

'The Court is aware of its functions without instructions from either side. Let us move along.'

Alex Moore was more accustomed to confronting the witness chair than sitting in it. In response to Nicoletti's questions he stated his name, profession, and association with Porterfield, Baker & Sheridan.'

'Who is the senior partner of that firm?'

'Mr Lucas Holmes Sheridan.'

'What is his relationship to the defendant?'

'He is Kenneth Sheridan's uncle and guardian.'

'Are you here in court voluntarily?'

'I am not, sir. I was served with a subpoena.'

'How long have you known the accused?'

'Since he was a very young boy, approximately fifteen years.'

'Has he ever been employed by Porterfield, Baker & Sheridan?'

'During the months of July and August of the last two summers.'

'Are you friendly with him?'

'I think so, considering the difference in our ages.'

'Were you also acquainted with the victim in this case, Miss Dolly Wayne?'

'I was.'

'No generation gap there, I take it?'

'None, sir.'

'How close was your friendship?'

'Exceedingly close.'

'To the point of sexual intimacy?'

Moore's face closed up. He waited for Paul's objection.

It did not come. Paul was pretending to examine papers. Allowing the questions to stand would open vital areas for cross.

Moore said quietly, 'I do not see the relevancy of that question.'

'It may become apparent as we proceed. Please answer.'

'Well, if it enlightens you any, I had asked Miss Wayne to be my wife.'

'May I take that as an affirmative response?'

'If you wish.'

'I call your attention to Wednesday, October eighteenth, the day Miss Wayne was killed. Did you have an appointment with her?'

'I did.'

'For what time?'

'Seven o'clock that evening.'

'You had specific plans?'

'Dinner and the theatre.'

'Did something occur to alter those plans?'

'Yes. Miss Wayne phoned me the day before and cancelled our date.'

'Did you ask her why?'

'She told me she had some family matters to discuss with her daughter and would be driving up to Poughkeepsie some time the following afternoon and would not be back until late.'

'You were annoyed by this change in plans?'

'I was.'

'And did you demand ....rification, why she had to go up there on that particular day?'

'I did. She said it was urgent and could not be postponed.'

'Under the circumstances, you wanted to know why it was so urgent, did you not?'

'I have no particular recollection.'

'Then perhaps you should reconsider your answer, Mr Moore. Bearing in mind that you are under oath and that Miss Wayne's maid, Elvira Wilcox, was in and out of the room and heard a large part of that conversation.'

Moore's eyes sought Paul's and flashed a warning signal.

Paul rose. 'Is the prosecution attempting to impeach its own witness?'

'Is that an objection, Mr Slater?'

'It is.'

'Overruled. In view of the relationships here, I am going to permit some latitude.'

Nicoletti pressed his inquiry. 'Once again, Mr Moore, why was it so urgent for Miss Wayne to drive up to Poughkeepsie to see her daughter?'

Moore shifted uncomfortably. His gaze fastened on Lucas Sheridan's blank face. He made an almost imperceptible gesture of helplessness.

Nicoletti's chin came up. 'She told you, did she not, that her daughter was pregnant?'

'Yes. She told me.'

'And in that connection did she mention the defendant here, Kenneth Sheridan?'

'She mentioned him.'

'As a matter of fact, she told you that he was responsible, isn't that so?'

'She believed that to be the case.'

'How did Miss Wayne sound when she gave you this information?'

'I am not sure that I can characterize her tone.'

'Well, sir, you had spoken to her often enough. Certainly you must be able to distinguish between a calm normal voice and one that is labouring under a severe emotional strain.'

Moore sat mute.

Nicoletti thrust his jaw forward. 'If I were to tell you that Elvira Wilcox claims she was overwrought, raging into the phone, would you contradict her statement?'

Paul came up growling. 'Objection.'

'Withdraw the question. I ask you again, Mr Moore, how did Dolly Wayne sound on the phone?'

Moore continued to take refuge in silence.

'Will the Court please direct this witness to answer?'

Chaffee bent over. 'Yes, Mr Moore, answer the question.'

'She was angry.'

So it was out. The People now had confirmation from a witness presumably not biased against the defendant. An admission untainted by self-interest carries great impact.

Nicoletti was not quite satisfied. He had one more question. 'Did you suggest to the deceased that she should drive up to Poughkeepsie in the morning and thus be able to return in time to keep her appointment with you?'

'I did.'

'And what was her answer?'

Moore looked down at his hands. He spoke with difficulty. 'She said she had an appointment with Ken Sheridan on Wednesday around noon and would not be able to leave until sometime later that day.'

Nicoletti bowed towards the defence table with caustic gallantry and sat down.

Paul's initial approach was bland and fraternal. As he again underlined the relationships between all the parties, Moore visibly relaxed.

'You had ample opportunity, did you not, to observe the defendant, especially during the summer months when he worked at Porterfield, Baker & Sheridan?'

'I saw him every day.'

'Including weekends?'

'Yes. I was a frequent visitor at Miss Wayne's summer home, which adjoins the Sheridan property. There was considerable visiting back and forth.'

'And he spent quite a bit of time with Miss Wayne's daughter?'

'They were constant companions.'

'So you saw him in his social environment as well as in business.'

'Yes.'

'Did you ever see him exhibit the slightest trait of violence?'

'No, sir, I did not.'

'Going back now to the call you received from Miss Wayne breaking her appointment with you, you were annoyed, is that correct?'

'Well, it had not been easy acquiring those particular theatre tickets.'

'And you remonstrated?'

'Pleaded would be a more accurate term, Mr Slater.'

'Weren't you bitterly resentful?'

Moore hesitated. He had detected a sudden change in tone, a subtle shifting of mood. 'No, I don't think so.'

'Now, Mr Moore, is it not a fact that for some weeks prior to her death, your relationship with Dolly Wayne had deteriorated to the point of open conflict?'

Moore sat motionless, his pulse accelerating wildly. Where in hell was the defence headed? How much had Elvira Wilcox overheard? Uncertain, loath to commit himself to an outright denial, he said, 'Some difficulties existed, the minor discord between any two individuals.'

'Are you telling us that nothing at all happened to threaten the security of your relationship?'

'Objection.' Nicoletti was on his feet. 'Immaterial and irrelevant to the issues in this case.'

'I am merely pursuing a matter opened by the People on direct, Your Honour.'

'I will allow it,' Chaffee said.

Moore answered like a man walking on eggshells. 'I can only admit that we were seeing each other less frequently. Both Miss Wayne and myself had been increasingly occupied with personal affairs. My own free time was severely limited by pending litigation. Miss Wayne was negotiating for a new stage show.'

'There was no other reason?'

'None I can think of.'

'I suggest, Mr Moore, that Dolly Wayne had formed a new attachment. To put it bluntly, she was giving you the gate and you knew it, did you not?'

'I had become vaguely aware of some change in her attitude.'

'We'll pass that for the moment. You were Brian Wirth's lawyer?'

'I handled his affairs. He was represented by Porterfield, Baker & Sheridan.'

'Were you intimate with Mrs Wirth during his lifetime?'

214

Moore was stunned. He sat very still, withdrawing into a cold shell.

Nicoletti flagged the judge with a weary gesture. 'Your Honour, I must restate my objection. Counsel is wandering pretty far afield with this line of inquiry.'

'My ruling stands.'

'Let me put it this way, Mr Moore. During her husband's long illness, did Miss Wayne ever complain to you that he was neglecting his conjugal obligations?'

'We did not discuss it.'

'Did his neglect result in your assuming those obligations?'

Moore's eyes flickered. 'Mr Slater, I am not going to answer that question.'

The refusal contained its own answer. Paul changed the subject abruptly. 'Do you consider that you have a fairly reliable memory?'

'I do.'

'Are you acquainted with a Mr Donald Baker?'

'Yes. He is an associate of mine at Porterfield, Baker & Sheridan.'

'Is he married or single?'

'Single.'

'Will you tell us where he lives?'

'He has an apartment on East 79th Street.'

'Does he also have a country place?'

'He has a small beach house at Hampton Bays.'

'I direct your attention to the July Fourth weekend of last year. Do you recall that Mr Baker left New York to spend the holiday at Hampton Bays?'

'He may have. I do not keep tabs on Mr Baker's excursions.'

'Do you remember your own activities over that weekend?'

Moore's mouth grew small. A faint tic was pulling at one eye. 'I'm afraid I would need time to look at my appointment book.'

'If I were to remind you that you borrowed Mr Baker's apartment, would that aid your recollection?'

'I'm not quite sure I follow you. I have my own apartment.'

'I suggest,' Paul said with knifing sarcasm, 'that you

215

borrowed it for a clandestine assignation with Dolly Wayne and that you used it to betray a man who was your friend and your client. That you——'

Moore came up out of the witness chair, white and shaking. At the same instant Nicoletti, bristling with anger, leaped to his feet, kicking his chair back.

'This is absolutely inexcusable, Your Honour. Counsel is making unfounded accusations without offering proof. Improperly designed to prejudice the jury. I object to this whole line of inquiry and I now move that it be purged from the record.'

'Mr Slater?'

Paul wheeled to the defence table. Abe Barish thrust a paper into his hand.

'Your Honour, I have here a statement signed by Donald Baker substantiating the charge. It will be offered at the proper time and I——'

'Not now, Mr Slater.' Judge Chaffee was firm. 'I will hear arguments on this in chambers. Court is adjourned until nine-thirty tomorrow morning.'

CHAPTER SIX

LUCAS HOLMES SHERIDAN, struggling to maintain an icy calm, took an elevator to the fourth-floor apartment and rang Donald Baker's bell. When the door opened, he stalked in and concentrated a withering glare on the bemused lawyer. 'Don, I'd like to know where in Christ's name you were hiding when they handed out brains?'

Baker's mouth flapped open. 'What—what——'

'Just shut up and listen to me. Only an accident of birth brought you into the firm. I've suffered your feeble-minded incompetence ever since you joined us. How in hell you ever passed the Bar examination is a mystery. For years I've kept you out of trouble with puerile assignments. And now it turns out you had the effrontery to do something on your own initiative. Naturally you pulled the prize boner of a monumentally cretinous career.'

'I—I don't understand.'

'Of course. When did you understand anything? Would I be after your hide now if you had a single gram of intelligence? You signed a statement about Alex Moore's activities over the July Fourth weekend last year. Don't stop to think about it. Just tell me what you said and why.'

Baker was humbly apologetic. 'I gave the statement to Burroughs because he said it would help Ken.'

'The contents, please.'

'Moore asked if he could use my apartment if I went away for the weekend.'

'Why not his own? Did you ask him that?'

'He said it was being painted and everything was covered with canvas.'

'So you gave him a key?'

217

'Yes. And on Friday I drove out to the beach. But Saturday the weather turned sour and it began to rain. The forecast said it would continue through Monday. It seemed pointless to stay out there alone, so I drove back to the city.'

'Did you attempt to call Moore first?'

'I didn't think he'd mind. There's enough room here for the two of us.'

'All right. What happened?'

Baker swallowed. 'It—it was terribly embarrassing. I never expected he'd be home at that hour, so I walked into the bedroom and he was in there with Dolly Wayne, the two of them, and they were . . . I turned right around and started to leave, hoping they wouldn't see me, but Dolly looked up and screamed. And Alex began to curse. I ran out. I can't tell you how I felt, Mr Sheridan. I walked around in the rain, and later when I phoned the apartment, they were gone.'

'So you put all this down in a signed statement and gave it to Burroughs.'

Baker nodded in numbed acquiescence. 'He told me it was standard practice in criminal cases to confuse the issues and create reasonable doubt. I knew our office had used Burroughs and I thought all the time he was working for you.'

'Why didn't you ask?'

'Because, Mr Sheridan, you are not an easy man to approach. Frankly, I try to stay out of your way.'

'Didn't it penetrate that skull of yours that every member of Porterfield, Baker & Sheridan holds our reputation in his hands? Or how it would affect Moore, an invaluable member of the firm?'

'I was only trying to help.'

'The only help I want from you is invisibility. I promised your father to make a place for you. Don't force me to break that promise. Just concentrate your efforts in the supply room, counting pencils.' He turned abruptly and left.

Quintus took his coat and nodded ruefully towards the study. 'Mr Stoufer, sir. He's waiting for you.'

Ernie Stoufer could have been drinking bile instead of

Scotch. He heaved himself erect, his face pinched and bitter. 'Jesus H. Christ, Lucas! That goddamned son-in-law of yours! What's he trying to do to me?'

'What are you talking about, Ernie?'

'Have you spoken to Slater?'

'Not yet. The judge wanted him in chambers, so I didn't get the chance.'

'Then you were in court and you heard. It's on the air already. That business with Moore; what's he trying to prove?'

'Reasonable doubt, I imagine. If Dolly turned Alex out, it might look as if he was implicated in what subsequently happened to her. So Slater wants to show that she was involved elsewhere.'

'Does he know who?'

'Probably. He's had a damned good private eye poking around.'

Stoufer looked sick. He threw his hands up. 'You've got to stop him, Lucas.'

'Why?'

'Good God, man! Can't you guess?'

Sheridan gave a short harsh laugh.

'*You*, Ernie? You and Dolly Wayne? That's pretty rich. How did it start?'

Stoufer sank back into a chair. He sat, deflated, hands hanging loose between his knees.

'Dolly came to see me. She was worried sick about money. Some silly ass had been handling her investments, churning the account, almost cleaning her out. She wanted me to take over, and I agreed.' He looked up, then averted his eyes. 'A damned attractive woman. She had always appealed to me and . . . well, somehow it just happened. We drifted into it.'

'Does Janet know?'

'Of course not. And I don't want her to find out.' Belatedly he added, 'She's a fine, loyal woman.'

Loyal, Sheridan thought, but unappetizing and soggy. Still, who am I to condemn? Haven't I conjured some feisty notions of my own?

'What do you want me to do, Ernie?'

219

'I want you to muzzle your son-in-law.'

'How?'

'Christ, Lucas! This trial is a circus. I've got to be kept out of it. You know what it would do to my marriage? To Stoufer, Wingate & Company? In a business that operates on trust? With all those stuffed shirts in the banking community? It could mean we'd be cut out of future syndications. I can't take that risk. I won't take it. You give Slater the message. Put the brakes on that sonofabitch.'

'He's a hard man to control.'

'Not for you, Lucas. He wouldn't dare turn you down.'

'He has in the past. He says his chief concern is Ken. And the boy happens to be my nephew. So the position you're asking me to take is vulnerable. He's already hurt Moore. Why should he protect you?'

'I don't give a shit about Moore. I'm worried about me. Ken is innocent and he'll be acquitted. It can be done without dragging me into it. Slater's made his point. Why go ahead now and crucify me?'

Sheridan deliberated, deep furrows etched across his brow. 'All right, I'll try.'

'Tonight. Lucas. We can't wait. He'll be working on Moore again tomorrow morning.'

'You want to come along with me?'

'If you think it'll help, yes.'

'I warn you, Ernie, we're dealing with a mulishly stubborn character.'

'He's got to listen.'

'Oh, he'll listen. Whether he yields or not is something else.'

Paul had reason to be pleased with his arguments before Judge Chaffee in chambers earlier that evening. He granted that he could not introduce Donald Baker's statement until it had been properly identified. On the other hand, he had no way of putting Baker on the stand until the prosecution had concluded its case. The sequence of proof for the People was Nicoletti's prerogative and Paul had no way of altering it. And Chaffee had agreed with him. He'd made his ruling over

220

Nicoletti's vociferous objections. The defence could proceed to impeach the witness.

Even so, Paul was troubled. He took no pleasure in what had to be done. To help one man, you sometimes injured another. Moore, he knew, had no inkling of what was in store for him when the trial resumed.

Paul was still exploring alternatives when the bell rang.

Dru appeared.

'Dad is here with Ernie Stoufer.'

He gestured wearily. He could guess what ailed them. There were no amenities, no handshakes.

'What are you drinking?' Paul asked.

'This is not a social visit.' Grimly, Sheridan closed the door behind Dru. He folded his arms. 'Why are you doing this to Alex Moore? What will you gain by spiralling off into his private life?'

'Not what I will gain, Lucas. What Ken will gain.'

'All right. So you've made your point. The jury is convinced. You can afford to drop it.'

'As soon as Moore makes the necessary admission.'

'Do you have to crucify him? He's not a murderer.'

'Are you sure?'

'Yes, damn it.'

'Then he's got nothing to worry about. But I have. I'm still worried about Ken.'

'And you think I'm not?'

'I know you are. But his defence is my responsibility. He's entitled to the best I can give him. Every other consideration goes out the window.'

Stoufer pushed forward.

'Do you know why I'm here, Slater?'

'Certainly. You're here because you panicked. You're scared silly your name will come up at the trial tomorrow. You appealed to Lucas. You want him to gag me.'

'Good God, man, for a dubious advantage at best, would you brand me in public as an adulterer?'

'Whatever you are, I had nothing to do with it. I'm willing to let the facts speak for themselves.'

It wrung a groan out of Stoufer's throat. 'Lucas, don't let him do this to me.'

Sheridan was suddenly very quiet and very grave. 'Paul, I'm asking you to reconsider, to be reasonable. You gain nothing by hurting Stoufer. There must be some other way.'

And what, Paul thought bitterly, is the size of your annual retainer from Stoufer, Wingate & Company? He was instantly ashamed. It was cynical, unjust, a disservice to the old man. He walked to the window and came back.

'This is not the first time I've tried to make my position clear, Lucas. I am not ruthless, not without compassion. But I don't pull punches when someone's liberty is at stake. There are ramifications in this case that you know nothing about. On the other hand, you should know that I had no intention of bringing Stoufer into it unless Moore left me no alternative. I'll make this concession—if it's at all possible to force an admission from Moore that he knew Dolly was dumping him because she had another lover, then Stoufer is home free. I don't need his name and I won't mention it.'

'I guarantee you'll have your admission.'

'How can you do that?' Stoufer demanded.

'I believe I still have some influence with Alex Moore.'

Stoufer turned back at the door. 'Listen, Slater. I make a far better ally than enemy.'

'That's unnecessary,' Sheridan snapped. 'And foolish.'

'Forget it,' Paul said. 'He's overwrought.'

Alex Moore struggled out of a barbiturate sleep and fumbled in the dark for the clamouring telephone. His brain was sluggish, groping for orientation.

Lucas Sheridan's voice brought him awake.

'Alex? I've been trying to reach you for hours. I gave up about eleven.'

'I was out, Lucas. What time is it?'

'Seven. You're due in court at nine-thirty. I'll be there in half an hour. I want to talk to you.'

Moore shaved and dressed quickly. His eyes were grainy and tired. He had walked the streets till midnight. At three a.m.

he'd taken a pill, and still felt its effects. He was finishing his second cup of coffee when Sheridan arrived.

'You look like hell, Alex.'

'I feel like hell. I need another couple of hours' sleep.'

'Sorry. I couldn't wait any longer.' Sheridan sat without removing his coat. 'Is Slater on the right track, Alex? Did you know that Dolly Wayne had another man on a string?'

'I suspected, but I wasn't sure. What troubles me is that Slater knows more than I do.'

'Burroughs.'

Moore flattened a palm against his chest. 'You mean Burroughs was investigating me?'

'He was investigating Dolly and he passed the information to Paul.'

'Then he knows who the man is.'

'He knows.'

'Do you know, Lucas?'

'What difference does it make, Alex? Dolly is gone.'

'I'd like an answer.'

'What will you do, challenge the man to a duel? Forget it, Alex. It's over. Done. It was bound to happen sooner or later. Dolly was about as exclusive as a politician's handshake.'

'I warn you, Lucas——'

'Look at the facts, damn it. She was tumbling you while Brian Wirth was still alive. And then she took this new one on too. And God only knows how many others when she was struggling for recognition. Be sensible. She never guaranteed you an exclusive.'

'Enough!' Moore turned away, trembling. After a moment he said, 'What did you want to see me about?'

'Dolly's friend was a Porterfield client. Linking their names would serve no purpose. If you force Slater to bring him into it, it would hurt the man's family and his business. A pointless waste. We owe him an obligation to——'

'I owe him nothing.'

'You owe something to the firm.'

'What about *my* name?'

'Alex, you're in it already. Nobody can do anything about

223

that. It was just plain lousy luck that you had to call her that day and the maid overheard.'

'This man, maybe he had something to do with Dolly's death.'

'Impossible. Forget it.'

Moore started to burn. 'Why not tell your son-in-law to forget it. Tell him to drop the whole damn subject. There's an idea for you, Lucas. Talk to him about it.'

'I have. He's made a concession. If you admit that Dolly was brushing you off, he won't identify the other man.'

'Are you asking me to make myself a suspect?'

'Don't be a fool. It would presume jealousy, not homicide.'

'Homicide is precisely what Slater *is* suggesting.'

'No. He's creating reasonable doubt.'

'At my expense.'

'Nonsense. You were nowhere near Dolly when it happened.'

'Are you sure?'

Sheridan was startled. 'This is nothing to joke about, Alex. And we're running out of time. I'm not asking you to go beyond that one minor admission. Slater is going to prove it anyway.'

'Then what have I got to gain?'

'For one thing, my gratitude. For another, if you compel Slater to establish it against your denials, it looks as if you had something to conceal. In exchange, all you get is disclosure of the man's name. Information that will fester and destroy your peace of mind.'

Moore slumped. The fight went out of him.

'All right,' he said tonelessly. 'Let's make Slater's job easy. He's got his admission.'

Sheridan stood. His hand chunked solidly against Moore's shoulder.

'You won't be sorry, Alex. I think we have time for a cup of coffee before court.'

It seemed anticlimactic.

When Paul Slater rose to confront Alex Moore, the court-room had subsided into a hushed expectancy. The working press felt a showdown was imminent. Instead, Moore made a conciliatory gesture.

'I may have given the wrong impression yesterday, Mr Slater. The fact is, I was reluctant to admit even to myself any possibility that Miss Wayne had developed a new attachment. Last night I had an opportunity to review my feeling. I must admit now that unconsciously I had drawn certain inferences. There had been a deterioration in our relationship and I attributed it to another man.'

Now it was on the record.

Paul nodded. 'You stated yesterday that you had asked Miss Wayne to marry you.'

'Yes.'

'I take it then you were in love with her. So this knowledge that you had a rival must have come as a shock.'

'I was not happy about it.'

'You were in fact crushed, heartsick, isn't that so?'

'I will not deny it.'

'Were you also enraged?'

Moore shrugged. 'People grow apart, Mr Slater. I never felt that I had a right to stand in her way.'

'Even though you had sacrificed your whole future for her?'

Moore had a sinking premonition. 'I'm afraid I don't follow you.'

'Well, now, isn't it a fact that you made yourself vulnerable, that you jeopardized your profession, that you practised fraud and deceit——'

Nicoletti stormed to his feet. 'Objection. Again counsel is making unfounded accusations. Highly prejudicial. There is absolutely nothing on the record that——'

'Yes,' Chaffee said curtly. 'The Court has been extremely lenient, Mr Slater. Such statements are inflammatory and improper.'

'I apologize, Your Honour. If the Court permits, I will lay a proper foundation.' He swung back towards Moore, whose face was swept with apprehension. 'You testified yesterday that you were the associate at Porterfield, Baker & Sheridan who handled Brian Wirth's legal affairs, did you not?'

'That is true.'

'Do you recall that he appeared at your office on March fourteenth, exactly two weeks before his admission to the hospital as a terminal case?'

'I do not remember the exact date.'

'If his name appeared in your appointment book for that date, would you consider it accurate?'

'Yes.'

'At any rate, he did appear at your office not long before he died?'

'Yes.'

'A professional visit, was it not?'

'It was.'

'For what purpose?'

'Objection,' Nicoletti said. 'Immaterial, irrelevant, and incompetent.'

Chaffee was still permitting a wide latitude. 'Overruled.'

'A further objection, Your Honour, on the grounds that conversations between attorney and client are privileged.'

'Withdraw the question,' Paul said. 'Without going into the context of your discussion with Mr Wirth, did he not ask you to draft a new will?'

Nicoletti exploded. 'The privilege still applies.'

'Your Honour,' Paul said, 'the rulings on this question are explicit. Whenever a client intends his communication to be disclosed to a third person, he waives the privilege.'

Nicoletti's voice was a growl of exasperation. 'What third person?'

Paul smiled sweetly. 'Did Wirth expect his lawyer to sit down at a typewriter and tap out the will with two fingers? He knew it would be dictated to a secretary and then typed by her. And he knew that ultimately it would become a matter of record when filed for probate.'

'Amazing!' Nicoletti flung his arms wide. 'Counsel is creating a whole new body of precedent to suit his needs.'

'The prosecution knows better, Your Honour. Mr Nicoletti exposes the poverty of his position by substituting mockery for logic. I cite Doheny v. Lacy, 168 N.Y. 213. If necessary we will establish the will and its provisions by calling the typist. Certainly Mr Nicoletti does not contend that any privilege extends to her.'

Chaffee's head had been bobbing back and forth between them. Now he rapped his gavel sharply. 'That is quite enough, gentlemen. Mr Slater's point is well taken. I am going to over-rule the People's objection.'

'But where is the materiality?'

'I ask the Court to take it subject to connection,' Paul said.

'And if we keep opening collateral matters, this trial will last into the next millennium.'

'The Court has made its ruling, Mr Nicoletti. You may have your exception.'

Moore had listened to the exchange with quickly rising alarm. The judge had granted Slater a licence to open the whole can of worms and his mind frantically sought a loophole. That Fern McFee, a traitor in his own office. And Don Baker, that damned dimwitted Judas. He felt trapped.

'Brian Wirth asked you to draft a new will, did he not?'

'Yes.'

'In what other way did he effect revocation of his old will?'

'It was in our files. It was brought in and destroyed in his presence.'

'So pursuant to his instructions a new will was drawn and signed that same afternoon, was it not?'

'Yes.'

'Who were the attesting witnesses?'

'Mr Donald Baker and myself.'

'Did this will call for a drastic change in the distribution of Brian Wirth's estate?'

'It did.'

'No bequest at all to Dolly Wayne, was there?'

Moore sat brooding, milking his thumb. 'That is true.'

'He was able to cut her off completely, was he not, because there had been an ante-nuptial agreement?'

'Yes.'

'Nevertheless, after his death she was appointed adminis-tratrix and inherited the bulk of his estate?'

227

'Yes.'

'Will you explain to the court how that could have happened?'

Moore's face was blank. 'Mr Wirth had revoked that last will too.'

Neat, Paul thought grimly. But what else could the man say? 'Who had final possession of that last will?'

'It was in the files of Porterfield, Baker & Sheridan.'

'And at the time of revocation, where was Mr Wirth?'

'In Manhattan General.'

'How, exactly, did he give you these instructions?'

'He called me on the telephone and told me that he had changed his mind again. He instructed me to tear up the will.'

'Do you have any confirmation of this call?'

'Not unless someone had been eavesdropping on the line. Why would I need confirmation?'

'Because destruction of that will enabled a woman you hoped would be your wife to inherit over a million dollars.'

Moore was a splendid actor. He glared, gripping the arms of the witness chair, his face mottled with anger. He said evenly, 'No one has ever doubted my word in the past.'

'The future may not be so gullible. You knew of course that Wirth was extremely ill?'

'Yes.'

'A terminal case, in fact?'

'I suspected as much.'

'Did you advise him that it would be unwise for a man of his substance to die intestate?'

'Naturally.' Moore was still simmering. 'He said that he would be in touch with me on the following day.'

'And did you hear from him again?'

'No, sir. He died during the night.'

'To be precise, at two a.m. on Thursday, April fifth.'

'I will take your word for it. I have not seen the hospital records.'

Paul knew that he had him now. The trap had been sprung. Somehow Burroughs had managed to acquire a xeroxed copy of the appropriate page from Alex Moore's appointment book.

But there was no pleasure in the knowledge. He knew that his father-in-law was in the first row, listening, and he had forced himself not to think of the effect on Lucas Sheridan of what he was about to do. The effect on Alex Moore, of course, would be shattering.

He took a paper from the defence table and handed it to Moore. 'Do you recognize this?'

Moore frowned. 'It appears to be a copy of a page from my appointment book.'

'It is. Please notice the single entry for the morning of Wednesday, April fourth. What does it indicate?'

'That I was in court that morning.'

'And when did you return to your office?'

'Sometime in the early afternoon.'

'No doubt in your mind about that?'

'Absolutely none.'

'If it please the Court, the original of this page is not in our possession, nor is it available to us. I offer the copy in evidence.'

'Let me see that,' Nicoletti said, advancing. He was puzzled as to its purpose, but had no objection.

'The Clerk will mark it,' Chaffee said.

'You say you returned to your office in the afternoon. So it must have been then that you received the call from Brian Wirth instructing you to destroy his will.'

'That is correct.'

'The will had left the bulk of his estate to various charities, did it not?'

'It did.'

'So that destroying it was a complete reversal. The charities got nothing; Dolly Wayne got everything.'

'It had that effect, yes.'

'A lucky windfall, wouldn't you say, this sudden inheritance through intestacy, at a time when her personal finances were in a deplorable state because of severe stock market losses?'

'It would seem so.'

'Is the name Fern McFee familiar to you?'

'She was one of my secretaries.'

'Is she still employed by Porterfield, Baker & Sheridan?'

'No. She left to get married.'

'Have you examined the Wirth file recently?'

'No, sir. It became inactive when the estate was closed.'

'Do you recall seeing a letter from a company calling itself National Appraisers offering to evaluate certain assets of the estate?'

'I believe so.'

'Would it surprise you to learn that the letter arrived within forty-eight hours after Brian Wirth died and that Miss McFee herself put it in the file?'

Moore knew what was coming. He seemed visibly to shrink, eyes hanging almost mesmerized on Paul, waiting numbly for the blow to fall.

'If Miss McFee testifies that she saw Brian Wirth's will in the file at that time, clearly indicating that it was still in existence *after* he died, what would you say?'

Moore felt as if he'd been clubbed. The room swam and he felt faint. His voice was barely audible. 'I—I would say she was mistaken.'

Paul swung back to the defence table for another document. 'I showed you a copy of Brian Wirth's hospital chart for that last day of his life when you claim he called you on the telephone.'

'Objection.'

'I am not offering it in evidence at this time, Your Honour. It will be properly identified when the defence makes its presentation.'

'Objection overruled.'

Moore took the paper and glanced at it. The blood drained from his face. He looked ill.

Paul said, 'The record shows that Wirth fell into a coma at twelve o'clock noon and never regained consciousness. Will you explain how a man in that condition made a telephone call later in the day, instructing you to destroy his will?'

No sound. Moore sat motionless, his eyes turned inward.

'I am suggesting,' Paul said, 'that you destroyed both the will and the ante-nuptial agreement of your own volition in order to protect Dolly Wayne's inheritance. And that after you

committed this breach of trust you learned that Miss Wayne
was abandoning you for another man.'

Moore's eyes were lost and bankrupt.

'No comment, Mr Moore? Then I have no further questions.'

There was a moment of silence.

Chaffee smothered a cough. 'You may step down. Please
call your next witness, Mr Nicoletti.'

Paul saw Lucas Sheridan rise and follow Alex Moore from
the courtroom.

CHAPTER SEVEN

'NO, SIR,' Nicoletti said to District Attorney Philip Lohman. 'I don't buy it. Not one syllable. Alex Moore may or may not have pulled some damn-fool shenanigans with Brian Wirth's will. My guess is that he did. But I don't believe for an instant that it goes beyond that. The man is not a murderer.'

'He stuck his neck out for the lady, John. He put his career on the line and she discarded him like an old hat.'

'If that motivates homicide, you'd have to increase the trial staff by a hundred thousand men in this county alone.'

'How in hell did Slater get this information?'

'He has an investigator working on it. Man named Burroughs.'

'One investigator? How many men have we got?'

'It was luck.'

'You have to admit he turned in some fancy footwork in court this morning.'

Nicoletti was stubborn. 'My money is still on the boy. I won't be stampeded. Slater's trying to raise a reasonable doubt.'

'And succeeding.'

'Because of Chaffee. They ought to kick his stupid ass off the bench. Half that testimony should have been excluded.'

'I'm not so sure, John.' Lohman pulled at his chin. 'You think old Lucas Sheridan knew what Slater was up to?'

'Not from his expression. There was murder in his eyes.'

'Directed at whom, Moore or Slater?'

'Both of them.'

Lohman shook his head. 'My God, a partner in Porterfield, Baker & Sheridan debauching a sick client's wife and violating a fiduciary trust. I wouldn't even take it to the grand jury if

232

Sheridan cancelled them both. You know something, I have to hand it to that Slater. It took guts, considering the old man is his father-in-law. There could be a family rupture.'

'It's Moore's career against the boy's neck. How would you choose?'

'I'm glad I don't have to make that decision. The question is, what are we going to do about Moore?'

'We leave him to the Bar Association. They'll chop him good. And we go right on with our case.'

'Slater has given the rug a hell of a jerk.'

'Sure, but we're still on our feet and we never expected easy sailing. We're not going to lose this one.'

Lohman smiled. 'Okay, John. Go back to work.'

In the spare bedroom of her grandparents' apartment, Peggy Wayne sat at a window, staring out, her mind failing to register any of the night-time sights. She was not able to understand why they kept her out of the courtroom. Something about testifying for the State. They were out of their minds if they expected her to say a single word that might harm Ken.

Tear tracks marked her face. She made no effort to staunch the flow. In a way, it was really all her fault. The doctor in Poughkeepsie had given her precise instructions. Take the pill on the fifth day of her period and continue for twenty-one consecutive days. And then, after the onset of her cycle, the count begins again. He had stressed the importance of accuracy. And if she had not been so careless her mother would have had no reason to drag Ken in from Cambridge. He would not have driven to New York. He would not have been in her mother's apartment on that ghastly Wednesday.

She remembered the two days she had missed. It was a Friday and Ken had called from school, saying he was going out to Sands Point for the weekend and could she meet him there. They had been apart for several weeks and she hungered for the sight of him. She had tossed her clothes hastily into a bag and quite simply had forgotten the pills.

She had meant to warn Ken. But that night in the boathouse when he reached for her they were both so eager and ready that

233

she had never given the pills a second thought. They had been waiting all day for a chance to be alone, secret glances fired with promise. There were times when she didn't think she'd be able to wait. All her senses were tuned and aching with need.

The memory surfaced, unsolicited. Alone at last in their own special blinding world, the boathouse tilting crazily, Ken hammering her against the canvas mat while she leaped and bucked beneath him, her breath a whoofing furnace, the electricity pulsing so deliciously along every fibre of her body. He was so tall, so hard-muscled and oh God, how she wanted him even now. . . .

She choked back a sob, feeling the rivulets running like hot mercury from her eyes. What was wrong with her? Was she losing her mind or something? Mother gone for ever and all she could think about was making it with Ken.

She put a hand down, cupping herself, thinking about the abortion. Her grandparents had talked her into it. She had wanted to ask Ken, but she had not been able to see him, so she had submitted. She couldn't really think clearly for herself these days. And afterwards, for the first twenty-four hours anyway, she was certain she would never let another man touch her. But that had passed quickly enough.

Perhaps she should have told her grandparents about the trip to Maryland.

It had been Ken's idea and she had leaped at it enthusiastically. They had driven down and found that little old pink-and-white justice of the peace. And after he had performed the ceremony he'd bussed her so soundly she had carried a welt on her cheek most of the next day. Ken didn't want anyone to know they were married. He insisted on keeping it a secret because his uncle was so emphatic about finishing school first.

Now she was uncertain. It was silly and maybe dangerous to keep secrets from one's lawyer. She really should tell Paul Slater. Indecision suddenly crystallized into resolve. She hurried to the shelf where she kept the box with her papers and letters. She found the marriage certificate and ran for her coat. . . .

*   *   *

The phone had been ringing intermittently all evening. Alex Moore heard it through an obliterating fog of alcohol. He did not think there was enough liquor in the world to blank out his consciousness completely.

He had come straight home to the bottle after leaving court. He vaguely remembered that Lucas had caught up with him in the street, but he had pulled his arm loose and broken away. He was in no mood to face the senior partner and the inevitable recriminations. Over and over again his brain kept repeating a bitter litany of resentment and self-pity.

How had it happened? What had brought him to the brink of disaster? An emotional bondage; nothing more, nothing less. Moving him to act on impulse, ignoring the hazards.

He knew that he had become aware of a troubling element in his relationship with Dolly. She had made herself increasingly unavailable. But he had refused to allow anything to break his faith in the ultimate success of his courtship. He had only to prove his devotion. He knew of Dolly's obsession with money. Perhaps if he could insure her financial security and somehow let her know what he had done. . . .

He remembered seeing her at Brian's funeral. Ostensibly she was in mourning. The public saw a stricken widow, but it was simply one more performance in Dolly's long repertoire of roles. Because at the time that Brian Wirth was gasping *in extremis* on his final voyage to eternity, Dolly was also gasping on a more turbulent voyage to her own little death. *La petite mort*, the French called it. Moore knew this as a memorable fact because just about that precise moment he had been locked in the frenzied vice of her thighs while she keened his name in the paroxysms that racked them both.

It was in the lingering afterglow of that episode that he had violated his trust. The taste of ashes had been in his throat because one does not alter the patterns of a lifetime without some reaction.

The same taste was there now. The anticipated appreciation had never materialized. In the months following Wirth's death the breach between them had widened. He knew now that if she had ever loved him at all, it was as an instrument of her

235

own pleasure. She had grown cold and remote, always finding some excuse to avoid seeing him. The thought that he was losing her sickened him to the point of nausea.

His thoughts turned inward at a bleak and empty future. For most of his adult life he had found sublimation in work. It had absorbed most of his energies. On those occasions when glandular urgencies made ungovernable demands he had called a number and they had sent him a discreet young woman. She was invariably well groomed, an expert technician who would accommodate him with all the artful subterfuges and sound effects of her profession. A business arrangement, lacking involvement, accompanied with the sterile precision of a surgical procedure. He would have the large bills folded in his palm and discreetly tendered as he showed her to the door.

It had been like that as long as he could remember—until the affair with Dolly Wayne.

Ironically enough, it was Brian Wirth who brought them together. Moore had been a weekend guest of the Sheridans at Sands Point when Wirth phoned from the adjoining estate. He had received an urgent call requiring his presence back in Manhattan. He wanted to draft Moore as escort for Dolly that evening. So Moore had accompanied her to a nearby dinner party and somehow the spark was struck.

She had taken him to bed that night and the experience introduced him to a new and vital ingredient, an emotional involvement that left him in a dreamlike trance, moonstruck as a schoolboy.

Every subsequent meeting had been planned with care and discretion. Except for that one lapse when Don Baker had returned unexpectedly to find them *in flagrante delicto* at his apartment. But Baker was easy to control and he'd been sworn to secrecy.

Moore was certain that Brian Wirth had never mistrusted him. Even when he came to the office to change his will, Wirth's suspicions of infidelity had been aroused by Dolly's newer liaison.

He recalled Wirth's bitter comment, 'She's shut me out,

Alex. Won't let me touch her. And I know Dolly; she needs it the way she needs oxygen. She's got a stud hidden away somewhere. I saw it in her eyes again last night when she came home, the sated look, the way she walks. Oh, she's getting it, friend, she's getting plenty, but not from me. So I'm cutting her off, cold cock, not one red cent. Now let's tear up that old will.'

He was referring to a will he'd made after the death of his only surviving son from a previous marriage, leaving his estate to Dolly despite an ante-nuptial agreement.

Moore had been shocked by Wirth's appearance. He was wasted and ravaged, the mark of death already on him. A racking cough had left him moist and trembling.

'All those doctors, Alex, the silly bastards. Soft-soaping me, assuring me I'll recover. One look in the mirror tells me more than all their goddamned diagnostic machines put together. They talk about this marvellous mechanism of a human body. Bullshit, Alex! DuPont has developed better material out of a test tube. God did a piss-poor job. Six days to create this ball of mud and the lice that inhabit it. Why in hell didn't He take His time and some pride in His craft?'

The phone rang again. Lucas, probably. Moore suffered a sharp twinge of conscience. After all the years of trust and confidence, he had betrayed the firm, blackened its name. Lucas would demand his resignation. And the Appellate Division would finish him in the profession. One mindless, bonehead error was all it took to cancel the long, hard years.

Finished. Shorn of dignity, stripped of self-respect, ego mutilated, disavowed by his colleagues. And Dolly for ever gone.

Alex Moore groaned. The glass slipped from his fingers. He rose unsteadily, walking with the stilted movements of a man on artificial legs. He stepped out on the small terrace overlooking the East River. Traffic lights glittered far below. He threw one leg over the rail, then the other, and hung there for a brief despairing moment, then he let go. . . .

CHAPTER EIGHT

PAUL'S MOOD often swung between extremes during a trial
—from elation to gloom. The cross-examination of Moore had
released considerable adrenalin. Now the reaction had set in
and his spirits were at low ebb. All through dinner Dru had
been remote and uncommunicative.

All right, he thought, she doesn't like what happened in
court this morning, and she doesn't trust herself to talk about
it. It saves me the job of justifying myself. I don't like what
happened either.

Half an hour later Abe Barish arrived with the day's
transcript. They retired to the study. Barish, too, seemed
detached and abstracted.

'Damn it!' Paul said irritably. 'What's eating you? Don't
just sit there brooding at me. Spit it out.'

'Ah, Paul, you didn't leave Moore very much, did you?'

'Moore didn't leave himself much. And any comment I have
about his actions will make me sound sanctimonious. But when
a man takes a calculated risk, he accepts the possibility of being
caught. So knock it off.'

Barish sighed. 'Dru looked unhappy.'

'Tonight she speaks only in monosyllables.'

'Have you heard from her father?'

'Not yet.'

'So he must have hit the ceiling and he has to come down
first.'

'Lucas has no monopoly on tranquillity. He'll learn to live
with it.'

'Such irreverence towards our aristocrat?'

'The only aristocracy I recognize is the aristocracy of
achievement.'

238

'Ah, he has achieved, most formidably. Prominent attorney, adviser to people in high places.'

'Abe, when you join a man's family, the perspective narrows.'

'You have detected flaws?'

'In him, in myself, in everyone I ever met.'

Barish smiled ruefully. 'Me, too?'

'Give me time. I'll find something.'

'Such cynicism. Disenchantment with God's masterwork?'

'In spades, my friend.'

'So much truculence today, Professor. I thought this afternoon in the men's room you were really going to tag that young journalist. You had mayhem in your eyes.'

Paul made a face. After Judge Chaffee called a ten-minute recess Paul had repaired with Barish to the washroom. They were discussing a touchy point of testimony when the door opened for a newcomer. Paul recognized him as a reporter who had been irritatingly persistent and nosy ever since the beginning of the trial. Instantly he barred the man's path. 'Where do you think you're going?'

'To one of the urinals, third from left.'

'Not now. Later.'

'What the hell are you talking about, Counsellor? This is a public facility. If you think I'm here to eavesdrop, then find some other place for a conference. Move it.'

Barish saw the danger signals and he quickly bulled his way between them, making placatory gestures. 'Easy, gentlemen, easy. The man is right, Paul. So please let us step outside.'

In the corridor, Paul cooled instantly. 'Thanks, Abe. I came within an inch of hanging one on that joker, and all the poor bastard may have wanted was to empty his bladder.'

'You're not sore at him. You're sore at yourself.'

'If you're trying to tell me something, Abe, save it. Let's get back to the courtroom.'

He had completely forgotten the incident. He said now, 'A lot of things make me angry. Who started all this, anyway?'

'I did.' There was a humorous quirk to Barish's mouth. 'I find your little aphorisms amusing.'

'But without truth.'

'With enough truth to be disturbing.' He opened the trial transcript. 'Enough. I want to show you something I find most interesting.'

They heard the doorbell ring. A moment later Dru appeared. 'You have a visitor,' she said, nodding at Peggy Wayne.

Paul saw that she had lost weight. 'Come in, Peg.'

'I have something to tell you,' she said, 'and I'd like Dru to stay.'

He nodded. Dru remained at the door. Barish clamped the pipe between his teeth.

Peggy stood for a moment, twisting her fingers. 'I guess you know, I had an abortion. It was my grandparents' idea.'

'You didn't really want an illegitimate child, did you?' Paul asked.

'That's just the point. The baby would have been legitimate.'

He was instantly alert. 'What do you mean?'

'Ken and I are married. It's almost eight months now.'

Dru's eyes widened. Paul exchanged a quick look with Abe Barish.

'Tell us about it,' Paul said.

'There isn't much to tell. We drove down to Maryland one weekend and found a justice of the peace in a small town, and his wife acted as a witness.'

'Do you have the marriage certificate?'

She took it out of her purse and handed it to him.

'Was it Ken's idea to keep it a secret?'

'Yes. Because of his uncle. Ken promised he'd finish school before he made any other plans.'

'Why didn't he tell your mother when she found out you were pregnant?'

'For the same reason, I guess. He was afraid his uncle would be angry.'

'Why are you telling us now?' Abe Barish asked gently.

'I had to tell someone. I just couldn't accept all the responsibility myself. And I thought it was silly to keep secrets from our lawyer, especially if there was some way it could help Ken.'

'You did the wise thing,' Paul said. 'It isn't going to hurt our case one bit.' He looked up. 'Dru, could we have some coffee?'

'An excellent suggestion,' Barish said.

The doorbell rang again and Dru went to get it. They heard voices. A moment later Lucas Holmes Sheridan stood at the threshold, white lines framing his grimly set jaw, his eyes cutting into Paul like twin scalpels.

'I hope to Christ you're satisfied.' The words were thorns in his throat. 'You finished Alex Moore—finished him for ever.'

'What are you talking about, Lucas?'

'He's dead. He killed himself less than twenty minutes ago. . . .'

City editors on two major dailies held up the morning edition while they changed the front-page make-up. Prominent space was allotted to the suicide of Alex Moore on the heels of what they termed a slashing cross-examination by defence counsel. The *News* had assigned a feature writer to the story and this journalist speculated on possible motives for Moore's act of self-destruction. An unendurable fall from grace, perhaps, or disbarment, and/or alarm at being implicated in the heinous crime of Dolly Wayne's death.

John Nicoletti had reached similar conclusions. And he was worried about their effect on the jury. He did not want them speculating on Moore's whereabouts at the time of the murder. Weighing his options, he decided to take countermeasures. He dialled a number and got through to District Attorney Philip Lohman, who was entertaining guests at home. He heard background noises of glassware and laughing.

'Let me take this on another line, John.' A moment later Lohman's voice was free of interference. 'Just heard about Alex Moore and I don't like the sound of it. You have something in mind?'

'I'm not going to let this sink us, Chief. I'd like authorization for a warrant to search Moore's office.'

Lohman exhaled. 'Lucas Sheridan will blow a gasket.'

'Lucas Sheridan doesn't deliver votes. We can leave him out of our deliberations.'

'What do you hope to find?'

'At the very least I'd like a look at his appointment book. Let's see how he spent his time during that critical afternoon. If Slater can use the appointment book, so can we.'

'All right. Judge Barrow is here now. If you draw the papers fast, you can still catch him for signature. What about your supporting affidavit?'

'We're investigating. We don't know whether Moore jumped or was pushed.'

'Good enough.' Lohman chuckled. 'I'll break open a bottle of Special Reserve and that ought to hold the judge until you get here.'

By midnight Nicoletti felt he had a lock on it. The night superintendent at the Broad Street building let two investigators into the offices of Porterfield, Baker & Sheridan. They found Moore's appointment book and it apparently cleared him of any involvement in Dolly Wayne's death. Moore had pencilled in a luncheon appointment with Donald Baker for twelve-thirty on the afternoon of October 18. It was between that time and one o'clock that Billy Clark had heard the noise of a struggle.

A subpoena was issued for Donald Baker's appearance in court and the production of his own scheduled appointments on that day.

Paul read the morning papers on his way to court. The implication that his cross-examination had broken Moore's will to live was deeply disturbing. The man's self-destruction was something he had not anticipated. Everything he knew about the man had led him to believe that Moore had enough starch to weather any storm. If Paul had been able to foresee the consequences, perhaps he would have acted differently. He told himself that Moore's act was caused more by desolation over the loss of Dolly Wayne than by exposure of his misconduct.

And yet, as he'd tried to explain to Lucas, it always came down to a matter of personal judgement. You can't ask anyone to share that responsibility. He had weighed all the factors and balanced them against his job as defence counsel. Must he condemn himself now for lack of omniscience?

Alone with Dru, he had sensed her constraint, the ambivalence of her position. He had asked quietly, 'Do you think I'm responsible for what happened?'

'Do you think you are, Paul?'

'He lost his woman; I had nothing to do with that. He lost his honour; the result of his own actions. I merely brought it to light.'

'And almost broke Dad's heart at the same time.'

'When you try to predict everything in advance, you often wind up doing nothing.'

'Is that so bad? It might have kept Napoleon on Elba and Hitler's panzers in his own back yard.'

Had his mood been different, he might have laughed.

The People's case was just about completed. Only a few loose ends remained and Nicoletti was prepared to clear them up this morning. Having excluded Peggy Wayne from the proceedings under the Rule, he decided now on a token appearance. His treatment as he guided her through the various relationships was courteous and considerate.

'Now, Peggy, I would like to take you back to the week commencing October sixteenth. I know the recollection may be painful and for that I apologize.'

She nodded and made no comment.

'You had been home from school that weekend?'

'Yes.'

'And you had not been feeling well?'

'Objection,' Paul said. 'He's leading the witness.'

Nicoletti rephrased. 'How was your health?'

'I was suffering from dizzy spells and nausea.'

'Did your mother ask you to see a doctor?'

'Yes. Dr Truscott.'

'Who arranged the appointment?'

'My mother.'

'And did you see the doctor?'

'Yes.'

243

'He examined you?'

'Yes.'

'He told you his diagnosis?'

She answered simply and frankly. 'He said I was pregnant.'

'Did he ask you to name the father?'

'Dr Truscott was very understanding. He did not pry.'

'Would you identify the father for us now?'

'It's no secret, I guess. Ken Sheridan is the only man who ever touched me.' Her eyes fell on the defendant and she smiled.

Paul applauded silently, pleased at the way she was acquitting herself. Tragedy had apparently endowed her with a new maturity and composure.

'Did you know that Dr Truscott intended to inform your mother?'

'I expected he would.'

'Is that why you went straight back to school?'

'Yes.'

'What reaction did you expect?'

'Objection,' Paul said.

'Sustained.'

'Are you still pregnant?'

'No, sir.'

Nicoletti cocked an eyebrow. 'Would you elaborate on that?'

'I had an abortion.'

'No further questions.' Nicoletti returned to the prosecution table, satisfied that for the Catholics on the jury her admission might tarnish the initial favourable impression.

Paul stood. 'This abortion, Peggy, who suggested it?'

'My grandparents.'

'Did you submit willingly?'

'I was terribly confused, Mr Slater, and worried about what they were trying to do to Ken.'

'Did the issue of illegitimacy play any role in your decision?'

'No, sir.'

'Will you tell the jury why?'

'Because Ken and I were already married.'

Nicoletti sat erect, frowning.

'Will you identify this paper?'

'It's a marriage certificate.'

'Where did the ceremony take place?'

'In Maryland.'

'How long ago?'

'More than eight months.'

'Before the foetus was conceived?'

'Yes, sir.'

'I offer it in evidence.' He turned and proffered it to Nicoletti, who scanned it briefly and nodded.

'Why didn't you tell your mother?'

'Because Ken asked me to keep it a secret. He'd promised his uncle to finish school first.'

'Thank you, Peggy.' Paul sat down.

'Mr Nicoletti?' Chaffee inquired.

The prosecutor shook his head.

'Call your next witness.'

It was a totally new experience for Donald Baker. He sat nervously on the edge of the witness chair, his round face bathed in moisture.

'You are a member of the firm of Porterfield, Baker & Sheridan?' Nicoletti asked.

'That is correct.'

'According to testimony already received, Alexander Moore was also a member of that firm.'

'Yes, sir, he was.'

'The subpoena commanding your appearance in court also required you to produce your personal appointment book. Do you have it with you?'

'Yes, sir.'

'Would you consult it now, referring specifically to the date of October eighteenth, and tell us if you had a luncheon engagement for that day?'

Baker flipped the pages. 'Yes, I did.'

'With whom?'

'Your Honour,' Paul broke in, 'I don't see the materiality of Mr Baker's feeding schedule, nor where all this is taking us.'

'Oh, he sees it, all right,' Nicoletti said acidly. 'And its materiality will emerge quickly enough.'

'I will allow it subject to connection.' Chaffee nodded at the witness. 'You may answer, Mr Baker.'

'On October eighteenth I had lunch with Alex Moore.'

'At what time?'

'To the best of my recollection we left the office about noon.'

'Where did you dine?'

'At the Bankers' Club.'

'And how long were you there?'

'At least an hour and a half. We ran into a client and he joined us.'

'Do you remember the name of the client?'

'Yes, sir. Mr Ernest Stoufer.'

'So you did not leave the restaurant until after one-thirty.'

'That would be an accurate appraisal.'

'Thank you, Mr Baker.' Nicoletti now had ammunition for his summation. He surrendered the witness with a wave of his hand.

Paul rose, his brain churning. Had he destroyed Moore for no reason at all? Had it been a monumental blunder?

'Did Mr Moore return to the office with you after lunch that day?'

Baker frowned. 'I don't really remember. I have a vague idea that he had another appointment.'

'Do you know what happened to Mr Moore last night?'

Nicoletti sprang instantly to his feet. 'Permission to approach the bench.'

'Yes, gentlemen, if you please.'

At the sidebar, out of earshot, Nicoletti said urgently, 'What happened to Moore is no part of this case. The Court deliberately sequestered the jury to keep them free of news media. Extraneous information of this kind can only serve to further confuse already complicated issues.'

'Your Honour,' Paul said, 'I don't see how we can keep it out.'

'I strongly suggest you try, Counsellor. Are you making an objection, Mr Nicoletti?'

'Most strenuously.'

'Sustained.'

Paul returned to the witness. 'Was lunching with Mr Moore a frequent occurrence?'

'Not frequent. We lunched occasionally.'

'Several times a month?'

'I don't think that often.'

'Several times a year?'

'Perhaps.'

'Would you examine your appointment book and show us one other occasion during the year when you did lunch with Mr Moore?'

Baker shifted uncomfortably. 'I—I'm afraid that may have been the only time.'

'Then it would be safe to assume, would it not, that this was a novel, in fact, an unprecedented event?'

Baker mopped his forehead. 'I—I suppose so.'

'Who extended the invitation?'

'He did.'

'Can you account for its purpose?'

'He said he wanted to talk to me.'

'On any special matter?'

'Well, it was about some litigation we had at the office.'

'Had he ever consulted with you on legal matters before?'

'Once or twice.'

'Once or twice in all the years of your association?'

Baker swallowed. 'That is correct.'

'Are you the same Baker named in Porterfield, Baker & Sheridan?'

'No, sir, that was my father, Asa Baker.'

'Then your position in the firm is due to inheritance, isn't that so?'

'I wouldn't put it that way, Mr Slater.'

'Would you describe your work there as an important or valuable contribution?'

Baker lifted his chin defensively. 'Yes, I would.'

'Have you ever been involved in actual litigation?'

'We have specialists for trial work.'

'Do you draft contracts, papers of incorporation, wills?'

'Well, no . . .'

'Briefs for the appellate courts?'

'That is not my function.'

'Do you consult with clients and advise them concerning the law?'

Baker squirmed, his meaty cheeks afire. 'Our work is all highly compartmentalized.'

'And which compartment do *you* fit into?'

'I—er—my duties are mostly administrative.'

'Checking the court calendar, supervising stenographers, purchasing supplies, defending the petty cash—is that what you mean?'

Baker suddenly deflated. 'Someone has to keep a large office like ours running smoothly.'

At that moment Paul loathed himself. And he hated Nicoletti for putting him in this position. Nor was he convinced that it was even necessary to diminish this impotent little man. Had he been tearing away at him in bitter frustration for the posthumous alibi Baker had provided Alex Moore? Was he being driven by some inexplicable motive to denigrate his father-in-law's firm? Or was he simply trying to discredit a prosecution witness?

'I have no further questions,' he said.

He saw the curiously disturbed expression on Abe Barish's face as he joined him at the defence table.

Nicoletti ducked into a whispered conference with his trial assistant. He stood and addressed the bench. 'Your Honour, the People rest.'

'This seems like a good time to recess for lunch,' Chaffee said. 'I will entertain defence motions when court reconvenes at two-thirty.'

CHAPTER NINE

THE STORM came without warning. The sky darkened and then a cannonade of thunder rumbled in the distance. Within seconds the clouds opened and a hard cold rain hurled by a driving wind swept the city streets. Water raced along the kerbs and drenched pedestrians huddled in doorways. Lights flickered on in the courthouse windows.

Judge Albert Chaffee liked rain, especially when he was snugly safe indoors. He had sent his law clerk out for lunch, and seated now at his desk in chambers, he attacked with vast relish a thick corned beef sandwich, pausing occasionally to bite off a chunk of tart pickle. Kosher corned beef. Truly a gastronomic triumph, he thought. Whatever else the Jews may or may not have contributed to civilization, this was one area in which they had never been successfully challenged. He topped it off with coffee and a Danish cheese. Its caloric content was sinfully high, but the conversion of starch to fat had never been one of his problems. A high rate of metabolism permitted him to eat with never a worry about his waistline.

He swept the paper plates into the wastebasket and swivelled back, fingers laced behind his neck. Chaffee was troubled. The publicity in the Sheridan case nourished his ego, but the complexities sharpened an awareness of his own limitations. He wondered again if he was on solid ground in admitting all that evidence about Alex Moore. If the boy was convicted, an appeal would be filed and the whole trial record would come under very close scrutiny. He read again the notes he'd culled from Richardson's text on Evidence and found the statement that had persuaded him to open the door: 'Circumstances which indicate motive for committing a crime embrace the whole range of human affairs.'

249

His finger tapped the phrase. There it is, he thought. 'The whole range of human affairs' would certainly include Moore's erotic obsession, a breach of trust for the woman's profit, and a consequent rage on learning that he had jeopardized his career in a hopeless cause.

These were certainly circumstances that indicated motive for a crime. But apparently not the crime of homicide, not if Baker's luncheon alibi were true. Would Moore have committed suicide, Chaffee wondered, if all that testimony had been excluded? Had he fallen into a quagmire, a damned hopeless quagmire?

He sighed and re-read his notes. The State's case against young Sheridan was based exclusively on circumstantial evidence. Unlike the average layman, Chaffee recognized its true value. Inferences from certain events were not only logical but inevitable. To impeach such evidence solely because of its indirect nature would be folly. He remembered an old maxim from his schooldays: *Circumstances never lie, although a witness can.*

His law clerk appeared at the door and said, 'It's that time again, Judge.'

Paul considered his options during the luncheon recess. On the surface, Don Baker's testimony seemed to disprove any implication of Moore's involvement in the actual murder, a point Nicoletti would certainly stress on summation. Still, there was no positive evidence on the exact time of death, and Moore's whereabouts after lunch were unknown. So he had decided not to alter his defence plan.

His first witness was Elizabeth Harmon, R.N. In the chic new outfit acquired for her courtroom appearance, she looked almost like a fashionable matron.

'What is your occupation?' Paul inquired.

'I am a registered nurse.'

'Were you on duty during the first week in April?'

'Yes, sir. I was employed as a private nurse by Mr Brian Wirth, a patient at Manhattan General Hospital.'

'What was his condition at that time?'

'He was a terminal case, suffering from carcinoma.'

'Is carcinoma the medical term for cancer?'

'It is.'

'Can you recall the precise time when his condition became hopeless?'

'It was hopeless before he entered the hospital. If you mean the final stage—well, he lapsed into a coma on Wednesday, April fourth, at twelve-oh-three p.m. I summoned the staff physician, but there was nothing he could do.'

'By coma, do you mean he lost consciousness?'

'Yes, sir. He was in a state of profound insensibility, unable to move or speak. The doctor told me it was just a matter of hours.'

'Did he receive any telephone calls?'

'A few. I took them and explained his condition.'

'Did he himself initiate any calls?'

'That would have been humanly impossible, Mr Slater.'

'Did he have any visitors?'

'Just one. His wife. She sat a while in the waiting room and then left.'

'Thank you, Miss Harmon. No more questions.'

Nicoletti remained standing behind the prosecution table. 'Am I correct in understanding that you did not leave Mr Wirth's bedside after he became unconscious?'

'That is right, sir.'

'No time off for lunch?'

'It was served to me on a tray in the patient's room.'

'What time were you relieved?'

'At five o'clock.'

'Are you telling us that you did not visit the bathroom even once during all the rest of that long afternoon?'

'Mr Wirth had an adjoining facility and I probably used it several times.'

'Did you close the door?'

She looked insulted. 'Well, of course I did.'

'Then you cannot be entirely sure whether or not he recovered long enough to make at least one call while you were out of sight and hearing, can you?'

'Yes, I can. He simply could not have done that.'

'Will you tell us why not?'

'Because,' she announced triumphantly, 'he was in an oxygen tent all that time and the clinical tests showed that he was making no response whatever to stimuli.'

Nicoletti knew that he had asked one question too many. But his face remained bland. 'You say you went off duty at five o'clock?'

'Yes, sir.'

'Then it is possible, is it not, that he may have used the telephone after you left?'

'If one believes in miracles, yes.'

Nicoletti wanted no more of Miss Harmon and sat down. Paul's next witness was the staff physician, who corroborated the nurse's testimony about the coma. The prosecutor passed him without cross.

'The defence calls Fern McFee.'

She was a crisp and competent woman in her middle thirties. She sat on the edge of the witness chair and submitted to Paul's preliminary questions with a faint suggestion of irritability.

'What is your present occupation, Miss McFee?'

'I am a housewife.'

'And before that?'

'I was a legal secretary.'

'Who was your last employer?'

'Porterfield, Baker & Sheridan, where I was assigned as secretary to Alexander Moore.'

'When did you leave?'

'Several weeks ago in order to get married.'

'How long did you work there?'

'Six years.'

'All of them as secretary for Mr Moore?'

'No, sir, just the last two.'

'Did your job require you to take dictation?'

'Yes, sir. It did.'

'Do you recall an occasion when he called you into his office and dictated the last will and testament of Mr Brian Wirth?'

'I do.'

'Can you recall the contents of that will?'

252

'Not all of them, no. But I do remember that it contained mostly a number of very large charitable bequests.'

'Was Dolly Wayne named as one of the legatees?'

'No, sir.'

'Was she named at all?'

'Only in one brief paragraph stating that for good and sufficient reasons no provision was being made by Mr Wirth for his wife and referring to an ante-nuptial agreement.'

'Who typed the will?'

'I did. Mr Moore asked me to do it during lunch hour because Mr Wirth was coming back to sign it that afternoon.'

'And was it signed?'

'Yes, it was.'

'Who were the attesting witnesses?'

'Mr Moore and Mr Baker.'

'What happened then?'

'Mr Moore handed it to me and asked me to file it with the rest of Mr Wirth's papers.'

'Now, Miss McFee, after Mr Wirth died, did you again have occasion to consult that file?'

'Yes, sir. We received a letter from a firm offering to appraise certain assets of the estate for tax purposes. The letter crossed my desk because Mr Moore was out of town for several days. I got Mr Wirth's folder in order to include the letter for future reference.'

'Was Mr Wirth's will still in the file?'

'It was.'

'And that was after he died, was it not?'

'Yes, sir.'

'Which specific member of the firm handled the estate?'

'Mr Moore.'

'Did he file the will for probate?'

'No, sir. He did not.'

'How was the estate conducted through court?'

'An application was made, stating that no will could be found and asking for the appointment of an administrator.'

'On whose behalf?'

'Mr Wirth's widow, Dolly Wayne.'

'Did that strike you as odd?'

'It certainly did.'

'Did you say anything to anyone about it?'

'No, sir, I didn't. This was a very prominent firm of attorneys, Mr Slater, and I did not think it was my place to challenge their actions.'

'Now, Miss McFee, did you subsequently volunteer information to a private investigator?'

'Yes, I did.'

'What brought about this change of heart?'

'Well, the situation had changed very drastically. Miss Wayne was dead. And Mr Sheridan's nephew was accused of killing her. It was no longer a sleight-of-hand problem. I simply could not remain silent while an innocent young man was on trial.'

'Objection,' Nicoletti said wearily.

Chaffee nodded. 'Sustained. Strike that last remark. Members of the jury, you will disregard this witness's characterization of the defendant.'

Paul smiled. 'You may cross-examine.'

'No questions.' Nicoletti waved her away as inconsequential.

Chaffee glanced at his watch. 'I believe we have time for one more witness.'

After shooting a quick encouraging grin at Ken, Cliff Eldon's expression shaded into a more appropriate solemnity. Paul's quiet manner gave him time to settle into his new role as a witness.

'You say that you and the defendant rented a small apartment together in Cambridge?'

'Yes, sir.'

'And how long have you known Ken Sheridan?'

'Ever since my freshman year as an undergraduate, something over four years.'

'Did you see much of him during that time?'

'This is our third year as room-mates.'

'Then you've had ample opportunity to observe his behaviour, have you not?'

'Yes, sir, I have.'

'What is his reputation as a peaceful and law-abiding student in the school community?'

'He has never been in trouble. He is one of the student leaders and he was on the varsity tennis team. Everyone, including the professors, admired and respected him.'

'Now, Mr Eldon, let us go back to the day that Dolly Wayne died, October eighteenth. Can you remember what time Ken Sheridan left for New York?'

'Yes, sir, eight o'clock in the morning. I was up early and had coffee with him.'

'What time did he return to Cambridge?'

'About four-thirty in the afternoon.'

'Was there anything strange about his behaviour? Did he seem nervous, edgy, excited?'

'No, sir. He was the same as always, cool.'

'How about his appearance? Did you notice anything unusual about his clothes?'

'Well his sweater was pretty muddy. He told me he'd taken a short cut across the empty field.'

'What else did he tell you?'

'He told me he'd been sitting behind the wheel of his car for more than eight hours since morning and he felt stiff as a board. He wanted to loosen up and wondered if we could start a game of touch football. We asked the fellows next door, Frank Hadley and Duke Pirie, to join us. We went out and tossed the ball around and then a couple of strangers came along and we got them to play too.'

'Will you tell the jury what happened during that game?'

'We were playing about twenty minutes, I guess. Ken had the ball and suddenly Duke Pirie tackled him and brought him down. The two strangers piled on top and that started a free-for-all. By the time we broke it up, Ken's nose was bleeding.'

'Did Ken suffer any other damage?'

'Only to his sweater. It was badly torn.'

'Please describe it.'

'There was a rip at the collar and one of the sleeves was

255

almost torn off. It was covered with mud and there was some blood on it from Ken's nose.'

'Did you ever see Ken wearing torn or damaged garments before?'

'No, sir.'

'Do you know what he did with this tattered and muddy sweater?'

'He said he didn't think it could be salvaged and he got rid of it.'

'How?'

'He tossed it down the incinerator.'

'Had he ever to your knowledge discarded other items of clothing in that manner?'

'All the time. Whenever shirts were a little frayed, they went into the incinerator.'

Paul did not belabour the point. 'Now, Mr Eldon, are you acquainted with Miss Peggy Wayne?'

'Yes, sir. Peggy is Ken's steady girl friend. She'd been out to Cambridge for all the college affairs and often spent the week-end.'

'How did he behave in her company?'

'He always treated her with great affection and respect and we all took it for granted they'd probably get married after he graduated from law school.'

Paul nodded. 'Thank you, Mr Eldon. Your witness.'

Nicoletti canted his head to one side and silently inspected the witness for a long moment. 'You are a close friend of the defendant, are you not?'

'Yes, sir.'

'His room-mate, you said?'

'Yes, sir.'

'Would you occasionally talk about your plans, the future?'

'Oh, yes, many times.'

'And was it your understanding that Ken Sheridan intended to join his uncle's firm, Porterfield, Baker & Sheridan?'

'There was never any doubt about that.'

'And on graduation, would you also like a job there?'

'If they accepted me, sir, I'd be proud.'

256

'A recommendation from Ken Sheridan to his uncle would help, would it not?'

'I can't say. I don't know if he has any influence.'

'Don't you think that testifying here in court on his behalf might induce his uncle to be favourably disposed to such an application?'

Cliff Eldon widened his eyes innocently. 'The thought never entered my mind.'

'Have you ever met Mr Lucas Holmes Sheridan?'

'Yes, sir, several times, when Ken invited me out to Sands Point as a guest.'

'Have you spoken to Mr Lucas Sheridan since the defendant's arrest?'

'No, sir.'

'But you have spoken to the defendant's lawyer?'

'Yes, sir.'

'Discussed your testimony with him at some length, have you?'

'I thought all lawyers discussed the testimony of their witnesses in advance.'

'Just answer my questions, Mr Eldon.'

'Well, you're trying to insinuate that——'

Chaffee tapped his gavel. 'The witness will refrain from gratuitous comments. A word to the wise, young man. . . .' He nodded at Nicoletti.

'You stated that Peggy Wayne came out to Cambridge a number of times to visit the defendant. On those occasions, where did she stay?'

'I don't think I understand the question.'

'It's phrased in simple English, Mr Eldon. You said they were weekend visits. Did she sleep in the park, in a hotel room —where?'

'Sometimes in a hotel.'

'And other times?'

'I—er—guess she stayed with friends.'

'You mean Ken Sheridan, do you not?'

'Well, when there were no reservations available . . .'

'She spent the night with the defendant, isn't that so?'

'Most of the time she slept on a sofa in the living room.'

'But you didn't have a living room when you were under-graduates, did you?'

'No, sir.'

'And they were not married at that time, were they?'

'No, sir.'

'Then I put it to you that since she was then under eighteen years of age, your characterization of Ken Sheridan as a sterling, law-abiding citizen was not entirely accurate, was it?'

Eldon coloured and started a feeble protest. 'Well, I don't know what they were doing in there. . . .'

'Come now, Mr Eldon, a red-blooded American boy and a healthy young girl, are you asking us to believe they spent the night in bed doing crossword puzzles?'

'I didn't say that.' He was turning sullen.

'But you did say that he was a student leader, didn't you?'

'Yes, sir.'

'Was he a member of any student council?'

'No.'

'Elected to any undergraduate organizations at all?'

'I don't think so.'

'Valedictorian of his class?'

'No.'

'Phi Beta Kappa?'

'No.'

'Then I suggest that your earlier portrait of this student paragon was wholly unjustified, isn't that so?'

Eldon sat sulking.

Nicoletti kept hammering.

'Well, then, Mr Eldon, how about you? Are you a peaceful, law-abiding citizen?'

'I think so.'

'Never fined for speeding or passing a red light?'

'Those are traffic violations.'

'Oh? So you take it upon yourself to decide which laws may be disregarded with impunity, do you?'

'I didn't say that.'

'Let's forget about traffic violations. Nobody gets hurt except maybe a few innocent pedestrians. Do you know if there is any law against the use or possession of marijuana?'

Cliff Eldon paused in the act of crossing his legs. He looked wary. 'Everyone knows there's such a law.'

'But not everyone obeys it, do they?'

'I guess not.'

'Do you obey it, Eldon?'

He sat still, grappling mutely with growing apprehension. Nicoletti's voice turned sharp. 'The jury can't hear you, Eldon. Speak up.'

'What—what was the question?'

'We were talking about the cannabis plant, boy. Hemp, the loco weed, pot.' Nicoletti produced a yellow flimsy and glanced at it. 'Have you ever been busted for possession?'

It fastened Eldon's gaze with sudden belligerence on his inquisitor. Words came in a torrent of defiance. 'Laws are meant to protect society and any law that doesn't do that is a stupid law. There's no harm in pot. Any doctor will tell you that. You can't legislate a person's freedom to do what he wants with his own lungs. I don't need protection against myself. Why don't you pass laws prohibiting cigarettes—or do they pay too much taxes . . .'

His voice faltered and died with the belated realization of how fraudulent his litany must sound to this jury of middle-aged squares. He managed a weak, conciliatory smile.

Paul's expressionless face masked exasperation. He knew that Nicoletti had deliberately suffered Eldon's harangue, allowing it to cast its own reflection on the witness.

'You still haven't answered my question,' Nicoletti said. 'Have you ever been arrested for the possession and use of marijuana?'

Paul objected, knowing the gesture to be futile. 'This line of inquiry is irrelevant to the issues.'

'Not to the issue of credibility, as counsel is well aware.'

'Yes,' Chaffee said. 'I will allow it.' He pointed his chin towards Eldon. 'Answer the question.'

'Yes,' Eldon said.

'Was the defendant also busted at the same time?'

'Objection,' Paul snapped.

'Sustained.'

Nicoletti shifted abruptly. 'When the defendant returned to Cambridge after visiting Dolly Wayne the day she was killed, what was he wearing?'

'Jeans, a sweater, and a windbreaker.'

'And later that day his sweater was ashes in the incinerator, was it not?'

'Yes.'

'Quite anxious to get rid of it, wasn't he?'

'Well, it was torn and filthy with mud and blood.'

'Whose blood?'

'His own.'

'And did you make the appropriate serological tests to determine that fact?'

'His nose was bleeding.'

'Wasn't that the result of a game and a fracas he himself was extraordinarily eager to initiate?'

'He didn't pressure any of us.'

'Well, at any rate, Mr Eldon, you couldn't see any blood on his sweater when he returned from New York because it was pretty much covered with mud even at that time, isn't that so?'

'He slipped on the wet field.'

'Yes. We know all about the mud. Yet at the defendant's request you were easily persuaded to go wallowing in all that muck yourself. Do you usually engage in that sort of activity?'

'Not often.'

'You were just accommodating the defendant?'

'He said he needed the exercise.'

Nicoletti showed his square teeth in a sceptical smile to the jury, and veered off again. 'You were not in the courtroom when Peggy Wayne testified. Did you know she had married the defendant?'

Eldon looked surprised.

'No, sir, I didn't.'

'He had not confided in you?'

'Not about that.'

'But he usually confided in you about other matters, did he not?'

'Yes.'

'And you knew that Peggy Wayne was his steady girl friend?'

'Yes.'

'He was always faithful to her?'

'Absolutely.'

'He never tomcatted around?'

'No.'

'A true-blue, one-woman man, was he?'

'Yes.'

Nicoletti sat, an inverted smile on his mouth.

Paul looked thoughtfully at the witness and shook his head to indicate there would be no re-direct.

Chaffee said, 'Court will adjourn until nine-thirty Monday morning.'

The gym attendant sat on a folding chair and quizzically nursed a bruised jaw. He had suggested putting on the gloves for a brief workout, but when Slater proved unexpectedly aggressive he had thrown in the towel. He watched Slater lifting weights, straining his muscles, inhaling huge gulps of oxygen.

On leaving the courthouse after the Friday session, moving with no conscious volition, Paul had suddenly found himself outside his health club. His customary visits had been suspended since the beginning of the trial. Now he was driving himself with an almost maniac intensity.

'All right, Mr Slater,' the attendant said. 'That's enough. A swim and then a rubdown. Okay?'

Paul lapped the pool ten times, climbed out, and went to the table. He submitted to the strenuous kneading of sinews and flesh, stood under the needle shower, then dressed and departed in a preoccupation so complete he forgot to leave a tip or return his trunks to the locker.

CHAPTER TEN

THE RED LIGHT on Flight 641 flashed on, instructing passengers to tighten their seat belts. Moments later the stewardess announced, 'We will be landing at Logan International in about fifteen minutes. Please remain in your seats until the plane comes to a full stop.'

Paul returned the transcript to his attaché case. He'd been trying to analyse all prosecution claims that needed rebuttal, but his mind kept wandering back to Cliff Eldon on the witness stand. Paul had stressed the importance of absolute truth. 'Don't lie,' he'd told the boy. 'Don't exaggerate. Don't colour. Nicoletti has a sure instinct for deception. He'll see through it and turn you inside out.'

But for some reason Eldon had thought it necessary to assert Ken's fidelity to Peg. Which did not tally with the gamey revelations given Paul on his first visit to Cambridge. Nicoletti had not challenged him; still, that secret smile on the prosecutor's face troubled Paul.

Lying in bed last night alongside a quietly remote Dru, he kept thinking about Ken's entanglement with the Kowalski girl he'd picked up in Newton. As the false dawn cast its first grey smudge across the sky, he had decided to pay the girl a visit.

The plane dipped a wing into the terminal leg of its landing pattern. He heard the thump of lowered flaps and felt the drag of diminishing airspeed. He took a taxi and they headed out the highway towards Newton.

He reviewed what young Hadley had told him about the girl. A bold and brassy piece. A beer-joint pick-up that had developed into superheated sex. Had it been exclusively physical? Unemotional? And was it completely ended now?

He found his destination on the far outskirts of town. Tract houses thrown together with no geography between them. Flaking paint and sagging beams on a potholed street. The Kowalski address behind a weed-cluttered yard.

A brass knocker hung on the door, incongruous, probably salvaged. Its hefty weight chunked solidly. When the door opened he saw that Hadley's description had rendered her accurately.

'Miss Kowalski?' he inquired politely. 'Miss Amy Kowalski?'

She stood, hip-shot, holding a transistor radio, swaying to the percussive assault of rock, furry little brows arched in insolent appraisal. Silvered hair fell straight to shoulder level. The deliberately provocative air belied her age.

'Amy Kowalski,' she told him. 'That's me. All hunert and twenty-five pounds. Who're you?'

'My name is Paul Slater. I'm a lawyer.'

It took a moment to register. Then she gaped. 'Hey, man! I read about you. You're Kenny Sheridan's mouthpiece.'

'You know Ken?'

'Used to.' She frowned suspiciously. 'Who tole you about us?'

'It's no secret, Amy. Would you mind turning that thing down and inviting me in. I'd like to talk to you.'

'About what?'

'Ken Sheridan. You may have some information that I can use.'

'In court, you mean? Me help ole Kenny?' She gave a short mirthless laugh. 'He must have a bolt loose, sending you here. I wouldn't lift a finger to help that prick. I'll tell you something, mister. I hope you bomb out. I hope they fry him or pack him away for life. He's strictly bad news. So just bug off, willya——'

She had started to slam the door, but it was suddenly yanked wide and a balding bull-necked man loomed behind her.

'Who is this joker, Amy? What's he want?'

'Never mind, Pop. I can handle it.'

'I asked you a question.' His meaty arm brushed her aside. He planted himself in front of Paul, distrustful and truculent. A black pelt showed through the open collar of a denim shirt.

263

'Don't talk to him, Pop,' Amy shrilled. 'He's a lawyer from New York—Kenny Sheridan's lawyer.'

The heavy muscles flexed. Kowalski had the look of a savage street brawler. Tangling with the man would be a profitless exercise in violence and Paul instinctively moved back a step.

'Throw him out,' the girl yelped.

'Butt out of this,' Kowalski told her. 'I don't need your advice. You want an earful, mister, come on in.'

Amy made frustrated, cawing sounds and ran back through the hall. In the narrow living room, Kowalski indicated an overstuffed chair and asked Paul if he wanted a beer. Paul thanked him, and the man shouted instructions to his daughter. She brought two cans, no glasses, and lounged resentfully in the doorway, emanating antagonism. Kowalski put his head back and gurgled off half his beer. He wiped his mouth with the back of his hand.

'Look, mister,' he said, 'I don't know if the Sheridan kid shelved that lady or not, but I sure would like to see him take the rap. I hope they strap him down and burn him good.'

'Capital punishment has been abolished in the State of New York, Mr Kowalski.'

'Yeah? Too bad. So do the world a favour. Dump him. Let him rot behind bars.' Kowalski nodded with satisfaction. 'I knew sooner or later he'd get his ass in a sling, and it don't give me no pain at all, mister. I seen trouble coming the first time he took up with Amy.'

'What kind of trouble?'

'Sex trouble, mister. Only worse than I expected. The little sonofabitch got his meat into her and knocked her up—and that ain't all——'

'Jesus, Pop!' Amy broke in fiercely. 'Listen, don't——'

'I told you to button up,' he barked, not looking at her. 'I know my kid ain't no angel, mister. Hanging out in bars, wearing them short skirts up to her keister, waving it around in front of the loafers, getting everybody all steamed up. So maybe that Sheridan wasn't the first. How in hell would I know? But she always took care of herself until that goddamn crotch jockey got her so hopped up she couldn't tell her ass from third base. If I told her once I told her a hundred times—give him the gate. Like talking to the wall.' The thick neck inched out of his collar. 'You name me somebody whose kids listen. Boy, I jumped if my old man so much as sneezed. Nowadays all you get is lip. They got all the answers. They know everything except how to make an honest buck. Life is short. You gotta live it up. Kicks, that's all they think about. I tell her to go to school, learn how to type, find a decent job. No, sir, she's satisfied with the five-and-dime and ballin' it up —and look what it got her, a fat belly and a lousy lock-picker.'

'Lock-picker?'

'Abortionist.' Anger mottled Kowalski's face, the frustrated parent choking on his own venom.

'Abortions are fairly common these days,' Paul said.

'Shit! I'm not complaining about that.' He gave a barking laugh. 'And me a card-carrying Catholic. I pushed her into it. That's all I need around here is a bastard kid yelling its lungs out all night. Who the hell would take care of it? My woman died six years ago. Amy, maybe? From the back seat of a motor-cycle. Aagh! So I dug up a croaker and he——'

'Oh, Pop!' Amy cried out in desperation. 'Don't you know it's against the law to——'

He wheeled on her. 'What's he gonna do? Squeal? Get his client into more trouble? Sheridan set it up with cash, didn't he? He laid out the dough. So clam up.' He swung back to Paul. 'It wasn't easy, mister. I had to go down to that college and lay it out for him. He denied the kid was his. Told me half a dozen guys were making it with Amy. But I knew goddamn well nobody else got near her after she started with him. I told him he had to do the right thing and he just stood there grinning at me.' Kowalski brandished a fist. 'I had to twist him a little.'

'What happened?'

'One of his crummy friends came in and squared off on me.'

'Frank Hadley?'

'He's the one,' Amy said disdainfully. 'He called me a couple of times after I broke up with Kenny, trying to make a date.'

265

'Yeah,' Kowalski said. 'Your boy friend must of passed the word and give you a good recommendation.'

'Jesus, Pop, you got a mind like a sewer.'

'You want a fat lip, young lady? Show some respect.' He appealed to Paul. 'You make a home for them and what do you get?'

'Some home,' she said.

'So clean it up. Get off your lazy ass and use a little elbow grease.' He lifted his chin at Paul. 'You got any kids?'

'Not yet.'

'Then don't. It ain't worth it.'

'What happened at the school, Mr Kowalski?'

He laughed once. 'All I did was wave a fist like I was gonna hang one on him and he backed off fast. I told Sheridan if he didn't cough up the dough for an abortion he'd have to marry Amy. And if he balked at that too, I'd get in touch with his family. That softened him. He needed a little time. I came back the next day and he handed me five hundred bucks. Hell, man, I figured she's lucky to be rid of him.'

'You said she was hopped up, Mr Kowalski. On what?'

'Pills.'

'What kind of pills?'

He jerked a thumb. 'Ask her. She's the expert.'

Paul looked at the girl. 'Amy?'

'Speed,' she said in an offhand manner. 'It has another name, I guess. Kenny told me once, but I don't remember.'

'One of the amphetamines?'

She looked blank.

'Methadrine?' he said.

'Something like that.'

Kowalski said, 'It drives them crackers. They freak out on the goddamn stuff. I know because I caught 'em one night right here in my home, on that couch there——'

'Pop!' she squealed. 'For Pete's sake——'

'I'm not talking to you.'

'*Jesus!*' It was a cry of anguish. 'You have to tell him everything?'

'I got nothing to be ashamed of.' But he was both torn and

266

goaded, unable to hold his tongue. 'I want this hotshot lawyer to know the kind of crud he's defending. Wasting his brain to save a skunk.'

She smothered a cry and fled. Upstairs a slamming door rattled the house.

Kowalski looked sour. 'All of a sudden she's sensitive.'

'You were saying?' Paul prodded him.

He rubbed his eyes, reliving the scene. 'It happened maybe two o'clock one morning. I came home earlier with a skinful, you know. Stopped off for a couple after work. This was a few weeks after the abortion. I didn't even know she was seeing him again. I guess they thought it was okay with me bombed out upstairs. Anyway, it was Amy's scream that woke me. Christ! It woulda bumped a dead man out of his coffin. And that Sheridan must of heard me tumbling down the stairs, because he was off her and diving for the window.'

'Ken Sheridan? You're sure?'

'It was him, all right. Making it right here under my nose. I would of broke his spine if I'd got my hands on him. You never seen a guy move so fast. He's goddamn lucky the window was open. I turned on the lights and I seen Amy half naked whimpering and bleeding like a stuck hog. He—he——' Kowalski choked, close to apoplexy.

Paul's mouth was dry. He gave the man time to collect himself. Kowalski held his fists to his chest. He had to clear an obstruction from his throat.

'The goddamn degenerate! He'd sunk his choppers into her thighs. Amy don't go for no funny stuff like that. He was chewing on her like a sonofabitch vampire.'

Paul's heart skipped a beat, then another. The recital had jolted him so violently, his face went blank, as if carved from volcanic rock. But inside, his stomach twisted with nausea, bile leaping into his throat. He felt cold and empty and sick.

'You said you turned the light on after he went out the window. How can you be so sure it was Ken Sheridan if the room was dark?'

'The hall light was on. I didn't go after him because Amy was in such lousy shape I wanted to get her to a doctor. She

267

raised hell, but I took her anyway.' He looked up. 'You think it taught her a lesson? Hell, no. Not Amy. She was still hooked on the bastard and she had to go tagging after him until he wouldn't even answer the phone or talk to her. She was mooning all over the place. So I had to smack a little sense into her.' He demonstrated his method by driving a fist into his palm. 'Anyway, the message finally got through. She knew they were washed up and good riddance.' He ducked his head in grim satisfaction. 'Look at the fix he's in now. It couldn't have happened to a more deserving guy.'

Paul had lost the thread. He felt oddly diffused, spread thin. He needed air and time to think. He mumbled something about plane schedules and thanked Kowalski for his time and frankness. The man followed him to the door, hurling his words like impotent weapons against unseen enemies.

Paul took a cab back to Logan International. On the shuttle flight back to New York he felt suffocated, as if the plane had suffered a leak and rapid depressurization was taking place.

John Nicoletti preferred to work in his office even on weekends while a trial was in progress. With the Sheridan case rapidly approaching its climax, he studied memoranda spread out across the desk and made tentative notes for his final summation.

At 3 p.m. visitors arrived. Detective Lou Schatz and a stranger. He lifted an inquiring eyebrow at Schatz, who introduced the newcomer.

'This is Otto Ganz,' Schatz said. 'Licensed hack driver. An independent, owns his own cab. He came in with a story and I thought you ought to hear it.'

Nicoletti turned to the man, a stringy adenoidal type with an acne-scarred complexion. Otto Ganz reached for a provisional smile, abandoned it, then brought a newspaper clipping out of his pocket and handed it to the prosecutor. Nicoletti saw a picture of Alex Moore published on the morning following Moore's suicide.

'I read this,' he said. 'What about it?'

Ganz produced the trip card required by the police department's Hack Bureau, which stated the place of pick-up and destination of passengers, with the times involved.

Ganz explained in a reedy voice, 'That man in the picture, I collected him at the corner of Broad and Wall and I delivered him to 65th between Park and Lex.'

That would be the immediate vicinity of Dolly Wayne's house. The date, October 18, when she'd been shelved. The time, he saw, was 2.20 p.m., and although that was considerably later than Billy Clark had heard sounds of a struggle, Nicoletti did not like it. He wanted no evidence that Alex Moore had been anywhere near the area on that day.

'You pick up quite a few passengers, don't you, Mr Ganz?' he asked.

'Yes, sir. No complaints. Business is pretty good. For a while there, after we jacked up the fares, it was murder.'

Nicoletti's spatulate finger tapped Moore's picture. 'Can you tell me what made you remember this particular face?'

'Well, he looked worried, kind of jittery, squirming around on the back seat. He kept lighting one butt after another and then grinding it out on the floor of the cab after a few puffs. I got to clean up after these jokers. Anyway, I dropped him off right across the street from that Wayne address. He gave me a ten-dollar bill and waved away the change, absent-minded like. When I drove off, he was just standing there, looking up at the house.'

'Why did you wait so long before reporting this?'

Ganz flicked a sheepish glance at Detective Schatz. 'Well, I'm a taxi driver. We're none of us crazy about cops, and I didn't want to get involved. But the missus, she's something else, she kept bugging me, said it was a murder case, it might be important.' His helpless gesture included the others in a long-suffering fraternity. 'You know how it is, the old lady gets on your back, forget it, you better give in. So I went down and told my story and this detective brought me over here to see you.'

'Have you discussed this with anyone else?'

'No, sir, just the missus.'

'All right, Mr Ganz. I want to thank you for coming in and

269

volunteering information of your own accord. If all citizens had a sense of civic responsibility our work would be a lot easier. However, your story doesn't affect the State's case. We don't want the basic issues cluttered with a lot of loose talk and rumours. I'm going to ask you to keep it under your hat for the time being. Will you do that?'

'You mean I don't have to go into court?'

'Probably not.'

Ganz looked relieved. 'Well, sure, if you say so, I'll dummy up.'

'Detective Schatz says you own your own medallion.'

'Yes, sir.'

'I'm going to hold on to this trip card. We'll xerox a copy for you. Lou, you know where the equipment is. Duplicate this, have Ganz sign the original, and give him the copy.' He stood up, offered his hand. 'We'll be in touch if we need you, Mr Ganz.'

Schatz took the man with him. Alone, Nicoletti swivelled back, his face long and brooding. He was mulling it over when Schatz returned and asked, 'What do you make of it?'

'It doesn't appeal to me one little bit.'

'Well, look, Ganz walked in after the State finished its presentation. Why can't we just sit on it?'

Nicoletti's face turned cold. 'Goddamn it, Schatz, you know how I operate. It's not my style to suppress evidence, even if it hurts the prosecution. And don't feed me any bullshit about the Supreme Court coddling criminals. If I can't nail 'em on the evidence, I don't resort to flummery. Maybe some others in this office do, but I don't.'

Schatz was only mildly chastened. 'He didn't give us much. Just how vital is it?'

Nicoletti shrugged. 'We know how Moore felt about Dolly Wayne. We know the risks he took, how he climbed out on a limb for her. And we know she gave him the gate. So the man had motive. And now we've got him located at the scene.'

'Almost an hour after the struggle.'

'What the hell, we have no proof she was killed at precisely that time. Her assailant may have left her unconscious.'

'We've got him located in the area, but not inside her apartment.'

'Don't split hairs. All he had to do was ring the bell and she'd let him in. Moore could have been half out of his skull with lust and anger. He's got teeth and he's got hands. So we wind up with that goddamn unholy trinity—means, motive, and opportunity.'

'Do we have to prove the defendant's case for him?'

'We only have to prove our own. What's eating me is this: we have Moore standing across the street from the Wayne apartment, watching it. We say the Sheridan boy was in there with her. Maybe Moore saw him leave.'

'No, sir. He got there too late.'

'That's just the point. Maybe he didn't. And yet he never spoke up, never said a word, even though it could have taken him off the hook.'

'How could he? If he saw the boy leave and said so, it would knock the props out from under Slater's timetable. That would help cook the boy. It would certainly finish Moore at Porterfield, Baker & Sheridan. So of course he'd sit on it.'

Nicoletti nodded slowly. 'All right, Lou, that shines enough for me to buy it.' He sat back and peered sharply at the detective. 'Tell me this: since the department wants a conviction, why in hell complicate it by bringing Ganz here?'

Schatz grinned. 'Fear. Lieutenant Varney said you'd peel our hides if we put the lid on Ganz and you heard about it. So we give you everything we have. And we got another lead that Barney Krehm is checking out this afternoon. Something about a little Polack hotbox the Sheridan boy was pronging.'

Nicoletti perked up. 'I'd be interested. Let me know. Now get the hell out of here so I can do some work.'

CHAPTER ELEVEN

FOR THE FIRST TIME since the trial had started Paul felt threatened, insecure.

When the guard at the Tombs delivered Ken Sheridan to the small conference cubicle he searched the young, amiable face, trying to keep his own expression from revealing a powerful conflict of emotions.

'Why so mournful, Counsellor? Something wrong?'

Paul said quietly, 'We're coming to the end, Ken. At this point we may have a slight edge, but no one can tell in advance what a jury will decide.'

'There's one way you can sew it up.'

'How?'

'Put me on the stand.'

He marvelled at the boy's conceit. 'You'd have to face cross against Nicoletti.'

'How can he hurt me? I've got nothing to hide.'

'Nothing at all, Ken? Not even one slight indiscretion in all your past?'

'Nothing he can blow up out of proportion.'

'The man's a tiger.'

'Tiger's have only a primitive intelligence.'

Paul stifled his anger. 'Climb down, damn it! Nicoletti's been chewing up wiseacre witnesses and spitting out the pips for almost half your lifetime. This is no mock trial in a make-believe world. That's a man-eating jungle out there and it isn't run by idiots. What makes you think you can handle a man like Nicoletti?'

Ken's smile was maddening. 'I didn't think you were sensitive about the man.'

'I'm sensitive about inflated egos. I'm sensitive to a first-year law student running down a crack pro who can ride over you like a bulldozer. You saw what he did to Eldon.'

'I'm not Eldon.'

'So you're smarter than Eldon. But before I'd let you testify I'd have to know everything you've ever done, every indiscretion, infraction, transgression, that could put you in a bad light. Otherwise I might have to keep you off the stand.'

'Don't I have anything to say about that?'

'Yes. You have a right to insist. And I have a right to announce in court that you're taking the stand against my better judgement.'

Ken shrugged, still serene. 'All right. What do you want to know?'

'Before Eldon testified I asked him if there was anything he should tell me that might impair his value as a defence witness. He said no. I accepted his statement and that was a mistake. Because he lied. He'd been busted for possession of pot and Nicoletti knew it and shot him down.'

'Come off it, Paul. Possession of pot is hardly a crime.'

'You may not think so, your contemporaries may not think so, but it's still on the books. Just how would you go about trying to persuade a jury of middle-aged squares that the lawmakers are all wrong?'

Ken shrugged. 'So Cliff Eldon smoked a joint. Can they hold that against *me*?'

'If you were there with him and collared at the same time. I can't check all the records. But I do have to know the truth.'

'All right. I was with him.'

'Did they take you in?'

'Yes.'

'What happened?'

'The charge was dismissed for lack of evidence.'

'Did your uncle know about it?'

'There was no point in telling him.'

'Does Eldon ever use anything stronger than pot?'

'You mean like acid or horse? Hell, no.'

'I mean like speed, Methadrine, any of the amphetamines.'

'You've got the wrong customer, Paul. Cliff even balked at

273

grass. He only tried it because everyone called him chicken.'
Ken chuckled. 'That's when he got busted, when they raided
that party, the first time he ever took a puff.'

'So you were off the hook that time. How about other times?
Do you ever use the stuff?'

'Not me. There's too much at stake.'

'I think you're lying, Ken.'

Ken raised his eyebrows. 'You must be joking. Cliff Eldon
and Frank Hadley corroborated everything I told you.'

'They're lying too, especially Eldon. He lied through his
teeth on the witness stand.'

'What the hell are you talking about, Paul?'

'I'm talking about perjury, false testimony under oath.
Eldon said you were a one-woman man, faithful to Peggy
Wayne.'

'So?'

'So Hadley claims otherwise. He told me you were pronging
some little tramp you picked up in a Newton bar.'

Ken shook his head disparagingly. 'Oh, that! I was feeding
Hadley a line. He's always avid about sexual exploits and I
invent stuff to make his mouth water.'

'You never touched Amy Kowalski?'

'All we did was gulp beer in local gin mills.'

'Nothing more?'

'Like what?'

'Like a roll in the hay. Like another knock-up. And another
abortion.'

'Who handed you all that stuff?'

'Amy's father.'

'You saw him?'

'Yes.'

'Amy, too?'

'Yes.'

Ken's mouth grew smaller.

'Just what are you trying to prove, Paul? Digging up that
pair, listening to their crap.'

'That's a bad hand, Ken. Throw it in. Kowalski had no
reason to lie.'

274

Ken spread his fingers in good-natured surrender. 'All right. So I fooled around with the girl. It was just a little extra-curricular homework and we got caught. No big deal.'

Paul shook his head. 'Her pregnancy is only one aspect. I could overlook that. You have a compulsion to go tomcatting around and taking a hack at all the available snatch, okay. None of my business. What's eating me is something else. The last night you saw the girl you were high on something. Speed, probably. Whatever, it knocked you off centre and you went at the girl with your teeth. It drew blood and frightened her and she screamed loud enough to yank her old man out of a half-drunken stupor. Instinct drove you out of there when he came bellowing down. You were lucky. He was in a murdering mood. And lucky, too, because he took her to a doctor who didn't blow the whistle on you. After that you decided not to see her again and that finished the romance.'

Ken took his time answering. He tilted back, lids half lowered over sleepy eyes. 'You know something, Paul. You worry me. Your judgement is bad if you can't read that pair. Amy thought she had me. They both did. I was money in the bank. I was going to be their passport to a new and richer life. And when I walked away they were pissed off. You know how that kind of mentality works. They had to get back at me, so they trumped up a pack of lies.'

'No, Ken. It won't wash.'

'How do you like that? The man refuses to believe me.'

'The doctor who treated Amy will have a record of her condition. It shows a pattern of behaviour that can sink you.'

'How? Boil it down, Counsellor.'

Paul lowered his voice. 'The injuries suffered by Dolly Wayne were exactly similar to those you inflicted on the Kowalski girl. I have a feeling Nicoletti may be on to it. He'll contend you were jittery when you called on Dolly and took something to bolster your confidence. You walked in there with your mind blown and your inhibitions gone. And you gave her the same treatment you'd given Amy Kowalski.'

'You're putting me on.'

'I'm giving you facts.'

'Suppositions, guesses. So that's what Nicoletti would say, *if* he knew about Amy. What would you say?'

'I'd say he could be right.'

'What motive would I have?'

'You didn't need one for the mutilation. For the murder, money, perhaps. You knew Dolly was loaded, worth over a million, and that Peggy would inherit. You never had any money of your own. Your parents left you nothing. You've always lived off your uncle. So you married Peggy, knowing you had her under your thumb and could always take control.'

Ken reverted to a mask face. 'I'll tell you something, Paul. You don't need anything to blow your mind. It's bizarre enough. It makes you sound more like a prosecutor than a defence lawyer.'

Paul put a hand in his pocket and brought out a fold of tissue paper. He unravelled it and displayed the contents. 'Recognize this?'

'It looks like a diamond ring.'

'Any idea who it belonged to?'

'Not a glimmer.'

'It's part of the loot stolen from Dolly's apartment the day she was murdered.'

Ken was watching him with an unblinking saurian intensity. 'Who found it?'

'Roy Burroughs, the private detective who's working for us.'

'The other stuff too?'

'Most of it.'

'Where?'

'Don't you know, Ken? Can't you remember what you did with it?'

Ken's face changed. A vein jumped in his forehead and he lowered his voice to a corrosive whisper, his teeth biting off the words. 'You're a goddamn crock of shit, Paul. Nobody can find Dolly's jewels. Nobody, ever. That ring is a sleazy dodge trying to trap me into an admission. It won't work.'

'It already has.'

'What are you talking about?'

'Only the person who took Dolly's jewels knows for certain

276

they will never be found. Because he knows where they are. Tell me, Ken. Sinking in the mud under the Charles River?'

The sudden withdrawal, the frozen expression, the lidless stare told Paul with a chilled certainty that he had scored a hit. He had not wanted verification. He felt a sickening revulsion. It abraded his spirit, staggered his mind with the enormity of his dilemma. He perceived with startling clarity the web of duplicity and lies his own cross-examination had produced, obscuring the truth.

In a wooden voice he catalogued an indictment, point after point.

Ken listened to him, one millimetre of elevation in eyebrows that indicated open mockery. 'You make noises like some pious hypocrite, Paul. You're frozen into a set of rules concocted by political hacks sucking up to a half-dead middle-class mentality. Don't expect everyone else to live by those rules.'

'I'm not going to argue philosophical concepts. The rules give you freedom, so long as you don't interfere with others.'

'Do drugs or sex interfere with others?'

'Drugs scrambled your brain and made you attack Dolly Wayne. Yes, it interferes with others.'

'All right. So Dolly Wayne is dead and you have some silly notion I'm guilty. So let the State prove it. Haven't I heard you sound off about the presumption of innocence? Isn't that your bag? Or were you double-talking the jury with that noble phrase? Don't you think I'm entitled to the presumption as well as any other defendant?'

'It's only a presumption. And presumptions die with knowledge.'

'You believe what you want, so long as you don't throw the ball game. Or would you prefer to withdraw from the case?'

'The idea has occurred to me.'

'How would you explain it to Dru? "Look dear, your little cousin is a fiend. I can't corrupt my lily-white integrity by defending him. Try to understand, dear, I have to dump the boy so the State can convict him and lock him away like a caged animal where he belongs." ' Ken smiled mockingly. 'Ah, Paul, Dru would love that. It wouldn't change your marriage at all, would it? And remember, emotional shock has been known to bring on miscarriages.'

For one precarious moment Paul almost clubbed a fist into the smiling face across the table. His chair scraped back; he turned without a word and strode past the guard into the corridor.

His hand tightened over the tissue-wrapped ring he'd borrowed from Dru's jewel box without her knowledge. Entrapment, he thought bitterly. Forbidden to the police and yet he himself was guilty. Guilty on all counts.

Dean Julian Farquhar looked harried. Wearing an ancient smoking jacket, he sat in his living room overlooking Washington Square Park, studying a sheaf of papers. He would have to call a faculty meeting. Which inevitably would produce heated debate. Any proposal for change always drove old Foster up a wall. Farquhar grimaced. Foster had been teaching Negotiable Instruments with implacable tedium for twenty years. Even the Dean's vaunted talent for arbitration often failed to pacify the apoplectic old reactionary. There would be fireworks.

For some inexplicable reason Slater seemed most able to handle Foster. He had been remarkably successful in smoothing the ruffled professorial feathers. It might be best to postpone any meeting until Slater was free of the Sheridan case.

Julian Farquhar was a pragmatist. He did not believe in mental telepathy. But when at that moment the house phone rang and Paul Slater announced himself, the Dean blinked rapidly and invited his visitor to come up. He was waiting at the open door when the elevator arrived.

'A pleasant surprise indeed,' he greeted. 'And in the midst of a trial too. Don't tell me you're here for advice. I'd be flattered, but not much help. Rusty, my boy, rusty. Too many years away from the courtroom.' He took Paul's coat. 'Brandy?'

'Please.'

Farquhar displayed the Courvoisier. 'Your gift—the last time you were here. Seems to me I was much younger then.' He noted Paul's abstraction and failure to smile. He poured, and waited with patient curiosity.

278

Eventually Paul spoke. 'If I may, Julian, I would like to pose a problem. Strictly theoretical, of course.'

'Naturally. Theoretical problems, *in vacuo*, as it were, are my exclusive province these days. A problem of considerable import, I take it.'

Paul stared at him.

'My dear boy,' Farquhar explained, 'an unheralded visit. A hint of gravity behind the impassivity. What else?' He twisted the stem of his brandy snifter. 'Proceed.'

'I ask you to assume certain facts,' Paul said. 'First, a lawyer defending a man charged with a capital crime. He has reason to believe his efforts may win an acquittal. Then, during the course of the trial, he comes into evidence that convinces him of his client's guilt.'

Farquhar raised a quizzical eyebrow. 'Well, now, obviously that cannot be the problem. You know the answer to that as well as I do.'

'Nevertheless, I want you to express an opinion.'

'Any decision as to innocence or guilt must be made by the jury. Your lawyer must not usurp their function.'

'What if our lawyer is in a better position to judge the facts.'

'Ah, but is he really, Paul? Would you substitute his judgement, a single individual's for that of twelve disinterested talesmen? And tell me, what would put him in a better position?'

'Knowledge of facts not available to the jury.'

'Available to the prosecution?'

'I think not.'

'Your lawyer has made an independent investigation?'

'He has.'

'Are you so sure, Paul, that his judgement of these facts is infallible?'

'He has good reason to believe it is.'

'For the sake of argument, let us grant your supposition. Even so, the Fifth Canon of Ethics prescribes a lawyer's right to undertake a defence regardless of his private opinion.'

'His right, yes. What about his obligation? What if his conscience dictates otherwise?'

Farquhar put his glass down. He stood and went to the bookshelves. He selected a volume, leafed through it, and came back. 'The autobiography of Sir Patrick Hastings. You know the name, of course.'

'One of England's great barristers.'

'Yes. I would like to read an appropriate passage. Quote: "The comment has often been made, how can counsel defend a cause in which he cannot honestly believe? The answer is simple. Counsel has no right to believe or disbelieve either his client or his case. He has a duty to perform; he must perform it. He has no right to arrogate to himself the task of forming an opinion as to whether his client is innocent or guilty, truthful or a liar. He must fight the cause to the best of his ability." ' Farquhar closed the book and looked up.

'I remember,' Paul said, 'that he also suggested a rule of conduct. The lawyer must be as honest in his practice as he would be in his private life.'

Farquhar smiled. 'I see we share a similar addiction to biographies. Then you must also know Boswell's *Life of Samuel Johnson.*'

'A long-ago favourite.'

'Do you remember Johnson's reply when Boswell asked him what he thought of a lawyer supporting a cause which he knew to be bad?'

'Vaguely.'

'It may be even more relevant. I quote from memory: "Sir, you do not know it to be good or bad till the judge determines it. If the lawyer's arguments are insufficient to convince himself, they might convince the judge. If they do, you are wrong and he is right. It is his business to judge." ' Farquhar aimed a finger. 'Substitute jury for judge and you have an answer.'

'Not one I'm willing to accept in this instance.'

Farquhar sighed patiently. 'May I offer one more quotation?'

Paul nodded.

'This time, verbatim. From G. K. Chesterton. "When a man has something unimportant to do, like build a bridge, he calls in a trained individual, but when he has a really important function to perform, like doing justice, he relies on twelve people with common sense." ' Farquhar spread his arms. 'Why not leave the whole problem to a jury?'

'Ignoring truth and justice?'

'Paul, Paul, what would you have our lawyer do? Expound his theories in court? Convict his own client? Turn his back and walk away from the case?'

'No, Julian, he cannot quit the case. At this stage of the trial the judge would not allow it. And there are other reasons, personal reasons that preclude such action.'

'Of course. The defendant's relatives still believe in his innocence. What's more, they're deeply attached to him. And you to them—or at least to her.'

Paul shot him an oblique look. 'Have we abandoned our hypothetical lawyer?'

'He's never been more than a figure of speech.' Farquhar's eyes were sympathetic. 'We both know whom we're talking about. You say you have special knowledge. Have you confronted the Sheridan boy with it?'

'Yes.'

'And his reaction?'

'More defiance than an outright denial. There were positive intimations of guilt.'

'Guilty or not, Paul, the defendant is entitled to acquittal on any charge the evidence fails to prove.'

'That's just my point, Julian. All the evidence may never appear.'

'Are you accusing the prosecution of incompetence?'

'No. I'm saying they do not have access to full information.'

'And since when is that the lawyer's concern?'

'But the lawyer knows the kind of man he's defending.'

'The lawyer's duty is not weakened by his client's character.'

'Even if the defence witnesses have perjured themselves?'

Farquhar bunched his lips in troubled deliberation. 'You're certain of that?'

'Dead certain.'

'As an officer of the court, shouldn't you take it to the presiding judge?'

'There's my dilemma, Julian. I should, but I'm not going to. Chaffee is unpredictable. He might make it public. I won't force Dru into a position of conflicting loyalties.'

Farquhar brooded. 'I see your problem. It would be an insuperable imposition.' He shook his head. 'I have no solution, no pat answers. I know only that every accused is entitled to his day in court. The Constitution itself gives him the right to assistance of counsel. *Every* accused. Not only those a lawyer believes to be innocent.'

'Assistance, yes. Is he also entitled to collusion in perpetuating a lie?'

'What lie?'

'The lie of innocence.'

Farquhar made a helpless gesture. 'Paul, I speak only as the devil's advocate. The lawyer can never be certain that he's right. He acts only as a surrogate, defending with zeal and eloquence.'

'How about an equal zeal to protect society?'

'Under an adversary system you leave that to the prosecutor. Your job is to blunt the thrust of overzealous police action—without, of course, wilful connivance or subornation.'

'Aren't there subtler definitions of connivance, Julian?'

'Such as?'

'Concealing evidence that could affect a jury's decision.'

Farquhar studied Paul carefully, pulling thoughtfully on his bottom lip. 'Would it distress you so much if a guilty man were acquitted?'

Paul's face was stiff with restraint. 'This guilty man sat silent and smiling in a courtroom while I ruthlessly sacrificed Alex Moore to save his skin.' The knowledge still rankled like an ulcerating sore. 'He knew that Moore was innocent of any crime beyond a clouded judgement and a breach of trust. Yet he never said a word. He sat mute and let Moore go down the drain to preserve his own freedom.'

'Are you demanding an eye for an eye?'

'No, Julian. It goes far beyond that. This was a crime of unspeakable violence. We live in a jungle society where survival is difficult at best. Is a lawyer nothing more than a gladiator entering the arena just for the sport of winning? Do you measure his worth by the sum of his victories? Does he owe no obligation to society? Are acquittals his only goal even if it tosses back into circulation a festering evil? Can he be free of responsibility for subsequent transgressions?'

'If you ask lawyers to bear that burden, Paul, how can they ever defend?'

'By all fair and honourable means. He must have some responsibility to justice, to the law itself.'

'The law is a philosophical concept created by man. Your client is a human being created by God.'

'By a biological act with normal results.'

'Whatever.' Farquhar smiled distantly. 'Let us not argue evolution too.'

'Agreed. Let us argue truth, conscience, responsibility. Withholding evidence may be clever trial tactics. But is it ever justified?'

'On some occasions it might be necessary.'

'In the pursuit of what?'

'Justice, Paul.'

'Exactly. Isn't that the whole purpose of a trial? A search for truth and justice? Or is it simply a jousting arena between opposing counsel?'

'If you limit my options, I must pick truth and justice.'

'In that case, Julian, shouldn't all pertinent data be given to the jury? How else can they reach a conclusion consistent with truth?'

Dean Farquhar sat for a long silent moment in deep thought. Finally he said in a quiet, troubled voice, 'I remember you as a student in some of my classes, Paul. It was a challenging experience. I followed your career with pride. We stayed in touch. When I was appointed Dean, I invited you to join the faculty. I was delighted you accepted. I understand your problem and I do not know how I myself would act under similar circumstances. You are the man of action. Your particular dilemma is so intensely personal that I would not presume

283

to offer advice. I offer only my sympathy and the assurance
that no matter what your decision, I will not sit in judgement.
Have you discussed it with anyone else?'

Paul shook his head.

'Then I'm gratified you came to me. Distressed at my
inability to help.'

'But you have, Julian. I needed a sounding board. And in
some curious way you've helped to clarify my own thinking.'

Farquhar eyed him keenly. 'You have a solution?'

'Nothing concrete. Only a vague notion, but it's taking
shape.'

The apartment was dark, silent, deserted.

He called Dru's name and received no answer. He went
straight to the bedroom and found it empty. Still wearing his
coat, he sat on the edge of the bed and dialled the Sheridan
number. Quintus informed him that Dru had been there and
had gone out to dinner with her father. My own fault, he
thought. I told her I had no idea when I'd be home.

It had been a long, eventful day, physically and mentally
exhausting. He wished he could forget it completely. Wipe out
all memory of Amy Kowalski and his confrontation with Ken
at the Tombs. Proceed as if the events had never occurred.
Could he live with it if he won the case? Live with the reality
of subverting justice and inflicting a malignancy on society?
Could he ignore the moral imperatives involved?

The phone rang. He snatched at it eagerly, longing to hear
Dru's voice.

'Paul?' It was Abe Barish.

'Yes, Abe. I was just about to call you.'

'Anything special?'

'Yes, Abe. A new development. You'd better sit down.'

'I don't like the sound of your voice. What is it?'

'Did I mention my plans for today, tell you where I was
going?'

'You did not.'

'I flew to Boston for a visit with a former flame of young
Sheridan's.'

'I thought his activities in that area were limited exclusively to Peggy Wayne.'

'You were mistaken.'

'But we supplied testimony to that effect.'

'The testimony was in error. Our boy was involved with a gaudy little punchboard who responded, and they got caught.'

'By whom?'

'Not whom. Caught by sperm.'

'My God!' Barish was nonplussed. 'Another one? Pregnant?'

'Yes. And another abortion.'

Barish made a clucking sound. 'Did Hadley know this when he testified?'

'He must have.'

There was a moment of silence. 'Then the boy lied.'

'Deliberately. But a minor consideration compared to what I heard from the girl's father. Listen to this, Abe.'

In a flat, uninflected voice he related the details of his visit to Newton and his subsequent confrontation with Ken at the Tombs.

Barish said in a hushed voice, 'Is it possible the boy is . . .?'

'Not only possible; it's more than probable. Identical injuries in both cases. Lies from our own witnesses. Lies from our client. And here's the clincher, Abe.' In a harsh voice he told Barish about Dru's ring and Ken's reaction. 'The boy knew I was lying. You could see it in his face. And he had a damned good reason. Because he himself had gotten rid of the loot where it could never be found. He sneered at me, Abe. He defied me to pull out, knowing I'm hobbled, locked into his defence. Our client is a poisonous little butcher who ought to be caged and——'

He heard a gasp and snapped his head around. His gaze fell on Dru, rooted in the doorway, staring at him in dismay, her face set in a grimace of pain and shock. Instantly the words stuck in his throat. How long had she been standing there? How much had she heard?

The pause seemed an eternity. The look in her eyes pulled at his gut. He whispered into the phone, 'I'll talk to you later, Abe,' and hung up.

Dru said accusingly, 'You were talking about Ken.'

He nodded. 'I've never lied to you, Dru. I can't lie now. This isn't easy for me. Please try to understand. I know how much Ken means to you. I've done everything humanly possible to help the boy. I even destroyed Alex Moore in the process, and that's something I'll have to live with. Ken watched me do it and he relished it. Our loyalty, yours and mine, was misguided, wasted . . .'

Her eyes filled. 'How can you say you helped him? You tried to trick him into an admission. I heard you. A helpless boy. How utterly despicable!'

'I had to know the truth.'

'What truth?' Her mouth was trembling. 'Dear God, I've known Ken all his life.'

'Isn't it possible you're prejudiced?'

'We've lived in the same home. I watched him grow. I helped raise him. And I know in my heart he's not the monster you just described.'

He rose awkwardly and she fell back a step, hugging herself as if chilled.

'Who do you think you are?' she said bleakly. 'Deciding a boy's fate on your half-baked suspicions and fantasies.'

He held his hands out, palms together in supplication. 'Ah, Dru, listen to me——'

'No.' She sobbed once and wheeled away blindly. He heard the door to his study close behind her.

Paul sank back on the bed, drained and empty, his heart leaden.

CHAPTER TWELVE

EARLY SUNDAY AFTERNOON Lucas Sheridan appeared at the Slater apartment. Paul was expecting him. Sheridan's manner was curt and inflexibly militant.

'Where's Dru?'

'In bed, resting.'

'She sounded damned peculiar on the phone this morning. You two having problems?'

'Nothing important,' Paul said, trying to minimize the discord. But it had lasted through a night of separate rooms, a morning of non-communication, except for a brief appearance at the study door to announce that her father had called and would be coming over to see him. He was certain that she had not mentioned last night's episode.

Lucas Sheridan made a peremptory gesture and headed towards the study. He remained standing when he spoke. 'All right, Paul, we're coming up to the wire. I can no longer stand on the sidelines. There's too much at stake. I insist on being heard.'

'About what?'

'I want you to put Ken on the stand.' He lifted his hand to forestall an objection. 'Hear me out first. We've brainstormed this thing at the office. Whatever you may think, we have some first-rate talent there. We've examined it from every angle and we've reached a consensus, I think it would be a serious miscalculation to keep the boy from testifying. Those jurors would wonder if he had anything to hide, regardless of any instructions from the judge. That is an immutable fact, and nothing you say on summation can change it. I cannot accept that risk. Ken will make an excellent impression. He's intelligent, capable of fielding questions and handling himself competently.' He punched a hole in the air with an emphatic fore-finger. 'I just came from the Tombs. I saw him less than an hour ago. We discussed it and he agrees with me. He's eager for an opportunity to confront his accusers. In fact, he insists on it.'

Paul nodded. 'All right.'

Lucas Sheridan was startled. 'You agree?'

'Yes. If that's his last word, I won't fight either of you on it.'

Sheridan had been braced for conflict. He rocked for a moment on the balls of his feet. 'One additional point. I am not unknown. My word carries a certain cachet. I want you to put me on the stand as a character witness.'

'Tomorrow morning,' Paul said. 'You'll head the line-up.'

It had been a long-established rule that evidence of a defendant's character is admissible on the theory that his disposition could incite or restrain him from certain acts. Paul knew that Lucas Sheridan had made a profound impression on the jury. His credentials were impeccable, his presence impressive, his unemotional voice convincing. In his recital of the events that had orphaned Ken, he had created a subtle bond of sympathy. He spoke of the boy's early years as a member of his own household, his exemplary behaviour as a summer apprentice at Porterfield, Baker & Sheridan. There had been no charge of nepotism. Indeed, colleagues and other employees had often remarked on Ken's amiability and diligence.

When, ultimately, he was turned over to the prosecution for cross, Nicoletti stood back and proceeded on a courteous note.

'You spent a number of years in various diplomatic posts, Mr Sheridan, did you not?'

'I did.'

'Which means, does it not, that you were generally out of the country during those periods?'

'Yes, sir.'

'Did your family accompany you?'

'My daughter and my nephew remained at school here in the States.'

'How long were you away?'

'Approximately six years.'

'And how often did you return?'

'Whenever I was called back to Washington.'

'Once . . . twice . . . ?'

'More than that, sir.'

'Three times . . . four . . . ?'

'At least once a year.'

'For brief periods?'

'Several days.'

'And during your visits to the capital you were mostly busy with the State Department, were you not?'

'I believe that would be a fair statement.'

'Would it also be a fair statement to say that during those six years, covering a major part of the defendant's youth and adolescence, you saw him only briefly and sporadically?'

Lucas Sheridan turned frosty. 'I had regular reports from my daughter and from the boy's headmaster at school.'

Nicoletti was peeling the silk gloves. 'But you personally did not observe his growth and behaviour, isn't that so?'

'If you wish to put it that way.'

'You returned permanently and resumed your stewardship of Porterfield, Baker & Sheridan about the time the defendant entered college, is that correct?'

'It is.'

'He was an undergraduate for four years?'

'He was.'

'Did he visit your home in New York on weekends?'

'Occasionally.'

'But not frequently.'

'Students often spend their weekends at school studying.'

'With all respect, Mr Sheridan, you're not being responsive. We now have an additional four years when he was not under your observation or your supervision.'

Lucas Sheridan bristled. 'I saw a great deal of him during summer vacations.'

'Two months out of twelve, sir. Was the relationship between you and your nephew very close?'

'We were and are extremely fond of each other.'

'If he found himself in trouble, would he confide in you?'

'No such occasion ever arose. Until this absurd charge, he never got into any trouble.'

'Not to your knowledge anyway. I wonder if we're talking about a normal boy or some saintly paragon. You heard Peggy Wayne testify that she and the defendant had been secretly married, did you not?'

'I did.'

'The first time you ever heard that particular bulletin was right here in court?'

'Yes.'

'Then you really know very little about what the defendant is up to most of the time, isn't that true?'

Paul doffed an imaginary hat to Nicoletti. Challenging a witness of Lucas Sheridan's stature was always a delicate problem. He admired, too, his father-in-law's control.

'There were reasons for the boy's lack of candour. He knew I wanted him to finish his education before he made any permanent commitments.'

'He knew, but apparently he did not respect your wishes. Did he mention the fact to your daughter?'

'I believe not.'

'Was she closer to the defendant than you were, Mr Sheridan?'

'I have no measuring device for such an evaluation, Mr Nicoletti.'

The prosecutor smiled ironically. 'I don't think we need go any further, sir. You may step down.'

Judge Chaffee lifted his chin in Paul's direction. 'Mr Slater?'

'The defence calls Kenneth Sheridan.'

Sudden excitement swept like a wave across spectators and officials alike. Nicoletti sat erect. Abe Barish took a sharp breath. Almost no one had anticipated the move. The whispering and shuffling faded as Ken mounted the stand and took the oath.

Paul could not help but marvel at the boy's composure. No trace of nervousness or apprehension. He looked sober, earnest, candid. Earlier that morning when Paul had informed him of the change in strategy, he had nodded without comment, smiling enigmatically. Now, seated in the witness chair, with all eyes focused on him, facing his lawyer, he waited patiently for the first question.

In a direct examination keyed deliberately low, Paul guided him through a detailed account of his early years, his schooling, his aspirations, and his courtship of Peggy Wayne. It was a long recital and although it parelleled to some extent the ground covered by his uncle, Paul saw from a visual poll of the jury that it held their attention and that they were favourably impressed.

He asked, 'Were you pressured into marrying Peggy Wayne?'

'How do you mean, sir?'

'Did you marry her because she was pregnant?'

'No, sir. I married her because we were in love. Peggy became pregnant afterwards.' He shrugged ruefully. 'She was supposed to be on the pill, but I guess something went wrong.'

'Did you feel that your uncle's request for a delay was unreasonable?'

'No, sir. The only excuse I can make is that we were both very young and impetuous.'

'Now, Ken, before the proceedings in this case, did you ever have any other trouble with the law?'

'Yes, sir.'

'Describe it to the court.'

'It was during my last year as an undergraduate. We had just finished midterm exams, and a couple of fellows got together for a little celebration. It was late, after midnight, and somebody suddenly brought out a joint . . .'

'By joint you mean a marijuana cigarette?'

'Yes, sir.'

'What happened?'

'Most of the fellows started to smoke, only a few puffs, and then suddenly we were being raided. I don't know how the police got wind of it, but there they were. It seemed strange to me at the time because the whole thing was unpremeditated. And they took us all down to the police station.'

'On what charge?'

'Possession and use.'

'Were you booked?'

'Yes, sir.'

'Convicted?'

'No, sir. The case against me was dismissed for insufficient evidence.'

'Did you ever smoke marijuana?'

'I tried it once and didn't like it.'

Paul stepped forward one pace. 'Now, Ken, let us go back to October the seventeenth, a Tuesday. Can you remember anything unusual that happened on that date?'

'Yes, sir. I received a long-distance telephone call from Dolly Wayne.'

'What was the purpose of that call?'

'She said she wanted to see me on a very important matter and asked me to drive to New York the next morning.'

'You heard the testimony of Gordon Frazer when he appeared in this courtroom as a witness for the People?'

'Yes, sir, I did.'

'He testified that he was with Miss Wayne at her apartment when she called you and that she was very angry. Does that concur with your recollection of her attitude?'

Ken shook his head. 'I can't imagine why he'd say anything like that. It just isn't true. Dolly may have been a little upset, but not at all angry.'

'You agreed to go to New York?'

'Yes, sir.'

'And you left Cambridge the next morning?'

'I started driving at eight o'clock and I got there around noon.'

'In your own words, Ken, I would like you to tell the court and jury exactly what happened on that visit.'

Ken leaned forward and looked directly at the jury. 'Dolly was waiting for me. She said she was sorry if I had to cut any classes, but there was something we had to discuss. She asked me if I knew that Peggy was pregnant. I was really surprised. Peggy hadn't mentioned a word about it to me. Dolly wanted to know if I was responsible. I said yes, there couldn't be any doubt about that. I knew Peggy wouldn't let anyone else touch her. Dolly asked me what I intended to do about it. Well, she was Peggy's mother and she had a right to be upset. So I told her the truth. I told her that Peggy and I were already married, that we'd been married for about six months. I told her about our trip to Maryland. She was so relieved that she laughed a little and cried a little at the same time. Then she threw her arms around me and kissed me on the cheek and said, "Oh, my God, I'm going to be a grandmother. There goes my career as a soubrette." I explained why we hadn't told anyone and asked her to help us keep it a secret until after I finished law school.' He looked around, grinning boyishly. 'She said she was perfectly willing to wait two more years, but she didn't think the baby could hold out that long.'

There was a ripple of laughter.

'Of course she was right,' Ken said, 'and I agreed with her. She thought an announcement was in order because people would soon begin to notice Peggy's condition. So I asked her to let me notify my uncle first and she said sure.'

'There were no arguments, no harsh words between you?'

'Absolutely none.'

'How long did you stay?'

'About half an hour.'

'Then you left Dolly Wayne's apartment at twelve-thirty?'

'Give or take a few minutes either way.'

Paul conducted him through a description of the events surrounding the praying-mantis pin, conforming it carefully with Peggy Wayne's account. It had to be obvious to the jury that only a cretin would have pawned stolen merchandise under the circumstances.

'You knew that Peggy's mother had given her the pin?'

'Yes, sir.'

'And that she had a right to sell it if she wished?'

'It was her suggestion.'

Paul nodded. Then, in precise detail, he led Ken along the route back to Cambridge, describing his arrival and the start of a touch-football game that ultimately damaged his sweater.

'It was supposed to have been a friendly game?'

'Yes, sir. But it got out of hand when Duke Pirie tackled me. He shouldn't have done that; it's against the rules. I fell flat on my face and that's when my nose began to bleed. Then I really got miffed when those two strangers piled on top of us.'

'Is that when your sweater got torn?'

'It must have been.'

'How badly was it damaged?'

'Well, the sleeve was almost off and there was a rip at the collar, besides all the mud and the blood from my nose.'

'Could it have been repaired?'

'I don't think so. It was a total wreck.'

'Is that why you got rid of it down the incinerator?'

'Yes, sir.'

'How did you generally discard worn and useless garments?'

'The same way, down the incinerator.'

Paul moved back one pace. 'Now, Ken, look at the jury and tell them whether or not Dolly Wayne was still alive when you left her apartment that Wednesday afternoon at twelve-thirty p.m.'

Ken faced the panel.

He said quietly and with deep feeling, 'She was alive and well, so help me God!'

Paul turned back to the defence table. 'You may inquire,' he said.

Judge Chaffee peered down at the prosecutor. 'Are you anticipating a lengthy cross-examination, Mr Nicoletti?'

'It will not be short, Your Honour.'

'Then I believe this will be a good time to break for lunch.'

Lunching at Conally's with Paul and Abe Barish, Lucas Holmes Sheridan was scarcely able to conceal his elation. 'Just as I told you. The boy made a splendid impression. Don't you think so, Mr Barish?'

'Yes,' Abe said.

'I was watching the jury and I tell you those women were beaming. They believed every word Ken said. Nobody can convince them otherwise. You've got them locked into an acquittal, Paul. And the men, too, were not unaffected. All in all, an excellent morning.'

In the euphoria of that moment, he seemed to have forgotten Alex Moore completely.

When court reconvened, Chaffee reminded Ken that he was still under oath. Nicoletti's initial approach was restrained and paternal. The large square teeth shone in a bland smile. Ken met his gaze with the earnest solemnity of a youthful novitiate.

'Now, Ken,' Nicoletti said, 'have you told us the whole truth and nothing but the truth exactly as it happened in Dolly Wayne's apartment on October eighteenth?'

'Yes, sir, I have.'

'So help you God?'

'Yes, sir.'

'Those were your exact words?'

'They were.'

'Are you religious, Ken?'

'We're members of the Episcopalian Church.'

'And when was the last time you attended services?'

'Not for some time, I'm afraid.'

'Within the past year?'

'No, sir.'

'The year before?'

'I don't think so.'

'Am I correct in assuming there is an Episcopalian church in the Cambridge area?'

'Yes, sir.'

'Then I take it you invoke the sanctity of God with some hypocrisy?' Nicoletti's voice had sharpened. 'Do you always speak the truth?'

'Most of the time.'

'But not *all* the time. Does that mean you sometimes lie?'

Paul saw the change in Ken's face as the forthright sincerity subtly shaded into wary caution. Now, at the very start of his cross, he was beginning to see the calibre of the man opposing him.

He said, 'I do not deliberately tell lies.'

Nicoletti's eyebrows soared. 'You do not tell lies. How refreshing! A paragon of honesty! Didn't you promise the deceased that you would notify your uncle about your marriage to her daughter?'

'Yes, I did.'

'But you did not tell him.'

'Well, I didn't have a chance. Dolly was killed later that day and everything blew up in my face.'

'Did you tell your cousin, Drusilla Slater?'

'No, sir.'

'She lives right here in Manhattan, does she not?'

'She does.'

'And are there telephones available on many of the streets here?'

'I suppose there are.'

'No, sir. You *know* there are. You've lived here and seen them. Are you devoted to your cousin?'

'We are deeply attached to each other.'

'And yet, having travelled all that distance, you could not spare the time to phone her or pay her a brief visit.'

'I was in a hurry to get back to school.'

'Are you sure you didn't have another reason?'

'I don't understand the question, Mr Nicoletti.'

'I am suggesting, sir, that you did not want to be seen by anyone at that particular time because of your appearance. Isn't it a fact that your sweater was already stained with Dolly Wayne's blood?'

'No, sir.' Ken stressed the denial with righteous indignation. 'That is not a fact.'

'Nevertheless, you were in a rush to get back to school?'

'That's right.'

'So that you could waste more time playing touch football? Was that so much more important than seeing your devoted relatives?'

'Well, it was a long drive and I needed some exercise.'

'We'll come to that in a moment. Let us get back to the telephone call you did not make. Isn't it a fact that you didn't think it necessary to notify your uncle or anyone else of your marriage because the pressure was off, because you knew that Dolly Wayne was dead?'

'No, sir. That thought never occurred to me because I knew she was alive.'

'You testified, did you not, that you left Cambridge about eight o'clock that morning?'

'I did.'

'And you got to New York about noon?'

'Yes, sir.'

'Four hours?'

'Yes, sir.'

'And how long to drive through the choked streets of midtown Manhattan on a weekday?'

Ken moistened his lips. Paul saw that he was growing increasingly uneasy.

'Not long,' he said.

'It took you some time to find a parking place?'

'I was lucky.'

'Lucky enough to park on a prohibited street?'

'Well, I didn't expect to be there long.'

'Even so, logic would seem to indicate that you could not have rung Miss Wayne's bell much before twelve-thirty.'

Ken shook his head. 'I really don't think so.'

'But you're no longer sure. Now, you heard your room-mate testify that you had coffee with him at eight a.m.'

'That's right.'

'Anything else? Cereal? Eggs?'

Ken smiled tightly, as if realizing that Nicoletti was trying to delay his departure. 'No, sir. Coffee was all I had and I left immediately.'

Paul saw it coming before anyone else, how neatly the prosecutor had sprung his trap.

Nicoletti said, 'And you drove straight to New York?'

'Yes, sir.'

'No stops for refreshments or lunch?'

Now Paul guessed that Ken's mind had leaped ahead to test his answer.

297

'I drove right through.'

'Did Miss Wayne offer you any lunch?'

'No, sir. I don't suppose it occurred to her. She was concerned about Peggy's condition.'

'And still no offer even after you reassured her on that score?'

It was obvious now that Nicoletti was trying to delay Ken's departure to coincide with Billy Clark's account of a struggle. Equally obvious was Ken's urgent need to clear out.

'Dolly knew that I was in a hurry to get back to school.'

Nicoletti spread his hands. 'But you must have been exceedingly hungry by now. Nothing but coffee since eight a.m. Are you telling us that you intended to drive at least another four hours without arranging for some nourishment?'

Ken took the bait. 'Well, as soon as I left Dolly's, I walked over to Lexington Avenue and found a lunch counter.'

'How many blocks away?'

'Not far. To the best of my recollection, just a few.'

'At that hour it must have been crowded.'

Paul visualized the alternatives racing through Ken's head. The more patrons, the more anonymous his own presence, should corroboration be required. Nicoletti wanted him back in the victim's apartment; Ken needed to place himself elsewhere.

'Yes,' he said, 'there were a lot of people there.'

Nicoletti capitalized on the answer. 'Then you had to wait, didn't you?'

Ken saw that he'd been boxed, and he back-tracked. 'Not very long.'

'Well, sir, just how long did it take to get you seated and served?'

'Maybe twenty minutes.'

'Pretty warm in there with all those people?'

'I suppose so.'

'But you did not remove your coat, did you?'

'I was wearing a windbreaker and I kept it on.'

'Naturally.' Nicoletti glanced significantly at the jury. There would be stains on his sweater the witness wanted to conceal. He would emphasize the point on summation. 'By your own figures then, that would take you back into the street about one o'clock."

Ken's timetable was being squeezed out of proportion. He had no choice but to concede grudgingly. 'Could be.'

'And by a more logical computation, it was probably later than that.'

'I don't think so.'

'At any rate, we have you tagged with a parking violation fifteen minutes later. At one-fifteen to be precise. So Patrolman Molloy's watch had to be fairly accurate, wouldn't you say?'

Ken groped for a satisfactory answer. Paul saw from the pull of sullenness at his mouth that he did not like the way his cross was proceeding. 'It might have been. I don't know.'

'What happened to the ticket?'

'I don't remember.'

'Did you throw it away?'

No, sir.'

'Did you pay the fine?'

'I never had a chance.'

'But you would have paid the fine under other circumstances?'

'Yes, sir.'

'You would not deliberately ignore a summons, would you?'

'No, sir.'

Nicoletti swung towards the prosecution table. His assistant had a sheaf of papers ready. 'I have here a record of eight citations for various vehicular offences issued against a Volkswagen registered in the name of Kenneth Sheridan, not one of them——'

'Objection,' Paul said. 'Immaterial to the issues in this case.'

'It goes to the credibility of the witness, Your Honour. They serve to impeach his testimony and to show disregard and contempt for the law.'

'Objection overruled,' Chaffee said.

Nicoletti brandished the papers. 'All of the fines assessed on these citations were ignored, Mr Sheridan. How do you explain that?'

The only possible response was a lame one. 'I must have forgotten about them.'

'Are you asking us to believe that each subsequent summons failed to remind you?'

'I guess I was busy at school.'

'What did you do with all those tickets?'

'I really don't remember.'

'So you're admitting now that your memory is unreliable.'

Ken chewed his lip. 'You're trying to put words in my mouth, Mr Nicoletti.'

'Not at all. I'm perfectly willing to let the facts speak for themselves. If you prefer not to answer, we'll let the jurors draw their own conclusions.' Nicoletti ambled towards them, leaning on the rail, compelling the witness to face in that direction. He wanted them to see the defendant's expression. 'According to the time on Officer Molloy's citation,' he said, 'it would seem that you reclaimed your car about one-thirty at the earliest.'

'I didn't check it, Mr Nicoletti.'

'And with the traffic still clogging the streets, it must have taken you at least half an hour to reach the Bruckner Expressway. That takes us up to two o'clock.'

'You're doing the arithmetic, Mr Nicoletti, not me.'

The prosecutor smiled coldly. 'You testified that you returned to Cambridge about four-thirty that afternoon. Will you explain to this jury how you managed to make a four-hour trip in two and a half hours driving a Volkswagen?'

Ken moistened his lips. There was perspiration on his forehead. 'I didn't log that trip minute by minute. I merely know when I left and when I returned.'

'Well, think about it. If you drove two hundred and thirty miles in two and a half hours you must have been travelling over ninety miles an hour. Will a Volkswagen travel at that speed?'

An edginess crept into Ken's voice. 'The only answer I can give you, Mr Nicoletti, is that I must have left earlier.'

'Or got back later. Now, you say you parked and crossed that wet field on foot, isn't that so?'

'Yes.'

'And you slipped?'

'Yes.'

'And that is how you got mud on your sweater?'

'Yes.'

'Were you wearing that sweater on top of your wind-breaker?'

Ken swallowed. A random tic pulled at one eye. 'No.'

'Then perhaps you can explain how you got mud on your sweater but not on your windbreaker.'

Ken's lips were compressed. He prised them apart. 'I—I took it off.'

'Why?'

'Because I felt warm.'

Again Nicoletti stalked over to the prosecution table. Like a trained seal his assistant handed him another document. He brought it back and handed it to the witness. 'Will you tell us what this is?'

'It looks like a weather report.'

'Correct.' Nicoletti grinned wolfishly. 'It's a certified copy of an official weather report for Boston and its surrounding area. Will you read the date, please?'

'Wednesday, October eighteenth.'

'Excellent. And what was the temperature on that day?'

Ken dropped his eyes. His voice was strained. 'Low, thirty-five; high, thirty-eight.'

'Pretty cold, wouldn't you say?'

'For some people, maybe.'

'Well, now, you're a college graduate. You know that water freezes at thirty-two degrees Fahrenheit, don't you?'

'Yes.'

'Then I think any intelligent person would assume that it was very cold that Wednesday. Will you please explain why you removed your jacket in near-freezing weather?'

Paul stole a quick glance at Lucas Holmes Sheridan and saw his father-in-law sitting rigid, his face carved in stone. The old eagle had wanted the boy on the stand. What did he think of his strategy now?

301

'Cold doesn't bother me,' Ken said in a pinched voice.

Paul stood. 'I think the district attorney should qualify that weather report.'

'If it please the Court,' Nicoletti said, 'this is a certified copy of an official report made by the National Weather Service, an agency of the United States Government, properly certified. If counsel for the defence insists on delaying the trial, we'll produce the appropriate official to verify it.'

'Mr Slater.'

Paul waved his acceptance. Further objection would accomplish nothing.

'Offer it in evidence,' Nicoletti said.

'The clerk will mark it.'

'Now, Mr Sheridan,' Nicoletti said, folding his arms, 'I suggest that you did indeed remove your windbreaker, but not because you felt warm, however. You took it off and crossed that wet field instead of using the paved sidewalk so that you could deliberately slip and roll in the mud. I suggest you did that in order to conceal evidence of Dolly Wayne's blood on your sweater.'

It brought Ken out of the witness chair, trembling with anger. 'You're a liar!'

'Sit *down*!' Chaffee snapped. 'I want you to control yourself, young man.'

Ken sank back, nervously biting his lips.

Nicoletti said, 'And you kept wearing that same sweater for the so-called friendly football game, didn't you?'

'Yes.'

'You knew there would be horseplay.'

'No.'

'You would have started some yourself if Duke Pirie hadn't accommodated you. I suggest that you deliberately pushed your nose into the ground and started the nosebleed yourself.'

'That's another lie.'

Paul saw the dilated pupils and knew that Ken was on the brink, dangerously close to losing all control.

'You didn't just toss that sweater into any handy old trash can, did you?'

'No.'

'You threw it down the incinerator to get rid of it for ever—wasn't that your reason? To preclude any test ever being made for your victim's blood?'

Ken's cheekbones were flat and white. 'No.'

'Did you suffer other injuries in that convenient little fracas?'

'My shins were bruised.'

'Black and blue, were they?'

'You saw them when I was arrested.'

Nicoletti's harsh tone was shot with contempt. 'And do you want the jury to believe that those bruises were *not* inflicted by Dolly Wayne trying to defend herself?'

'You don't have to believe anything.'

Nicoletti had made his point. Abruptly now, he shifted his attack. 'Are you a scholarship student at school?'

'No.'

'Who pays your tuition?'

'My uncle.'

'Your parents did not leave you much of an estate, did they?'

'Objection,' Paul said.

'Your Honour, this line of questioning goes directly to motive. In his cross-examination of Alex Moore, defence counsel himself endorsed the admissibility of such evidence.'

'I will allow it subject to connection. The witness may answer.'

Ken glared. 'My father was very young when he died.'

'Nevertheless, you have no money of your own.'

'I expect to earn what I need.'

'You already have, haven't you? You married Peggy Wayne, who inherits her mother's considerable estate.'

It wrestled Ken to the edge of his chair. Anger reverberated in the suddenly high nasal pitch of his voice. 'That's a damned filthy insinuation. You're trying to twist and distort everything that's happened. You wouldn't have the guts to re**peat** that outside this——'

Chaffee's gavel hammered him into silence. Paul felt Abe Barish's fingers gripping his arm. He sat impassive, while Nicoletti continued implacably.

303

'You knew Dolly Wayne was a rich woman.'

'I never counted her money.'

'It's common knowledge she'd been a stage star for many years and the widow of a millionaire. By marrying the daughter and eliminating the mother, you would eventually control that fortune. You knew you had Peggy Wayne under your thumb, didn't you?'

Ken took refuge in a trembling silence, strain cutting white lines around his mouth. Nicoletti did not wait for an answer. He kept boring in.

'You married the girl. Were you in love with her?'

'Yes.'

'Were you formally engaged?'

'We had an understanding.'

'For how long?'

'Ever since we entered college.'

'Were you faithful to her all that time?'

'Yes.'

Paul held his breath, aware of a throbbing tension.

'You're sure of that?'

'I'm positive.'

'Does the name Amy Kowalski mean anything to you?'

The sky fell in. It froze Ken into immobility, turning him ashen. In full pursuit, Nicoletti was relentless.

'The court can't hear you. Speak up.'

Ken's gaze scattered in all directions. He could not deny it and he nodded in numbed acquiescence. 'Yes,' he whispered, 'I know her.'

'A young girl who lives in Newton, not far from school?'

'Yes.'

'You were friendly with her?'

'We had a few beers from time to time.'

'That's all? No physical contact?'

A dry swallow moved Ken's throat. 'I—I don't know what you mean.'

'I mean exactly what the words imply. Physical contact. Getting into bed with her, fornicating, copulating, making her pregnant.'

304

Impotent fury bent the boy forward. 'If that's what she told you, she lied.'

'Her father confirmed it.'

'He lied too.'

'Everybody lies except Ken Sheridan. You have a monopoly on the truth, as amply demonstrated, since you swore on the Bible and took that witness stand.'

'They hate me. They'd say anything.'

'Is it a lie that she was pregnant?'

'I don't know if she was or not.'

'Didn't you pay for an abortion?'

'To get them off my back. It could have been anybody. The girl's a tramp.'

'You know that at first hand, don't you?' There was knifing sarcasm in Nicoletti's voice.

'Yes, yes.' Words were pouring out in a heedless torrent. 'She was no good, a bum who'd put out for anybody. And her old man was no better. The bastard mousetrapped me. He threatened a paternity suit unless I ponied up. So I paid him. It was extortion. I should have turned them over to the police, both of them, the whore and the blackmailer. But I—I . . .' He choked it back, one eye twitching.

'Did you see Amy Kowalski again after that?'

'No. I was fed to the teeth. I'd had enough.'

'You're under oath, Sheridan. Think hard. Did you see the girl again?'

He prised his teeth away from his bottom lip. 'Well, I—yes, maybe I did.'

'Do you remember the occasion?'

Ken seemed dazed. 'Not very well.'

'Then let me refresh your recollection. You were out with her. You brought her home, some time around two in the morning. You had her on the sofa and you did things to her. Things that hurt her and frightened her and made her scream out in terror——'

Paul came to his feet, shouting, 'Objection, Your Honour. There is nothing on the record, no evidence, no foundation to warrant these accusations.'

305

'Counsel will please approach the bench.' Chaffee looked bleak.

Their footsteps echoed in the deathly still courtroom as ears strained to hear the sidebar conference.

'What about it, Mr Nicoletti?'

'The State has witnesses to prove each and every assertion, Your Honour.'

'Where were they during your examination in chief?'

'The evidence was unavailable at that time. It came to light only over this past weekend.'

'Are you making a motion to reopen?'

'If necessary, yes.'

'The prosecution has rested its case,' Paul snapped. 'The defence would object most strenuously.'

Nicoletti allowed himself a thin smile. 'Mr Slater is making noises for the record. He knows the rules as well as I do. This court has discretionary power to permit additional evidence even after the prosecution has closed. In the interests of justice, such evidence would be essential to People's case.'

Chaffee looked at Paul. 'The Court would rule favourably on the motion, Mr Slater. You could have your exception.'

A fat lot of good it would do, Paul thought, striding back to the defence table. 'They have the Kowalskis,' he told Abe, 'and they may reopen.'

Barish closed his eyes prayerfully.

Nicoletti resumed his attack at once.

'That night on the sofa, Mr Sheridan, do you recall escaping through the window when the girl's screams awakened her father?'

Ken sat mute, the bones growing more prominent in his shrinking face. His eyes burned feverishly. He can't take it much longer, Paul thought—this Italian immigrant's son proving smarter, sharper, tying him into knots. An uneasy tension gripped the courtroom, like the calm before a storm. The jurors stared at the witness, faces starkly impenetrable.

Ken found his voice in a hollow litany he had convinced himself would be his salvation. 'You're blind, all blind. You need a scapegoat because you can't reach Alex Moore. He did it. Moore killed her. He lost his head and he couldn't face the music. That's why he jumped off his terrace . . .'

Nicoletti overrode him. 'It won't wash, Sheridan. You heard the testimony of the medical examiner. You heard him describe in detail the injuries suffered by Dolly Wayne. Explain to the jury how it happens that you mauled and savaged the girl Amy Kowalski, inflicting on her injuries of an identical nature? Are you asking the jury to believe it a coincidence?'

The words were a catalytic agent, almost wrestling Ken out of his chair. Dark blood suffused his face. All restraint abruptly gone, he was purging his fury in shrill, foam-flecked obscenity. Chaffee sat back, thunderstruck.

Nicoletti's voice cut through like a scalpel. 'Do you know anything in Moore's background that would cause him to use his teeth, to disfigure and lacerate the deceased?' He levelled an accusing finger. 'Isn't that your pattern, Sheridan, only yours?'

Ken suddenly went limp. He collapsed into the chair, drained, his face bloodless. He kept shaking his head numbly from side to side. 'I don't have to answer that. You can't make me. I won't answer any more questions. I take the Fifth . . . the Fifth . . .'

He kept repeating it, his breathing ragged, his eyes dazed and lost.

Chaffee recovered and rapped his gavel. 'Court stands adjourned. I want to see counsel in chambers immediately.'

The room was in turmoil. Among the seething spectators, Lucas Holmes Sheridan sat, bowed over, his face in his hands.

CHAPTER THIRTEEN

WALKING NOW was difficult. Dru had not been sleeping well
and a mild sedative prescribed by her obstetrician had proved
ineffective. Her ankles had been swollen for some time and the
abdominal heaviness emphasized her discomfort. Nevertheless,
she kept trudging, aimless, distracted, heedless of other
pedestrians and the surrounding traffic.

It had been impossible to remain home after the newscast.
The walls of the apartment seemed to be closing in, suffocating
her. She had been listening to the radio when sudden excitement caught the announcer's voice:

'We interrupt this programme to bring you a special bulletin.
Kenneth Sheridan, the young law student on trial in Manhattan's Supreme Court for the first-degree murder of stage
star Dolly Wayne, brought the case to a dramatic climax late
this morning. During an annihilating cross-examination by
Assistant District Attorney John Nicoletti, Sheridan suddenly
erupted uncontrollably to curse the prosecutor. Then, confronted by the introduction of new incriminating evidence, he
took refuge behind the Fifth Amendment, refusing to participate further in the trial. In a scene of utter chaos, Judge
Albert Chaffee adjourned court to discuss this new development with Nicoletti and defence counsel, Paul Slater. Stay
tuned to this station for additional bulletins.'

It had left her aghast, paralysed with shock. As the full
implication slowly penetrated, a wave of nausea swept over
her and she stumbled blindly to the bathroom, where she
emptied herself in wrenching spasms. She sat on the edge of
the tub, chilled and sick, huddling herself in misery.

Now, the first moments of shock gone, she felt oddly
diffused. Why had it happened? What had gone wrong? Who

was to blame? She searched for answers and found only confusion. She thought of Paul and suffered a twinge of acute pain coupled with a sense of loss. What she had found with Paul was in such sharp contrast to the unhappy time with Gordon Frazer.

It all flooded back. . . .

God, what a chastening experience! All the romantic illusions of adolescence so rudely demolished. The storybook dream of illimitable raptures seemingly gone for ever. It had soured her to the point of cynicism. The men she'd met seemed carved of clay, one-dimensional, single-tracked in their pursuit of erotic gratification.

It had been an aimless, arid time. She had felt cheated. Instinct told her there had to be something more. She wondered whether all the furry and mindless little animals weren't better off, feeding and multiplying and living out their brief span untroubled by the follies and the imbecilities of human beings.

Then, with her depression at its nadir, Paul had appeared on the scene. Life suddenly took on fresh meaning. Colours became more vivid. Food tasted better. The air smelled cleaner. There had been such a totality of giving and response, such a vast sense of fulfilment. Their love-making so lusty, so bawdy, yet so wonderfully flavoured with tenderness.

And now the pain and loss seemed intolerable. Her eyes stung. . . .

'It's no use, Lucas,' Paul said. 'We can't reach him. He won't talk to anyone. There's been some kind of regression; he seems catatonic. Nicoletti thought he was faking, now he's not so sure. Chaffee's ordered a psychiatric examination. And he's allowing us to bring in our own doctor.'

Lucas Holmes Sheridan had aged visibly. His face was haggard, his eyes deeply socketed. He'd been waiting in the corridor for Paul to finish his conference with the judge.

'Do you know a good man?'

'Yes. Max Beaudette. I've already set it up.'

'And after that?'

'I just don't know. But I have a feeling that Ken isn't going back on that witness stand.'

'Perhaps that's best.'

'It creates a problem, Lucas. We examined the boy on direct and Nicoletti is entitled to a full cross. We cannot abridge that right or limit it by the defendant's refusal. It's a mess.'

Sheridan suppressed a groan. Pain shadowed his eyes. 'It's my fault. I insisted he take the stand.'

'No, Lucas. You're no more to blame for what happened in that courtroom than I am for Alex Moore's suicide.'

'Is—is there anything that we can do to salvage the situation?'

'We'll have to play the cards as they fall.'

His eyes searched Paul's face. 'I want the truth. Do *you* think the boy is guilty?'

'I'm not going to answer that, Lucas. You were there and you saw what happened.' Paul caught sight of Abe Barish hurrying along the corridor. 'You'll have to excuse me now, Lucas. I'm pressed for time. I won't be able to get home for a while and I think someone ought to be with Dru.'

The old man nodded and walked heavily towards the elevators, moving like an automaton.

Barish beckoned Paul into a corner. 'I finally made contact with your detective. I told him you'd never received his chemist's report on those tablets you'd taken from Ken's bathroom cabinet. He checked it out and got back to me. He said they'd been analysed and a report mailed to the office. We never received it.'

'Goddamn mail.'

'Yeah. And the cost of postage keeps going up. Anyway, it's just as you suspected. Amphetamines. Speed.'

Clouds scudded across the sky, leaching out the last remnants of daylight. Maximilian Beaudette, M.D., member of the New York Psychoanalytic Society, sat back and shook his head at Paul.

'Had to cancel all my appointments so I could see your boy.

My patients do not take kindly to postponements. You look lousy. I thought only doctors work hard.'

'It's tough on everybody, Max. Especially trial lawyers.'

'I believe you, Counsellor. I've seen you at work.'

Beaudette had in the past appeared as a witness on behalf of certain clients. He was a sallow, easy-mannered man, resourceful, intuitive, and surprisingly free of the cabalistic jargon that generally characterized his professional colleagues. Paul marvelled how, after being exposed hours on end to abusive, bedevilled, and guilt-ridden patients, he still managed to retain a semblance of equanimity and wit.

'How's Dru?' he asked.

'After what happened in court this morning, I don't know. I haven't seen her yet. The trial has her on edge.'

Beaudette eyed him shrewdly. 'You two been feuding?'

'A little.'

'This is not a good time for it. Her term must be well along. What's the ETA?'

'About three months.'

Beaudette shook his head sympathetically. 'Fatherhood is not an unalloyed pleasure. Prepare yourself for howling in the night and changing diapers and other assorted pleasantries.'

'You do not discourage me.'

'Enjoy while you can. You may have to cope with even worse later on.'

Paul leaned forward. 'Are you finished with the amenities, Max? Can we get down to business now?'

Beaudette sighed. 'As you know, I saw the Sheridan boy. It was not an especially productive session. Incidentally, I spoke to the State's psychiatrist. Dr Ivan Maslick. A good man. We find ourselves in complete agreement. The boy is not faking. First, let me make one thing clear, Paul. Whatever I tell you is on the basis of a single examination. I prefer not to indulge in offhand diagnoses. Nevertheless, from all indications, the boy is suffering from what we call hebephrenic catatonia.' He made a face. 'In simple English—total alienation from the outside world. The symptoms are a stuporous condition, lack of facial expression, incoherent response. Some of this may be due to schizoid tendencies. I have no information about his genetic traits, but there could have been some predisposition, with the breakdown precipitated by the stress of trial and what seems to have been a relentlessly destructive cross-examination. I suspect he's been coddled by over-indulgent relatives to the point where his vision of reality became flawed. He's been nursing his adolescent ego on sports and girlie conquests.'

'None of this was visible before the trial, Max.'

'Not visible to you, perhaps. At any rate, it broke through clearly enough when his stress apparatus started to malfunction. Right now, there has been a return to some infantile level.'

'How long will it last?'

'Who knows? Treatment may or may not bring him round. He should be institutionalized.'

'Would he be capable of knowing what's happening in court?'

'Are you kidding? At this moment there's a total vacuum north of his sinuses. He doesn't know enough to lower his pants for the toilet.'

'You'd swear to that before the judge?'

'Hell, yes. And so will Dr Maslick.' Beaudette cocked his head. 'What happens if we do?'

'The judge would probably declare a mistrial and commit the defendant for treatment.'

'Seems like a good solution.'

'There are no good solutions, Max. It may be the least painful.'

'You said something on the telephone about amphetamines.'

'I have reason to believe he was using the stuff.'

Beaudette exhaled sharply. 'Damned fool! That speed is very dangerous merchandise. Some doctors prescribe it in diet control. Stupid. Utterly asinine. I've seen patients who developed a dependency and then patronized several physicians in order to get additional prescriptions.'

'You know what the boy is charged with, Max. Is it possible the drug could have influenced his behaviour?'

312

'I know this much. It has a terrifying potential. Investigators claim that it disorganizes personality, drives its users to grotesque and aberrant behaviour, and sometimes generates sexual fantasies that result in marked deviations. It's a chemical invasion of the psyche. And a meth-freak on a bad trip is unpredictable, erratic, and frequently violent.'

'How far can the violence go?'

'All the way—including suicide or homicide.'

Paul shook his head. 'And you say its use is widespread?'

'Over eight billion tablets manufactured every single year in these enlightened United States. It's almost a cult among the younger generation.'

'What in Christ's name is the attraction?'

Beaudette shrugged. 'The desire for a new experience. An escape valve. Contempt for the establishment, alienation, frustration, boredom. You put me on the stand with your hypothetical lawyer's question and I'll deliver a lecture to the jury.'

'That may not be necessary, Max. It depends on what happens in the next few hours.' Paul glanced at his watch. 'I'm due for a conference at the district attorney's office in half an hour. Dr Maslick will be there and I want you along too.'

Beaudette groaned. 'My wife is going to love this. We're having dinner guests tonight. Ah, well,' he said philosophically, reaching for the phone, 'I warned her about marrying a doctor. I told her she'd be better off with a plumber.' He started to dial.

John Nicoletti was not a vindictive man, nor an inflexible one. He listened carefully to Dr Maslick, then turned to Max Beaudette. 'Okay. It's your turn. Shoot.' When Beaudette was finished, Nicoletti shook his head. 'First time I ever ran across two shrinks who agreed with each other. Sounds like collusion.'

'Dr Maslick is *your* man,' Paul reminded him.

'So he is. Jesus, what a snafu!' He heaved a deep sigh of resignation. 'If the defendant is incompetent at this time, I'm prepared to take it to the judge and move for a mistrial. Provided you set up no obstacle against his commitment to Mattawan.'

'Couldn't we find some institution a little less——'

'*No*, goddamn it! What the hell do you want, Slater? Blood? We're not dealing with some mild neurotic here. I want that boy under lock and key.'

'All right,' Paul said mildly. 'If you insist.'

'Damn well told.' Nicoletti shuffled his papers together. 'It's settled then. Let's go sell this bill of goods to Chaffee.'

It was late when Paul entered the apartment. He felt gutted, wrung-out. He knew that in the desperate scramble from crib to casket there would be few days more calamitous than this one. A single light burned in the living room. He found Dru huddled in a chair, a stillness in her face, utterly immobile. She looked at him with an expression he could not translate.

He sat close. Carefully marshalling his words, he told her of the judge's decision.

'What will they do to him?' Her voice was flat, toneless.

'He's sick, Dru. He needs care. They'll put him in an institution and there may come a time when he'll be eligible for release.'

'He wanted to be a lawyer.'

'That's not the only profession. He'll have to adjust.'

'Does Dad know?'

'Yes. I called him. He seems satisfied.'

Her eyes were expressionless. 'And you, Paul? Are you satisfied too?'

'What do you mean?'

'You didn't really want him acquitted, did you?'

He had a premonition. 'Why do you say that?'

'Because Dad was here. He couldn't stop condemning himself. He said the outcome might have been different if he hadn't insisted on letting Ken testify. He said he should have listened to you. But it wouldn't have made any difference, because you would have put Ken on the stand anyway, even if Dad hadn't interfered, wouldn't you, Paul?'

'Probably.'

She closed her eyes. 'Oh God, I've heard you hold forth on the jury system, praising it and defending it. But the jury

314

system wasn't quite good enough for you in this case, was it? You decided on your own that Ken was guilty and so you deliberately put him on the stand. You knew he overrated himself. You knew he was green and no match for a man like Nicoletti. You knew he'd be cornered and confused and cut to pieces. You pitted that inexperienced boy against a seasoned, implacable adversary. Isn't that exactly what happened, Paul?'

He looked into her swollen eyes, the taste of ashes in his mouth. 'It isn't quite that simple.'

'Then perhaps you have a different explanation, Paul. I need one badly. I need one very badly.'

He measured his words. 'Listen to me, Dru. Try to understand. I could have denied your accusation, sworn my innocence. And maybe even convinced you. But I don't want a lie holding us together. We all keep referring to Ken as a boy. When does a boy become a man? At what age? When does he have to accept responsibility for his acts? But whatever he is, Dru, you've closed your eyes to one central fact—his guilt. You've forgotten what happened to Dolly Wayne. Your vision is blurred by devotion. Ken lied to me. His witnesses lied. Our defence was riddled with perjury from the start, and that was something I could not ignore. I had a duty to inform the judge, and I reneged on that duty. I knew you still believed in his innocence. I thought all right, let him prove it. Maybe I'm wrong. Let him testify in his own behalf.'

'But he didn't have to prove his innocence. *They* had to prove him guilty.'

'I know, Dru, I know. That's what chewed at me. And I might conceivably have won an acquittal. But at what cost? Did you really want me to connive at deceit and perjury to get him off? Return him to circulation? Inflict him on a vulnerable society? Ignore other potential victims? Quite literally help him get away with murder? A boy in his condition, sick, hooked on speed? No, Dru, he had to be isolated. He had to be treated. That was the problem I faced. And I tried to solve it in a way that would serve justice and help you to accept whatever happened.'

She said in a muffled voice, 'He trusted you.'

315

'No. He trusted only his own inflated ego. He felt himself above the law. Infallible. Sacrosanct. No sacrifice too great to save his hide. He sat in court and watched me sacrifice Alex Moore and he never stopped smiling. My God, Dru, you think I enjoyed this? You asked me for the truth. It's something you always cherished. All right. I wanted the truth to emerge in this case. Because if perjury is fundamentally wrong, when if ever can it be applauded? When is it justified? And from whom? From a man accused of a crime because he's related to my wife? From his witnesses? I don't think so, Dru. Truth is not a matter of expediency.'

He saw a shift in her expression, the beginning of uncertainty, and he pressed his argument.

'My colleagues may think I pulled a boner by putting Ken on the stand. So be it. I didn't take this case to enhance my reputation. I took it to help a boy in trouble. But the bargain never included a sacrifice of my own principles. Maybe Ken should have been defended by someone else. There are lawyers who'd stop at nothing to win a case. I've never been able to see eye to eye with them. Should a man bankrupt his conscience for fear of losing his wife? Would you want such a man? Would you really be able to love him?' He took a breath. 'Maybe I'm trying to justify the unjustifiable. I don't know. And I can't ask you to forgive me because I think that what I did was right. I ask only for your understanding, and to remember that no matter what happens, I love you, Dru. I will always love you.'

She looked at him, her face tear-streaked, a fullness in her throat preventing response. She stood suddenly and turned and walked away. He watched her leave, feeling drained and hollow and unutterably desolate. He could not believe that this was how it would end. He stood, tense, listening. He heard her footsteps, but he did not hear the bedroom door close behind her.

He followed her, feeling humble, knowing it would not be an easy time.